"A moving tale of mourning and revelation . . . this spare and vivid debut brings together wrenching personal and political histories."
—*Publishers Weekly*

"[A] beautifully rendered glimpse into the persistence of cultural identity even through tragedy . . ."
—*Booklist*

"Mysteries unfold across time and space in this spellbinding journey into Latin America's tragic past and unsettled present. With grace and verve, Sylvia Sellers-García dissects the baroque heart of a rural village and finds the emotional tissue that binds it to one man's soul."
—Hector Tobar, author of *The Tattooed Soldier*
and *Translation Nation*

"Sylvia Sellers-García has invented a rich and strange place, and her novel is possessed of a narrative voice that brings to mind the atmosphere and tension of Gabriel García Marquez's *No One Writes to the Colonel*. *When the Ground Turns in Its Sleep* is an extraordinarily assured novel. It's a mesmerizing debut."
—Katharine Weber, author of *Triangle* and *The Little Women*

"Sylvia Sellers-García writes a marvelous prose: spare, cinematic, utterly compelling. The story—the slow revelation of meaning out of unspoken knowledge and hoarded memories in a Guatemalan village—unfolds with ceremonious dignity. But it is this young novelist's superb control of pace that astonishes."
—Inga Clendinnen, author of *Reading the Holocaust*
and *Dancing with Strangers*

"The novel investigates the very nature and value of truth—a question that, to its credit comes off not as academic but as meaty and salient . . . It's a smart inflection in the searching-for-roots trope. History plays not as something to dig up but as something to be."
—*San Francisco Chronicle*

"This impressive debut is narrated by Nítido Amán, a high-school teacher born in Guatemala but brought up in America. Reading about the atrocities of the 1980s warfare in his homeland, Amán returns there, in order, he says, "to fill the silences" left by his parents and by "the wide margins of the newspaper." Arriving in 1993 in an isolated village near his parents' birthplace, he is mistaken for the town's new priest, and finds himself furthering the illusion. Sellers-García is concerned with the jigsaw nature of violent history. The villagers confess mysterious illnesses; Amán gives refuge to an injured priest from a neighboring town that no one will talk about; and the stage is set for the dramatic unravelling of near and distant savageries." —*The New Yorker*

"There is nothing in this impressive first novel to suggest that the author is a UC Berkeley PhD candidate in Latin American history . . . her spare, graceful prose is anything but cerebral or academic. . . . Part folktale, part noir mystery, part meditation on the burden of history, this is a remarkable debut." —*San Francisco* magazine

"Some first novels give the feeling of having grown in a chrysalis, only to emerge at the very height of readiness. Sylvia Sellers-García's *When the Ground Turns in Its Sleep* is just that kind of novel. . . . In graceful prose [Sellers-García] offers in narrative form an insider's look at the Guatemalan conflict, how it turned neighbors into enemies and ruined the lives of families. And in what might be the book's best asset . . . [she] evokes compassion as she describes historical events on the ground level." —*BookPage*

WHEN THE GROUND

Turns in Its Sleep

SYLVIA SELLERS-GARCÍA

✦

RIVERHEAD BOOKS

New York

RIVERHEAD BOOKS
Published by the Penguin Group
Penguin Group (USA) Inc., 375 Hudson Street, New York, New York 10014, USA •
Penguin Group (Canada), 90 Eglinton Avenue East, Suite 700, Toronto, Ontario M4P 2Y3, Canada
(a division of Pearson Penguin Canada Inc.) • Penguin Books Ltd., 80 Strand, London WC2R 0RL,
England • Penguin Group Ireland, 25 St. Stephen's Green, Dublin 2, Ireland (a division of Penguin
Books Ltd.) • Penguin Group (Australia), 250 Camberwell Road, Camberwell, Victoria 3124,
Australia (a division of Pearson Australia Group Pty. Ltd.) • Penguin Books India Pvt. Ltd., 11
Community Centre, Panchsheel Park, New Delhi—110 017, India • Penguin Group (NZ), 67
Apollo Drive, Rosedale, North Shore 0632, New Zealand (a division of Pearson New Zealand Ltd.)
• Penguin Books (South Africa) (Pty.) Ltd., 24 Sturdee Avenue, Rosebank, Johannesburg 2196,
South Africa

Penguin Books Ltd., Registered Offices:
80 Strand, London WC2R 0RL, England

The author gratefully acknowledges permission to reprint Humberto Ak'abal's "Tiznada" from
Poems I Brought Down from the Mountain translated by Miguel Rivera and Robert Bly, Nineties Press
© 1999. Reprinted by permission of the publisher.

First Riverhead hardcover edition: December 2007
First Riverhead trade paperback edition: December 2008
Riverhead trade paperback ISBN: 978-1-59448-336-3

The Library of Congress has catalogued the Riverhead hardcover edition as follows:

Sellers-García, Sylvia.
When the ground turns in its sleep / Sylvia Sellers-García.
p.   cm.
ISBN 978-1-59448-954-9
1. Guatemalan Americans—Guatemala—Fiction.   2. Guatemalan American
families—Fiction.   3. Guatemala—Fiction.   I. Title.
PS3619.E467W47   2007   2007008683
813'.6—dc22

PRINTED IN THE UNITED STATES OF AMERICA

10 9 8 7 6 5 4 3 2 1

A los que, en esos tiempos, se dedicaron a la cura.

Tiznada	Blackening
El fuego ardía, ardía, ardía . . .	The fire burned, burned, burned . . .
A veces tronaba.	Sometimes it cracked.
"Alguien está hablando de nosotros."	"Somebody is talking about us."
Las ollas y los tenemastes	The pots and hearth stones
tiznados.	blackened.
La noche	The night
no entraba a la cocina,	would not go into the kitchen,
¿porqué?	why?
¿para qué?	For what?
Si adentro	If inside
estaba más negro que afuera.	it was darker than outside.

—HUMBERTO AK'ABAL

WHEN THE GROUND
Turns in Its Sleep

PART I

One

HARDLY A DAY PASSES that I don't recall the moment when
the Río Roto I'd always imagined was suddenly replaced by the
Río Roto I encountered arriving at the end of August of 1993, on
the first dry morning following a week of rain. I'd pictured the
river as a clear ribbon lining the green hills, an image that later
seemed roughly as prescient as the hundreds of other slight and
colossal suppositions that had driven me there. Instead I saw the
brown waters ripping trees from the banks and a car pinned to
the skeleton of a flooded bridge. Half a mile from the entrance to
the town a mud slide had buried a quarter-mile of road, and the
bus from Rabinal had to try three routes before finding a connecting passage. When I got off the bus I could hear the water
half a mile away, gorging itself on the branches and rocks that
had fallen into it. The process of displacement had begun while I
was riding, as each corner glimpsed through the dirty pane belied
expectation, but when I stepped onto the road, the Río Roto that
had existed in my mind until then was irrevocably lost. The place
I'd invented despite your silence and believed in for years sud-

denly disappeared, and I had no recollection of how the town, and I in it, were meant to be.

I stood in the road, holding my suitcase and looking down at the mud. The bus honked as it departed, leaving me and a handful of other men who scattered noiselessly. I stood facing west, overlooking the town center: a soccer field that was severed by two main roads leading north and drowned, on the side farthest from me, in a long, muddy pool. Stores lined the street on the east side of the field. A cement church, buckling under the weight of a brick bell tower, occupied the south side. While the streets around the field preserved a certain symmetry, the dozens of houses behind them staggered more and more crookedly into the surrounding hills, as though crushed against one another by an encircling arm.

A man in the grocery chewing a stubby pipe told me where to find the post office. I carried my suitcase around the block and introduced myself to Tomás Morelio, a thin man with a mustache whose shirt pocket sagged under the weight of half a dozen pens.

"Good morning," I said to him. "I'm Nítido Amán." I held my hand out.

He raised his eyebrows and looked at me, glancing at my crumpled pants and the jacket tied around my waist. "A week late."

I paused. "I'm sorry? Didn't I say September?"

"Felix," he called over his shoulder. "I'm walking over to the sacristy." A chair in the back room squeaked in reply and Tomás led me out of the post office and onto the road. "Here," he said, as soon as we were out the door. "I'll carry that."

"I can carry it."

He raised his eyebrows. "After that bus ride?"

"All right," I said. I handed him the suitcase with some embarrassment, thinking that it probably weighed as much as he did. "It has been a long trip."

He walked off half a step ahead of me, easily carrying the heavy suitcase, and I followed him toward the plaza and around the church. The sun had only begun to dry the dirt roads; my shoes were caked with mud after ten paces. He led me to a white house with a door varnished orange and took a set of keys out of his pocket. "The sacristy is the only house with a lock. And everyone has a key." He smiled. He opened the door and put my suitcase on the threshold. "I'll show you the boxes."

I followed him to the back of the house, where a narrow passage covered with zinc roofing connected the house and the church. He'd stacked the boxes neatly against the wall. Nevertheless the rain had already disintegrated several of them. I could see the spines of my books through the broken cardboard, swollen to bursting with water. "Thank you," I said to Tomás. "It looks like they're all here." He turned and walked with me the way we'd come and paused at the door. I glanced into the dark hallway and then back at Tomás, expecting him to offer some sort of explanation. For several seconds we stood there uncertainly, our arms at our sides.

"Would you like to go in?" he asked.

"All right."

He motioned with his hand. "I'll wait here."

I hesitated for a moment before walking in. The house had four rooms, including the bathroom; the others were a kitchen, a bedroom, and a front room meant as a living room that felt more like a furnished hallway. The furniture had just been purchased; the sofa stood on foam pads, still wrapped in plastic. A set of folded sheets, cardboard backing included, lay at the foot of the mattress. In the corner of the bedroom a table the size of a bathroom sink had been repurposed by a cockroach for its final resting place. Its legs stretched limply toward the ceiling. I stood in the doorway and looked at the bedroom with some concern. I made an effort to recall exactly what I'd written to Tomás Morelio before arriving, but I couldn't remember. A picture of a blond Christ wearing a crown of thorns hung a few inches above the headboard. When I stepped toward the foot of the bed his eyes rolled upward and when I stepped back to the door they closed. I moved back and forth, watching his eyes flicker.

Tomás stood waiting by the front door. "This is the sacristy?" I asked.

He held his hands together and nodded, smiling demurely. "I hope you like it. Everyone's pitched in."

I felt embarrassed. "It's very comfortable. Much more room than I need."

He nodded again.

"Am I going to share the house——"

"No, no," he said. "Luz brings your meals. She's across the street. You should have sheets and towels. She'll take those too."

"That's not necessary," I said.

"You'll find your time taken up with other things," he said.

I hesitated. "Yes, probably."

"We're glad to have you," he said. He coughed into his hand. "You're much needed," he said in a low voice.

"Mr. Morelio," I said.

"Please," he said. "Tomás. You really are." He looked at his feet and then in through the doorway of the sacristy. "It's been empty too long."

I didn't say anything.

"Far too long," he murmured.

I stared at the pens in his shirt pocket, which as he bent forward had begun to tip out. "Tomás, I just want to make sure we're clear." I hesitated, unsure of how to be clear myself. "You did receive the letter I sent last month?"

"Of course." He smiled. "I saved the stamp."

"Ah," I said.

That would have been the moment to press further, but I didn't. Instead I smiled at Tomás and nodded.

"Well," he said. "I'm sure you'll want to rest. When you're settled you'll have to come have dinner with me and my wife." He shook my hand and walked off into the road. I turned back to the house and realized I'd forgotten to ask him for a set of keys.

I AWOKE in a dark room to the sound of knocking. My neck hurt from the folded sheets under my head and I didn't recognize the bed. I touched the figure-eights imprinted on my arms and chest by the mattress. Then I remembered—the bus, the mud, Tomás Morelio—and I swung my feet to the floor and stepped into my shoes. I pulled a shirt on and combed my hair with my fingers as I walked to the door. The knocking stopped. When I opened the door I found a plastic chair facing me on the doorstep. There was a tray of food on the seat: a bowl of beans, a tamale, a hard roll, a teacup covered with its saucer, and a glass of water. In the twilight I could barely distinguish the woman crossing the road toward the other side. When I opened the door her long braid spun around as she stopped to turn.

"Thank you," I called out. "This is really not necessary," I said to myself. She waved and stepped into the house across the street. I took the tray inside and set it on the plastic-wrapped sofa and flipped the light switch. A single bulb three inches over my head glared on the plastic and filled the hallway with shadows. I turned it off again and ate in the dark, wiping the bowl with the hard roll and swallowing the tea in gulps before it had time to cool. After washing the dishes in the sink I made the bed and crawled under the covers.

I AWOKE at seven in the morning to the sound of knocking again. This time I knew where I was. I put my shirt on and tripped to the door. The woman with the braid stood there holding another tray. "Good morning," I said.

"Good morning, Father Amán."

I thought I'd misheard her. "I'm sorry?" I said. I squinted at her. It was either not yet dawn or the sky was overcast; I could barely see her face in the shadowed doorway. "I'm the American—maybe Tomás Morelio told you." I put out my hand. "Are you Luz?"

She looked down, disconcerted, and put her limp hand briefly in mine. "Could you give me your tray from last night, please?"

"Of course, I'm sorry. Come in. I washed everything."

She stood without moving on the doorstep. "I'll wait here. You don't have to wash. If you just leave the tray outside when you're done I'll pick it up."

"It's really no trouble to wash."

"Just leave it out when you're done."

"Won't it get full of ants?"

She frowned. "I can see the front of the house from my window."

I turned away, flustered, and went to get the tray. I'd stacked the dishes and thrown away the tamale leaf and teabag. She took it silently and handed me another tray with a plate of scrambled eggs and a cup of coffee on it. "Leave it outside when you're done," she said quietly.

"All right," I said. "Thank you."

I ATE BREAKFAST standing in the kitchen. When I'd finished eating, I stacked the dirty dishes and placed the tray on the chair outside. Then I closed the door and stepped to the edge of the window and watched the walkway. A moment later Luz opened her door. She took the tray and glanced at the window and walked back across the street. As she was reaching her doorstep I heard a sharp whistle and she turned to look over her shoulder. A man leading a mule stopped by the stick fence and pointed in my direction. Luz shifted the tray to her hip and walked up to him and they talked for some time, gesturing, their faces serious.

Even though I'd slept more than twelve hours, I felt exhausted. From the bedroom window, I stared out into the passageway at the boxes sitting in the shadow of the church. I knew my books had begun rotting, but I couldn't bring myself to unpack. There'd clearly been some misunderstanding, and after sorting things out with Tomás Morelio I would probably have to move. There was no point in unpacking the books until then. As I stood there staring, the church door across from me opened and a woman stepped out holding a short broom. She shook the broom briskly and then she paused, holding it aloft, and took a few steps toward the boxes. After a moment's hesitation she crouched on her heels to examine the books that showed through the wet cardboard. She ran her hand slowly along the spines, turning her head as if to read them.

Suddenly she looked up and peered at the window. I stepped away from the curtain and sat on the bed. For some minutes I sat there, listening. Then I stood up and walked to the back door and opened it quickly and looked out, but the woman was gone and the church door was closed.

I took a shower, dressed, and prepared to leave the house. On the front doorstep I found a green plastic basket. As I put it on the chair, the door opened across the street and Luz's head appeared in the doorway. "Laundry," she said.

"I don't have any, thank you," I said.

Her head disappeared and the door shut silently. At eight the sun had already begun baking the road, cracking the mud puddles. The post office was closed, so I decided to walk around for an hour before returning. I headed north, past the central plaza. At the side of the otherwise empty field an old woman sat on a bench, poring over the contents of a plastic basket. Most of the houses had their doors partway open and through them came the hoarse buzz of the radio, the rushing of faucet water, and the sound of wood being split, though the sources of these sounds were invisible. The street climbed uphill. The open sewer next to it ran with muddy water that choked on clots of garbage and, at one corner, over the immense haunches of a speckled toad.

The town ended abruptly on the north side in a line of houses. A cistern partly blocked a footpath leading uphill into the brush. From that vantage point, most of the shallow valley was visible; it sloped east, plunging sharply to meet the river. Beyond it and on the other three sides of town, the hills spread outward in ever-tightening creases until they met the horizon. There seemed to be no roads through them, and yet the maps I'd brought showed footpaths traversing them in every direction.

No doubt it was the sense of vastness provoked by the view that made me suddenly, incautiously confident. The openness of the valley gave the impression that anything I looked for would be there, just within view. I turned and walked past the houses to the other end, where a road led northeast. An old woman sitting on a three-legged stool peered out at me from behind her stick fence. When I greeted her she clucked and grinned, tucking her toothless smile behind her hand. "Resting," she said, as if to account for herself. She squinted at me. "Off to work?"

"Not yet," I said, vaguely.

She laughed warmly at this and murmured, "Lazy, lazy."

I smiled and pointed at the road that led away from town. "Is this the road to Naranjo?"

The woman's wrinkled face froze. She scowled, her dark eyes puckering. For a minute she didn't say anything. Then a hoarse sound formed in her throat. "Go to hell," she growled. She pushed herself up with difficulty and leaned tremulously on the fence. For a moment she muttered to herself and then she said again, "Go to hell," as if unable to think of anything stronger. She shook the stick fence for emphasis and turned away and hobbled to her door. At the doorway she turned and her voice shook. "You've no respect," she said.

I stared at her, realizing that she must have misunderstood me. "I'm sorry; you heard me wrong." I walked up to the fence and spoke over it so she would hear me clearly. "I'm just wondering where Naranjo is. Is it here, in town, or somewhere else?"

She looked at me with apprehension, as if I'd threatened to kick down her fence. Then she shook her head at me and shut the door.

I stood in the road, my face burning, staring at the crooked door on the other side of the fence. The woman was now on the other side of the thin wall, stomping to the back of the house. There was no one else on the road. I repeated the question to myself, thinking about the words I'd used, the way I'd taken hold of the fence. I thought about going to the door to apologize.

But instead I looked away, turning my back to the road north, and walked toward town. The houses on the east side varied only in their color—turquoise, pink, yellow, white, green—and in their state of disrepair. Cement blocks, roofed with zinc and cluttered with tiny windows, they faced one another through their back and side doors as much as they did the main road, with knotted footpaths linking one to another through the coarse grass. A woman hanging laundry on a line strung up to her neighbor's window stopped and watched me pass. Out of nowhere a pair of little girls appeared, holding hands, following me, halting each time I turned, until we reached the plaza and they braked as if against an invisible wall. I walked past the stores and then south beyond the edge of the soccer field.

Beyond the church the houses grew smaller and shabbier, as though everything south of the plaza had been rained on too hard, too often. Two blocks south of the center an entire square block stood abandoned. The grass grew unchecked; a bougainvillea rooted in the corner had engulfed a fragment of cement wall. The floor of whatever building had once stood there still clung in pieces to the ground, partitioned by weeds and the crumbling remains of walls at regular intervals. I stepped onto the grass and walked toward the middle, where a world map painted onto the cement years earlier had broken up into cracking, faded continents.

I heard a bell ring then and a man came up the road pushing an aluminum barrel on a wheelbarrow. As soon as he saw me he stopped, still holding the handles of the wheelbarrow. He stared at me.

I watched him for a moment. "Good morning," I said. He was silent. "I'm Nítido Amán."

He put the wheelbarrow down and pushed the brim of his hat back. He didn't offer his name. "What are you doing?"

"Just looking around."

He went on staring. "What are you standing in the school for?"

I looked down at my feet and then at the ruins of the rooms around me. "This is the school?"

"Was."

"I didn't know what it was."

"It was the school."

"Where's the new one?"

He didn't say anything for a moment. "I don't know."

We were silent. I realized he was waiting for me to leave. I began walking away from the map and toward the road. "What happened to the school?"

"You're not from here," he said, squinting.

"No. Just got here yesterday."

He picked up the handles of the wheelbarrow and prepared himself to keep walking. "Fire, I think," he said. "Can't really remember." He walked away and the bell started tinkling and he stopped at the corner of the burned schoolyard as a woman came out of her front door holding a plastic pitcher. He filled the pitcher with milk from the barrel and handed it to her and she went back into the house. Then he pushed the wheelbarrow up the street toward the other houses.

When the milkman was gone, I noticed an old woman sitting on a plastic chair two houses away. She was watching me and smoking, holding the short pipe with her thumb and forefinger. She nodded at me when I looked up and I walked toward her slowly, turning back to look at the ruined schoolyard. When I reached her walkway, she pointed to the chair next to her and I thanked her and declined. "I heard about you." She frowned. "But you don't look so much like a foreigner."

"Thanks," I said.

"You dress like it, though."

"I can't help it."

She smiled and her brown teeth showed around the stem of the pipe. "Walking around?"

"Yes."

"What do you think of the church?"

"I haven't been in yet."

She leaned back and crossed her ankles. "We haven't had a priest for years."

It had slipped my mind that Luz had called me "Father" that morning on the doorstep, or perhaps I'd willfully ignored it. But now it returned to me, and the confusion I'd started to feel seeing the ruined school was compounded. I answered the old woman vaguely. "That's what I hear."

"You don't know how hard it's been without one."

"I can imagine."

"I used to go to services twice a week. Now——nothing. I can barely remember the Lord's Prayer." She smiled and winked.

I smiled back. "How'd the fire start?"

"What fire?"

"At the school."

She frowned. "Can't recall." She stood up. "Can I get you some coffee?"

"Thank you, no. I'm just heading back."

"Well, welcome. We're glad you're here."

WHEN I RETURNED to the sacristy I sat on the bed, watching the curtains sway against the open window. Río Roto had no telephone, and there would be no buses for Rabinal until the following day. I decided to unpack some of the things I needed. I could always pack them again.

Luz knocked on the door at twelve and handed me a plate of chicken and rice, and after I'd eaten I left the tray outside and went behind the house to look through the boxes. The books I left mostly untouched, though I couldn't help taking the ones that looked most damaged and setting them on the walkway to dry. I found my coffee press in one of the boxes along with the letter from Tomás Morelio that I'd received before leaving. I'd remembered it somewhat differently. It read only,

We are delighted that you have had the great kindness to accept the post. Everything will be prepared and made ready and comfortable for your arrival. I am at your service to receive the boxes that you mention in your letter and although there is no telephone in Río Roto I may say that we have a very reliable postal service as long as no cash or checks are sent in which case I can vouch for our locality but not the officials in the capital so you may feel free to use the postal office here as your future forwarding address.

Cordially,

Tomás Morelio.

I was reading the letter for the second time when I heard a knock on the door, which I'd left open.

I stepped into the corridor. "Amán?" the man said. He was a head shorter than I, with a full beard and glasses. His shirt was tight around the waist. He held out his hand to me. "Estrada. Doctor."

"Come in," I said. I cleared the papers off the plastic-wrapped sofa and offered him a seat, which he declined, and then coffee, which he agreed to, following me into the kitchen as I went to put the press together.

"I like the books on the walkway." He grinned. I replied with some embarrassment that I'd probably brought too many. He looked around at the small kitchen and walked into the hallway, then the bedroom. "I'll help you put some shelves together."

"Thanks, I don't think I'll need them."

"Course," he said. "You have all that room in the vestry. Where are you from?" He picked up the bag of coffee I'd brought, and opened it and sniffed it. "Bring coffee to the land of coffee. Don't blame you. They export the good coffee. Local they mix with blood to darken it." He laughed. "Chicken blood, usually."

I took the coffee from him with some confusion. "I wasn't thinking when I packed it."

"Your accent's a little funny," he said.

I looked away. "I was born here, but I moved to the States with my parents when I was young."

"Ah." He laughed. "That explains it. Worst of both worlds— our looks and their personality. Right?" He laughed and clapped me on the arm.

I flushed. "I guess so."

"When did you get in?" I told him I'd arrived the day before and that I'd spent the morning walking around. I fumbled with the coffee press. "Let me do that," he said, taking it from me. I filled the kettle that I'd found in one of the cabinets and put it on the stove. "Electric stove," he said. "All the luxuries."

"It's very comfortable."

"Not saying I envy you though," he said. "There." He handed me the press and I spooned the ground coffee into the glass base.

"Do you live in town?" I asked.

"Northeast corner. Come by sometime. So what made you pick this place?"

I looked around at the nearly empty kitchen. "Tomás Morelio brought me. He made all the arrangements, I think."

He laughed. "Right. But seriously, you might still reconsider. I'm saying after a few months, a year. Costa Rica is beautiful, right around the corner, nice beaches."

"Oh, that. Just my parents."

"They're from here?"

"Somewhere around here."

"There aren't any Amáns in Río Roto."

I turned away. "Maybe in the other towns nearby."

He shook his head. "I've never heard the name."

I lowered and then raised the heat on the kettle. Estrada silently inspected my coffee and I thought about how to bring the conversation around. "Just now," I said, "I saw an empty lot with some old foundations, and someone told me it was the school."

The doctor looked at me over his glasses. A smile spread slowly across his face. "Crazy, isn't it?"

"Where's the new one?"

His smile grew broader. "What new one?" He laughed. "We

haven't had school here in ten years. I tell you. They like to stay dumb." He pulled his thumb and forefinger over his lips, zipping them shut, and then tapped his temple. "Dumb and dumb, you know?"

I looked down at the floor.

He patted my shoulder and I resisted the impulse to pull away. "Wait a few days. You'll believe it."

I looked back up at him and the kettle whistled. I turned to make the coffee and the doctor laughed again in a tired, rumbling way. "Don't even mention the school. They look at you like it's a dirty word."

I poured the water into the press and watched the grounds float.

"I don't take sugar," the doctor said.

"All right."

"But if you do you should use your own. The sugar here tastes like fertilizer."

It took me a moment to grasp what he'd said. "Don't they grow sugar here?"

He shook his finger at me. "They grow cane, not sugar."

Two

It wasn't what I'd had in mind for my first visit to Guatemala. I'd always meant to go for a shorter visit—a vacation rather than an indefinite stay. I would have spent some time on the lake, maybe, and seen the volcanoes. The ruins alone would have been worth the plane fare. But the trip to Guatemala never took place while you were still alive. I never mentioned to you that I wanted to go, and you never suggested it or asked.

You didn't have to; I could see for myself that you were doing everything possible to move us in the opposite direction. At the beginning I couldn't figure out what we were meant to be leaving behind. I finally realized, when I left for college and you moved to Oregon, that you and Mamá simply fell, every few years, into a panic of restlessness that you could only cure by repeating, again and again, that first flight northward. It surprised me when you showed no sign of wanting to leave Oregon despite your dislike of the rain, Mamá's complaints about the neighbors, and the house's demand for constant repairs.

At the time, I didn't understand why you stayed. As far as I could tell, you could have moved again whenever you wanted to. During my visits you must have either purposely or inadvertently hidden your symptoms. Mamá described the signs to me—how you spoke differently, looked at her differently—but I hadn't seen them. My visits were too short for me to notice the changes myself. I would have needed to see you more often— several weeks at a time—to pick up on them. Even after you'd been to the doctor I had difficulty believing it. You were younger than all of my friends' parents; when I thought of you and Mamá, in my mind you were only middle-aged.

Not until I moved back to be with you, for the last year in Oregon, did I realize how much time had passed. You and Mamá were both completely different people by then; I took over bathing, dressing, and feeding you, and I pushed the wheelchair when we went for walks. But these tasks had already distorted Mamá's impression of you so greatly that she spoke to you like an infant when she spoke to you directly, and, with greater frequency than she realized—sometimes she caught herself—she spoke of you to me in the past tense.

During the long, rainy winter, Mamá often sat by the sliding doors to the yard, staring out at the bird feeder. The knitting in her lap rarely progressed, but she seemed to require an hour or two with the unaltered fringe of blue and white on her lap nonetheless. I discovered early on that you preferred my reading aloud to anything else. I would read from the sofa while you sat silently in your easy chair. You would watch me with interest and something like your old concentration, seemingly content. It didn't matter what I read. You liked the sound of my voice, so I read from whatever I was reading myself at the time. One afternoon, Mamá got up from her chair when we'd settled down to read, and she handed me something from her knitting basket. She smiled shyly. "I found it on your shelf," she said. "Would you mind?" From then on I read to both of you from the books she chose: *Just So Stories, The Wind in the Willows, The Phantom Tollbooth*. I'm not sure whether she realized that you'd already read most of them to me more than twenty years earlier.

A few months after I arrived, you began speaking differently. You rarely formed complete words any longer, and when you did, they usually seemed entirely out of context. But at times—Mamá must have experienced the same thing—you had disjointed moments of lucidity that unnerved me; they seemed not so much nonsensical as uncannily subtle. Just when I'd accepted the idea that you were unaware of everything going on around you, including me, you would say something—only a word or two, perhaps— that with its oracular precision caught me completely off guard. I never babbled with you, as Mamá did, but knowing how much you liked to hear my voice I tried to speak to you frequently, even though you usually responded with only sounds. On one occasion, as I turned down the bed while you sat by in your pajamas, I told you how cold it was. "You picked a rainy place to live," I said.

You made an appreciative noise.

"But I'm glad to be here with you. I don't know why I didn't come earlier. Not like the weather's better in Rhode Island."

You laughed lightly, as you often did. Then you said, quite clearly, "Nothing to forgive."

I looked at you, and you smiled mildly. You held your hand out to me. I took it and squeezed. I hadn't believed that you could grasp anything so concrete, but it seemed suddenly possible that you had another, more instinctual way of comprehending my thoughts. I had the momentary impulse to speak to you frankly, as

I'd heard Mamá do when she thought I wasn't listening. Instead I kissed you on the forehead. "Time for bed," I said. I lifted you out of the chair and put you between the sheets.

MAMÁ REACTED as though she hadn't seen it coming when you passed away. She stayed shut up in her room for days; she lost weight; she clung to your clothes and wouldn't leave the apartment. Then, after a month, she began to feel different. She decided she couldn't stand the apartment any longer. It grieved her, weighed her down. Everything that had belonged to you or that even reminded her of you had to go. She threw away all the unfinished knitting projects and talked about moving to Canada. In the afternoons she took longer and longer walks, insisting that she needed time alone.

While Mamá was out walking, I packed. I got rid of your wheelchair and all your medicines. Most of your clothes I gave away, and the neighbor ended up with your fishing equipment. When I boxed your books, I came across some that I remembered and others that I hadn't known you owned. Your copy of the Popol Vuh was falling apart. It was as I packed your books and flipped through them, seeing in some of their margins your cryptic annotations, that I began seriously considering the trip to Guatemala for the first time. There weren't any plans for me, anymore, in Oregon. It was too late in the year to think about a new teaching job, and I had no idea what other job to look for. What I'd always wanted to do and never thought possible was suddenly a realistic option. You hadn't given me any reason to think that anyone from your family was still alive, but I had nothing to lose by trying.

The only difficulty, I knew, would be bringing it up with Mamá.

She still wasn't well. And I knew from the little she'd ever said about Guatemala—and the enormity of what she hadn't—that she wasn't going to take it well. I began by mentioning, every few days, that I wanted to travel, to take a vacation. She seemed to accept this and showed no inclination to go with me. Then I told her I was considering different alternatives: I would probably buy an old car and drive south, down the California coast and into Mexico and then—leaving unsaid what lay in between—all the way down to Patagonia. Or perhaps I would fly directly to Mexico and travel from there. She grew sufficiently accustomed to the idea for me to mention, offhand, that I would travel in Central America. And then it only remained for me to communicate, as delicately as I could, that the bulk of my time would be spent in Guatemala.

She'd taken the same tone with me every time I discussed my plans, and when she heard this new development she responded, to my relief, with her usual skepticism. "Do you really think your Spanish is good enough?"

"I'll get by."

"You've never taught in Spanish."

"I've taught Spanish classes."

"But it's different. You'll have to practice. Maybe if you teach younger children."

"Yes." I felt grateful to her for taking it so well. "You know, it's only for a little while. I'll just go until the end of their school year. In December I'll look for another job near you."

She didn't say anything. We were walking from her car to the grocery store and she wore a hat that hid her face. Her feet in their plastic covers clicked on the wet pavement. "Why do you have to go to Guatemala at all? Couldn't you just go back to the school in Rhode Island?"

I looked up at the heavy mist; the hill at the end of the street was entirely invisible and the shops seemed to end in a cloud. When I spoke my voice sounded muffled. "They filled my position a long time ago."

We stood by the entrance of the grocery in the drizzling rain. Mamá tilted her umbrella so that her face was hidden from view and then she moved it back, sharply. "Where in Guatemala?"

"I'm not sure."

"You're not," she said. "You wouldn't go anywhere near Rabinal."

I didn't say anything.

Her expression was strained. "There's no one left, Nítido," she said.

"Do you know that for sure?"

"I can't believe this," she said. "You've already planned it."

"If there's something you want to tell me—"

She cut me off. "I have never thought there was any point in going back to Guatemala. I don't and never will think it's a good idea for you to go."

I took a deep breath. "Mamá, you know I've wanted to go for years."

She looked at me with surprise, as if she'd just realized what I was talking about. Then she looked away. "No one will know you're American. It won't make you safe."

I watched the fine drizzle fall on her lashes and along the edge of her cap into her hair. Her chin was trembling. I put my hand on her arm. "I'll be careful."

She looked at me quickly. "It's not going to be easy finding a job just like that. In the middle of the year."

"I've written a few letters. There seem to be some possibilities."

"You would be much better off staying in the city."

"I can't be sure that I'll find a job there."

"I see. And I can't stop you from going." She sniffed quietly. "You'll be back in December."

"Yes, I will."

We walked into the store, and I knew that, as with everything pertaining to Guatemala, we wouldn't speak of it again.

In early June we made a trip together to Seattle and stayed for a week on Bainbridge Island. The inn stood only a short block away from the wooden steps that led to the sea. From the window of my mother's bedroom we could see the water over the immense blackberry bushes that divided the road from the rocky descent to the shore. Mamá's eyes gleamed as she watched the sun set from the window. We found a house near the water with an in-law apartment for rent. The couple had moved from Seattle, renovated the house themselves, and arranged their rooms on the first and second floors. The basement apartment, invisible from the front of the house but with a beautiful view, wedged as it was into the slope leading to the water, had its own entrance at the side. They took to Mamá at once, and it only remained for us to pack her belongings in Oregon. She flew back, and I drove a truck with her things after sending mine to the postmaster of Río Roto. We spent the end of July and the beginning of August arranging her apartment, buying furniture, finding our way around the island. At the end of August I put the few things I had with me in a suitcase. Feeling finally settled in her new place, she seemed to have no more need of me. I told her I would return to see her for Christmas and she said, "You know you're always welcome." She stood out on the road to watch the taxi leave and she waited, not waving, until we'd turned the corner.

Three

THE SECOND NIGHT in Río Roto I hardly slept at all, and in the morning I got up early. I began writing a letter to Mamá, telling her that I was safely in Guatemala. Luz knocked at seven. I opened the door with the intention of telling her that I'd already eaten, and then I noticed that she wasn't carrying a tray. Her face looked even blanker than it had the day before. "Dr. Estrada needs to see you right away," she said.

My first thought was to wonder why he hadn't come himself. I found myself thinking back on the conversation we'd had the day before, and I tried to remember what I'd said to him as he was leaving. I could think of nothing significant.

"He said it was urgent," Luz said.

"Yes, I'm sorry." I walked out onto the step and closed the door behind me. "I'll follow you."

Luz took me at my word and walked, silently, a few paces ahead of me. We took the main road, northward, passing the plaza and then the knot of houses at the base of the hill. Luz turned left in between a pair of white houses and threaded through a number of others until we reached a one-room house with no door. She motioned toward the empty doorway and watched me step in.

There were no lights, only a candle on the table by the bed. The walls and floor were made of packed dirt. Chipped bowls covered the surface of the corner table, and a large plastic basin by the foot of the bed was filled with milky water. A cluster of flies attended the basin, filling the room with a gentle hum. Estrada sat on a low stool, his back to me, leaning over a low bed. When he turned around, I was shocked to see his eyes filled with tears. He swallowed and looked away. "She wants last rites." He walked brusquely past me, stepping out of the doorway into the sunlight. He crossed his arms and looked out toward the town.

I followed him as far as the doorway; it had taken me that long to realize what Estrada meant: she wanted last rites from me. Estrada didn't notice me standing in the doorway. He wiped his eyes roughly and cleared his throat. Then he shook his head and took a few wavering steps. He wandered away, arms crossed, seemingly lost in thought. I looked back into the house. The candle in its glass container diffused a yellow light. I stood still for more than a minute, and then a voice emerged from among the blankets. "Father?" she said.

I will never be able to explain to you how that word sounded to me then. Perhaps to you, having heard it from me for many years, it would have sounded ordinary. But to me it was a revelation. This one word, which I'd always heard and never really heard before, left me speechless. If she'd said my name, and called me to her side, and unfolded like a conjuror every moment of the last year I'd lived, she wouldn't have unearthed what lay buried in me as easily as she did with that one word. For a moment it left me paralyzed, and I had a sensation of precipitous, uncontrolled falling. The darkness of the room lay before me, and in the bright rectangle of sunlight that fell through the doorway onto the floor, I cast a dark shadow. The angle of the sun made me appear wider, more stooped. I moved my hand to the door frame and the shadow responded with a gesture of infinite calm. It stood in the doorway, waiting. The sense of dizziness passed, and the room composed itself around me. I looked once more over my shoulder at the sunny grass beyond the doorway, and then I turned and walked into the room.

I sat down on the stool next to the bed. Despite the dim candlelight, I could see the bed, the room, and everything in it with incredible clarity. The old woman's white hair had been braided and then combed; it rippled out over the soiled pillow and onto the blanket. She gripped my hand as soon as I reached the bedside. The skin of her face was thin, as if composed of the dead leaves that become nearly transparent with the onset of winter. "Thank God you're here, Father."

When she smiled, the skin near her lips seemed to want to break. She spoke slowly. "I was always devout, Father, though my attendance wasn't the most regular. But I've always prayed for the humility and guidance to live as I should."

I said nothing and held her hand tightly.

"It's such a relief to me that you're here." She smiled. "Just in time. I wouldn't presume to believe I'm so important, but it almost seems He sent you for me."

Her eyes were wet and they blinked slowly, like a child's. Their heaviness, the careless grace of her hair, and the fragile creases of her smile all struck me as extremely beautiful. I smiled back at her.

"Will you take my confession?"

I placed my fingertips briefly on her forehead and she closed her eyes. Then I took her hand in both of mine, and she squeezed back gently, still present.

She opened her eyes. "Bless me, Father, for I have sinned."

Afterward Estrada was waiting for me outside the house. He nodded at me and pressed my shoulder. "Thank you," he said. "I'll come by later." I watched with wonder as he stepped into the house. He seemed completely unlike the doctor I'd met the day before; he was a different person. I turned away from the house and wound my way back to the road.

I SAT BEHIND the sacristy, next to the cardboard boxes full of books, and stared at the spines that showed through the broken cardboard. It had seemed like such a good idea, when I was packing, to take them with me. I'd imagined a comfortable routine: teaching in the mornings and afternoons, reading in the evenings. The arrangement seemed so certain in my mind that I'd even made a reading schedule, and I'd thought carefully about which books to bring. It seemed, in retrospect, laughable to have planned it all with such certainty.

In part because I could think of nothing else to do and in part because the familiarity of them calmed me, I began to sort mechanically through the books, moving them out of the boxes and into meaningless piles that I then took apart and reordered. I flipped through them, examined their warped pages, set them out to air, closed them again, moved them into the sun, reopened them, and moved them onto another pile. Some of the books, which I'd brought from Oregon, you would have recognized, and others I'd had since college. But most of them I'd bought since then. They were unread, and taken together their titles reflected the unsystematic habits of an amateur. Long after the possibility of going to graduate school faded, you continued to discuss it—with the kindest intentions, I know—as a serious alternative. You once asked me with considerate gravity, I remember, whether I subscribed to any scholarly journals. And though I said yes, it wasn't until after you asked me that I subscribed to two of them. I kept the subscriptions for years when I lived in Rhode Island, and, incredibly, I would sometimes take them with me to school intentionally, so that the students and other high school teachers would see them on my desk. In reality I never read them. I always meant to, but the journal would sit around in different places and then by the time the next issue arrived the previous one seemed not worth reading. And it went on that way until a teacher from one of the other sections once pointed to the latest journal sitting on my desk and asked, "What do you think of their annual symposium?" It seemed that she read the journal with genuine interest; she, at least, was not a fraud. I spent twenty minutes discussing the symposium I'd never read, with my face hot and a dead feeling in my stomach.

I canceled my subscriptions the next day. It was not, I thought then, a feeling I wanted to get used to. You wouldn't know—you never willingly deceived anyone. The fear of discovery isn't the problem. Within a very little time the story begins to seem believable, and after that it soon appears as true as anything else. Then it is only a matter of time before you don't know who you are without it. The sun moved across the roof of the church, and the shade cast by the zinc siding above me eased over the packed dirt. I might have sat there for two or three hours, feeling numbed, staring blindly at one of the open books before me.

Finally I roused myself, and I realized that the book I was holding was ruined. The pages were covered with thick, jagged waves where there had once been words.

IN THE AFTERNOON I arranged wooden planks and bricks for shelves in the hallway. The books smelled of mildew; a pale green fungus had begun to discolor their edges. I ran a laundry line through the house and hung them to dry, but there wasn't space for all of them. I thought about taking them to the church and went through the stack of those that were still damp, separating some that might go into the vestry. But then when I looked them over I began to wonder what people would think of them if they understood the titles. I thought of the woman I'd seen behind the sacristy, peering at my books through the seams of the cardboard boxes. I didn't know what kind of books a priest was supposed to have. Perhaps my books wouldn't look out of place, but I couldn't be sure. On the other hand, depending on how the shelves in the vestry were arranged, the books might not even be visible.

I went out behind the house and tried the back door of the church. It was open. I walked into the rear of the vestry. The high ceilings made the room appear narrower than it really was. At the end of it and to my right, an open door looked onto a patch of grass, and next to the door stood a sink filled with cut flowers. Someone had left the water running. It fell over the flower stems through the plastic bag attached to the faucet nozzle. I walked through the room and looked up at the figures that filled the room, crowding the floor and threatening to pitch forward from where they rested upon one another. Saints cut life-size out of blackened wood darkened the corners; processional figures made of plaster, their long robes cascading onto the wide platforms, stared into the room with their pale complexions. Their smell of decay, their broken features, made the room seem like a place just unearthed. In the corner opposite the door a Virgin Mary leaned forward, as if attempting to step into the air. The thumb on her right hand was missing. Her blue robe had crumbled at the edges and the lace trim that had once been golden was now tinselly gray. Her lower lip was chipped just where it met the upper lip, as if she'd bitten down too hard. She was about five feet tall and her feet were fastened to a painted platform that came up to my waist.

I couldn't understand how she managed to hover midair. Then I wondered at her skin—its luminous surface. Reaching out over the platform, I lifted the edge of her blue robe. Her feet were undamaged in their brown sandals. Her tiny toes had pale, shell-colored nails. The sandals—of leather rather than plaster—and the careful separation of the toes gave me the sudden impression that she was made of flesh. I reached out quickly to touch her ankle and felt the cool, slightly damp, plaster. Behind her feet metal rods cut cruelly into her calves; she'd planted one foot ahead of the other, stepping forward, and the rods kept her erect. I lifted her skirt and leaned closer to look at the metal rods and then someone spoke to me from the doorway.

"What are you doing?"

I dropped the robe and turned quickly. The woman standing in the doorway had a pair of pruning shears in her hand. I'd seen her before, looking at my books in the passageway. Her long hair was pulled back loosely and her eyes were flat, calm, reflecting none of the sharpness in her voice. She stood very straight and held the pruning shears lightly against her hip. "She's in good condition," I said.

The woman didn't say anything for a moment. "You think so?"

"Yes. I was just inspecting the base—of some of them—and they look very solid."

She turned to the sink and she began cutting the stems of the flowers. "I'm Xinia," she said.

"Nítido Amán," I said. I looked past her through the doorway and spoke to the patch of grass. "Father Amán." You would have been surprised at how natural it sounded.

"Are you finding the house comfortable?"

"Yes, thank you."

"We're all very glad you're here."

"Thank you."

"You haven't come to look at the church yet," she said quietly.

"No, well, I only arrived a couple days ago."

She nodded. "Should I show you around?"

"Thanks, yes."

She cut the stem from a lily and placed it on some newspaper that lay on the counter. "I work here afternoons," she said, looking me in the eye. She washed the shears in the water and turned the faucet off. Then she wiped the shears on her skirt and put them on the counter.

She dried her hands. "Follow me. I change the flowers every other day. I clean the inside of the church and polish the pews. I straighten the hymnals and prayer books and clean the holy instruments. I don't prepare the sacraments, that's for whomever you get to be the sexton. I have a key, so I unlock and lock the church for services, but I don't do any repairs or laundry. You can give the laundry to Luz. And if you want me to, I can keep the books. I know how."

We'd walked out of the back room into a short hallway. She

showed me a small room equipped as a study to the right and another room with a wardrobe to the left. At the end of the short hallway a set of steps led to a door that opened directly onto the chapel and we came out behind the altar. "You can look around," she said. She took the flowers she was holding to the altar and placed them there and then set about arranging them in vases. I walked down among the pews, my steps echoing. There were four arched windows on each side and a set of double doors at the entrance. Instinctively I looked toward the right, where we had always sat in every church we'd ever attended; you liked to be near the windows. The dark wood of the rafters, almost black against the white ceiling, mirrored the dark pews. The room was clean and peculiarly cold.

Near the doors I turned around to look back at the altar. Xinia had arranged the vases to the left and right of it. The lectern stood off to the side. Apart from the lectern, the vases, and a pair of chairs, only a large crucifix carved from a red wood decorated the altar. I walked up to the altar to look at it more closely. "It's very striking," I said, indicating the crucifix.

Xinia paused to glance at me and then went on picking up the stray leaves and petals from the altar. "My brother made it," she said.

"He's talented."

She took the bundle of leaves and walked back toward the vestry and I followed her. "When will you start holding service?" she asked.

Instead of answering I picked up some of the leaves that had fallen by the sink. "Can I help you?"

"No, thank you, I'm just going to clean up." She took a broom out of a closet near the sink and started sweeping the leaves and water out onto the grass. "When will you hold the first service?"

"Well, I think I'll need a week or two." I stood with my back against the Virgin.

"How about the other towns?"

"What other towns?"

"The smaller towns nearby. You're the only one for all of them." The leaves were wet and they stuck to the floor. She swept hard, then bent over and picked them up one by one and flicked them onto the grass. "You'll have to go there on weekdays. That's what Father Antonio did."

"I didn't know."

She glanced at me. "You can do whatever you want, of course."

"Yes."

She put the broom under the faucet and tousled it with her fingers and then turned the faucet off and tapped the broom handle on the rim of the sink. "Though they'll be expecting you."

I put my hands in my pockets and took them out again and crossed my arms. "So what towns did Father Antonio go to?"

She unscrewed the head of the broom and laid it on the grass and propped the handle up in the corner beside the sink. "He went to Murcia on Tuesdays and Los Cielos on Thursdays."

"And how far away are they?"

"Murcia is about an hour south of here. Los Cielos is two hours northwest. You have to walk because to those towns there are no roads for cars."

"All right, I guess I'll walk, then. Tuesdays and Thursdays." I walked around to the side of the sink so I could see her face. "And what about Naranjo?"

For a moment she paused, holding the rag she'd taken off the shelf, and then she began wiping the sink down, running the rag slowly around the edges. "It's more than two days away on foot."

"I guess that's too far. But won't they be expecting me as well?"

Xinia locked the closet next to the sink and then closed the door that led to the yard. The room became suddenly dark; only with the door closed did I notice the round window far above it near the ceiling. The sun came in through it, casting a dusty ray onto the feet of the saints at the other end of the room. "Who knows what they expect," Xinia said. "But keep in mind that people here expect you not to go there." She held her arms at her sides. Her face was serious, and for the second time since I'd met her she looked me in the eye rather than at my shoulders.

I took a step back and knocked up against another platform. "Why is that?" I asked.

She looked at me for several seconds without speaking. "Just Murcia and Los Cielos."

"All right," I said.

Xinia led me out through the short corridor into the chapel and then out through the double doors that led onto the plaza. She locked them behind us. "The church is always open but I lock the vestry."

"And how should I get in to reach the vestry?" I asked.

"I'll let you in," she said. "I'll be sure to get here before you."

When I returned to the sacristy I found a man standing on the walkway, not sitting or leaning but standing with his hands clasped, waiting patiently.

"Father Amán?" he asked as I came up the walkway.

"Yes." I put my hand out.

"Aurelio Beltrán."

"Pleasure. Have you been waiting long?"

"No, not at all."

I moved past him toward the doorway. "Come in," I said.

Aurelio coughed and shifted his weight. "No, thank you. If you don't mind. It won't take long."

"All right."

Aurelio coughed again and cracked his knuckles. "I was wondering if you'd hired anyone to do the work at the cemetery." His hands were large and muscled, and the thin wrists that swam inside the cuffs of his button-down seemed too small to support them.

"No, I haven't. I didn't know there was one."

"There is."

"I mean, I didn't know where it was."

"It's on the southern edge of town. On the way to Murcia." Aurelio blinked and looked down. The skin of his forehead was deeply wrinkled, giving him a look of perpetual concern.

"Has that always been your job?"

"No, Father." He took a deep breath. "But I'm sure I could do it."

"No doubt. I just—I was wondering who had the job before."

"I wouldn't be taking it from anyone. I'm sure no one's doing it now." He put his hand over his mouth as if to stop himself from running on.

"Then," I said, "I'd be grateful if you'd do it."

He let out a breath and his brow cleared. "Thank you."

"Xinia's keeping the books—I'll check with her about pay."

"Thank you."

"Thank you for mentioning it. I might have gone weeks without going there."

"Would you," he hesitated, "would you like to see it?"

AURELIO WALKED without speaking, slowly and with his hands in his pockets. His trousers were worn at the bottom; he wore rubber boots a size too large that slapped lightly on the road after each step. As we walked south past what had been the school, two men who stood talking by a guava tree stopped to watch us pass. One of them, who looked younger than the other, cradled a plastic bag in his arms and looked down at the ground as we approached. Aurelio kept his head down and I nodded at them. The older man made the slightest hissing noise with his tongue, as if he'd just tasted something bitter. I said good afternoon and he looked back and forth from me to Aurelio without saying anything. Aurelio stared ahead unconcerned, his fists balled in his pockets.

At the cemetery he swiveled the rusting gate and held it open and then closed it behind us. He was right; no one had maintained the cemetery for years. It was possible no one had even visited, so thickly had the weeds crowded the graves. The gate led to a long path that cut across the center of the cemetery and split in four directions at the middle around a dry fountain. Each quadrant was laid out in rows, with mausoleums, raised tombs, and headstones all intermingled. The trees around the perimeter leaned inward, encroaching on the tombs, and weeds choked the brick walkways. Wild grass grew around the fountain and at the base of the grave-stones, which appeared here and there as only slim borders of stone.

At the edge of one of the walkways the ground had ruptured,

forming a deep, ragged hole. The dirt scattered around it looked dark and fresh. I looked down into it. "That isn't a grave?" I asked Aurelio.

He shook his head. "There used to be a mimosa tree. Someone took it away."

The size of the hole suggested that the tree had been enormous. In places, its broken roots jutted out of the earth, severed or ripped and gleaming white against the dirt. I turned to Aurelio. "Is there anyone at the cemetery with the name Amán?"

He looked at me for a moment. "Family of yours?"

"I don't know—maybe."

He shook his head. "I've never heard the name."

I looked back at the ground. "Who would steal a tree?"

He smiled and crouched down by the hole. "People sell them in the city, sometimes."

I nodded. Aurelio wandered off to inspect a broken stone and I stood near the fountain and looked in all four directions. The layout was beautiful in its precision; with the tombstones squared smartly, the ones in the north half facing the ones in the south, the cemetery resembled a chessboard, its pieces elongated by the setting sun. No two tombstones were the same shape, but they were all raised; none was like yours, sunk deep into the grass. The gate at the end of the walkway swung on its hinges, creaking mildly. A firefly dipped past one of the tombs, and then another appeared just next to my elbow and vanished. Aurelio came up to me with his cheeks flushed and his hands full of weeds. "I guess I'll come back with a hoe tomorrow," he said.

"Does this fountain still work?"

"I'm sure it does," he said, running his finger along the bottom. "Just too many dead leaves."

Four

WHEN PEOPLE WHO KNEW Guatemala inquired, you always asked in return whether they'd been to Rabinal. Very few had. You told them we'd come from a small town near there, a town they'd never heard of, and they took your word for it. I could remember only one person, a Guatemalan you befriended in Los Angeles, asking further. "Do you mean Río Roto?"

You nodded noncommittally: "Very near there."

After we left Los Angeles we didn't meet many Guatemalans, and I never heard you or Mamá say anything more specific. Then when I packed your books and papers in Oregon, I came across another name—one I'd never heard. The description you'd written was of the Mojave Desert, and the place I thought belonged to Guatemala received only passing mention:

The dry air makes my throat itch. The earth seems dead, stretching out in every direction like a dusty slab. When the sun sets the world goes blind. On the mountain, in places like Naranjo, it's completely different.

When I'd first read it in Oregon, it had seemed like an unmistakable reference to a place from your past. But when I reread it in Río Roto, it struck me differently. There were towns called "Naranjo" all over the hemisphere, and no one in Río Roto recognized our name. Besides, your writing didn't specify what the place meant to you. You might only have been passing through. You might have been there only once. Clear as it had seemed to me in Oregon, I realized in Río Roto that it probably meant nothing.

I could have asked you directly, sometime before the last year. But for the longest time I didn't even have questions. I began having them only when I went to college, and as a consequence the first version of Guatemala that I discovered came from reading newspapers; in this version the armed conflict of so many decades sounded like a thing belonging to the natural course of human life. I read repeatedly the articles that seemed to best describe the contours of that unknown region where I'd been born, though they sometimes made it more, not less, incomprehensible. The headlines my senior year flashed warnings, as if transmitting to the readers of the *New York Times* periodic updates on the state of a sinking ship. October 13, 1983: "Guatemalans Publish a Guerrilla Statement." November 9, 1983: "Guatemala Missionaries Accused of Subversion." November 18, 1983: "Guatemala Mobilizes 700,000 Civilians in Local Patrols." The stories themselves confounded me with their incongruous sense of detachment: the reporter was there, looking at the bodies and speaking to the heartbroken relatives, but he was undistracted. The war unfolded before him, its smells and sounds filling his ears, and he wrote of it with perfect correctness, so that the text—read at breakfast tables and on buses all over the United States—would be unspoiled by the humanizing touch of confusion, distortion, and dismay. There was no explanation of when the war had begun, or what was contested, or why, in page after page, death formed the only constant, appearing and reappearing in seemingly infinite forms.

I read further—interviews, books, magazine articles—and at one point I realized, as I arranged the dates in my head, that you were still living in Guatemala during the coup of 1954. Until then I'd unconsciously assumed that the papers, for all their inexplicable myopia, had more to say than the two of you, closeted away as you were in Oregon, hearing and seeing nothing. But I suddenly saw it differently. I realized clearly for the first time how little I knew about your lives during that time.

Almost at the same moment I became conscious of the possibility that my not knowing might be intentional. Other people I met in college whose parents had immigrated to the United States seemed to know much more than I did about their past. In some cases they had even gone to those other countries, those places that had been left behind. When friends asked me about your background, I found myself giving general replies that derived, as a matter of course, from things that I'd read. And the more I read, the more the place started to take shape in my mind. I began imagining it, first only interrogatively, as a matter of experiment and curiosity, and then intentionally, in order to fill the silences left by you and the wide margins of the newspaper. I'm not sure whether I was reading in order to avoid the necessity of imagining or in order to imagine better. My purpose became lost along the way when I realized, finally, that the reading would not satisfy, and that my own writing would have to pick up where the reading left off.

I wrote the first story about you during my second year of college. I began with your early years, projecting onto that distant screen the light of your present selves to create the images that would explain them: palpable reasons, in an accident, a hard year, an untroubled summer, to account for who you were. It came easily—too easily, I later realized—and in the years that followed I wrote and rewrote enough to describe every moment of your lives before the time I was born. I could even trespass on the early years of my life that I had no memory of, inventing where I was born and how you left Guatemala with me. But the time that brought with it a scattering and then a consistent stream of recollections, which I could trace back to my fifth year, formed an impenetrable barrier. I couldn't bring myself to contradict what I remembered with invention, and I couldn't reconcile what I wanted to invent with what I recalled. So my efforts rounded out to become the story of your first quarter-century with Mamá, the fiction of your early life as I wanted it to be. The writing offered some answer to all that I hadn't asked. It also made it all the more impossible to ever again contemplate asking; unlike before, there would have been something to lose.

At the university I became proprietary, making Guatemala the subject I claimed to know best and allowing no one to speak of it without giving my piece. It was assumed, by them as well as by me, that I had some hereditary claim; I had the last word. In reality, I had only a textbook knowledge of it, and I arrived in Guatemala with nothing more. Though in my more honest moments I surveyed the ground I'd staked and found it absurd, in retrospect there seemed to be more than a little justice to my position. I spent half my waking time inhabiting that faraway place, even though, like everyone else I knew, I had no understanding of it.

When i returned from the cemetery with Aurelio, the long habit of assuaging my sense of ignorance by burying myself in a book intervened, predictably, and drove me to the bookshelf. The hole of the uprooted mimosa had brought to life a passage from the Popol Vuh that I remembered imperfectly. It was the story of Zipacná and of how he'd been lured into a pit by his enemies.

"How shall we kill this boy?" they said to themselves. "Let us make a big hole and push him so that he will fall into it. 'Go down and take out the earth and carry it from the pit,' we shall tell him, and when he stoops down, to go down into the pit, we shall let the large log fall on him and he will die there in the pit."

Though the meaning of the story has changed for me, and it is now laden with implications I couldn't have imagined, in one regard Zipacná appears the same to me now as he did on that day. I recognize that the words, as they appear here, would sound like broken stutters to the Maya who, hundreds of years ago, watched their creation stories performed in an explosive splendor of sight and sound. But perhaps because I was fortunate enough to first encounter the Popol Vuh as something heard, not read, my opinion of its potential for majestic display has never wavered. Your reading of the Popol Vuh stayed with me, populating my mind with images of suns and jaguars, rabbits and turtles. Later readings only intensified that first impression. When I lay in bed listening to the exploits of the K'iche' lords, the battles played themselves out over my head in undiluted colors. The blood flowed in brilliant ribbons, and death clouded the air like a fog.

Outside the desert air would grow cool. You sat in a dark corner with a tiny light that came over your shoulder. Every once in a while the sound of the cars on the highway would reach us, disturbing the silence. I began by sitting with my back on the headboard, and gradually I would slide farther and farther under the covers until my pajamas were bunched up under my arms. Your voice rolled out slowly, describing a hole in the earth. A great hole, made single-handedly by Zipacná. His enemies, the four hundred boys, planned to trap him in it and make it his grave. But Zipacná knew their minds and he hid in a corner of the pit, calling out:

"Come and take out and carry away the dirt which I have dug and which is in the bottom of the pit . . . because in truth I have made it very deep. Do you not hear my call? Nevertheless, your calls, your words repeat themselves like an echo once, twice, and so I hear well where you are."

The four hundred boys rolled a great log into the hole, and Zipacná pretended to be dead. He gave bits of his hair and finger-nails to the ants, who crept out of the hole, parading the evidence of Zipacná's death. I felt very tired. The noises in the kitchen ceased, and Mamá turned out the light. I heard her footsteps go by as she walked to the bedroom. But Zipacná was still alive, and on the third day of hiding he sprang out and killed the four hundred boys, who, in their ecstasy, had drunken themselves insensible.

Five

ALMOST ONE IN THREE of the houses in Río Roto stood empty. Even some of the houses on the central square had been vacant for years, and they served as corridors for children seeking shortcuts and dogs wanting cover when it rained. The church, too, had fallen into disuse. Xinia had maintained the building, but the administrative structure had long since fallen apart. She told me I would have to look for a sexton and an acolyte, and there would have to be a new church committee. "Besides," she said, "people are used to the music, and we don't have a musician anymore."

The music was an electronic keyboard she kept stored in the wardrobe of the vestry, covered with a white sheet. After showing it to me, Xinia sat on the edge of the chair in the vestry. I'd moved some of my books from the makeshift shelves into the church, intending to make paper jackets for them, and they sat in a pile on my desk. "I've made a start," I said to her. "I hired a man named Aurelio to restore the cemetery."

Xinia looked at her hands in silence. Then she looked up at my desk. "You have an interesting collection of books," she said.

"Yes," I said, turning the spines away from her. "Well, they're mostly in English."

She looked at the other end of the desk. "I could have suggested someone for the cemetery."

I turned the books around absently and re-sorted them, putting another one at the top of the pile. "He offered. No harm done, right?"

She was silent again. "He'll mostly be down there, then?"

"Yes."

She stood up. "I can give you a list of names—people I recommend that might be interested in working with the church."

"All right, thank you."

"If you stop by anyone's house, they're sure to invite you in. They'll want to say that they had the priest over."

After lunch Xinia knocked on my door with a list of names. I asked her to come in and she said, "Let's sit in the vestry," and turned back down the walkway.

Of all the people I'd met only Estrada had crossed the threshold of the sacristy. Nevertheless I continued to ask people in, assuming only politeness kept them from accepting. With some irritation I followed Xinia to the study and sat across the desk from her. She handed me the list, first names written in capital letters. "I'll tell you where they live," she said, "so you can go see them."

I agreed and looked over the short list. In her hand the capital A's were triangles.

"You don't have to see all of them now, but Sunday is only two days away."

I looked up. "Sunday?"

"Morning service." Xinia sat very straight with her hands clasped in her lap. There were red smudges on her fingers, as if from a pen.

"I was thinking I would start next week."

Xinia looked at me. "I should think you would want to start Sunday."

The chair clattered as I pushed it back to stand up. "But there haven't been services for years. One week won't matter." I realized as soon as the words were out of my mouth that it was the wrong tack to take.

She paused. "I'm surprised to hear you say that, Father Amán."

"What I meant was it will take some time to get the congregation together after so long."

"On the contrary. Everyone is looking forward to it. We're eager for you to begin services right away."

"But still, we have to get the word out. Most people in Río Roto probably don't even know I'm here."

"Everyone knows. The whole town will be here on Sunday." She hesitated a moment before going on. "I don't know what you're accustomed to, but from my experience that means you'll at least need an acolyte."

I took a deep breath and sat down again. "I see. You must know."

She pushed the list toward me. "The boy at the top, Claudio."

"Was he the acolyte before?" I looked at the list again, running my eye over the names that meant nothing to me, as if looking at them closely would make things clearer.

"No, but he's happy to do it. You'll find him two blocks south of the plaza on the main road. On the corner."

"Across from the school?"

"The empty lot."

I looked up to stare at her. "The empty lot," I echoed.

"If I were you I'd go down there today or tomorrow. I've told them you'll be by."

"And he said he'd do it?"

"Yes."

I looked at her. "I'm sorry, I don't understand. He's already said yes?"

Xinia paused. She set her mouth in a line and spoke to my hands on the desk. "It's an honor if you ask."

"All right. Yes," I said. She glanced up at me and looked away quickly, her expression vexed. "Of course I trust your recommendation," I said. "But could you give me some idea why?"

"You don't have to trust me. It's only a suggestion."

I gave her a strained smile. "Why do you suggest him, in particular?"

She spoke slowly, stating the obvious. "Because he'll be a good acolyte."

I nodded. "But he's never done it before."

"No."

I looked down at the list again. "Then what? I'm just wondering."

She let out a short breath. "He just needs something like this."

"I don't follow you."

"Something to interest him."

I was quiet for a moment. "Maybe school."

She shifted in her chair. "Something more significant."

"School can be significant." I smiled inadvertently and looked away, but she'd caught my eye.

"No doubt for you it was."

"Actually for me it wasn't. At the beginning."

"So I don't know much about you. You know even less about us."

I leaned forward. "That's why I'm asking."

Xinia frowned and looked down at the desk. "I know enough, Father Amán. You might speak Spanish but you grew up American. That's obvious."

I waited, watching the muscles in her tensed hands. "I'm the first to admit I don't know how things are done here. But I'm trying to find out."

She was silent. I stood up and went to look out the window at the patch of grass. I had a diagonal view of the plaza, where the wind was blowing a sheet of newspaper across the street. When I turned back toward her, Xinia was still frowning. "I have trouble imagining how different they could be elsewhere." She stuck her chin out slightly and looked me straight in the eye. "It occurs to me, Father Amán, that we don't have your letter of introduction from the bishop."

I stared at her. "I assumed Tomás Morelio had received it."

"He may have received notice of your arrival. But don't you have a letter of introduction from the bishop yourself?"

"No, I don't."

She crossed her arms. "Do you have anything with you? A letter from your parish in the United States? From the bishop there?"

I didn't say anything. I looked away and thought for a moment. When I turned toward her again I avoided her eyes. "I do have a letter from my last appointment in the United States. But it's in English." I shrugged regretfully. "Sorry."

She blinked. "Perhaps you could give it to me anyway."

"Now?"

"Why not?"

"Well, it won't be any good to you, but I'll look for it." I sat down and opened the drawer of the desk where I'd thrown all my papers, including the letter from Tomás Morelio. My pulse remained steady as I looked for the recommendation letter the principal had given me when I'd left Rhode Island. I had a single folder with all my important papers: my birth certificate, some letters from you and Mamá, a number of informational press releases from the American embassy. I found the letter I was looking for toward the back of a file folder and looked it over briefly. The letterhead looked official, the signature was impossible to decipher, and the dense writing would be entirely incomprehensible to someone who didn't speak English. It described my teaching responsibilities and my credentials in the overwrought language of a professional reference letter. I handed it over to Xinia, irritated to see that my hand was trembling slightly.

She looked at it for several minutes with a blank expression. "Who is this from, exactly?" she finally asked.

"My last supervisor. I was living in Rhode Island, which you probably haven't heard of. It's a small state on the east coast of the United States."

She looked at me for several seconds and then down again at the letter. "This date at the top is from more than a year ago."

"Yes, I spent the last year taking care of my father. He died just a couple months ago. I came here because"—I paused—"after he passed away."

She looked at me closely. "I'm sorry to hear of your loss."

"Yes. He—my mother and I miss him very much."

I thought she would ask me something more about you, but she didn't. After considering me carefully for a moment she stared down at the desk and sat lost in thought. Finally she handed the letter back to me. "You can keep this," she said. "Thank you." She sat back in her chair. "You were asking me about Claudio."

I took the letter and turned it facedown on the desk. I'd lost all interest in Claudio, but I struggled to focus my attention on what Xinia was saying. Her tone had changed completely. "Yes," I said.

She nodded. "Well, I can't tell you much. But you know his only living relative is his grandmother."

"I didn't know." We both sat in silence for a moment. "When did he lose his family?"

"Some years ago."

I waited, but she didn't go on. "What happened to them?"

"They got sick."

"I'm sorry to hear it. All of them?"

She looked down at her lap. Her voice was very quiet. "Yes. All of them."

I tried to think of what else I could ask, but I'd lost the thread of our conversation.

"You shouldn't mention it," Xinia said, looking up. "To him or others."

"Of course—if you think I shouldn't, I won't. Thank you for telling me."

She nodded. "Not at all. Please come to me first, Father Amán, with all such doubts you may have."

I wasn't sure whether Xinia was making an offer or a request, and before I could make up my mind she'd risen from her chair. Moments later I heard her running water in the sink.

◆ ◆ ◆

THAT AFTERNOON I followed Xinia's list to the house by the abandoned lot. I had no reason to doubt Xinia's explanation, and Claudio's grandmother seemed to confirm it with her extravagant descriptions of maladies and remedies and the careful, almost overbearing watch she kept on her grandson. She was the woman I'd met on the day I first saw the schoolyard, and when she saw me coming she raised her pipe and waved me in, as if she'd been expecting me at any moment. Claudio agreed instantly to be an acolyte and waited for Josefa to ply me with coffee, rice pudding, and sweet bread. Josefa talked while I ate, and she talked so much that I ventured to speak more myself. I wondered aloud, when she finished telling me about the house she'd grown up in, whether she knew any Amáns. She shook her head and said she'd never heard the name.

I nodded. "I don't know anyone else who has it either. In the States, I mean. But I thought maybe here. Or maybe they've all passed away."

She shrugged.

"I might look in the cemetery. Is everyone from Río Roto buried there?"

She looked away. "It's such a small town that there are only six or seven names. Everyone's family." She told me the names of the neighbors on either side and the names of their parents and their parents' parents and how each generation had gotten old and passed away, and she never failed to itemize their various illnesses and the precautions they'd overlooked.

"You seem to know everyone," I said.

She laughed. "Not many people to know."

Claudio sat on his hands in a corner, kicking his legs out in front of him with impatience. When I finished eating, he popped out of his chair. His grandmother sighed. "He'll be wanting to show you the horse," she said to me, winking.

Claudio took my hand and pulled me out of my chair. "Do you have time to come see it?" I thanked his grandmother, and she extracted a promise from me about dinner on the Monday following the first service.

"Claudio, I don't have to remind you not to go near the sugar mill," she said as we left the house.

"No, Grandma," he shouted. I followed Claudio out the door onto the main street. He walked ahead of me, tripping along at a rapid pace and turning occasionally to wave me on. After a few blocks we cut across to the other side of town, away from the river, and continued west onto a path that climbed up into the hills. The route was steep but fairly dry, and I made my way up a few yards behind Claudio, who had to stop and wait for me. After climbing for half an hour, we reached a level spot with a view of the town. I turned to look out over the small valley. The soccer field and the empty lot where the school had been stood out like footprints. A cloud hung over most of the town at that moment, darkening the streets south of the plaza. The cloud drifted slowly north, setting the zinc roofs sparkling, until the whole town cast off a metallic light. A few people were walking past the stores in the center. A woman quite close by, near the entrance to the route we'd taken, sat on her back doorstep, leaning her head against the door frame. A dog moved her way—rounding the house sulkily and then hurrying over when it noticed her—and she shooed it away without moving her head. Claudio pulled me on, saying we were almost there.

The sugar mill had been abandoned for years. The pile of dried-out cane had stood by the grinder through countless wet and dry seasons until it had faded into a feathery mass. No one had removed the wooden molds—some of them still sat in rows on the long tables, others lay scattered on the floor. The cart attached to the ox's harness had come to a halt by the entrance. And all around it the cane had grown farther and farther inward, until it threatened to overrun entirely the machines that once ground and juiced it. Claudio winked at me as his grandmother had done. "She doesn't like me to come up here."

"Why not?"

He shrugged. "My father used to work here."

"Ah," I said. I looked again at the broken machinery of the mill. "Could be dangerous."

"No," he said. He turned away. "Come see the horse."

The donkey was tied to the guava tree with a frayed red rope. As we approached, the animal looked at us indifferently and went on chewing. Claudio ran his hand over its back, slapped its behind. "What a magnificent horse," I said. He smiled at me. He sat down near the tree and pulled out two sodas that he'd smuggled into his pockets. I sat next to him and took one. The warm soda tasted like bubble gum. From where we sat on the side of the hill near the sugar mill we could see the whole town below us.

Claudio waved his arm expansively, as if offering me the place. "From farther up you can see the river," he said.

"You come here a lot?"

"Every day. Farther up there's more cane and oranges."

"You found a good spot."

He nodded.

I looked in either direction—no other towns were visible in the hills. "Claudio," I said, "you seem to know these paths well."

"I know all of them."

I smiled. "That's impossible."

"I do."

"I don't believe you."

"Try me."

"Do you know a route to Naranjo?"

Claudio scoffed and looked away. "I know all the paths to real places."

"What do you mean?"

"My grandma's always talking about Naranjo. Just to scare me."

I turned to look at him. He tore at the grass by his feet and threw the green pieces into the air. "What does she say?"

He shrugged. "Some story about people from there. The evil eye. They look at you and you get sick or something. She just makes it up. I've never met anyone from there, anyway."

I looked away. "I hadn't heard that story."

Claudio curled his lip. "It's stupid."

The climb had made us dusty. There were dark creases of dirt in the skin of my hands. "What about a *naranjal*? Is there an orange grove somewhere?"

He nodded. "Yeah. It's in the Malvinas." He pointed to the right. "Over there. You go south on the main road, then go right where they've put planks over the stream."

"Thanks. I'll go see it sometime."

Claudio rested the soda on a flat rock. He took a dirty pocket knife out of his pants and walked over to the cane nearest us. With short, steady thrusts he sawed a stalk of cane off at the base and after sitting back down he cut the other end of it off and then split it down the middle. He offered me half. I took it and watched as Claudio sank his teeth into the wet, fibrous pulp at the center of the stalk. I did the same with mine and sucked out the grassy syrup. The white marrow was tougher than I'd imagined and I came away from it with my lips raw. When we were through Claudio finished his soda and then he drank mine and we sat back on the grass, feeling the sugar burn in our stomachs. After a while, he said, "I don't know how to be an acolyte."

"Don't worry about it too much. It's not hard—I used to be one a long time ago."

He looked at me. "You can teach me, then?"

"Sure. Though I'm not sure you do everything the same way here."

"That's all right." He made a sharp little shrug.

Claudio put the empty soda cans back in his pockets and we climbed down the path. I checked when we passed, but the woman who'd been sitting on her back doorstep had disappeared into her house. The dog I'd seen lay sleeping in her place.

I took Saturday afternoon to walk in the Malvinas, the hilly area Claudio had pointed out to me lying west of the river and south of town. I left after lunch, taking the main road south until it dwindled into a narrow dirt road. A dairy stood on the left, and an abandoned house across from it seemed to have tumbled down the side of the hill. After a mile the road dipped and intersected a stream that fed into the main river. On that afternoon the stream was almost dry and I walked over to the other side on a battered plank that lay across it. The path climbed steeply past a pair of empty houses. Farther up, the stream fell in rapids, throwing up mist and forming pools large enough to swim in. Trash floated downstream erratically, swirling and catching against the rocks: a detergent bottle, a plastic bag with something inside it. The houses farther up were smaller and made of wood with foundations on raised platforms surrounded by trampled mud. A few hens made their way through it, their scabbed feet brown. The buzzing whine of a radio and loud thwacks, as if someone was slamming a knife onto a cutting board, sounded from one of the houses. Past the houses two boys in their underwear lay on a rock beside a pool. An older girl who hadn't gone swimming sat near them in the shade, and she followed me with her eyes as I walked past.

At one corner, where a narrow band of water cut through the rocks and then across the road in a thin, brilliant strand, a swarm of black butterflies suddenly came around the corner toward me. I started and then made myself stand still. They approached as a cloud and with their peculiar, agitated movements, as if threaded together, brushed against me. Seen through their restless dance, the green hills of the Malvinas appeared to blur and drop away. For a moment I felt a kind of superstitious lightness—as if privy to a distant vision of dread—and then the butterflies passed. I turned and saw them dropping, descending to the stream like scraps caught on the wind. I walked on.

Most of the hilly area called the Malvinas was uninhabited. Some of the people in Río Roto had plots of coffee or pastures in it. I passed a few cows grazing in a square of barbed wire, and where the stream was finally inaudible I reached a depression in the hills that had been mown or burnt bare. It was a view you would have liked; you would have observed the stillness. Only the

passing clouds betrayed any movement. The town below lay hidden from view and the hills all around made dense folds, so that I
felt that I'd been dropped into their wrinkles. At the edge of the
cleared pasture stood a shack bleached gray from the rain and
sun, and at first glance it seemed abandoned. A moment later,
looking at it again, I saw smoke rising from the narrow chimney.
Half a dozen cows watched me arrive and began to converge on
the shack as I moved closer. I sat in the shade of a tree to rest.

I stood up to move on when a man emerged from the shack
and began making his way toward me. I'd thought for a moment
that he meant to go see the cows, and he did, but then instead of
going back into the shack he began walking across the pasture in
my direction. He wore rubber boots that came up to his knees.
His shoulders were wide but his face and arms were thin, giving
the impression that he'd once been much larger. When he stood
about ten feet away from me, he stopped and put his hands in his
pockets.

"Am I trespassing?" I asked.

"What?" he said. His face was pockmarked, his mouth set in
a line.

"I thought I might be on your land."

He shrugged. "Possibly."

"It's a beautiful spot."

He turned to look around him. "Good for grazing."

"I'm Nítido Amán."

He nodded. "The new priest."

"Yes." I'd walked closer to him, and we both stood with our
hands in our pockets, looking out over the pasture. I turned to
him, waiting, but he didn't offer his name. "Is there an orange
grove around here?"

He glanced at me. "You're in it. The orange trees are along-side the road all the way up."

I smiled with embarrassment. "I don't know much about trees."

He shrugged. "You can tell from the smell," he said. "Sweet smell. The air here puts the cows to sleep. I sleep better up here, too."

"You camp out in the shack?"

He nodded. "It doesn't get too cold." We were silent for a minute. The cows took a few steps, continued grazing. "How long have you been here?" he asked.

"Came from the States less than a week ago."

He murmured something to himself that I didn't understand.

"What?" I said.

"My mistake."

"About what?"

"You look like you're from here."

"I am. But I grew up in the States."

He nodded and seemed to think it over. "You preaching tomorrow?"

"Yes. First sermon."

He gave a hard smile and glanced at me.

"Are you going?" I asked.

"I'm not much for church."

I nodded and thought about what I was supposed to say to that. He moved away. I thought he was going say goodbye, but instead he beckoned with his left hand and I followed him over the grass to where the cows grazed and a handful of trees grew next to the shack. Without looking at me he walked among the trees and reached a tall, narrow sapling of something I didn't rec-ognize. I stood by, watching. He grasped it with both hands and crouched and pulled with his legs and his back until the ground burst and the roots came free in a bundle of dirt. Holding the roots up he smiled faintly and I nodded, not knowing what he meant me to say, and he walked back to the side of the shack and plunged the roots in a bucket of water. He worked the roots with his hands underwater, breaking the clumps of dirt loose. When he pulled the roots out again I could see dangling from its ends what looked like oversized peanuts. He took his machete out and hacked at them, cutting them free. He handed the largest one to me and I held it, thinking it weighed several pounds. "Cassava," he said.

"Thank you."

"Don't mention it." He squinted at me and smiled grimly. "You know how to cook it?"

"Like potatoes."

He shrugged. "Can be. They're best fried."

"All right. I'll try it."

"Take these too." He picked two oranges off the tree nearest him and with the machete cut a cross on the navel of each. "To peel."

"Thank you."

He walked out to where the cows stood. I stood next to him, waiting, but he didn't turn to me again. I looked at my armload and wondered whether he thought I'd come up on purpose to see him. "I didn't know anyone lived up here," I said, breaking the silence.

"No one does live up here." He didn't smile, but his eyes blinked slowly in acknowledgment. I thanked him again and walked back the way I'd come. When I turned back to look he was gone or inside the shack. The fire seemed to have exhausted itself, because once again no smoke rose from the chimney.

Six

SINCE MY ARRIVAL in Río Roto I'd almost always understood, in a literal sense, everything people said to me. I never had to ask anyone to repeat or rephrase what they'd said. But I often had the impression, as I had in the Malvinas, that I'd nevertheless failed to grasp the meaning behind their words. I can only describe it as a kind of unaccountable incompleteness, as though every time someone spoke to me a few of the words fell away before they reached me. Everything I heard seemed to have pieces missing.

Before arriving in Guatemala I hadn't expected language to be a problem. Though I spoke English and they spoke K'iche', Spanish would be our middle ground. I envisioned conversations taking place in the Spanish I knew, with words that were clear and familiar. But after spending less than a day in Río Roto I realized that the words could be clear and familiar while their meanings weren't. People spoke to me in nothing but direct, unambiguous Spanish, speaking K'iche' only among themselves, but I nevertheless could never quite follow. I increasingly found myself attempting to make sense of what people said to me by repeating it to myself—by translating it—in English.

I hadn't realized until then what should have been obvious to me all along: regardless of what language I was speaking in, my thinking always happened in English. And yet, as I reflected in Río Roto, I must have learned to think in English over time, because I didn't always speak it. For at least those few years before I started school, I must have thought in Spanish. Most of my time during the first year in school I spent by myself; the clearest memory I have is of myself alone in the playground. The garden walkways branched out from a central circle, separating the herbs, in triangular wedges, from the roses at the edges. Between the garden and the school building stood a bay tree, a swing set, a seesaw, and a wooden boat with two oars. The other children mostly played inside and no one showed any particular interest in the boat. Its paint curled at the slightest touch and the handles had so cracked from the rain that on every visit I lodged a penny in the fissures without ever running out of room. I remember sitting in the boat, paddling the oars in the dirt, glancing occasionally at the nun who watched me from the window. She would always be there when I sat down, and then a few minutes later she would be gone, called away by someone else.

The dirt, the bay tree, and the rose garden—none of them seemed incompatible with pulling on the oars and coasting out onto imaginary waters, farther and farther from the school. I was always surprised to step out and find myself on land, only a few feet away from the building, after it had been receding steadily for fifteen minutes. Sometimes I dropped the oars and allowed the boat to drift. My mind would wander, and I would become absorbed with something—picking the paint off the seat or cleaning the dry leaves out from the bottom. Below the indentations made for the oars, dime-sized holes just large enough for my fingers had been drilled into the sides. At first I'd used these as windows for observation but I later realized they were meant for tying the oars in place, and when my mind wandered and I forgot to row, I often slipped my fingers into these absently, until on one occasion the bell sounded and I found that my forefinger was stuck in the left side of the boat. I tried to pull; my finger swelled and turned red. When after several minutes I couldn't dislodge it, I panicked. The nuns passed the window without looking out. No one else was outside. I didn't want to shout or cry, but I had to make myself heard. I spoke as loudly as I could. For several minutes, no one came. Then someone must have realized that I was missing. I saw Sister Catharine peer out through the window. A moment later she was running out toward me. "Speak English, dear. What is it?" Five minutes later all the nuns were clustered around me; they had poured dish soap on my hand. I wiggled my finger, Sister Catharine gave it a little tug, and my hand came free. I was about to hug and kiss her in relief, but her face was stern and worried, and so in my confusion I kissed my finger and they all laughed. "Nítido," Sister Catharine said to me, "you must try to play with the others so you learn English. And don't talk to yourself so much. That's not going to help either." She spoke very clearly and slowly, and I understood her perfectly. By the end of the year I spoke as fluidly as the other children, but the difficulty of speaking clearly and being nonetheless misunderstood had always returned, a continual problem that I couldn't always account for.

It had never occurred to me, as it did for the first time in Río

Roto, that the difficulties of translation were almost indistin-
guishable from the difficulties of comprehension inherent to
reading and listening. As the man in the Malvinas spoke to me,
I couldn't help translating the meaning of his words, but in
translating what he—and everyone else in Río Roto—said to
me, I sometimes had the impression that I was choosing blindly,
arbitrarily, from among the possible translations. Perhaps as I did
so, the real meaning of what people said to me was lost.

Long before I would reflect upon these questions, you encap-
sulated for me, in a single moment, the very point I later discovered. I was just on the verge of learning to read; the books
that most captivated me did so with their suggestive images
rather than with their words. I can no longer recall their titles,
but even now I can remember perfectly the illustrations, the place-
ment of the text, and the changing sensations I experienced turning their pages. One in particular, which I later bought and then
lost during one of our moves, still has the ability to move me
deeply whenever I think of it. The book was a puzzle; three stories ran in parallel to a single set of illustrations. For days, when I
first found the book, I could only study the pictures and stare at
the three blocks of text next to them. When the librarian discovered what I was doing she went through the book three times,
reading each of the stories aloud once. Then she checked it out in
my name and sent it home with me. By the time I reached home
I remembered the ideas but not the words, and I wanted to know
them again. I showed the book to you and Mamá; you both
exclaimed at the beautiful illustrations. I didn't think my request
strange, since you read aloud to me almost every night, but when
I pushed the book toward you and asked you to read it, you
paused, and Mamá got up a moment later and left the room. You

took up the book with a somber expression and told me the story, turning the pages slowly so that I could inspect the illustrations. I interrupted you halfway through. "Papá," I said. "That's not how it goes. You're changing it."

You were silent for a moment. "The story is in English," you said. "I am translating it."

"But the stories are totally different in English."

"Yes," you said, after a pause. "That doesn't surprise me."

It may be that you were already learning. You must have been cowed by how Mamá, who wasn't as shy and spent more time with English speakers, had a greater facility with the language. But perhaps the picture book had some effect; by the time I was older and reading on my own, you kept pace with me, so that I often found you reading my books when I was through with them. But you never read to me aloud in English, and I wondered whether you were simply embarrassed or rather meant, purposefully, to make certain I continued to hear Spanish. When I was too old to be read to, you continued to put the Spanish books on my shelf. "You'll forget if you don't practice," you would remind me.

Nevertheless, it had never occurred to me that your concern about forgetting the language extended to yourself; certainly I never dreamed that you were writing. But in Oregon I found the cabinet in your room full of spiral-bound notebooks crammed with your tilted cursive. For some time I resisted the temptation, because you'd clearly meant to keep them hidden, but as the months progressed I felt myself forgetting how you used to speak. I wanted, you see, to hear your voice. I allowed myself to look at them, thinking I would skip the parts that you wouldn't have wanted me to see.

As it happened, there wasn't anything to skip. Even though you wrote journal entries, you rarely wrote about yourself, or even about Mamá and me. I couldn't find, in all that I read, a single line of introspection or reflection. Some passages detailed a situation you'd observed or a person you'd spoken with, but your greatest subject was the physical landscape, and on this subject you were exhaustive. You described the drive through the central valley, and then a few pages later, described it again in almost the same way, as if trying variations. On occasion an entirely new description would spring up between one paragraph or another; then other versions would be exactly the same, repeating twice, three times, four times, the thirty-minute glimpse of the coastline, or the middle of the day in Sacramento. I thought you might have been experimenting with style, or that you were returning to the memory again and again, trying to recapture the original impression it had made. But it occurred to me for the first time in Río Roto that you may have been translating: interpreting the landscape around you to make it familiar, rendering it in a language that would give it a clear meaning. As I do that myself, now, I can only imagine the small victories, the more frequent sense of futility, that you must have experienced. Even though this exercise allows one to recreate the place in one's own language, it doesn't prevent one from misunderstanding the place in its original language, and it may even run the risk of concealing, through the semblance of coherence, a total lack of comprehension. Sometimes, in reading your descriptions, I would not have recognized the places you described at all, had it not been for a name or some other marker.

Mamá didn't know about the notebooks, or if she knew she didn't mention them. When I moved her things, I packed most of them with her books and hid them in a trunk in her new apartment. But some of them I took with me to Río Roto, packing them in my suitcase, which I was glad of later because they hadn't been ruined by the rain. I still have them, and though I've read all of them repeatedly, there are passages in them that continue to move me deeply every time.

Seven

THE RITUALS OF MASS, familiar to me from childhood, were simple enough to perform. Writing the sermon, however, was a completely different question, and as I delivered it, I felt keenly the small errors of phrasing and the greater errors of content and tone. Even this effort, however, soon came to seem insignificant. The afternoon of the first service I began taking confession, and the confessions released—in a trickle and then a wave—concerns that would sweep me away, nearly obliterating my original purpose in Río Roto. At first the confessions struck me as only further instances of failed comprehension, but as they began to repeat themselves, not in their specifics but in their general contour, they came to suggest a meaning I couldn't ignore.

Because on that Sunday the first woman who came for confession, Carmen, began by talking about the sermon, I was distracted at the very moment when the nature of the confessions first made itself apparent. Only later, when I considered it in light of other confessions, did I consider the significance of what she'd said. Carmen's braided white hair coiled over her forehead, giving the impression of a dented crown. She held her hands with her bent and callused fingers curled in her lap. The dress she wore still bore the stiff creases of the packaging, though it had been ironed; from its pocket she pulled a white handkerchief embroidered with blue flowers.

"Father, I'll leave this for you," she said. "You might ask Claudio to tie it around your thumbs."

"Thank you. I hadn't thought of that."

She nodded. "My sister used to be incredibly clumsy. We'd tie her thumbs together. But next time you won't be as nervous."

I looked down at my knees. "I hope so."

"You shouldn't be. You can't expect us all to understand it." She smiled. "I'm so slow, myself."

I looked at her through the screen. She folded and refolded the handkerchief and then spread it out over her knee. I didn't know what to say.

She looked up at me briefly and smiled. "You must be very intelligent."

"Not in the least. I'm sorry, I'm not always as clear as I mean to be."

"I'll have to try harder next time," she said.

I wasn't listening as she started her confession. I began going over the sermon in my mind, trying to remember certain parts of it. I would have to ask someone about it—perhaps Estrada. And yet I thought I hadn't made any obvious mistakes. Most of the collected sermons I'd brought with me were of no use: Ralph Waldo Emerson, William Clancy. They were philosophical tracts, and reading them before writing the sermon had evidently not put me in the correct frame of mind. I did have the two John Perry volumes you'd picked up at a garage sale in Oakland. I'd only brought them because you'd made some notes in the margins, but now it seemed worthwhile to read them through. From the little I'd read of Perry, however, it seemed I would be incapable of writing anything like his sermons.

I looked up, hearing Carmen pause. She seemed unable to go on. I hadn't heard any of her confession. "Go on," I said.

She put the handkerchief against her mouth and her lips turned faintly white. I was surprised to see tears in her eyes. "Father," she said.

"Yes?"

"I've been very ill."

I didn't say anything for a moment. I had the impression that she'd finished confessing and had gone on to speak of something else. "I'm sorry to hear it," I said.

She sighed deeply. "I have headaches. They start at the back near my neck. Then they spread out, filling my whole head. I have to close my eyes. If I don't, I see a blinding light around the edges. Everything I try to look at seems far away. Very far away, and then the light puts them out completely. Sometimes the pain goes on for hours. The longest one lasted two whole days. My daughter puts a cold towel on my head and I sit against the wall. Lying down makes it worse."

She waited for me to speak. I said the first thing that occurred to me. "How long have you been having them?"

Her voice shook. "For many years."

"Isn't there anything you can take?"

She glanced at me, surprised. "I've tried everything. Nothing helps." I waited, hearing in her silence that she expected me to say something else, but I couldn't think what. After several minutes she spoke again. "Forgive me my sins, Father."

When Carmen left I thought nothing much of it, but her confession struck me as I listened to Luz, who was waiting to confess afterward. Luz had never gone farther than the door of the sacristy and she rarely spoke to me. She purposely collected the dishes and laundry when she thought I was out. When she left my meals, she knocked twice and then slipped away, so that no matter how quickly I got to the door she'd always reached the street by the time I opened it. At confession, she seemed more at ease. She spoke unhurriedly. I noticed a ring on her finger and corrected myself; I'd only ever seen her in the house across the street with her mother.

"Father," she said, after a long pause, "I've been very ill."

I was silent for a moment, feeling a pang of surprise and waiting for her to continue, but she didn't. "I'm sorry to hear it," I said.

She looked at me curiously and I knew I'd said the wrong thing. Then she dropped her head. "I feel nausea and pain in my stomach. It happens suddenly, at any time of day. Most often when I go to bed. But sometimes when I'm in the middle of something. Then I have to stop what I'm doing and curl up until it stops."

"How long does it last?"

"Sometimes just a few minutes. Sometimes an hour or more. Just as suddenly the pain's gone."

"Have you seen the doctor about it?"

"No." She paused. "He doesn't know what it is. I was with my mother walking to the bus stop once and the pain came over me suddenly. It was raining out, hard. As soon as the nausea hit me I dropped my umbrella and fell to the ground. My umbrella rolled away. My mother stood over me, trying to cover me with her umbrella. Everything was an inch under water. All my clothes were soaked. When I got home they were so heavy I could barely lift them off. I threw up in the bathroom. I coughed up rainwater and gravel. It looked like the water that runs in the sewers, but I couldn't have swallowed so much water so fast."

I struggled with what to say. None of the formulaic responses I'd prepared seemed adequate, and the discordance between her words and her tone left me entirely at a loss. "I'll have to talk to the doctor," I said.

"Don't, Father."

"I didn't—I meant for myself."

She paused. "You're sick?"

"I'm sorry—that's not what I meant to say."

She looked at me in silence.

"When was the last time you felt this way?" I asked.

"Thursday."

I looked at her hands and noticed that her knuckles were raw. "I saw you on Thursday."

"Yes," she said quietly.

"You were sick then?"

"Yes."

I loosened my collar. The air stifled me. "Is there anything else you want to tell me?"

Luz glanced at me and hesitated. Then she sighed deeply. "Forgive me my sins, Father."

Of all the people who confessed that afternoon, nearly half spoke to me of illnesses. I had no idea how to consider their confessions, much less how to respond adequately to them. The only thing that came to mind was how a few years before I moved to Oregon, when you'd already been diagnosed but were still in the early stages of the disease, you sometimes spoke to me on the phone of certain changes, or, more accurately, you confessed them. I could never tell what, if anything, you meant to communicate to me, because Mamá was always on the phone. In admitting things to me, you were really apologizing for them to her, and as I listened—to your apologies and her responding protestations—I always felt as though I was somehow eavesdropping. You had, for instance, told me about going to the shopping center once; Mamá had gone to do her own errands and returned to find that you'd left without her. You confessed it ashamedly: not because you'd done anything intentional, but because it had inconvenienced her so much, and no amount of assurances from her could make you think of it otherwise. But the confessions in Río Roto were altogether different: they didn't seem to be confessing the burden of their illnesses upon others; they were rather confessing the illnesses themselves, as though sickness itself were a sin.

I HADN'T SEEN Aurelio after our visit to the cemetery, and I'd been meaning to walk down to see him again. As it turned out, he came to me on Monday after I finished taking confessions. I was working in the office of the vestry, and Xinia had directed those who wished to request prayers to see me there. No doubt she had some idea of what would occur, because she arranged a row of folding chairs in the corridor and placed a table with a pitcher of water and plastic cups next to the door of the study. I watched her and said nothing. When she was through she came to the door and said, "If you get tired, I don't mind taking over."

"Thank you. I'm sure I'll be fine."

She hesitated. "You know you can ask me for help with whatever. If for the sermon—" She paused.

"Thank you. I don't need help with the sermons."

She nodded and went to the back room. I looked at the things on my desk and pushed them around and then stacked them and then spread them out again. I took a pen out of the desk drawer. A moment later the first person arrived. He'd written a list of five names on a slip of paper. Without speaking—he nodded solemnly and held his hat against his chest with his left hand—he handed the paper to me and stood waiting. "Thank you," I said. "Are your loved ones ill, or are they far away and in your thoughts?"

"Deceased," he said, with some difficulty.

"I'll be sure to say a prayer for them during the service."

He stood uncomfortably, waiting. "You're to write them in the book," he said.

"Yes, of course. I'll do that before Sunday."

He looked at his feet, his expression anguished. Finally he took a deep breath. "Would you write them in?" he said. "So I can see."

I stared at his down-turned face. "All right. If you'd like." I took the bound journal that Xinia had given me—the pages at least twice the size of letter paper—and opened it. I'd looked at it earlier, when Xinia first told me of it, with the idea of looking for people with our name. I found your first name repeatedly and Mamá's twice, but the name "Amán" never appeared. What appeared were hundreds of other names, which I hoped, in some way, to make sense of. Almost half the pages in the ledger were full. The names were written in a careful, tiny hand: first names alone or first names and last names, rows and rows of names, four columns per page. Every few columns a date interrupted them. The most recent entry had been in August of 1990. I turned to the first empty page and wrote the date. Then I wrote the five names on the man's slip of paper: Otilio, German, Felix, Angel, Luis.

When I looked up I realized someone else was already waiting at the door. She sat on the chair Xinia had set up, holding a piece of paper, looking in expectantly. The man standing before the desk nodded his thanks and left. Then the woman came in and handed me her list. Three names, all women, all deceased, she told me when I asked. I wrote her names down and she thanked me.

I couldn't see the line from where I sat behind the desk, but every time I looked up, the chair by the doorway was occupied. I took names from half a dozen people before noticing something unusual about the lists. Though they hadn't been at first, they all now bore the heading "deceased," underlined and in capital letters. And they were all written in the same hand; the A's were little triangles. The man standing in front of me had given me two names. I wrote them down and handed the piece of paper back to him. He stared down at me coldly. He wore canvas pants and a machete in a sheath strung around his waist. His shirt was stained under the arms. I looked at his face and down at his list again and neither one made any sense to me. I assured him the names would be read, and he nodded and left the room.

It was as he left that I realized the next person in the chair was Aurelio, and I saw his face only briefly because then the man's back blocked it. The moment passed very quickly. As the man with the machete reached the doorway, Aurelio stood up to enter, and then—I was certain of it at the time—the man spat at his feet and turned the corner. Aurelio walked into the room, his face blank. He smiled at me briefly and handed me a piece of paper.

"Aurelio?" I asked, searching his face. I would have said something more, but his expression stopped me.

"Father Amán," he said, staring hard at the ledger in my hands. "The cemetery is looking better."

I glanced down at the paper he'd handed me, feeling unsure. "I've been meaning to go see it," I murmured. The paper read "deceased," and listed the names of two men. I wrote them in carefully and handed the paper back to him. He looked me in the eye and smiled. "You'll see the fountain's running," he said. Then he turned to go. At the door he stopped to thank me.

I stood up from my desk and walked to the other side. The woman who'd been waiting in the chair stepped into the room. From the doorway, I could see Aurelio disappearing down the corridor in the direction of the back room. The folding chairs in the hall were full. The people sitting there nodded when I came out and a few of them wished me a good afternoon. The line, as far as I could tell, extended into the back room and around the corner toward the door. I walked down the hallway and stopped when I reached the narrow back room. The line went out the door and onto the grass. I couldn't see where it ended. Xinia sat in a folding chair by the sink, holding a notepad and a pen. Everyone past her in the line had a slip of paper and everyone behind her didn't.

"Xinia," I said.

She looked up. "Yes?"

"You're writing the names?"

She looked at me. There was an uncomfortable silence. Everyone around us looked back and forth from me to Xinia. "Some people are unsure of their handwriting," she said.

I stared at her. A woman standing in line ahead of her laughed lightly. "Some people."

"Well," I said, looking around us, "couldn't you just say the names to me?"

Xinia's face clouded over. She stood up. "I have to get another pen," she said. She walked down the hallway toward the study and I followed her. The woman I'd left behind stood by the desk with her hands clasped on her belly. When we walked in, Xinia said something to her in K'iche' and the woman left, closing the door behind her.

Xinia looked at the ledger and I waited. "You're doing very well," she said.

"Why do it twice?"

"Father Amán, not everyone knows how to write."

"I know. That's why I'm saying—they can just tell me the names."

Xinia frowned and turned the ledger toward her. "They will. Eventually."

"All right." Her attempt to encourage me had left me tongue-tied. I didn't know what else to say.

"When they know you better."

"All right. I understand," I said, trying to make it seem so. I took the ledger and I walked back to the other side of the desk. "Thank you, then."

She left the room, the next woman came in, and I took her names. After two hours, the line dwindled, and by dinnertime, only a few people remained. I'd filled two pages of the ledger and written more than two hundred names.

A MAN named Oscar who'd agreed to be the sexton walked with me to Murcia the following day for the first service there. When he told me he was a carpenter, I asked him if he worked with Xinia's brother, and Oscar said, after a pause, "He was an artist."

I looked at him. "He was?"

Oscar shook his head. "Died years ago."

I looked at him. "How?"

"He got sick."

"I'm sorry to hear it," I said. "He must have been quite young."

He nodded without saying anything more and we walked past the abandoned dairy in silence.

Oscar pointed at a flattened piece of scaled skin in the road and began telling me about the snakes he'd seen on the way to Murcia, warning me that the one with scales like black velvet had a poisonous bite. He described the snakes that slept beneath the coffee shrubs, waiting for anyone who picked coffee barefoot, and the *come-caballo*, a spider rumored to crouch inside a horse's shoe and eat away at its hoof. We walked south, in the direction I'd taken to reach the Malvinas, but instead of turning up to the right we continued on the main road, which joined with the other that ran parallel to it through town so that we walked alongside the river.

I told Oscar I'd been to the Malvinas, and he agreed that it was beautiful. When I told him I'd seen someone up there, who kept cattle near a shack, Oscar nodded. "So you met Hook."

"I didn't know his name."

"We just call him that. I hope you didn't talk to him."

We'd paused by the side of the road. Oscar took a drink of water from his thermos and offered me some. I drank and handed it back to him. "No," I said, "I didn't. Why?"

"Best not to."

"Why's that?"

He shrugged.

"It did seem," I said, "that there was something funny about the air there."

Oscar laughed. "There's something funny in the air anywhere he goes. Poor man."

The path took us closer to the water and Oscar walked quickly. I was having difficulty hearing him. "Why?" I asked.

"He's completely lost it, that one," Oscar said, raising his voice.

"What do you mean?"

"You didn't talk to him?"

I struggled to catch up so I could hear him. "No."

"Well, that's best."

We'd reached the footbridge. Buried in weeds by the foot of the bridge stood what looked like a twelve-inch cocoon made of stone. Oscar tapped the top of it: a statue with bunches of decaying flowers strewn at its base. "Some people fell off the bridge years ago," Oscar said.

"What was it?"

"What was what?"

"The statue."

"I don't remember. A Virgin Mary, maybe. Or San Antonio."

The bridge trembled as we walked across the river; it was narrow, and I held on to the wires at either side. Even though it hadn't rained heavily for days, the brown water churned violently, eating at the roots along the banks. On the opposite side a narrow path ran alongside the river. Murcia was far above us, embedded in the hill, beyond what seemed like an impenetrable wall of sugarcane. Oscar wandered off to the left and peered into the cane, as if trying to see something through it. "The entrance is here somewhere," he shouted over the water. I walked along the edge of the narrow path in the other direction, staring into the cane. Moments later, Oscar gave a shout and waved and I met him at the entrance of a tunnel barely wide enough for a single person that cut upward through the cane. "It's fastest this way," Oscar said. "The flatter path takes hours."

The stalks grew far above us—the sun was still out, but setting, and only the surface created by the cane a foot above me received any light. Oscar walked quickly; he said that after dark it would be impossible to see and that we would have to take the long route or ask for a light. Smoothed by water and the passage of the cane-cutters' feet, the path wound blindly through the tall cane. After a few minutes Oscar outpaced me, and I walked on without catching sight of him. The blades overhead shone dully in the orange sunlight, though at their base they already lay in shadow. I could no longer hear the river. I had the sense that I walked in place and that the film of light above me would remain long after the sun had set. Without stopping, I glanced to either side of me into the cane, transfixed by how its dense stalks obliterated everything in every direction. The steepness of the path began to affect me; I breathed heavily and the sweat ran off my chin.

We reached Murcia as the sun was finally setting. Below us, the cane stretched toward the river in what seemed, from that vantage point, like a scant half mile. Fewer than a dozen houses, all recently painted, were scattered on the flattened side of the hill. The chapel was the largest building and well maintained, though as far as I knew it hadn't been used for years. There were only about twenty people in the pews, but I nonetheless found myself feeling nervous.

I'd decided to try something different with the sermon, after coming to the conclusion that another performance like Sunday's would raise questions. The sermon I'd read to the congregation in Río Roto had quoted Scripture, but it was correct only in this particular; its style, argument, and structure were more suited to a college English paper than a sermon. In preparing the sermon for Murcia I'd tried first to read the Reverend John Perry's sermons and then to formulate something in his style. But with the text beside me, I found it difficult to think beyond his limits. He'd pinpointed precisely the most pertinent meaning of each reading; all my attempts to improvise beyond him resulted in poorly phrased renditions of his ideas. In places you had translated or underlined some of Perry's metaphors; reading them I was surprised by their lucidity and power. I couldn't resolve the question of why or whether it should be, but there was no doubt that Perry's turn-of-the-century stringency could speak more truly, more directly to the congregation than anything I could write. The idea of having to use his sermons chilled me. The difficulty wasn't that anyone would notice the plagiarism or, much less, recognize Perry—who would? Translated into Spanish, he would be all but unidentifiable. Rather the problem would be with knowing: standing there, reading someone else's words, knowing that I had the capacity to pretend they were mine. I had told myself that with the smaller congregation at Murcia it would be easier to try the Perry sermon for the first time.

I was distracted during the service by a pale green insect that appeared on the lectern halfway through the sermon. As long as my forefinger and with delicate, veined wings like the leaves of a sapling, it stood on the corner near the edge of my papers. I inspected it as I spoke, watching the thin line of its belly, a ribbon of green and white stitching, rise and fall with its breath. Several times I lost my place in the sermon, looking to see whether it clung to me or perched somewhere nearby.

When the service ended I pointed it out to Oscar, who scooped it up and held it in his palm until the daughter of the woman who gave us dinner asked to see what he held, and she exclaimed in delight at the good-luck omen, taking up the *esper-*

anza carefully and holding it aloft in her cupped fingers. Two men with flashlights guided us back through the cane to the bridge, and then Oscar and I made our way back to Río Roto in the moonlight. The flashlights of the men, walking back uphill, were entirely swallowed up by the cane, and the houses above seemed to have already extinguished their lights. The angle of the road on our return gave us a view of Río Roto, and as we approached, the few lights that guided us disappeared gradually, until only one remained. Oscar entered his darkened house on the southern edge of town, and I walked on toward the church, disoriented by the stillness of the evening. Though we'd returned before nine, the town was already sleeping.

I remembered as soon as I saw it that I'd left the bulb by my front door burning. At first I couldn't make out the peculiar shadow that darkened the front of the house—something corrosive had apparently bored through the door and the ceiling around the bulb and the walkway, leaving a black, irregular hole—but after coming to myself and walking on I realized that every insect in the valley had been drawn to the bulb, the last one to go out. The writhing swarm that covered every illuminated surface seemed to be not crawling over but devouring the entrance of the sacristy. It carpeted the ceiling around the bulb so thickly that I could make out no single insect; they formed an undulating mass of legs, wings, and glittering eyes that emitted a dull murmur. Beetles the size of my open hand crawled on the walkway; a green insect I'd never seen with a long body and spidery legs dangled from the doorknob; dozens of moths with enormous wings wavered or rested by the bulb. A desperate fluttering sounded from the moths, like the pattering of fingers on a closed door. Their eyes glinted metallically in the light and their furred bodies collided against one another recklessly. Before the door and facing outward, as if on guard, crouched a harlequin beetle as big as a sewer rat. Its legs spread easily to the edges of the doorway. The other insects moved around and under it, insensible to its size. I stared at it in horror, thinking that it might not be real, until its immense left antenna jerked upward and I stepped back, repulsed. A dozen other insects clung to the chain for the light, dangling perilously as they crowded against one another. As I stood watching, a giant moth with wings as wide as my outstretched hands flew out of the entryway and toward me. I ducked down and batted my arms wildly, feeling its wings everywhere at once. When I was able to stand calmly once more I rounded the house and checked the windows, which I'd locked. Then I checked the door to the vestry, which Xinia had locked. I thought of going to her for the key but felt immediately that I would prefer to sleep outside. The sight of the insects had filled me with disgust; I felt the urgent need to leave, not caring where I spent the night. I walked out to the road and looked at the house from the street.

It was difficult to tell, because the house lay in darkness, but I thought I saw the curtain in the front room of Luz's house fall. A moment later, the light by her door went on. Within seconds, a moth flitted across to it, batting at the bulb. I waited, but she didn't appear. I heard Luz's voice from the front window. "Turn your light off," she called out.

I looked at the chain, still covered with insects. "Thank you," I whispered toward the window. Taking the sermon out of my bag, I laid the papers flat over the insects in a row, as far as possible from the harlequin beetle. The bodies underneath the papers cracked and gave way under my feet as I moved forward. I held the rest of the sermon in my hand and swatted at the chain, batting the falling moths away from me, until only a few remained. Still holding the papers I curled them around the chain and pulled, feeling the insects breaking under my fingers. The light went out. I shuddered and jumped away; perhaps I imagined that the insects would rush past me, as one, to the light across the street. In fact it took nearly half an hour for them to fill her front door, and when I finally forced myself to light the bulb of my house again, there were still a few stragglers. But the harlequin beetle had gone. I turned the light off and got inside as quickly as I could, checking to see how many had followed me into the house. There were none.

Though it drew them to the glass, so that I heard their hard patter on the window, I felt unable to turn out the bedroom light. I wouldn't have been able to sleep regardless. Instead I sat in bed reading until the sky lightened behind the curtain.

The walkway was clean in the morning when Luz knocked with the breakfast tray. I thanked her, and she smiled and told me I would get used to it. "I hope you don't mind," she said. "I threw your papers away." She looked down at my feet as she said it. I thanked her again, and she waved me off as if it had been nothing. "And someone left these for you." She handed me a plastic bag with oranges, their navels marked with crosses.

A MAN I RECOGNIZED from the day I'd written names in the ledger came to confession that morning and spoke with me. It seemed he often had difficulty with his right arm. "It's sudden," he told me. "There's no warning—it goes limp. I can still feel it, but I can't move it. I think about moving it, and nothing happens.

But when I pick it up with my left hand, it feels my fingers on the skin."

He spoke with embarrassment, his eyes on the ground. I asked him whether he'd ever injured it. He held it out and rolled up the sleeve. "Do you see anything?" he asked. I shook my head. "I don't either," he said. "A few weeks ago at the market I was unloading crates of tomatoes and suddenly—limp. I had to pull it out from between the crates with my other hand, and then it just hung there."

"What did you do?"

"Nothing. I couldn't lift the crates with one arm. Everyone knows it happens sometimes. So I just stood by the truck, watching everyone else do the work, while I waited for my arm to come back."

"How long does it last?"

"Sometimes just a few minutes. Sometimes more than a day. Once I went a whole week without it. I've gotten used to doing things with my left hand, but it's not the same." The muscles in his arm moved slightly. He sighed. "What bothers me is that I can still feel with it. When I touch it with my left hand, or when it brushes against something, I can feel it. But since I can't move it, it feels like the arm isn't mine. It feels like I have someone else's arm." It occurred to me, listening to him, that you must have experienced something similar when we moved you from chair to chair and propped you up at the kitchen table: as though you were suddenly accountable for an entire body that you couldn't control. The man shook his head and held his right hand up in front of him, comparing it with the other hand. "Then when it comes back to normal it's a little slow, remembering how to do things. I'm clumsier than usual." He half-smiled sadly. "Whoever it belongs to when it's not mine must be careless."

The man who came to confession afterward and introduced himself as Oso was shaped like a barrel. His hands and arms were covered with thick hair, and during confession he tucked his shaggy head down to whisper, bent as if expecting a blow. It didn't happen to him very often, Oso told me, but when it did he was useless for days. His feet would swell, puffing up slowly until they resembled loaves of bread. Then he had to sit back and wait for them to shrink.

"The first time it happened," he told me, "I thought it would only last a second. I was wearing rubber boots. I felt my feet swelling, and I thought they'd fallen asleep. I'd been sitting still for a while, milking, and when I stood up I realized something was wrong. My feet pressed against the sides of the boots. I couldn't move my toes. I tried to take the boots off to see what was wrong with them, but it was too late. The boots wouldn't budge. With my feet like that I limped back to town—it was like wearing iron casts—and when I got home my wife cut the boots off with a pair of shears. She got blisters cutting through the heavy rubber. Then she cut my socks off with scissors. My feet were the color of eggplants. My toes stuck out like stiff little teats on an udder; my foot and ankle were just a pulpy mass. For days they stayed that way. I tried soaking them in cold water, hot water, salt water. The pain was steady, but not intense. It wore me out. Just before they finally began to shrink I thought the pain would drive me crazy, like a toothache. As soon as I feel the swelling now I pull off my shoes and socks and sit there, waiting for them."

Another woman had told me about a similar swelling that took a more unusual form. She was slow to get started. In her hands she held a handkerchief, which she folded over and over again. She hunched forward in her seat, her ankles crossed, rocking herself agitatedly when she described the painful aspects of her illness. It seemed that she had, some years earlier, begun to feel a violent pain on the skin of her back. At first she only recognized it as a burning tenderness—she couldn't lean back in her chair or lie on her back; she had to sleep on her stomach. It felt as though the skin of her back were on fire. She stood under the cold water of the shower for some relief, but it eventually burned through the water, too, so that the abatement of pain was only ever temporary.

It didn't occur to her at the beginning to look at her back, so only on the third occasion did she take off her shirt, hold a small mirror in her hand, and look through it over her shoulder at the larger mirror behind her. What she saw caused her to drop the mirror, and it took her a while to pick it up and look again. She told me, in a whisper and on the verge of tears, that long red welts covered her back. She'd never suffered an injury that might produce them and she had no idea what caused them. The pain eventually died away; she awoke some days later lying on her back and she looked in the mirror. The marks were completely gone. Each time it occurred in the same way—the pain began, the red welts appeared, and then they vanished.

THE CUMULATIVE WEIGHT of the confessions, the names of the deceased, the absence of any defined date or event, and the mention, here and there, by Xinia and Oscar of people who had succumbed to illness all suggested that some contagious sickness—a plague, an outbreak—had swept through Río Roto in the recent past. What I'd heard combined with what I'd read— books describing the contagions visited upon the Americas by the Old World in the sixteenth century—suggested that the town struggled with some kind of repeating epidemic. I couldn't help but think, as I heard the confessions, that an old sickness was once again returning. I say this so you understand that I honestly never tried to blind myself to what lay behind the illnesses; on the contrary—I believed I'd hit upon the explanation by bringing my observations and my reading knowledge to bear.

"You're ill?" Xinia asked, when I told her I was going to see the doctor.

"No, I'm just going to visit him."

She studied me. "He's really out there, you know."

"Yes, I know what you mean," I said.

"Really. He lives in a different world."

Her emphatic tone surprised me. "You think so?"

She shrugged. "He thinks it's the rest of us who are crazy. See what you think." She told me he lived on the north side, in a field near the road to Los Cielos. "You're still going?" she asked.

"Do you not want me to?"

She gave me a look and seemed to lose interest. With a wave of her hand she walked down the corridor.

I left for the doctor's and found his house as Xinia had described it. The porch ran halfway around the building. The doctor sat in a wicker chair by the door, smoking. He waved to me as I walked up to the house and smiled when I reached the steps.

"Sick already?" He grinned.

"I'm just saying hello."

"Hello, then." He pushed himself out of his chair. "I'll get some lemonade." I sat in the other wicker chair and he disappeared into the house, coming back a few minutes later with two bottles of beer and a glass of lemonade. "I changed my mind," he said. "You'll want the lemonade."

I hesitated. "Yes, thanks."

I took the glass and leaned back in the chair. The porch had a view of the hills beyond the town where the Malvinas lay. The house closest to his had a hexagon of laundry line strung up in back. A chicken coop littered with hay stood by a stump with firewood stacked next to it. We drank and looked out over the field. I held the glass against my forehead and felt it grow warmer.

"Dr. Estrada," I said, "I'm worried about how many people seem to be sick."

The doctor took a swig of beer and swallowed loudly. "Are they?"

"They tell me in confession—they have all kinds of illnesses."

He grinned. "The privacy of the confessional is sacred, Father."

"Yes." I flushed. "I won't say anyone in particular. But I wondered if you knew."

"That they talk about being sick in confession?"

"That so many people are sick."

The doctor didn't answer me right away. He drank his beer and looked out toward the hexagon of laundry. After a while he put his beer down and said he would be right back. He went into the house and came back carrying a guitar. He smiled at me, sat down, and ran his fingers absently over the strings. I'd stopped drinking the lemonade and I stared at him, thinking about what Xinia had said. Soon his strumming revealed a discernible melody and he said, "Father Amán, tell me."

"Yes?"

"Anyone told you about an illness came through here—ten years or so ago?"

"I've heard something about it, I think."

He nodded and continued playing the melody, something in

the minor key that unraveled quickly. "Anyone in particular they said?"

"Who died?"

"Yes."

I'd thought about it before going to see the doctor, but I waited a moment before saying anything. "Xinia's brother, I think. Oscar told me he got sick."

The doctor nodded, ended his melody, strummed twice, and began another tune. I took a sip of the warming lemonade. "Vicente," he said, playing slowly. He spoke rather than sang, as if the words and the music were unrelated. "Grows orchids in a greenhouse. Drinks rainwater from his boot." The doctor's beady eyes blinked slowly. He smiled to himself. "Vicente"—he strummed—"twenty-four." My stomach lurched and I took another sip. "Vicente makes cabinets and furniture. Pews for the church. Saints for the wealthy. In the city. Eleven years old, he goes to the dreamer. The dreamer in Los Cielos, in a house built himself. Three floors. Balconies on every floor. Wooden gargoyles on every corner. A garden full of statues. Varnished so they wouldn't spoil. Over the door the sign says, 'House of the Dreamer.' Vicente's his only pupil. When the dreamer gets old, it's only Vicente. Working, working. Chiseling, carving, sanding. The dreamer does nothing but miniatures. A crèche that fits in his palm. A rosebud the size of a fingernail. Eyes, you know, good to the end. You can go see the house. Still there.

"Last time I saw Vicente alive, he was coming back from the Malvinas with a bag full of orchids, wrapped in wet towels. The day was dry. He was covered with sawdust. Where did I see Vicente next?" He looked at me.

I swallowed and shook my head.

"He was a statue. A statue at the dreamer's house. The dreamer gone without a trace. Vicente a fallen statue. No varnish for the rain. Lying in the grass, arms at his sides and his legs curled up. A statue of infancy. Of youth, perhaps. Of death, certainly. Gone almost a day. And yet no way to know. Only mark on him, apart from the calluses, the blisters—always forgot to wear socks—were small cuts. Tiny cuts. Little cuts in his mouth, on his lips. Like he'd bitten into a glass. A mirror, maybe. His sister said go ahead. I opened him up. What did I find?"

I stared at him.

He smiled. The melody he was playing tinkled to a close. "Two meters of barbed wire, coiled up in his stomach, all the way up his esophagus." He raised his eyebrows. "Two meters. Amazing."

My hands were trembling. I put the glass on the floor and held my hands together.

The doctor looked up at me. "You don't like my playing?"

"You're very good," I said.

"I saw it myself," he said softly. We looked at each other. He laughed, suddenly. "Peculiar illness, don't you think?"

"Yes."

"Peculiarly contagious, I'd say." He laughed again and struck up another melody, tapping his heel on the wooden floorboards.

I listened to him for a while, trying to make out what he was playing. "Does anyone know why he did it?"

He played on, smiling at me. "Did what?" He laughed. "You think he got hungry?"

I stared at him.

"He didn't get to pick the menu." He chuckled to himself, shook his head. "Poor Amán," he murmured. "Thinks he gets to pick the menu." He looked at me and winked. "But you don't, do you?"

"Don't what?"

"Pick the menu."

"No, I guess not." I reached distractedly for the glass, and looked at it and took a sip.

"That's right," he nodded. "I give you a lemonade. Drink it. Luz at the door. Eat chicken. Eat rice." He shook his head again. "Poor Amán. Poor Amán." He sighed. "I bet in the States you got to pick the menu."

Eight

THE LEDGER had accumulated many Vicentes—two in my handwriting. I didn't know who they were; I didn't know who anyone was. The names I would read aloud on Sunday were only names. The slips of paper in Xinia's hand seemed to fall in a flurry before me; the expressionless faces of their bearers had already become blurred in my mind so that they appeared less as the agglomeration of a hundred people than the hard, anonymous substance of their core, which while pushing me away as a stranger began also to erode the details that made me the particular stranger that I was. I felt the danger of losing, in the effort to understand their inscrutable and nameless commonality, the qualities that allowed me to see it as something I lacked. I would drift, and become lost, and when I reached the center of their mystery I would arrive as a blank page, with a hundred dimly recognizable names written upon me.

After returning from Estrada's I'd spent an hour leafing through the ledger, and I had no better sense of what his words meant. The next time someone arrived for confession I would be as much at a loss as I'd been before. Then I remembered, with a flash of surprise, a passage from Eric Thompson's *Rise and Fall of Maya Civilization* that spoke of the priesthood in relation to sickness. I found Thompson's book and flipped through it until I found the right page. The passage was just as I'd remembered it.

> An important duty of all members of the priesthood was divination. . . . Forms of divination . . . survive to this day as part of the training of village shamans or calendar priests. These are used principally for ascertaining such matters as the causes of sickness or the names of those who have caused it by black magic, the location of lost articles, whether a sick person will recover, or whether a girl will make a good wife. . . .
>
> The treatment of sickness was an important part of a priest's duties, the first task being to divine the cause of the sickness, often found to have been "sent" by an enemy or to have been caused by "evil winds" or failure to make the required sacrifice and prayers to the gods or to carry out some ritual correctly.

I saw in Thompson's description a series of implications that I hadn't considered before. When I read his words in Río Roto I finally understood the connection between illness and the priesthood that I should have understood, from personal experience, years earlier. As I reread Thompson's passage I recalled my last month of college, when I'd been sick with vertigo. To most people vertigo means a faintness brought on by the fear of heights, but it also manifests itself as an imbalance of the inner

ear causing dizziness, disorientation, and nausea. In my case it
was accompanied by fever. I'd at first dismissed the symptoms,
thinking they were due to lack of sleep. For days, I would open
my eyes in the morning after lying sleepless all night and
my head would spin so that I had difficulty sitting up. I would
reach for the clock and my hand would land on the pillow. The
extreme disorientation worsened when I stood up or made a
movement of any kind. The only relief came from lying, sitting,
or standing perfectly still.

I was taking medication to little effect, and it was your suggestion that I see Marie. I barely remembered her, but you and
Mamá had only good things to say about the time you'd spent
with her in California, and from her position as chaplain at my
college she'd kept a friendly eye on me over the years. Not until
I was sick with vertigo did I take up her long-standing invitation
to stop by. I sat in her office, waiting for her and admiring how
the room was more like a living room than a study. There were
armchairs and a pile carpet; she'd laid out things for tea on a long
coffee table. The sun came in through the windows behind her
desk and the beams of light, descending vertiginously to the
floor, caused my stomach to lurch violently. Just then Marie
walked in, smiling, a kettle full of hot water in her hand.

"Don't worry if you need to just rest your head back and close
your eyes," she said. "I know you're not ignoring me."

Though her voice was oddly sharp, even sour, there was no
mistaking the gentleness behind it. She walked over to the window with the kettle still in her hand and lowered the blind, then
turned back toward the room. Remembering the kettle, she set it
down on the rug and muttered something about a potholder. She
went off in search of it, tucking her graying hair back into her

hairpins as she walked around the room. Marie seemed to have all the time in the world. Her slow, somewhat absentminded movements immediately calmed me and I felt easier than I had for weeks. "Thank you for seeing me," I said.

"I'm delighted to see you," she said. She filled the teapot with boiling water and set the kettle aside on the potholder. "What a rough month it's been for you."

I nodded and my stomach lurched again. I closed my eyes.

Marie made a sympathetic noise. "I can't imagine what you've been through. But you're getting the degree; that's good. They would have to have hearts of stone to expel you at this point."

She had a way of speaking that was so unembarrassed and matter-of-fact that I couldn't feel ashamed. I realized, as we went on talking, that she was able to speak this way because she believed me implicitly. Unlike the professor who'd first called me into his office to point out the plagiarism or the administrators who'd interrogated me endlessly, Marie assumed that I was in the right before I'd even explained myself to her. It astounded me. I found myself describing to her what had happened with perfect honesty and none of the confusion that had made things so difficult with the administrators.

"I think," I said to Marie, "part of me really believed that what I was writing could be true of my parents. Since they never told me anything, I always made it up. And when I read about other people coming to the U.S., I guess I filled in the blanks. And then I just wrote that way."

Marie nodded. "Of course. That makes perfect sense."

I looked at her, feeling fully the injustice of it. "Some of those books I don't even remember reading."

"Cryptomnesia," Marie said. "I've read about it."

"It's like they were gone from my head, but then they came out when I was writing."

"Isn't that amazing?" Marie looked at me in wonder, as if marveling at some ingenious feat accomplished by my brain. "I'm surprised anyone even picked it up. It must be unusual in creative writing."

I sighed. "Actually the professor said I was the fourth case this year. But the only one in the senior creative-writing seminar."

Marie knew precisely what I was thinking. "But you're not like them. It's totally different when it's unintentional."

I realized then that these were the words I'd been waiting to hear for an entire month. I felt suddenly, immeasurably relieved. "I won't get the double major—just history. And all my recommendations for grad school have been withdrawn." But even as I said it the thought of it no longer bothered me as much.

Marie made a face. "So you'll miss grad school. Poor you."

The vertigo lasted for another two weeks, and in other ways, of course, the underlying condition never completely disappeared. But the most extreme symptoms began to dissipate after the visit with Marie. At the time I saw no connection between the two things; only in Río Roto did they appear to me in an altogether different light. Still, I knew that I didn't have the skill for either the kind of divination described by Thompson or the kind practiced by Marie.

Furthermore, there was the suggestion in what Thompson had written that illnesses could be brought about not only by internal anxieties but by external causes—by an "enemy," as he put it. His words suggested that another explanation might better account for what Estrada had told me. I searched for the part in Murdo MacLeod's *Spanish Central America* that explained how such external provocations occurred. It required no modern medical knowledge to believe, as people had for centuries, that illnesses could be inflicted by peoples upon each other. Diseases are not always neutral, their carriers blameless. The organism itself might be, but the one who spread it to others, particularly in a state of immunity, could be considered to bring the disease upon a people as an act of war. I'd once read that in the Brazilian jungle, anthropologists and explorers had provoked among the Yanomami of the twentieth century something similar to what the Spanish had created centuries earlier in Mesoamerica: unintentional, perhaps, but nonetheless responsible. MacLeod's description in *Spanish Central America* is unclear in its use of "holocaust," though as I read it I presumed, insofar as he considered the epidemic genocidal, that he also considered it culpable. On the other hand, his treatment of guilt is complicated, and it's difficult to say where he lays the principal blame or whether he thinks of blame at all. He describes the smallpox and plague brought by the Spaniards to Guatemala as the "shock troops of the conquest," forces that devastated the population before any armed battles began.

Indian accounts of these first epidemics in Michoacán and Guatemala are quite explicit. Such diseases had not been known in the region before; the death rate was catastrophic, and demoralization and illness were so widespread that the piles of dead were left untended and unburied for the vultures. Native sources in Yucatán, where a similar epidemic struck, called this time of sickness "oc-na-kuch-il" which is to say "when the zopilotes come into the houses," that is, when the dead lie about everywhere untended. . . .

Given present day knowledge of the impact of smallpox or plague on people without previous immunities, it is safe, indeed conservative, to say that a third of the Guatemalan highland population died during this holocaust.

It was an entirely different matter, I decided, putting the books back on the shelf, if the illnesses confessed to me pointed to the marching progress of troops I was unaware of.

Nine

I USED THE SAME SERMON in Los Cielos on Thursday, and
on Friday I ate with Aurelio, his wife, and his twenty-year-old
daughter. At one point, because Aurelio's wife asked, I found
myself telling them about you and where we'd buried you in
Oregon. I tried to describe to Aurelio the design of the garden
cemetery: the way the stones lay flat; how the curving drives were
bordered by pine trees. He asked me to stop by the Río Roto
cemetery when I could, so that he could show me something. I
promised him I would visit on Saturday, and without mentioning
to him that I would bring her, I asked Xinia to go with me. She
agreed to go, thinking, perhaps, that I wanted to show her the
progress Aurelio had made.

He'd cleared the central walkways of weeds, and the fountain
was running. Xinia sat on the stone lip of the pool while I went in
search of Aurelio. I thought I'd seen him as we were approaching,
but when we reached the fountain there was no sign of him anywhere. Xinia had pinned her hair back above her ears and I saw
her readjust the barrettes as I returned. Under her blouse she

wore a silver necklace with a pair of rings, which she fiddled with as she waited. I'd never seen her idle; there was something uneasy about the way she rested, as though she didn't know what to do with herself. For a moment, when she turned toward me to see who was coming, her expression lacked its usual composure, and I almost felt sorry. But then her face hardened, and I made myself continue. "Xinia," I said, "is your brother buried here?"

Her cheeks flushed and she looked away. I couldn't see her face; her arms were tightly crossed. She got up and began walking away from me, toward the gate. I thought she was going to leave without a word. But instead she turned left halfway up the walkway. She didn't look back and I hurried to follow her through the mausoleums toward the northern edge of the cemetery. We passed a number of tombs whose borders still looked raw from the clearing of weeds. One to my left had just been doused with water. The hose lay coiled beside it and the etched walls were dark with moisture, but Aurelio wasn't in sight. Xinia stopped in front of a plain headstone and stood with her arms crossed, looking down at it blankly. It read, "Vicente Mora, 1959–1983." Next to it was another identical stone reading, "Constancia Mora, 1961–1983."

I looked at Xinia and her eyes stayed on the stones. "I didn't know you had a sister," I said.

"His wife," she said. "She was two years older than me."

We stood there for some time, and I thought about the things I'd rehearsed, none of which I could get off my tongue. Xinia made no effort to hide her face from me, and I watched her mouth settle wearily. I tried to be watchful, to read some sign in her smaller movements, but I had difficulty noticing anything beyond my own agitation. Instead of exultation I felt a burning on my cheeks, embarrassment for what I'd meant to say; nevertheless I had to say something, and the impulse to provoke from her some unintended declaration faded into the definite necessity of making my curiosity seem the result of a misunderstanding. Finally I just said, "The doctor told me about him."

"Estrada talks a lot," she murmured.

"I thought— Someone else said—" I hesitated. "I had the impression he'd died of an illness."

"He did."

I paused, felt myself redden again, and said in a rush, "A peculiar illness, then."

Xinia's eyes hadn't moved from the headstones. As I spoke she looked above them to the wall of the cemetery and her expression sharpened. I looked in the same direction and saw a pair of pigeons rustling in the shade. "It came," she said, "from Naranjo."

I was silent as I watched her reach under the collar of her blouse for the rings that hung against her breastbone.

"The illness came from Naranjo," she said again.

I stared at her. "Estrada made it sound like something different."

"He would." Her eyes were bright. "Estrada doesn't understand about some illnesses. It's not his fault." She looked up briefly and spoke to the wall. "No one in Río Roto is to blame." The pigeons on the other side of the wall suddenly shot into the air, hesitated over the wall, and then scattered, flying over our heads toward the cemetery. She turned to me abruptly. "Let's go back now."

"All right," I said. My embarrassment had died away, and I began to wonder how much more she might have said. Her expression was elated, as though she'd gained a point in our conversation. We walked back toward the walkway and headed for the gate.

As we reached it Aurelio came through in the other direction, carrying a hoe. His face flushed as he wished us a good afternoon. "Thank you for coming," he said. I complimented him on how much had changed.

"Anything else you think of that I might do"—he inclined his head toward Xinia—"anything that occurs to either of you, I'll see to it."

"Thank you, Aurelio," I said.

Xinia nodded. We left him standing at the gate, holding his hoe in one hand and a bundle of weeds in the other.

ON THE SUNDAY of my second sermon in Río Roto I awoke from a dream in which I watched men working below me in the firelight, fortifying the walls with sandbags and smearing the ground around the embattled stone building with sheets of tar. The alarm clock read three o'clock. There were voices coming from just outside the front door, and I struggled for several seconds to distinguish them from the men in my dream, but I couldn't make out what they were saying. I stared into the darkness, watching the remaining traces of the dream—the smell of tar, the uncertain light of the fires—recede like condensation on a mirror, and before I could lean back again I heard a knock on the door. It took me only a few seconds to put on my shirt and shoes, but by the time I reached the front room the voices had died away.

I opened the door and, after a moment, looked down. The man lying faceup on my doorstep had his right hand on his heart. His eyes were closed, and his left arm lay in the wrong place. Blood that looked black in the silver light covered his face and arms; his clothing was shredded. I stepped over him and looked out into the road. The men I'd heard had gone.

I looked more closely into the face of the wounded man. His nose was broken and pools of blood had gathered in his eye sockets. I didn't recognize him, but it would have been hard to. I took my flannel shirt off and covered him with it. I stared at him with the sense that if I thought hard enough I would comprehend why he was there. You would have known what to do; I could only stand there.

"Father Amán," someone said. Xinia came toward me from around the church.

"Xinia," I said. I watched her come with a certain dizziness, realizing at that moment that I was still half-asleep. I'd dreamt of Xinia, and I couldn't recall what she was meant to do next.

"I told them to bring him to you," she said.

"What?"

"It doesn't matter. Get him inside. I'll get the doctor."

I looked down at the man by my feet. "Help me carry him."

She turned away. "I'll get the doctor."

I watched her leave; she walked quickly and disappeared around the church in a moment. I turned to look at Luz's house. There was no sign of movement there, though I knew she had to be awake. The man on my doorstep groaned. I went inside and pulled the flat sheet off my bed and took it outside and placed it next to the man. I lifted him onto it by moving first his head, then his shoulders, then his waist, and then his legs. They were thin and hard, ropelike. I moved him toward the middle by pulling the sheet under him. Gathering the sheet in two fistfuls over his head to make a limp stretcher, I pulled him over the tile floor into the front room, down the corridor, and into my bedroom. It took me almost ten minutes.

I heard the sound of feet pounding on the dirt road as I was wondering how to get him onto the bed. A moment later the doctor ran in, wearing his pajamas and a coat and carrying a bag in one hand and his glasses in the other. "Turn on the light," he said, breathing hard. The sheet was already heavy with blood. The doctor jammed his glasses on and held the man's face and neck, then lifted his arms and opened his shirt. The worst cuts were to his face and arms and back. He'd curled himself up to receive the blows. "Get the shower curtain," the doctor said. I ripped it off the curtain rod and laid it over the bed. We each took two corners of the sheet and lifted him onto the plastic. The doctor glanced at me. "Does it make you sick?" I shook my head. "Help me get his clothes off, then." I lifted the man's head and torso and then his legs as the doctor stripped him. He asked me for a bucket of warm water and a towel. Estrada washed the man quickly, wrapping the shallower wounds with strips of gauze. In places the skin was cut in deep flaps. The lower half of his left ear was missing. His head bled the most, his hairless scalp hardly more than a veil swimming over his skull.

The man hadn't regained consciousness by the time the doctor finished stitching and wrapping his wounds some two hours later. There was gray sunlight at the window. My arms ached as though I'd carried the man all night. We put the bloody sheets and clothes in a garbage bag and washed the bucket and the floor. The doctor used my shower and then I did the same, adding my bloodied clothes to the garbage bag. When I went to the kitchen to make coffee I saw that my front door was still open. Xinia sat in the chair outside the door, sleeping peacefully, her head resting against the window. Her hands were folded in her lap and her hair was loose, falling over her eyes. She woke up when I came back with coffee and she pressed her eyelids with her fingertips, as if trying to keep her eyes in place. The doctor and I sat on the doorstep.

"Looks like cuts from one machete," the doctor said.

"Do you know him?" I asked.

The doctor looked at Xinia. "He's the priest—the *mayordomo* from Naranjo," she said.

The doctor said something under his breath to his coffee cup. I thought I heard him chuckle.

"Who brought him?" I asked.

"They found him that way," she said.

"Who?"

"My cousins were on their way to the Malvinas. He was by the road for Murcia and I told them to bring him here." She looked at me. "He'll be safe with you."

"I don't mind," I said. Xinia looked at me and then looked at her coffee. "Though it's far for Estrada," I said.

She turned to him. "It's safest. No one will come close."

Estrada smiled faintly. "It's no trouble to come down here." He paused. "Are you sure, Amán—" He stopped, hearing a noise from inside.

The doctor and I stood up and went to the bedroom. The man's eyes were barely open. I reached him first and leaned in so that he could see me.

"Diego?" he said uncertainly.

"Nítido. Nítido Amán." He blinked at me. "This is Dr. Estrada."

The man ignored the doctor. He gave me a weak smile. "Nítido," he said, slowly. "Santos. From Naranjo."

PART II

Ten

THE NEWS OF SANTOS'S unforeseen arrival swept through Río Roto like a current of cold air over a pond, freezing the mud from the edges inward, molding the soft center into a fixed, brittle suspension. I stepped onto it unwillingly, trying to make the sermon I'd prepared sound as inconspicuous as possible, thinking, of each word, that it could have an additional meaning I hadn't thought of and checking, with careful glances at the still faces of the congregation, for the first sign of cracking under the accumulated weight of my phrases. I read from Perry's *On the Shortness of Life and the Length of Eternity*, which I'd translated the night before.

I no longer have the Spanish version that I wrote, but I did keep the copy of Perry—as a kind of penance, you might say. Though which of them is not a kind of penance? Perry, MacLeod, Tedlock, Thompson, the Popol Vuh: I recognize that collectively they are a consolation, a link with the past. When I return at the end of the day, seeing them on the shelf is the only thing that reassures me: yes, I've returned to the right place; this is where I belong. But as soon as I open one of them, every word seems to be a rebuke: of each mistake, misstep, of everything not yet known or known too late. Perry, whose gloomy appeals once seemed fabulously gothic, now strikes me as deliberately and maliciously ironic. If the significance of his words could vary so greatly for a single person, over time, then it's impossible to doubt that Perry's sermon meant something very different to the congregation in Río Roto than it did to me that day.

The reading on that Sunday was from John 16:17: "Then some of His disciples said to one another: What is this that He saith to us? A little while, and you shall not see me; and again a little while, and you shall see me." Perry had, as usual, divided his sermon into two complementary points. As I read the first point, on the shortness of life, before the congregation, it struck me that Perry's writing consisted less of original thought than of compilation. I thought to myself, then, that copying a bibliography was not the same as copying prose.

It is not very difficult to convince men both of the shortness of the present life, and of the miseries that attend it. The ancient Patriarchs, who lived to a much greater age than we now do, had, equally with us, a feeling sense of this truth. We read in the book of Genesis (xlvii.8), that, when Jacob was asked by the King of Egypt: "How many are the days of the years of thy life?" he answered: "The days of my pilgrimage are a hundred and thirty years: few and evil." Indeed, as St. James says (iv.15): "What is your life? It is a vapour which appeareth for a little while, and afterwards shall vanish away." The Psalmist compares it to a spider's web, which the least accident may break. (Ps lxxxix.9) Yes, Man is here today, and gone tomorrow.

You had underlined "a spider's web" and drawn a star in the margin. I thought, as I read the sermon, about the accidents suggested by the psalm.

But, on this subject, it will be sufficient to appeal to your own experience, What does your past life now appear in your eyes? Does it seem to you much more than as a dream? Does not your review of the past, when you look back upon it, make you feel the truth of those words of holy Job, that "man liveth but for a short time, and is filled with many miseries"? (xiv.1)

I'd brought the ledger with me, and I said prayers for the deceased for the first time that week after the sermon. In later weeks, I would realize that the unusual stillness that fell over the room was due to the reading of names, but on that first occasion I only took notice of the silence without knowing what caused it. They'd filled the seats and the day was warm. Though Xinia had opened the windows the room grew stuffy, so that the smell of incense became rancid and heavy. As I began, even the children grew quiet. Every eye was fixed upon me in silent concentration. I read slowly, to give each name its due, reading for half an hour, then an hour; by the end of an hour I had not yet read half the names and yet the perfect stillness continued. There had been a frigid stillness throughout the sermon, tense and perilous, but during the reading of names the congregation's attention was careful, almost expectant, so that I had the confused impression more than once that it was their names, not others, that I read aloud. An old woman in the front pew dressed in black held a handkerchief over her face and looked up from time to time, only to cover her face again. Sitting next to her, a couple held hands tightly. In the pew behind them, three boys sat with their mother; their wide eyes never left my face. A pair of pigeons flew in through one of the windows and settled in the rafters. Their murmured coos were the only sound apart from my voice. I read on and on, feeling the sweat drip down the back of my neck and my feet swelling in my shoes. The names swam on the page before me.

I finished reading the names at the end of two hours. The congregation moved again and the sounds of shuffling feet, opening collars, and fanning handkerchiefs filled the room. They all funneled out through the front doors—they spoke to one another on their way out; I heard two women speaking quickly and children calling to one another, their high voices sharp as whistles.

THE MAYORDOMO of Naranjo was awake when I returned to the house. The doctor sat sleeping in a chair by the foot of the bed. He woke up as I walked in and I told him to go home. He said he would return in the evening. In the daylight Santos looked older. The skin of his face visible through the bandages was wrinkled in a few deep creases that ran across his cheeks and brow. His hands, too, seemed worn, but his fingers were delicate and his palms smooth. We were silent for a moment after Estrada left. I went over to the table and looked over the bandages and other supplies that he'd left.

"The doctor tells me I'll be all right here," Santos said.

"Yes, that's the idea."

"So you have to be nurse and bodyguard." He smiled.

"It's not that." I sat on the chair in the corner and watched his unbandaged eye following my face. "I don't know how to put it." I looked at the window and back at him. "Most people won't come into the house. I think that's the idea."

He nodded, watching me. "Why is that?"

"I don't know."

Santos nodded again. Then after a pause, he said, "It doesn't matter." I stared at the parts of his face that I could see. His one eye closed slowly.

"I'm sure you'll recover," I said.

He smiled. "I didn't mean that."

I watched his hands move to cover each other over the sheet. "You saw them?"

He turned his head toward the window, where the curtains let in a pale blue light. "No." He paused. "I'm just as safe here as anywhere."

"So you have some idea?" He didn't say anything. I followed his gaze to the window and saw nothing there. "Now that you're here I hope you'll stay."

He opened his mouth as if to say something, but his eyes were closed. When I spoke to him again he didn't answer. His breathing grew heavy and his mouth fell open.

SANTOS AWOKE more than two hours later. I stepped out of the room briefly to eat lunch, but I spent most of the time watching him sleep. He seemed unsurprised to see me when he found me sitting in the chair by his bed. I waited for him to speak. He tried to sit up and couldn't, so I lifted him up as carefully as I could by the arms.

"Thank you," he said. "How long did I sleep?"

"A couple hours." He rested his head against the iron headboard. I took one of the pillows and set it behind his head. "Do you want some *atol*? I have some in the kitchen to warm up."

"Thank you, yes."

I went to the kitchen and heated the *atol* that Luz had brought with my lunch. There was enough of the porridge for several meals. I brought it to him in a plastic bowl with a flat spoon. "I have instant oatmeal too—that I brought with me. If you want."

Santos nodded. "*Atol* is fine. But I'm afraid I can't—" He held up his partly bandaged hands.

"That's all right." As I used to with you, I pulled the chair up next to the bed and fed him the *atol,* spooning it carefully into his mouth. We didn't speak while he ate, and when he was finished I went back to the kitchen and washed the bowl and the pot. I returned to the bedroom with a glass of sugared water and he drank it slowly with a straw.

"Let me know if you want more," I said.

"Thank you."

I sat down again by the window and watched him sip the water. When he was halfway through the glass he leaned his head back and regarded me. "So Estrada tells me you came from the States," he said quietly.

"Yes. At the end of August."

"Assigned by the bishop, were you?"

I didn't answer but stood up to open the curtains, which were fluttering against me. "Is the light too strong?"

"No, that's fine." He paused. "Or do you have some arrangement with a church in the States?"

"No, it's not through another church," I said.

He nodded. "I'm glad the bishop finally assigned someone." He took another sip of water. "Have you been to the other towns?"

"Yes—Murcia and Los Cielos."

"You haven't been to see us." He smiled.

I looked down at the blanket. His knees and feet seemed to hardly dent its surface. "It's far, isn't it? They told me it was about two days."

"That's about right. It took me two days."

"It's a long walk."

"It's not so bad. I used to do it often."

I looked up at him again. "People from here don't go very often, though. To Naranjo."

"No," he said. "Some people have never been. But they've doubtlessly told you about it."

"Yes."

"Well, that's a shame," he said.

I hesitated. "How's that?"

"All you know of Naranjo is secondhand. From people in Río Roto." He smiled.

"That's true."

"You'll have to come see it yourself. We could do a service together."

"Yes," I said. "I'm certainly—I'd certainly like to go. I hope you'll tell me about it."

He'd kept his eyes on me, and when I stopped speaking he smiled again. "Yes, I will sometime." He put his hand on his chest. "I seem to be opening up again."

I looked at the bandages on his ribs and realized that they'd begun to show blood. I stood up. "We should change them," I said. "Estrada left these." I turned my attention to the supplies on the table. After I changed his bandages Santos slept again, and in the evening Estrada returned to check his progress.

EVEN JUST after his injury, Santos spoke with his hands, using slow, fluid gestures to punctuate, as if the words wouldn't carry through on their own. The doctor thought the wounds serious, particularly those to his head, and yet while he stayed with me at the sacristy he never complained of any pain. He spoke warmly to me; I supposed at the time that it was because I took care of him. When I spoke, I would often look up to see him smiling, seeming charmed in the way that one is charmed by a child.

It was exactly how you used to look at me in your more lucid moments in Oregon. The habits I'd acquired taking care of you returned to me with Santos. I would carry him to the bathroom and wash him with a sponge. While his bandaged hands gave him difficulty I fed him *atol* and oatmeal, fruit milkshakes and pureed soups. At times, when I folded the blanket over his legs or propped him up in bed, I momentarily forgot who I was with, so that I found myself absently plucking his hands away from his face when they got too close to his injuries, and once I caught myself patting him on the arm.

You never demonstrated any surprise at the familiarity with which I treated you. At the beginning I often found myself worrying what effect it would have if you realized, momentarily, how much had to be done for you. I came to understand that such moments of clarity were long in the past. When I put your hands at your sides you left them there. If you slumped while sitting in the bath and I straightened you up, you would stay put or look up at me, smile, and slump again. It was difficult to tell whether you felt better in one position or another, or whether you felt physical comfort, discomfort, pleasure or pain, at all. I could only think about what would or wouldn't be comfortable for me. Once I discovered that you'd been sitting on a fork for two hours without protesting.

But there was always the possibility that you could feel pain, and it worried me in a way that it didn't Mamá. She seemed to think that your cries would sound a kind of alarm whenever anything was the matter. I, on the contrary, sometimes thought you'd forgotten what pain meant. One evening in February I'd put you to bed and gone to my room to read. When I turned out the light an hour later, I saw your light on; I remembered having turned it off before leaving you. I walked down the hall and looked into your room. You sat on the edge of the bed, your legs dangling over the side. The shade for the lamp on the night table lay on the floor and the bulb shone brightly. You were squinting at the light and pressing your fingertips against the burning bulb, as if trying to get at something inside of it.

I cried out and you jumped back. I walked into the room and took your hand. You stared at me in amazement. The tips of your fingers were red—they would begin to blister in a moment. I scolded you, but when your face grew alarmed I softened my voice and you smiled. You murmured something, and then you said, or I thought you said, "Empty." I washed your hand in cold water and put ointment on your fingertips and covered your hand with an oven mitt. I worried afterward that you would try to hurt yourself again, but that wasn't your intention. You were just curious about the things you no longer understood and as a consequence would hurt yourself inadvertently.

I often unconsciously treated Santos with the caution that had seemed necessary with you, and I would sometimes become confused and realize with a start that the hands, knees, weight of the man I was dealing with were unfamiliar. At times I became so absorbed with what I was doing that I failed to hear what was going on around me. It happened that way on the second day of Santos's stay, when I was making the bed. I'd just finished folding down the sheets and was placing him on them when he pointed over my shoulder.

"There's someone here," he said. I hadn't heard anything. As he spoke, a man stepped into the doorway.

"Santos," he said quietly.

The *mayordomo* nodded. "Tulio." He paused. "You look well."

Tulio grimaced. He stood in the doorway, glowering, his huge frame apparently struggling against the impulse to rush into the room. Santos's face was calm. The illusion of similarity between you and Santos was violently dispelled. Though Santos was a wounded man twice my age and ostensibly my guest, he showed no sign of counting on me to handle the sudden intrusion. Rather I looked to him, expectantly, and I thought of the fond smile with which Santos sometimes watched me.

The man I'd met in the Malvinas, whose real name I hadn't known until then, smelled like mildew and smoke. I looked at the *mayordomo* and forced myself to stand up. There was no reason I couldn't ask the man to leave. I cleared my throat, feeling the pulse in my neck.

Before I could say anything, Santos spoke without looking at me. "You don't have to go, Father Amán." Until then he'd called me nothing but "Nítido."

I hesitated. "All right."

Tulio took a step into the room and stood, staring at Santos. "I'm surprised to see you here," he said.

Santos was silent. "I'm surprised to see you," he said, after a long pause. "I heard you were ill."

"I'm still on my feet."

"You'd be better off staying in the Malvinas."

Tulio scowled. "I'll go where I want to, now. You're the one who broke your word."

"My coming here has nothing to do with you," Santos said. "You should stay in the Malvinas."

There was a long silence, as the two men stared at each other. Then Tulio gave a hoarse cough and I realized he was laughing. "You're threatening me?"

"I'm saying you're making a mistake."

Tulio's face was impassive. "I want to know why you're here."

Santos gave a thin smile. "Say I was sent on an errand." He put his head back then and closed his eyes.

Tulio took a step back and his face settled into the expressionless gaze that I'd first seen on him. "You shouldn't have come." Santos ignored him, and after a minute Tulio looked up, appearing to see me for the first time. For a moment he didn't recognize me. Then he blinked in acknowledgment. "How was the cassava, Father?" His voice was flat.

I nodded sharply, feeling the blood in my cheeks. "Good."

"Did you get the oranges?"

"Yes." I swallowed. "Thank you."

"There's always more."

"I don't—I don't need more. Thank you."

"I haven't seen you in the Malvinas recently."

"I've become busy. With services."

"Services. All the better for us." He turned back to Santos. "What will Naranjo do without the *mayordomo?*" Santos was silent. "You'd better hurry back to them."

"You've been very lucky, Tulio," Santos said, his eyes still closed.

Tulio turned suddenly toward the door. He adjusted his pants and looked back toward the bed. "So have you," he said. He nodded at me from the doorway. "Father."

"Good afternoon," I said, and Tulio was gone. Santos raised his hand to silence me when I turned toward him, and afterward he lay for an hour with his eyes closed, not sleeping.

AFTER CONFESSIONS on Tuesday, which ran late into the afternoon, I took a notebook and went down to the cemetery. I walked for a few minutes among the tombs, realizing that there were far more than I'd thought. It would take me several days to look at all of them. I looked at them idly, noticing the recurrence of a name or two, but didn't see anything of particular significance. I turned a corner and was surprised to see Aurelio.

"Aurelio," I said.

He was clearing weeds from around the base of a slate-colored stone, and he looked up when I said his name. "Father Amán," he said. He stood up and hastily wiped his face and hands.

"You're working late. I didn't think you'd still be here."

He smiled. "It's nice out. I thought I'd clear this row." He indicated the stones to his left and I saw that the dirt was smooth and dark around the base of each. "Did you see the fountain?"

"Yes—you were right. Makes the place much more alive."

He smiled again. Then he pointed to my notebook. "Are you working?"

"No, I just had this with me."

He nodded. For a moment we stood there, silently, and then he inclined his head to the left. "I'm glad you're here," he said. "I wanted to show you something." He looked at me expectantly.

"Oh? Yes—all right."

He walked away from me toward the southern edge of the cemetery, and I followed him past several rows of tombstones, a pair of stunted pine trees, and a tall jacaranda. "The *mayordomo*," he said to me over his shoulder. "How is he?"

"The doctor's done a good job putting him back together."

Aurelio nodded. "The service was good on Sunday, Father. Very good."

I watched his slim back for a moment. "Thank you."

He stopped, suddenly, by the southern wall, and he pointed to a square of stone that lay embedded in the coarse grass. It was the first grave I'd seen like yours—sunk in the grass and invisible from a distance. There was no inscription on it.

"Who's this?" I asked.

Aurelio wiped his forehead with his sleeve. "I wanted to tell you about Father Antonio. You never met him—he was here before you. For about five years. He went back home to Italy two or three years ago, I think."

"No, I never did." I thought of the cramped, tidy handwriting in the ledger.

Aurelio leaned to the side, resting his hand against the cemetery wall. He gazed thoughtfully at the blank stone by his feet and then up at me. "He was a good person."

"Is this his grave?"

"No, no. He's still alive, God willing." He paused. "A good man. And a very careful man. I mention it because it's important to know that he was a very good, very careful man."

"I'm sure he was."

"Very careful." He thought for a moment. "You haven't had a chance to do this yet, and I don't mean to say you should, though people would probably like it, but Father Antonio always had a raffle at Christmas, and I always went with him to the capital to buy the prize—a radio, or a television one year."

"A raffle?"

"I'm just talking about how it was then. We went to the capital every year, and we made the trip in a day, so it was a long drive, and the drive back was always at night, when it was dark. And a couple years before he left—I think it was five or six years ago—we were driving back close to midnight, and we were high up in the mountains, and the fog was thick. You've noticed how during the day people walk by the side of the road. At night there's never anyone. Unless they have no reason to be there. I mean, unless they have a bad reason to be there. No one wants to walk on the road at night.

"Father Antonio was taking the curves slowly, because there's only room for one car at a time and when a car comes in the opposite direction you have to pull to the side. The truck drivers know the routes and they drive too fast. Father Antonio was going slowly, but he must have let the car go a little bit on one of the turns because we came around the corner and there, suddenly, where the road had been empty a second earlier, a man stood in the middle of the road in the fog. He seemed to just appear out of nowhere. Father Antonio didn't have a chance to stop. He ran right into him and then braked and swerved, so that the car hung over the edge of the road.

"We got out and ran over to him and we could see right away that he'd been drunk—which is why he must have jumped out into the middle of the road like that—and when we looked at him more closely we knew he was dead. Father Antonio—I had never seen him that way. He took the drunk man's head in his arms and cried as if his heart was breaking. I kept trying to get him to put the man down so that we could get him into the car, but he wouldn't let go. He rocked the man back and forth—you would have thought he'd known the man his whole life.

"I finally got him to let go and we put the man in the back seat and drove to the nearest town. We woke the priest, who didn't recognize him. It was the only town for miles. We couldn't understand how the man had come to be on the road at that hour—he was well dressed and his shoes were clean. He wasn't carrying a bag or a suitcase. He couldn't have been walking long. And yet he'd been miles from the only town, a town he didn't belong to. Neither of us could understand it. My idea was that the man had been dropped from the sky and put in front of the car on purpose, but Father Antonio thought differently: someone had left him by the side of the road—maybe meaning to leave him there but maybe meaning to come back—and now they'd lost him.

"We left the man with the priest. He promised to bury him and find out if anyone knew him. Father Antonio wrote to him, hoping someone would come forward, but no one ever did. And it ate away at him, even though it was clear enough to me, as it should have been to him, that it was an accident he couldn't have prevented. I would have hit the man in just the same way if I'd been driving. Anyone would have. But Father Antonio couldn't get over not knowing who he was, knowing only he'd ended the man's life. I think it's the reason he left." Aurelio looked at me.

"He left town?"

"He left town, and he left the Church." He leaned forward and spoke confidentially. "He wasn't born a priest, you know. No one is."

I blinked. "Yes. That's true."

Aurelio nodded. "He wasn't born a priest," he said again, "and he didn't stay a priest. For some years he gave it everything he could—more than some men do in a lifetime. He carried that heavy burden for a time, and then he set it down." He looked at me silently.

"I had no idea," I said.

"That's how it is. Anyone would have done the same thing. No one can carry such a load forever." He looked at me in silence for a moment. "No one could have been more careful. But when he saw that man in the road, he thought it meant something particular about him. He never recovered."

"How terrible," I said.

Aurelio crouched down by the blank stone. "Father Antonio had this stone put here for him."

I crouched down as well and put my hand briefly on the rough surface. "If you find out, sometime, you can still put his name here."

Aurelio smiled at me. "Yes, that's the idea." He stood up.

I looked at the darkening sky. "Well, I should head back."

He nodded. "I'll go with you."

We stood silently for a moment. He seemed to be waiting for me to say something more, so I said, "Thank you for telling me."

"You're welcome," he said, nodding gravely.

We walked back through the cemetery in silence. I thought of Father Antonio as we walked home and for a moment more as I entered the sacristy, and then what Aurelio had told me slipped to the back of my mind.

Perhaps it was the art of divination acquired during his training as a *mayordomo* that permitted Santos to identify, so easily, thoughts of my own that I hadn't been aware of and even circumstances beyond our knowledge. At times he described things I knew he couldn't be apprised of with a kind of casual, instinctual comprehension. Though he never left the house and no one but myself and the doctor ever spoke to him, he seemed to understand better than I did the effect he'd had in Río Roto. "They're wondering," he said to me, "who it was."

I was sitting in the chair by his bed then, reading. He pointed vaguely at the window. "What?" I asked, standing up to look out. "What is it?"

"They come and look. You haven't noticed?"

"No."

"They're wondering whom to blame."

I stared at him. "What do you mean?"

He waved his hand over his body. "Wouldn't you wonder— don't you, Nítido—who it was?" He laughed softly. "Who says it's in the blood." He shook his head. I did wonder, or at least I had initially. But I had given it up. I suppose I'd assumed that, as with so much else, what seemed inscrutable to me was well known to others in Río Roto. It came as a complete surprise: the idea that silences in Río Roto could arise not only from secrecy but also from doubt.

Santos, at least, seemed to have no doubts; all his silences were intentional. He would not, for example, speak to me about Naranjo. As I lifted him from the bed and back again, changed his bandages, and sat for hours in the chair beside his bed, Santos must have been reading my thoughts, seeing in the jumble of unending questions something that warned him, because though I tried to ask casually from the first about Naranjo and the people who lived there, he was slow, cautious, and deliberate, so that when each conversation ended I realized I'd told him more about myself and still learned nothing from him. Only much later did it become clear to me that it must have taken him those long weeks—hours of daily concentration—to compose what he wanted to say. At the time I thought only that he had an uncanny tendency to make me speak of things I hadn't intended to discuss.

I'd believed until I spoke with Santos that I didn't know about your and Mamá's early years because you'd never spoken of them, but when I had difficulty answering Santos's questions about your life in the United States, I began to reconsider. I'd been present for all of it, but many things about our time in California I couldn't recall or hadn't known to begin with. At some point, I knew, you'd had taken the trucking job, which required us to move from the desert town north of Los Angeles to Santa Cruz. You'd opened the dollar store with Mamá afterward, and I had the feeling that it hadn't lasted more than a year, but I couldn't be sure. I had no clearer sense of chronology for the period of my adolescence, even though I ought to have recalled it well. I could remember what I'd done during those years. But how you and Mamá spent your time, I realized as I tried to answer Santos's questions, I couldn't explain. I remembered the Russian piano teacher with the two grand pianos, but not how you'd paid for the lessons. I recalled trying to do homework with the sound of your saw in the background, but I couldn't say what you'd been doing, or why you worked on it so persistently, or what became of it in the end.

When Santos saw that I couldn't account for why we'd moved so much, or for the changes in your occupations, or for the gradual improvements in our standard of living, he asked me about other things. "But did they like it?" he would ask. "Were they happy?"

I had never thought to myself, "Papá hated trucking," or "Papá loved trucking." I'd never considered the point, really. To answer Santos I had to recall what I could of specific episodes. Mamá would sit on the bed in the windowless bedroom of the house in Palo Alto, staring intently at the paneled wall. Once, in Santa Cruz, you'd fallen asleep while eating dinner and we hadn't noticed until you fell forward onto the table. Mamá had tried to grow roses when we lived in the desert, even when there was no water. She came in from the backyard wearing her gardening gloves and a straw hat, her face coated with yellow dust.

And then there was the time in Oregon. Did you like Oregon? Was Mamá happy in Oregon? Was she happy now, living on the island? I wasn't sure. I told Santos that Mamá didn't like Palo Alto, that you worked too hard in Santa Cruz, and that both of you thought we would stay in the desert. I hadn't realized any of it at the time, and as I said so to him, I wasn't sure it was true even then, considering all of it in retrospect. It might have been possible to know if I'd asked you, or if I'd remembered more, but both means escaped me. I have difficulty, even now, determining whether the two of you were really as reserved as I remember or whether, in reality, I was simply too unobservant, too self-absorbed, to see you plainly. The thought that you may have wanted to or tried to undo your reserve, only to find me uninterested, causes me to dwell upon certain moments that I now remember imperfectly. They are worn out from repeated reconsideration, and can tell me nothing of what you may or may not have meant.

It occurred to me a few days after Santos arrived that I could look at the journals, and I did, but I already knew what they contained, and when I read them again nothing surprised me. When I mentioned them to Santos, he asked me whether any part of the journals described what you felt about the changes you and Mamá went through. "I don't think so," I said. But I wasn't sure. It was my suggestion to read parts of the journals to Santos as a way of telling him about those changes and acquainting him with the places we'd lived in. Santos took me up on the idea at once. So it came about that at the end of the week I began reading aloud to him, and since I took some pride in your writing it didn't surprise me that Santos listened with rapt attention and growing interest.

At one time you must have made the train trip between Sacramento and Palo Alto quite frequently. There was one section—a portion of the trip—that you returned to repeatedly, sometimes omitting one detail or another. The ships you wrote of, for example, didn't appear in every version. It may have been that you sometimes fell asleep. Or it's possible that on days when the landscape looked different—say, if it was raining—you would fail to describe the inconsistencies. Because the entries weren't dated, it was difficult to know how much time elapsed between each trip. It's even possible that you wrote all of the versions in a single day, writing the first one on the train and the rest later on, repeating the trip to yourself again and again until you exhausted yourself, or until you had it committed to memory.

I'm on the second story of the train, at a table, looking out the window. We passed a dry gully that glimmers with broken glass. Now we're passing a dry field—might be alfalfa—has been cropped in rows. A wasteland of auburn and mustard grasses—all dry. In the distance, the highway, built on stilts like combs arranged in parallel, one after another, with a long ribbon of road on top. No clouds, a weak, hazy, white horizon and a deep blue overhead. A narrow dirt road alongside the tracks and workmen in orange vests walking along it. We pass groves of eucalyptus.

The train is going more slowly than it should, but it doesn't matter.

Mace Boulevard. Best Western hotel. Homes by the side of the highway in rows, all identical. Empty office buildings for lease. Arriving at Davis. Passing Davis Diamonds. And the Buckhorn steak house. And an abandoned Armco factory. Olive Drive. A freight train, going in the opposite direction, all rust. Dried palm fronds fallen by the side of the tracks. Horse farms set among the dusty trees. Beige hills to the west, frosted green along the tops and edges. The trees run down the sides like fur. Ross Noonan Livestock. The power lines to the right and the deep, dented hills the color of burnt butterscotch to the right. Any number of empty freight containers. At the crossroads, the cars line up and wait for the train to pass. A heron, standing on a mound of weeds in the middle of a bog. Here the telephone wires are low to the ground and tilted, as though being sucked down by the mud.

Far in the distance, gray ships like the ghosts of abandoned cities. Silhouettes—hundreds of riggings jutting up into the pale sky. They look not like boats but islands, overcrowded to the point of collapse and then abandoned.

Martinez—a town seemingly made up entirely of oil rigs and water towers, empty freight cars and miles of pipeline. I haven't the words to describe the strange devices of this place. The houses seem to be toys set among the machines.

Santos was visibly intrigued by the journals. After I had read to him for some time, he stopped me. "Is that what they're all like?"

"In what way?"

"Descriptions as he travels."

"Not always of traveling, but they're all descriptions."

"What about his thoughts or recollections?"

Surprised that he'd pinpointed the very quality about the journals that had first stood out to me, I looked at him with interest. "He didn't write that way, it seems."

Santos appeared to think about this. "You can't tell, from the journals, anything about his past—anything about Guatemala?"

I shook my head.

"He says nothing about Guatemala at all?"

"I don't think so." We sat in silence for a moment. "I thought he would. I hoped he— I know so little about Guatemala, really."

I looked away from him and felt his eyes on me. "He didn't tell you about it?"

"No—not really. He— There were a few things I picked up." I looked back at him for a moment and then away again. "But it wasn't the same. Without having been here that I could remember."

"I see what you mean." He smiled. "And now that you're here? Is it what you expected?"

I smiled back at him. "No—I can't tell. It's hard to know. I wish people would tell me more. About the town, I mean."

He raised his eyebrows. "I can't imagine why no one has told you. The history of Río Roto is well known." He spoke again before I could think of a response. "I'll tell you if you want."

I was too surprised to say anything for a moment. "Would you?"

He shrugged. "I know it as well as anyone else."

He sat for a minute without speaking, and when he began he spoke evenly, fluidly, as though he'd related the story many times.

Río Roto, Murcia, Los Cielos, and Naranjo, he told me, had not always been four towns. Centuries earlier there'd been only one town, and it had a different name, a name no one remembered any longer. The Spanish name "Río Roto" had probably been invented by Alvarado during the conquest. It was said that his soldiers arrived to find the houses not abandoned but suspended, as though the inhabitants had vanished in place. Plates of food lay on the tables, wet clothes rested on the rocks, fires burned in all the houses, and smoke streamed uninterrupted from the chimneys. This unsettled the soldiers, who'd already grown suspicious of the peculiar quiet that moved through the jungles, paralyzing everything. They turned to the river, thinking they would find there evidence of flight; they saw no canoes, crafts, or moorings. Instead their eyes were drawn to the currents themselves, currents unlike any they'd ever seen. The water split mid-river around a massive and invisible obstacle. Something like a boulder, which the currents swept up against and parted over, seemed to sit midstream, but where the boulder should have been only a blankness divided the water.

This story was confirmed centuries afterward by an army

officer who told Santos that he'd flown over the area repeatedly
in a helicopter and been unable to locate the town. He described
a moving light that shone like the reflection of a mirror and
blinded him as he flew overhead. The light shone from the direction of the river, and when he attempted to look beyond it he
glimpsed faintly some obstacle that divided the waters mid-river.
What the obstacle was he couldn't say.

In the mid-nineteenth century, the town of Río Roto, as if finally
discovering the nature of the obstacle, took its cue from the river
and split four ways. The eventual rupture was attributed to a man
named Coc, though inevitably, if not Coc, another man like him
who tended his *milpa* in the hills between what became Murcia and
Los Cielos would have done the same thing. Everything on the west
side of the river and the town, including the Malvinas and the hills
north of them, was cultivated by people who walked there by foot
and worked their crops year-round. Coc owned a plot on the land
that in the next century became the sugar mill. He grew maize and
beans, as did Santos's grandfather, and he made a decent living by it.

Coc's fate, and Río Roto's with it, was sealed the year the
locusts arrived in Río Roto. Unlikely as it seemed that the locusts
would discriminate, they left some crops untouched while
destroying others, as if by design, and as a consequence people
who had been sure of their yield could only wonder at the selec-
tive destruction and rely on their neighbors to make it through
the season. During the year of the capricious locusts, Coc, whose
plot was among those destroyed, began his dealings with Baer,
although no one knew of it at the time. People had seen the
German, who came through town on a horse and rode into the
crops, trampling the new maize, but no one had spoken to him
and they had the impression that he was just an adventurer.

On a day about two months after the sighting of Baer, Coc disappeared, along with his wife and two daughters. People later conjectured that he'd taken his money and walked several days to the city and from there traveled to the coast, where he bought a house and lived like an exile for the remainder of his days. A week after Coc disappeared, Baer arrived with thirty men from another part of the country. They didn't speak any language the people in Río Roto recognized, but they worked hard, tearing up the plots of fifty farmers all the way from the Malvinas to the northern edge of town. When Santos's grandfather and the others whose plots were destroyed confronted Baer, who sat in a hammock watching a dozen men lay the foundations for his hacienda, he pulled from his pocket a piece of paper, which he said was a deed, and which he claimed guaranteed him ownership to the four hundred acres that his men were clearing for coffee and sugar. He'd bought the land from Coc, he said, and the land wasn't registered in anyone else's name. Santos's grandfather and the others thought about having it out with Baer, but there were the dozen men, and probably more behind them in the trees, holding machetes, sweating under their straw hats, staring at them with inexplicable hatred, and they had the disadvantage of having been on the wrong side of the surprise.

There was disagreement about what to do. Some favored the expulsion of Baer and his men. Some argued that he could hardly be expected to stay very long, and he would soon be gone. Others pointed out that their crops were already ruined, and even Baer's expulsion wouldn't recover what had been spoiled. Over a period of weeks the disagreement grew rancorous: those who wanted to stay accused the others of abandoning Río Roto; those who wanted to leave argued that people with undamaged crops were not in the position to point fingers. Santos's grandfather took such a view, and soon more and more people began to like the idea of starting over somewhere far away, where it would be possible to forget all about Baer.

They could move, but they couldn't forget Baer, as Santos's telling me of him testified. How far away it was necessary to move was a matter of debate, and in the end the fifty families whose plots had been destroyed by Baer or the locusts plus a number of others who worried that their lands would be likewise devoured divided into three groups. Some moved to Murcia, where they could access the river and return easily to Río Roto, some went to Los Cielos, where it was thought that the higher altitude might provide better water, and the largest group, including Santos's family, set out east across the river in the direction of a place someone had heard about long ago where the water was sweet and the crops grew untended.

The soil was rocky and the groundwater was scarce in Naranjo but they stayed anyway; Santos's grandfather built a house there under the canopy that lasted more than a hundred years. In Los Cielos there were a few years of heavy rains that all but washed the new houses off the hillside, but then in the next year of moderate rain the houses were repaired and the town flourished. In Murcia, likewise, the corn would not grow on the steep decline to the river and for the first few years everyone went hungry. But then they turned to planting cane, and the little town above the river sprang to life. Only Río Roto, the most populous of the four, did not prosper. Baer squeezed it dry, buying up more land where he could, sending his hired men to destroy the *milpa* people planted elsewhere. Children could be seen picking coffee there from the time they could walk. The men's backs grew bowed because Baer was too tightfisted to buy oxen. They heard how people in the other towns—those who had abandoned Río Roto—were thriving, and they turned bitterly away from them and to the task of surviving Baer.

Baer did well with the plantation. For fifty years it profited, and only in the 1930s, when his nephew took over, did it begin to dwindle. Still, it was made to struggle on, though much of the land fell into disuse. Most of the coffee plants were spent, and what beans did drop from the dusty leaves didn't sell for much. The abandoned cacao plants took over, growing wild in the shade of taller trees, giving all the air around them an aroma of fermentation. And bit by bit it was possible to see small clearings made, tentatively, amid the abandoned shrubs. A tiny plot of maize appeared here, a couple of cassava plants threw roots there. Far beyond the reach of Baer, pieces of land devolved to the people who'd lost them fifty years earlier.

When the laws changed mid-century, these encroachments became less tentative. Baer died in 1947. His heir wanted nothing to do with the crumbling hacienda and the long avenues of coffee bushes rife with snakes. The building and the rest of the crops were abandoned. Later it burned, harmlessly, and no one ever determined whether or not the fire began by accident. With the destruction of the plantation, the reason for Río Roto's splintering also vanished, but the four towns did not merge back into one. They had grown apart from one another, and the people of Río Roto still resented its desertion. With the closer towns, Murcia and Los Cielos, it was possible to visit frequently and accept grudgingly, over many decades, that the people of these towns were not to blame. But the distant Naranjo could not expiate itself through close contact, and it came to represent, for Río Roto, all that was untrue.

Eleven

WHEN I LEFT OREGON I thought I was going to Guatemala
out of general curiosity. But after hearing what Santos had told
me, I knew that I'd had only one purpose in mind. I wanted to
step into the world you'd left behind, and since arriving in Río
Roto I'd continued to expect, without even being aware of it, that
such a place existed. Santos made me realize that it didn't. When
he finished speaking it suddenly struck me forcibly that I had no
reason to be there.

The idea of returning to the past must have settled in some corner
of my mind, staying with me throughout the year in Oregon and sug-
gesting, when I left, that the solution lay in understanding the past by
seeing it firsthand. I knew where the idea came from. It had first
fallen into my hands when I read Thompson's powerful argument
about cyclical time; he believed that the Maya had understood time
as a series of burdens, carried one after another by the gods.

One god raises his hand to the tump-line to slip it off his
forehead, whereas others have slipped off their load, and

hold them in their laps. The night god, who takes over when the day is done, is in the act of rising with his load. With his left hand he eases the weight on the tump-line; with his right hand on the ground he steadies himself as he starts to rise. The artist conveys in the strain reflected in the god's features the physical effort of rising from the ground with his heavy load. It is the typical scene of the Indian carrier resuming his journey familiar to anyone who has visited the Guatemalan highlands.

I'd been seduced, I recognized, by the possibility of seeing time as a fixed object, to be carried and borne and set aside. Imagined that way, periods of time could be discrete and distinct. They could be taken up one by one, each offering the clarity and immediacy of a fossil. I'd thought that arriving in Guatemala would allow me to take up the burden of time you'd lived there; I would truly grasp it—examine it, trace its smooth shape, feel its weight. And at the same time I would leave behind in the United States my own burden of time; I would set it aside, and the stone burden would roll away and out of sight.

I had to admit, however, that neither of these expectations had as yet been fulfilled in Guatemala. Only once in my life, and very briefly, had I been able to set aside my burden of time. It was the last month before I left for Oregon. After nearly six weeks, I'd finally finished packing up the apartment and it was almost empty. There was nothing else for me to do. Most of the teachers I knew from the high school found it awkward to continue their friendships with me, but even those I was still close with had far too much to do in the middle of the term. I didn't know many other people in the area. My house seemed at times suffocating and at times too vast, and anything I could have done in the city to fill the time would only have prolonged it.

I rented a house for a week on Block Island, where in March it was still too cold for tourists. The ferry arrived in the morning. I took a taxi to the house, putting my bicycle and my bag in the trunk. The driver took the roads slowly, passing through the empty streets into wintry fields the color of old paper. He pointed out a cranberry bog that would in later months be scarlet. The air smelled of wind and rocks dried by the sun.

The house didn't sit on the water, which suited me better. It was submerged in a gray field, with no other houses in view. On the first day I bought a week's supply of food. I took off my watch and buried it in my bag. I took the clock off the kitchen wall and put it in a drawer. The purpose of the exercise was to reset my internal clock: to determine how long I needed to sleep, when I ought to wake up, when and how often I needed to eat. As soon as the first morning, I awoke with no sense of the hour, and at first the disorientation unsettled me. Daylight stretched on monotonously. I had to resist the impulse to check the time. As the day wore on, I continually felt certain the sky would begin to darken, and yet it didn't. For a while I walked outside, thinking that the time would pass more quickly that way, but still the day wouldn't spend itself. I had the feeling that it had gotten stuck and that unless I looked at a clock it would stay that way indefinitely. Finally, when I began to grow used to the motionless light, the sky seemed a shade grayer than it had before. The wind became colder, and the sun began to harden behind the clouds. When evening fell I was exhausted, but I couldn't sleep for the desire to keep track of the passing time.

I awoke to a room filled with daylight. Something had shifted in me during the night, and though I looked at the night table instinctively, I felt relief at seeing only my book and the lamp. The second day, too, prolonged itself, but by the afternoon it had ceased to bother me. And by the next morning I'd forgotten the day of the week. It felt as though I'd been in the house already for several days, and that was all. When I was tired, I slept. I had the impression that I ate very rarely, but I couldn't be sure. Each time I said to myself that I would have to get groceries delivered, I looked in the cabinets and found that I had more than I needed. It occurred to me one afternoon that I wouldn't know when the week had ended. In fact, I thought to myself, the week had possibly already passed. The owner of the house wasn't expecting another tenant until May, and no one on the island other than the taxi driver knew I was there.

One morning I walked out to the water—a distance of about half a mile—and watched the gulls. A thought had been surfacing in my mind at odd moments during the last few days. It would be possible to continue to live as I had that week. I tried to imagine it: passing all the time that lay ahead of me in that way, not knowing what hour or day it was, then losing track of the year and my birthday, with the rest of the world aging somewhere else without me. But I was unable to grasp the idea; the sense of it was inconceivable. Something in the prospect caused me such longing that I felt tears in my eyes. If I wanted to I could be completely lost.

That evening I checked my watch, certain I'd overstayed by at least a few days. It was Friday—only five days had passed. I tried to slip away again on the weekend, but I'd been fished up from the deep. They were ordinary days, with mealtimes and things to finish. I cleaned the house, and it took no more and no less time than I had expected it to. As soon as my sense of timekeeping returned, so did the thoughts I'd lost track of—not quite forgotten—during the week. I had to decide what to do with myself. Much as I wanted to spend time with you and Mamá, I couldn't remain jobless in Oregon indefinitely. After the trip cross-country, I'd be there, with all my things, with no other responsibilities. The whole future stretched out before me, changeless and interminable.

I couldn't believe on such scant evidence that periods of time were isolated from one another. Either they weren't at all or they were greater than a lifetime—perhaps even centuries long—and thereby impossible for me to make out. There was no doubt that I'd carried my burden of time all the way to Guatemala with me. Nor had it been possible to find, as I'd expected, some version of the time you'd lived there. It's not that I'd expected against all reason to find you and Mamá living as you had almost half a century earlier. But I'd imagined that other aspects of that time would be preserved and that I might pull together, by some small effort, a world composed of the remnants.

After speaking with Santos, I knew this was impossible. The past he described had nothing to do with you. Whatever fragmentary piece of the past you'd left in Guatemala lay buried, all but invisible and entirely inaccessible in the present. Guatemala had gone on without you—without us—while we were gone. And we had likewise gone on without it. I felt compelled to consider the possibility that the burdens of time did not move smoothly from hand to hand in cyclical progression; rather they crumbled, dispersed, and accumulated like layers of debris, amassing infinitely with terrible determination.

If this was true, then Thompson's view would not hold, and I had to seek another explanation. The answer came from Barbara Ted- .

lock, who through her training to be a daykeeper with the K'iche'
had reached precisely the opposite of Thompson's conclusion.

Quiché resistance to the replacement of old customs with new
ones is based, in part, on Quiché conceptions of time. As in
other matters, thought proceeds dialectically rather than ana-
lytically, which means that no given time, whether past, present, or future, can ever be totally isolated from the segments
of time that precede or follow it. This does not mean that
innovations must be resisted but that they should be added to
older things rather than replacing them. My own teacher . . .
summed up his own position by flatly stating, "One cannot
erase time." The net result of this attitude is that the burdens
of time do not so much change as accumulate.

Perhaps, it occurred to me after speaking with Santos, you
and Mamá had understood this dilemma long before I even began
to consider it. You may have been attempting to set aside the burden of past time. You'd moved away from Guatemala, stopped
speaking of it, allowed the stone to roll away and rest. But you
must then have realized that such efforts were futile. The stones
cannot be left behind; they fill your pockets, their added weight
affecting slightly the manner of each new step.

Guatemala was not the place you'd left behind, and whatever
traces I might find of you would be unrecognizably altered by
the accumulation of so many decades. Just as the Río Roto I was
living in had no bearing on the place Santos described to me, so
the present Guatemala was nothing like the country you'd lived
in. The hope of finding a clear, telling past had vanished. With it
my entire purpose for being in Guatemala vanished also.

Twelve

THERE WERE THINGS Santos didn't know. He knew who
Xinia was but hadn't met her, and I could see that as his wounds
began to heal he felt a greater restlessness to see her in person,
though I didn't know why. I thought at first that he meant her
cousins, who'd found him injured, but he meant Xinia herself.
He brushed my question aside, saying, "It's because you always
speak of her."

"Do I?"

"Yes."

"I don't think," I said, "that she'll come into the house."

He didn't say anything for a moment. "Then will you take
her a message?" he asked. He waited for me to finish arranging
the sheets. "Tell her that Hilario lives with Noé, one of my
neighbors. Don't forget the name. Hilario."

I watched his good eye blink slowly. "All right. That's it?"

"Yes. She'll know what it's about." He sighed and lay back on
the pillows.

I didn't find Xinia in the vestry, and I could have gone home and waited to talk to her the next day, but I wondered, as I stood in the changing room staring at the yellow apron that she wore when she was working, what she would do if she wanted to speak to Santos in the sacristy. As I thought of it I caught myself smiling. Don't think I was being malicious; it was only because she was always so insistent. Perhaps she would speak to him through the window. Or she might stand at the door and ask me to take messages back and forth to him. Perhaps, I realized, surprised that it hadn't occurred to me before, she would enter the sacristy as long as I wasn't inside.

There was another reason for going to Xinia's house, which I'd never been into but had seen from the road a few days earlier when, by coincidence, I found myself walking a ways behind her toward the north side of town. I didn't call out to her or walk any faster, but we happened to be walking at the same pace, and after crossing the short bridge near where the road branched off toward Los Cielos she'd turned into a walkway on the right-hand side and walked into a wooden house. It sat only a short distance from Estrada's house, so I'd seen it before without knowing who lived there. On that evening it was almost dark, and as I stood in the road the lights went on in the front rooms and nonetheless she didn't draw the curtains as she walked into the bedroom and put her things on the bed and then stood in the living room, staring down at something in the middle of the floor. For that very reason it surprised me to observe, when I walked by another time in the middle of the day, that though the sunlight would have made it much more difficult to look into the rooms, Xinia kept all the curtains drawn. Even the back rooms were veiled in the heavy, red cotton that made it just as impossible to see in from up close as from far away.

When I arrived to give her Santos's message, I found the front door closed. I called her name, but it seemed likely that she couldn't hear me, and no one answered. As expected, the curtains were drawn in the front windows. I went to the back of the house to call in through the kitchen. As soon as I stepped toward the door, I saw that it was open, which I wasn't expecting, and I saw Xinia in the kitchen. She sat staring at a notebook that lay in front of her. On the other side of the table sat a man I knew from church as Eliseo but whom I'd never spoken to.

They hadn't yet heard me. I stood for a moment, watching them. Xinia's hair hung over her face and down her back; she'd just washed it, and the tips of it were making small wet dots on her shirt. Eliseo stared too, leaning in so far that his face hung only a few inches away from hers.

"Hello," I said.

They both sprang back. Xinia put her hand to her throat when she saw me. She glanced at Eliseo. He smiled at me and put the notebook under his arm.

"I'm sorry," I said. "I'm interrupting you."

"No, it's nothing," Xinia said. "We were just going over some work of Eliseo's."

"Ah," I said.

Eliseo stood up. "I don't think we've met," he said. He smiled. "I'm Eliseo." We shook hands.

"Well, I don't want to interrupt," I said. Eliseo stood by the table; Xinia remained seated and looked at the floor. "I have a message for you from Santos."

Xinia looked at me quickly, and for a moment her features pulled together in apprehension and then her face went blank. "Yes?"

"He says to tell you that Hilario lives with his neighbor, Noé."

Xinia's expression didn't change. She stared past me through the doorway. Eliseo sat down and reached across the table and took her hand. He murmured something, and she shook her head, pulling her hand away. "I'll go myself," she said.

For several seconds the two of us watched her, and she looked at the sky in the doorway over my head. "I'll go," she said to me, standing up.

"Let me talk to him, Xinia," Eliseo said.

She shook her head again.

"I'm sure he'll be glad to talk to you," I said.

Xinia put her hands together and pulled them apart and looked at them, as if surprised to find them empty. She glanced up at me. "I'll be just a minute," she said.

"Eliseo, good to meet you," I said, smiling. I walked away from the door and around to the front of the house and waited in the street. A moment later Xinia came out to where I stood, and I saw Eliseo leaving the house from the back, heading in a different direction.

We walked in silence. Xinia pulled agitatedly at her hair with her fingers. When we'd walked a few minutes I cleared my throat. "I was thinking," I said, "that if you wait in the chair outside I can push the bed out to the front room. As long as he doesn't mind I'm sure it'll fit through the door."

Xinia stared at the road in front of her and her cheeks slowly flushed. "Thank you," she said.

"It's no problem."

I looked ahead, but I could see that she glanced at me. When we reached the house, she stood by the doorway and waited. I went into the house and wrapped the sheets around Santos so that he wouldn't roll. I took hold of the iron headboard and pulled the bed away from the wall. Then I pushed the whole frame across the room and through the door into the corridor. The angle at the door gave me some difficulty, but by sliding the bookshelf to the side I made the turn and was able to push the bed all the way up to the door. The feet of the bed slid easily over the tiles and onto the entryway, so that Santos lay half in the house and half out.

I asked Santos if he was comfortable. Xinia stood with her hands clasped together before her. I prodded her again to take the chair. She sat absentmindedly and thanked me. "I think I'll go to the vestry and work on some things," I said, looking at Xinia. "You can call me from here if you need anything." She raised her eyes to meet mine and nodded.

I PLACED the chairs in the corridor and set up the table with water just as Xinia had the two Mondays before. Afterward I went to the study and took out the ledger and looked over the names. From another drawer I took an empty notebook and opened it to the first page. I began copying the names from the last two weeks into the notebook. I hadn't had the chance the last time, but I wanted to compare them with the names at the cemetery. I'd reached the halfway point when I heard a soft knock on the open door, and I looked up to see a man I recognized—either from the other Mondays or from services.

"Father Amán?" He couldn't have been more than twenty. He had a soft mustache and when he sat down I thought I smelled cologne. He reached over the desk. "Cruz," he said.

"I wasn't planning to take names until three, but go ahead," I said.

"Oh, I came to speak to you about something else." He smiled and ran a hand over his hair and cleared his throat and wiped his hand on his jeans.

"Please," I said, making a gesture as if offering him the chair he'd already taken, and I too cleared my throat and took my hand back and put it in my lap.

He looked at the ledger and the notebook. I closed one and then the other casually and stacked them. "I heard," he said, glancing back and forth between me and the window, "that you were going to do a marriage in Murcia tomorrow."

The couple had approached me on the first day in Murcia and had since then come twice to Río Roto to speak with me. "Yes, I am."

He smiled and his lip caught on his teeth and he licked his lips quickly. "I was wondering if you would—my fiancée and I, Sabina and I—we have been waiting to be married as well."

"Congratulations," I said. He sat back a little and tried to smile again. "Wouldn't you rather have it here?" I asked.

"Well, that's the thing," he said, lowering his voice. "It's a little difficult. My parents and hers don't really have the means for a big wedding."

"Of course, I understand."

He went on quickly. "We thought that if we were married in Murcia they wouldn't feel obliged to have a celebration. It would all be over before anyone heard about it."

I watched the sweat gathering in beads on his nose and between the soft hairs of his sparse mustache; he looked very young. "That's true."

"So you'll do it?"

"Well, it's soon. I haven't spoken to the two of you together at all."

He leaned forward onto the desk, his hands sweeping back and forth. "We could come tomorrow morning," he said. I thought for a moment and watched him clasp and unclasp his hands. I hesitated, trying to remember where and when I knew him from, but I couldn't recall.

"Or maybe," he said, "you wanted the chance to practice." He looked at me unsmilingly.

I glanced up. You will think I should have understood him at once, but it took me a moment.

He lifted his chin. "People from Murcia hardly ever come to Río Roto."

I pushed my chair back. "No. I wasn't thinking of that." I stood up and turned to the window.

"I just mean I'd understand. Your first marriage."

I turned back to the desk and looked over his head. My voice sounded distant, as though the words came out of my stomach. "Oh, I've done hundreds."

He smiled appreciatively.

I glanced at him and sat down. "All right. Come by in the morning with Sabina."

"Thank you, Father." He reached across the desk quickly and shook my hand and got up. He thanked me again from the doorway. For some minutes I stared after him.

Then I remembered where I'd heard the name Sabina—I had, in fact, met Sabina. On the Friday when I'd gone to their house for dinner, she'd been helping her mother in the kitchen while Aurelio and I sat in the front room, and during dinner she spoke very little. Cruz's name hadn't come up that evening. Although, as I recalled, Aurelio had said something to me about how much she liked children, and I might have guessed something from the way she blushed and looked down as he said it.

"It's new to me," I'd said, "to have neighbors." We sat at the table they'd set up in the living room for the purpose. They'd dimmed the lights so that I couldn't see into the kitchen, but I could hear the wood burning in the stove on the other side of the thin wall.

Aurelio protested that he'd read how in cities people lived on top of one another. "You must have more neighbors in one building than we have in the whole town."

"But we don't talk to one another," I explained. They didn't understand it, and the image of people living six feet from each other without speaking began to sound inexplicable to me as well. "I can't explain," I finally said. "Here everyone knows one another. I see people going in and out of one another's houses as if they all belonged to everyone. Who lives next door to you here?"

They were silent for a moment, and Aurelio looked at his wife and then said, with some hesitation, "Victor and his wife, Oso, his mother . . ." He trailed off.

"Yes, that's just what I mean," I said. "You probably spend half your time there. Or maybe not you, Aurelio, since you're working at the cemetery."

"Yes," he said slowly, "although the truth is we mostly keep to ourselves."

"You're right," Sabina said quietly, "that many people do come and go as you say."

I nodded. "Must be nice," I said.

Aurelio glanced at Sabina and said evenly, as if with pride, "Sabina has managed to make friends with some of the children. They really can't resist her." And Sabina looked down into her lap, and there was a pause, and then her mother asked me something about Luz taking me my meals.

"Yes," I said. "Though it's not the same with the sacristy," and this seemed to throw the conversation off. No one spoke for a while, and then Sabina began picking up the plates.

There was no doubt that I'd misunderstood—or at least understood incompletely—the significance of the comment about children during the dinner with Sabina and her parents. Just as I had that evening, I'd clearly failed to grasp the full weight of people's words on other occasions as well. I gave up the conversation with Cruz as just another instance of my imperfect comprehension.

XINIA ARRIVED just before three. Her face was flushed. I gave her a pad of paper and a pen, and she left to sit in the corridor and take names. Over the previous two weeks the people who came on Mondays had varied little. The number had grown somewhat, but so had attendance at services—perhaps it had taken some time for word to get around after all. On the third Monday, I recognized the faces of the people who came. And I knew more of them by name, since many had seen me in the confessional. Aurelio was among them. When he came in he walked up to the desk, held the piece of paper against his stomach, and told me the two names. When I'd finished writing, he didn't turn away immediately. He looked at me for a moment and then seemed to make up his mind. "My younger brother. And my cousin."

I looked at him, surprised. "They must be much in your thoughts," I said.

He nodded. "Thank you, Father." He folded the paper and put it in his pocket.

"They will be in my prayers," I said. Aurelio nodded again and left the room.

Four others said their names aloud—one, like Aurelio, telling me who they were, the other three content to say the names slowly, as if pronouncing foreign words, while watching me write them in the ledger. I told Xinia of it afterward and she glanced at me and looked away as though she wanted to smile. "You see," she said.

After we put away the chairs she followed me into the study and took a seat without my having to ask. We sat silently for several minutes. I looked over the names in the ledger and Xinia sat against the wall with her ankles crossed, looking out through the window behind me.

I thought of something then and stood up. "Santos," I said. "I left him in the doorway."

She smiled then and looked at me quickly and shook her head. "The doctor came by. He pushed the bed in."

"Ah." I sat back down. To prevent myself from talking I looked down at the ledger again and read through the names I'd copied into the blank notebook.

It took her nearly five minutes. Then she said, "Thank you for arranging it."

I looked at her. She stared into her lap but her lashes flickered. "You're welcome," I said. I fidgeted, turned back to the ledger, and waited again.

She got up abruptly and went to the bookshelf and stood looking up at the books. I watched her put her finger up to their spines. Then she turned around and spoke. "Did you know I went to the university for a year?"

"No, I didn't."

She made a quick gesture toward the bookshelf, as though she'd just been reminded of it. "Yes. I had to get up at four to catch the bus. I only lasted a year."

"You must not have slept much."

She nodded, moving back to the chair, and I kept my eyes on the desk. "I only made two or three friends there. By now I've lost touch with all of them. But that year I visited them once in a while. One of them lived between here and the city—about an hour away."

She paused, and I closed the notebook slowly and kept my eyes on its mottled green cover.

After a long pause she went on. "Only about an hour away. She lived with her mother. She talked about her mother all the time when I saw her at school, but didn't tell me much about her—it's just that her mother came up often, and I could see that the old woman relied on her.

"The first time I went to see her, I thought it was right to bring something—I think I brought some cakes. Her mother was only about sixty, but she may have aged rapidly. I did notice that she didn't get up from her chair when I came in, but I leaned down to kiss her cheek and didn't think anything of it. My friend had coffee ready. She put the cakes I'd brought on a plate and then she put everything on the coffee table. For her mother she pulled up a little round table and put the cake and coffee on it.

"I liked the old woman right away. She was quiet at first, and I thought she seemed a little depressed. But as my friend and I talked she grew livelier, and by the end she was talking and joking with us. It was a Sunday and I had to leave early. After a few hours I said goodbye.

"When we saw each other at school, the first thing my friend did was to put her arms around me. She drew back and there were tears in her eyes. I was surprised; I asked her what the matter was. She said, 'I can't thank you enough for visiting us. My mother liked you so much. There are other friends of mine she's tolerated, but she really loved you. It's so kind of you to be so natural with her.' I had no idea what she was talking about, and I said so. 'Can it be that you really didn't notice?' my friend said. Her expression changed; she seemed disappointed and a little unsure. 'I don't think I should tell you, then,' she said, more to herself than to me. I urged her on. And she told me about her mother's illness. It had cost her both her legs—they were amputated at the knee—and they would probably have to cut higher up. 'She thinks it's starting in her arms now. No one wants to go near her. It's not contagious. But people are thoughtless.' The old woman's skirts had covered her legs and draped to the floor. My friend looked at me, worried about what I would say. So I spoke quickly—I said I wanted to see them again. That very next Sunday even.

"Over the year I went to see them at least once a month. If they noticed any change in me, they didn't show it. It's true that sometimes I'd forget her condition, and I'd talk to her without thinking of it. But most of the time, the idea of her rotting legs—they were rotting, and the smell became overwhelming—terrified me. I forced myself to make those visits every few weeks, even though they were more and more uncomfortable. I came to dread the weekends even more than the weekdays. When I had to quit the university, I wasn't sorry. I let myself drop out of touch with her. I don't know anyone else from her town, so I don't know what happened to them—how long the old woman lived or what her daughter's doing now."

She stopped talking. Though I'd tried not to, I'd been watching her. The way she spoke about the university, the fact that she described her thoughts to me, made me feel less hesitant. But when she finished, she turned her eyes toward me and I had to look away from the calm aversion in them.

We sat in silence for a minute. Then I made up my mind, emboldened by how she'd waited until everyone was gone and by how much she'd told me. "My feelings won't change," I said.

She shook her head immediately. "To you—you think it's a little town with pretty scenery."

This threw me into confusion. She was looking through the window and didn't seem to notice. "If that's what you mean," I said.

"What did you think I meant?"

I didn't answer her. "Maybe," I said, "your friend liked you so much because when you were there, she forgot for a few hours about her mother's sickness. Then she wasn't using you fairly."

"It's not like that."

"It seems that way to me."

"No one here forgets for a moment," she said, her voice hard.

I didn't say anything.

"It's nothing against you. But we can't go into the sacristy." After a sharp intake of breath she said quickly, "If it were up to me we'd tear it down."

All her nervousness, her effort to speak openly, I realized, were about this: she'd waited until we were alone to tell me about the sacristy, not to tell me about herself. To you it will seem obvious, perhaps, but I wasn't expecting it; I was hoping for something different. I sat back in my chair. "The doctor doesn't have a problem with it." She looked at me and tilted her head, her expression pained. "I'm not afraid of an old woman's skirt," I said.

She turned away. "You should be."

◆　◆　◆

THE ONLY PEOPLE from Río Roto who had entered the sacristy were Tulio and Estrada, but the two were very much not of a kind. In fact, the doctor's tone, when speaking of Tulio, made it evident that Estrada viewed him with the same mixture of contempt and pity as did everyone in Río Roto. "Orchitis," he said, smiling broadly, when I made the mistake of asking him once about Tulio. "Poor son of a bitch. Each of his testicles is the size of a grapefruit." He laughed, throwing his head back and patting his knees with his clean hands. Santos eyed him coldly. "You'd think he wouldn't feel it but he whimpers like a puppy," the doctor said. "The funny thing is, he used to swagger like that even before his balls blew up. Now he has to come see me for injections."

"What will happen to him?" I asked.

"Nothing. His balls will just go on swelling."

I could see that Santos didn't want to continue the conversation, but, as usual, the doctor seemed unaware of it.

"You should watch out," the doctor said to me. "Have you crossed him off your list?"

I stared at him. "What do you mean?"

Estrada laughed and looked at Santos, who went on staring at his hands. "Aren't you making a family tree? You never know— he might be halfway down the trunk."

Santos looked up, taken aback. His expression was pained.

"No—no I'm not," I said quickly.

"Oh, is that right? You gave up?"

I glanced at Santos again, and his face seemed more composed. "There's just no one here—I was wrong."

"You haven't been methodical." He looked at me over his glasses.

I blushed, beginning to feel irritated. "I didn't need to be. My family is obviously from somewhere else."

He shook his head. "Well, I think you could have gone about it more methodically. Showed us pictures, looked up records. Now you'll never find them."

I didn't say anything for a moment. "Yes, I know," I finally said.

After the first day in Río Roto I'd made my inquiries more carefully, and after the visit with Josefa and Claudio I hadn't so much as mentioned to anyone that I was looking for family at all. I'd hoped that, like so many other things I'd done that first week, the remarks about finding our relatives had been forgotten. Estrada made it seem as though, far from being forgotten, they were actually cause for continued speculation.

When Estrada was gone, I could see that Santos had something on his mind. He began in his roundabout way, so that I couldn't anticipate what he was going to ask me. "The doctor has put me back together better than I could have hoped."

"Yes," I said.

"Don't you think?"

"Yes, you're healing quickly." I looked away, feeling no desire to talk about Estrada.

"He must be a very accomplished doctor."

"No doubt."

"You haven't consulted him for anything?"

I shook my head. "No. But I'm sure he's good—as you say. There's only so much you can do in a remote place like this, anyway."

Santos cocked his head to the side. "There are always greater forces at work, aren't there?"

"Yes. He can't be expected to prevent and cure everything."

Santos nodded. "He seems to come to terms with his dilemma quite well."

I looked at him. "What dilemma?"

"I mean the one you just said. Working so remotely. With so much going against him."

"Yes, I guess so." I felt myself frowning. "He seems unworried enough about it."

Santos smiled. "His sense of humor must be his best resource. I find his manner very amusing."

It seemed to me that Santos usually found it all but amusing. "You think it's amusing? Not abrasive?"

"You mean that he's direct."

"He's direct. But he's—He says—At times he's completely thoughtless."

Santos shrugged. "I'll admit that it's difficult to be considerate. To be both direct and always considerate."

"Exactly." I nodded. "He just says whatever occurs to him."

He smiled. "But most of what occurs to him is true."

I found this difficult to take. "I wouldn't say that. He gets something in his head, is what happens, and then decides it's true."

"You don't think his observations today were right?"

"No, I don't, really."

"Well, I wouldn't know."

"I might have had some idea when I first came—I'd thought there might be relatives. But I realized right away that there weren't, and I haven't mentioned it since."

Santos seemed surprised. "I thought you said you weren't looking for family."

"I'm not now—I just thought, at the beginning."

"So then your family is from Río Roto?"

"No. Clearly not. There's no one named Amán—no one living,

that I know of, and the name doesn't appear anywhere at the cemetery."

He squinted, as if trying to help me see the problem more clearly. "Do you know any other names—first names?"

I stood up and went to look out through the window. The door to the church was ajar, and the darkness of the vestry was visible through it. "It's not important now. I'm not looking for anyone anymore."

"I understand." He didn't say anything for some time. Eventually I turned away from the window and looked at him, warily. He had his eyes closed, but he opened them when I turned around. "I hope you don't think I was prying," he said. "I'd forgotten all about that comment. When I asked whether you thought Estrada was right, I actually meant whether you thought he was right about Tulio."

I sat down. "Oh—I'm sorry." Santos leaned his head back, calmly, and closed his eyes again. "I don't know," I said. "What about Tulio?"

He smiled. "Estrada seems to find him a little pathetic."

"I really don't know. I've only talked to him a few times. I hardly know him." I tried to organize my thoughts. "He doesn't strike me as pathetic, I guess."

Santos nodded softly. "I'm sorry; I'm falling asleep again." He made an effort to open his eyes. "But yes—I agree with you. It's hard to know someone you've only seen a few times."

AURELIO'S DAUGHTER, Sabina, sat next to Cruz in the vestry. She seemed calm, almost tired. Cruz sat on the edge of his seat and made his knee bounce. For this occasion he'd used more cologne and a liberal amount of hair grease. Sabina wore a white and yellow dress with a sash. She held her hands on her lap palm-up, as if she'd turned them off for a while, and watched me carefully. I felt a little sorry for her, but I told myself that it was only the cologne.

Later I would try to remember whether I'd mentioned the two of them to anyone that afternoon or the day before. I felt sure that after they'd been to see me I'd talked to Santos about them. I thought I'd said, "What do you know about Cruz and Sabina?" but I must have just said, "What do you know about Sabina?" because it was Sabina who was on my mind.

Santos stirred his pureed beans with a spoon and looked at me out of his unbandaged eye. "Aurelio's?" he said. He shrugged.

"They don't have much money," I said, somewhat questioningly.

Santos shook his head, meaning either that he agreed they didn't or that he didn't know.

I watched them walking together on the way to Murcia and thought to myself that Sabina appeared to be the older of the two, though she wasn't. She carried a canvas bag under her arm. We were quiet on the way—Oscar didn't go with us, and I only tried to speak to them once or twice. At times Cruz would take Sabina's hand and raise it to his lips. She continued walking, looking ahead, not blushing. Cruz's hair was stiff and shiny; by the time we reached Murcia it drooped. Sabina didn't know anyone in Murcia, but while I changed at the back of the church and Cruz sat in the front pew, clasping and unclasping his hands, she disappeared for a while and returned ten minutes later wearing a white cotton veil and white flats. There was a small gold cross on a chain around her neck that I hadn't noticed before. She put the canvas sack next to my things and walked around to the entrance of the church, her new shoes leaving small round dimples in the dirt. It will seem absurd to you, but I was actually pleased with how I carried the ceremony off. I thought I was finally doing something right.

Cruz had built a house on the southern edge of Río Roto. On the way back they held hands the whole time. Sabina asked me to stay for dinner and I made my excuses, but as I said no her expression wilted and I changed my mind. On her first night in her new house Sabina walked around barefoot, the back of her heels raw from the white shoes, which had disappeared into the bedroom as soon as we walked in the door. Cruz showed me the house as Sabina took out what she'd prepared earlier. The bedroom was long and narrow, with slits of windows at either end. Over the bed and its blue bedspread hung a white canopy of mosquito netting that Cruz said Sabina had made. A few other things I could see they'd bought in Rabinal. They had a small blue rug to put by the bed and blue curtains for the window slits that matched the bedspread. The bathroom had a stuffed poodle holding a box of tissues on the toilet. Over the open shower hung a showerhead like a dinner plate, and the soap on the tile beneath it was still in its paper wrapper. Instead of plastic-bound sofas there was wooden furniture with cushions in the front room. On a table meant for a television stood a vase of paper flowers.

Sabina set the dinner out in the kitchen. We had cold *curtido* and tortillas. I gave them a bottle of champagne, a tablecloth with napkins, and a portable radio I'd brought with me, new and not yet opened. It took some time to persuade Sabina that she should accept them. I pressed her. "To thank you," I said, "for the honor of being your first guest." Her expression was anguished.

Then Cruz leaned in and whispered something in her ear. She nodded, looked up, and attempted a smile. The champagne was stored, the tablecloth put to immediate use, and the radio placed next to the paper flowers. After dinner we had coffee in the living room and they both seemed to relax.

I left them late, at about nine-thirty, and I remembered on the way back to the house where I'd seen Cruz before I knew who he was. I'd seen him holding a plastic bag, standing by the side of the road. Next to him had stood an older man who, as Aurelio and I passed on our way to the cemetery, had hissed, quietly, as if surprised by his own breath. By the time I got home the doctor had already come and gone; Santos was snoring through his broken nose.

It was dark when I awoke to pounding on the door. "Father Amán. Father Amán." It was Xinia's voice, but Xinia never shouted. As soon as I opened the door, she shouted at me, "Is it true?"

I felt the ground drop away. In a split second I imagined myself going back inside, packing my suitcase, walking in the dark to take the bus for Rabinal and never returning. I'd been imagining it every other moment of the last few weeks. It was only a matter of time. But if you can believe it, I felt no relief.

My voice came out in a whisper. "I'm sorry."

"You married them?"

It took me a moment to realize what she was talking about. "Sabina and Cruz," I said. I looked down at my bare feet on the walkway. Then I looked up. "Are they all right?"

"It's true then?"

"What?"

"You married them."

"Yes," I said, my head spinning.

For a moment I thought she would hit me, but she held her fists at her sides. "You—" she said, and faltered. She turned and moved away down the walkway. I ran after her, feeling the pounding in my feet and my chest and my head. I watched the white of her soles leaping into the air ahead of me.

The lights of their new house were on, and the insects had begun to flock toward them. The fluttering black shapes, silhouetted from where I stood, stood out despite the commotion on the road. I saw Sabina first. She crouched naked in the dirt. She held her face down toward the road and pressed her chest against her folded legs. Her arms hung against her sides and her hands rested on the ground before her. She was perfectly still, almost remote, as if she'd crouched there to listen or pray.

A few feet away from her a knot of men tried to separate Cruz from a shirtless man who struck out wildly. For a moment they remained entangled. Then the three men who stood around him pulled the shirtless man back and they came apart. Cruz stumbled backward and stood limply, his arms at his sides. The blood was smudged on his face and neck and his naked limbs were covered with dusty dirt.

The shirtless man stared at him. His bearded face was wet with spit and his immense stomach trembled as he fought to free himself. They stood, breathing heavily, staring at each other.

"Papá, please," Cruz said, quietly.

At this the shirtless man flung the other men aside and lunged forward. His hands took hold of Cruz's face and the weight of his body knocked him into the dirt. They rolled, wrapped around each other, Cruz's frail legs kicking against his father's boots.

As the other men rushed toward them I took the shirt of my pajamas off and dropped it onto Sabina's back. She didn't move. Her open eyes seemed to concentrate on something on the road that lay between her thumbs. I looked up to see Xinia coming out of the house with a blanket.

Others had started to arrive, and they stood at the edges of the circle made by the light: expressionless, watching. Xinia crouched down and wrapped the blanket around Sabina. "Stand up," she whispered. "We're leaving. Get up." Sabina didn't move.

The men who'd arrived had moved in to where the others lay in the dirt, and now several of them lifted Cruz's father, dragging him away, his boots still kicking. He righted himself and tried to push them off. They continued to hold him and he finally stood, tense but winded, never taking his eyes off his son. Cruz had gone completely slack. The men on either side of him still held him loosely.

Then Cruz's father noticed me. The men who held him tightened their grip, their thin arms covering his chest and shoulders. I recognized him as the man I'd seen standing with Cruz by the side of the road. He turned away, abruptly, as if the sight of me sickened him. "Get him out of here," he said, his voice forced.

Everyone looked at me. I didn't say anything.

"Get out of here," he shouted.

"They haven't done anything wrong," I said. "They're married." He made a choked sound. "Behind my back."

"No," I said. "No, it wasn't." I felt a shudder in my stomach. I looked around. Cruz wouldn't look me in the eye.

The man lunged at me, suddenly, but it was halfhearted, and the men around him held him back.

"I'm sorry," I said.

The fat man laughed abruptly. Then he spat in my direction. "You're an incompetent," he said. "Go back to wherever you came from."

A woman somewhere behind me began crying Sabina's name. The men held Aurelio back, but his wife came up and threw herself over Sabina. She tried to pull her up and instead fell over her, weeping. Between her efforts and Xinia's, they managed to make her stand. Sabina, wrapped in the blanket and half-crouching, looked terribly small. Aurelio's face was blank. The men at his sides held their hands out in front of him as if reluctant to touch him. Cruz's father laughed harshly at him. "You're shameless," he said.

Aurelio glanced at me. "I didn't know," he said.

"No one knew," Sabina said abruptly, clearly, from inside the blanket. Her voice seemed to bring everyone down. Cruz's father stared at her and at her mother, at Xinia whose face was gray, at me and at Aurelio, as if he suddenly couldn't recall what he was doing there. Then without looking at Cruz again he turned and walked away until he was beyond the reach of the dim house light. The crowd gradually disappeared from the edges in, until Cruz stood alone, his hands at his sides, and Aurelio came toward me and the three women.

Thirteen

No one came to confession on Wednesday, and Xinia didn't appear in the vestry. There had been days in the past when only a few people came to confession, but it was the first time no one had come. On Thursday it was the same. I went so far as to stand in the doorway, looking out over the soccer field, as if by standing there I might see what had taken everyone away. Xinia had nothing in particular to do at the church on those days, but I still noticed her absence, and I couldn't remember whether she'd stayed away on other weeks.

It had been similar during my last month as a teacher in Rhode Island. They were days in which I had a lot of time on my hands, and the people I knew were unaccountably never around. I'd only talked to a few people about the conversation with the new principal, but I knew that among the teaching staff the outcome of it was common knowledge. When she'd first called me in to meet with her I'd assumed it would be like the personal meetings she'd been having with the other teachers. They were friendly, informal chats. With me the conversation immediately took a different turn.

To begin with she sat behind her desk, not next to me, and she crossed her arms the moment I walked in. "Nítido," she said briskly, "as you know I have some plans for us to be more competitive among private schools. I want us to really draw students from all over New England, if not from all over the country."

"Yes," I said to her. "I think it's a great plan."

She smiled. "One thing that really draws students, apart from the facilities and class size, is the quality of the teaching. Of the teachers."

"Of course."

She looked directly at me and held her pen up, as if checking an imaginary box that hung in the air in front of her. "As you must know, advanced degrees are really a large part of what makes a teacher attractive to prospective students and their parents."

I was silent, suddenly realizing what the conversation was about. "I think experience counts for a lot as well."

She nodded. "It does, and I know how many students have benefited from your teaching over the years." She gave me a tight smile. "Nevertheless, it is one of my goals to have a teaching staff entirely composed of teachers with advanced degrees."

"I see." But I did not, entirely. "I would be glad for the opportunity to work on an advanced degree. As I understand it, some people get advanced degrees by correspondence."

The principal put down the pen and opened a folder that was sitting on her desk. She looked through it, frowning, as if my proposal to take a degree by correspondence lay in front of her. "Nítido," she said, looking up. "I really want to have a teaching staff with impeccable credentials, to meet the highest standards. I'm looking at your file," as she said so she picked up the pen again and waved it over the file like a wand, "and there's something here about your undergraduate degree. A qualification about your creative-writing major."

She didn't need to say anything further. I nodded. "When I was first hired by Harris," I said, "he was kind enough to observe that the circumstances of my undergraduate degree would probably make me an understanding teacher. I think he was right. But I can see how being able to learn from your mistakes might not be, for purposes of competitiveness, the most desired quality in a teacher."

The principal didn't say anything. She squinted slightly, as if searching for my point.

I went on, "My father has been very ill, and I would be glad for the opportunity to move back to Oregon to be with him. Perhaps the end of the school year would be a good time."

She inclined her head in what was meant to be a sympathetic gesture. "I'm sorry to hear about your father. That sounds like a wonderful idea to go spend time with him. I'm sure, then, considering the circumstances, you must feel that the sooner you see him the better."

"I'll be seeing him over the break. I think at the end of the school year will be perfectly fine."

For a moment she didn't say anything. "I'm afraid, Nítido, that we actually have a new teacher arriving after the winter break. I know it's relatively soon, and I apologize for that. But as you know, I've only been here for a couple weeks myself."

There were two other teachers who were leaving at the end of the year, I found out afterward. But we avoided one another even

more than we avoided the teachers who were staying; it was as
though we didn't want to be thought of, by others, in the same
terms. I doubt my students learned anything from my classes
during those last two weeks. My co-teachers were so busy with
work at that time of year and so preoccupied with their own concerns that I never had the occasion to discuss what had happened
with any of them.

It was similar in Río Roto after the wedding in Murcia. Oscar
didn't arrive for the walk to Los Cielos, so I went by myself and
preached to the five people who sat in the pews. No one offered
me dinner, and I walked home early. The doctor had left Santos's
light on. I'd spoken to him as little as possible, but on Thursday
night I took a blanket into the bedroom and put it over my
shoulders and sat in the chair in the corner. Santos lay propped
up in bed, snoring. In the weak light he looked just the way you
used to, huddled under the sheets, unconscious of everything. If I
let my eyes close halfway it almost seemed as though I were back
in Oregon with you. I sat watching Santos until I fell asleep, the
laces of my shoes untied and my head resting against the wall.

I awoke on the floor, looking up at the edge of the bed, where
Santos's face peered over at me. I sat up and stretched; my right
arm and leg had fallen asleep, and I pushed myself back with my
other leg until my back was against the wall.

Santos watched me and when some feeling came back in my
leg I stood up shakily and sat back down again as a sharp pain
shot through my back. Santos said, "I'm feeling much better."

"I'm glad," I said.

"I walked around the house yesterday. Sat outside."

"Good."

"I'll be ready to leave in a couple weeks."

I looked at him. "That seems soon."

He flexed his fingers and looked at them, and then he folded his hands in his lap. "Did you want to tell me something?"

I stood up carefully with my hands on the wall and stretched and lifted the curtain to look out at the closed door of the vestry. The sun hurt my eyes and I let the curtain drop. "I made a mistake," I said.

He shrugged with one shoulder. "I'm not surprised. You're very trusting."

I sighed. "I'll be leaving in a few days." He stared at me. "As soon as I get my things together."

"Leaving for where?"

"Back to the States."

He lifted his right hand to his head and touched his bandaged cuts. He'd tossed in his sleep. A spot of blood like a red eye stained the bandages above his ear. He held his fingers there a moment, as if gathering his thoughts. "Don't do that."

I shook my head. "I'm sorry. You'll have to stay with Estrada."

"That's not what I mean."

"The whole thing was a mistake," I said quietly, more to myself than to Santos.

He spoke slowly. "Don't leave yet. Come back to Naranjo with me."

I looked through the window to where a few pieces of sodden cardboard still littered the grass. "I would have. Before."

"I'll be able to soon."

I shook my head again. "No. I've already made up my mind."

"Nítido, you can't go yet."

"I'm sorry." I pulled the chair up by the side of the bed and sat down.

For some time he was silent, and when I looked up he was still studying me. "Why did you sleep on the floor?"

"I have bad dreams on the sofa." I smiled.

He smiled faintly, sadly, and put his hand out toward me. "Let me tell you why you can't go."

"I'm sorry." I stood up again and began to move away.

He put his fingers around my wrist. His hands were strong, stronger than I would have thought possible. "I didn't tell you everything last time."

I didn't try to pull away.

"You know I didn't."

I stared at him in silence.

His face was very serious, more serious than I'd ever seen it. Usually his eyes seemed to smile even when his lips didn't, but as he gripped my hand his eyes were fierce. "Sit down and I'll tell you."

I've thought so often about what Santos told me next that whole pieces of his story play themselves out, uninterrupted, in my head. Nevertheless, I know that there are parts of it that I've forgotten. At one point Santos told me how he'd become a *mayordomo*, and though I recall the fact of it—he came from a long line of priests and *curanderos*—I can't remember how or at what point he described it. And some of what he told me I only seem to remember in English. Certain phrases in Spanish I can vividly hear him saying: "*los hombres de la montaña*," he says, pronouncing *hombres* loudly, hollowly. But then there are whole episodes that I hear in English, in a low, neutral voice that is neither his nor mine. This voice must belong to a translator—the translator in my mind. He has preserved the meaning of Santos's words, but he has obliterated the words themselves. How would it be possible to remember, exactly, what someone said a year ago, or two, or ten?

"Before I tell you I have to go back," Santos said, "to something else. To explain about the men from the mountain."

"Who are the men from the mountain?"

"Maybe to you," he said, "this place seems like the end of the world. It's nothing compared with the jungle—what we call the jungle. No one goes if he can avoid it. But there are things that will drive a person to live on the mountain. You have to think for a moment what kind of desperation would make the jungle—constant rain, dark canopy, spiders that burn through you with acid piss—seem like a livable place. For some years there were only rumors of strangers passing through. No one ever saw them.

"As it turns out I met one of them once, but I had always imagined them differently. It never occurred to me to think she was dangerous. I was about seven miles from Naranjo, in a narrow valley where as a boy I saw the only quetzal I've ever seen in my life—they hardly survive any longer in the wild—and I was heading home. The sun was hot and I walked slowly, trying not to fall asleep in the sun. When I reached the lowest point in the valley I gave in and sat in the tall grass, leaning my back against my bag. Ordinarily I notice everything, the smallest thing, but maybe the drowsiness dulled my senses, because I closed my eyes for a moment and when I opened them a woman was sitting only a few yards away from me, staring at me from the tall grass. I started, and she stayed perfectly still. Her eyes were glassy—I felt a cold chill at the thought that she might be dead. Then her eyes rolled back in her head and she fell backward with a soft noise in the grass.

"When I approached her I saw that she had gotten as far as removing her shoe and sock and rolling up her pant leg. A snake had bitten the thin skin on the outside of her leg above her ankle. Her pants were brown, her white shirt was very dirty. She wore her hair loose. I'd never seen a woman like her before. I crouched down and picked up her foot and began drawing the poison out of the flesh with my mouth. When most of it was out, I splashed water from my thermos on her face. She came to calmly, as if she'd just awoken from a nap. 'I shouldn't have wandered,' she said.

"'You'll be fine,' I said.

"She stared at me and then looked at her ankle. 'Thank you,' she said. 'I did know what to do, but I couldn't reach it.' She put her sock on, tied her boot, and stood up shakily.

"'Where are you going?' I asked.

"'I have to get back,' she said. She began walking away. 'I was going to leave, but,' she paused, 'now I don't want to.' She looked tired.

"I thought she'd come from Río Roto. She wasn't heading toward Naranjo, and she seemed not to need my help. 'You're going the wrong way,' I said. 'Río Roto is that way.' I pointed.

"She stood at the edge of the tall grass, where the trees began. As I spoke she turned around to look at me again. 'I'm going this way,' she said. Then she waved, and turned and walked off into the trees.

"Even after I heard about the guerrilla and knew about their passing through Río Roto, it didn't occur to me that the woman with the snakebite had been one of them. It wasn't until years later, when I walked through the valley again, that I realized she'd been living with the guerrilla for a long time—that she was, of all things, a man from the mountain. That time I walked through, thinking of her and watching for snakes, when I felt something solid underfoot that made me jump before I could think that it was too hard. I'd stepped on an ammunition shell, and the tall grass of the valley was littered with them.

"Their commander then was a man named Zúñiga, a student of

philosophy who didn't finish his degree. He had a beard and short fingers and he walked like a parrot, which made him ridiculous to me as a source of inspiration. Zúñiga was the one who made friends in Río Roto, finding people who would stockpile supplies, others to store ammunition, others who carried messages—to the capital or to other cells, for all I know. They rarely came up to where we were, or we, too, might have been taken in. But Zúñiga had Río Roto in the palm of his hand. They say—I don't know who they were— that some people actually went off with him to the mountain.

"Then one month, in the summer, Zúñiga and the others vanished. No one in Río Roto saw them for a while, and when they reappeared a month later they were fewer in number. A helicopter raid—Zúñiga and a dozen others had been traced, hunted down, killed. Someone in Río Roto spoke up." He stopped speaking and looked at me, waiting. "Do you know who it was?"

I stared at him. "No."

"You have no suspicion?"

We looked at each other in silence. "Aurelio would never do that," I said.

Santos considered me carefully. "Río Roto disagrees with you."

"I don't believe it."

Santos smiled, as if he'd expected as much. "Has Aurelio told you about the sugar mill?"

I didn't say anything for a moment. "No," I finally said.

Santos nodded. "The sugar mill," he said, "had been running from the time the German died. It ran with only eight men and an ox, which carried the cane in from the field. They fed the cane into a grinder, the grinder extracted the juice, and the juice ran off into buckets. Then they poured the juice from the buckets into a cauldron and one man stood over it, stirring constantly, as the sugar thickened. When the sugar ran like glue they poured it into wooden molds, where it hardened and drew the bees. The bees would swarm over the brown liquid and fly too close. Their legs and wings became trapped in the sticky surface and their bodies were pulled down by the struggle until the sugar enveloped and preserved them. The man who ran the sugar mill, Felix, had lost a hand to the grinder. He worked as well with his other hand as most men do with two. He hired only one man over thirty, Bartolomé, who was even older then than I am now. All he did was work the cauldron, and his hands and arms had so toughened that he could lay his palm flat on the surface of a stove. I knew him well because he was the *mayordomo* in Río Roto, and there were times when I would stay with him for months at a time.

"He made his own alcohol from the cane, and we would sometimes drink it together, sitting up near the sugar mill looking out over the town. One night we'd been drinking for a while when he stood up suddenly and walked over to the ox, which he fed and took care of, and which watched us drink with an expression of inconceivable exhaustion. He wrapped his arm around the ox's neck. 'You are more beautiful than the stars in the sky,' he said to the ox. 'I want to fall asleep in your eyes.' I laughed until my stomach hurt, and when I caught my breath I asked him how long he'd been in love. He regarded me seriously. 'You shouldn't laugh,' he said. 'This ox has seen things you and I can't even imagine.' I wasn't sure then whether or not he was sober.

"I mention it because I never found out who ended up with the ox. A week after the guerrilla came through wanting to know who'd given them away, the men from the sugar mill disappeared. The people who went to look for them found the sugar burning in the cauldron, the grinder stuffed with half-milled cane, and the molds full of hardened brown syrup. The ox stood alone by the edge of the mill, his head drooping so low that his tongue was dusted with dirt. For days they searched and found no one. And when they'd given up they found Aurelio, where he'd been the whole time, shut up in his house. As he told it, he'd arrived late to the sugar mill that day, and the men were all gone by the time he arrived. You can see why no one believed him.

"In the following weeks people left for Los Cielos, Rabinal, or, if they could afford it, the capital. Río Roto was divided all over again. Most people left. Not everyone was going to wait around for the guerrilla. Some did, because they were too far gone to turn back. Others stayed just to see what they could get out of it, thinking, maybe, when it was all over they'd have more than they started with. Tulio was the only one who came to stay with us. He stayed with Noé, the head of the patrol. When he arrived we heard from him what we'd long feared: the guerrilla were no longer just a rumor. They wouldn't touch us because of the patrol. It was only a dozen men with secondhand army rifles, but that can be enough. And who knows—since they never saw us themselves they may have heard something different: twelve men; twenty men; a troop of men armed to the teeth. I'll admit that if there were exaggerations, they became truer after Tulio came. Some men who hadn't wanted to before suddenly saw what it was about, and the patrol got bigger. We lived from day to day, thinking we would be next.

"A couple months after going to the sugar mill the guerrilla went back to Río Roto. Many people had left, but not all of them. Maybe the guerrilla were looking for Aurelio or maybe they thought they would make the town give him up. They went door to door. They rounded up a dozen people at random and took them back to the sacristy. All of them, along with the priest, were hung from the beams. You can see how sturdy they are. They cut crosses on their stomachs. Let gravity do the rest.

"I don't blame them for giving up then. They had no choice. In the months that followed, the guerrilla all but took over Río Roto. They slept wherever they wanted, took whatever food they wanted. Only a few months after they'd first gone to the sugar mill, they had the whole town at their feet. It was so fast—think of it—in a matter of months. We knew all about it from Tulio, who'd gone back, thinking the worst was over, only to turn right around. It was a difficult time, because much as we wanted to do something, we didn't know how many guerrilla there were, or whether they would expect us, or how many people in Río Roto we could count on.

"As it turned out we waited too long. Tulio kept urging us to go but we were too slow, too cautious. It took us almost three months to make up our minds. There were so few of us, you see. Only twenty men or so. When we finally decided to take the patrol to Río Roto, the place was beyond us. From the road you could see the cone of smoke that opened up into the clouds. The town was almost empty. It was impossible to tell from what remained of the school building how many people had been inside. Or how many people had escaped."

"Who was it?" I asked him.

Santos waved his hand. "Maybe the guerrilla decided to cut their losses. Maybe they'd been betrayed again. Maybe someone in Río Roto finally decided they'd had enough. And then paid for it."

"Then you don't know?"

He looked at me intently. "You have to understand, it was total chaos. Almost no one on the street, just buildings burning everywhere. We got there too late. They were all gone by then. Our only thought was to save whoever was still alive.

"We searched house by house and found almost all of them empty. Only once did we see any sign of life. In a house by the edge of town Noé heard cries coming from inside. The woman was crumpled on the floor. The man was sitting in a chair, his head hanging by the skin of his neck against his back. His right arm rested on the table, and his right hand was a couple feet away from it, lying palm-up. On his lap sat an infant, his face red from screaming. He held on to the man's shirt with his fists. When Noé walked in, the boy rested his head against the man's chest and screamed louder. The woman was barely alive. With her last breath she asked them to take the boy. A boy named Hilario. Noé had to rip the shirt off in bunches to get the boy away from the man he clung to.

"We left, taking Hilario from that place where there was no longer anything for him. Noé took him in, raised him. We never told him anything but the truth—how Noé had saved him. But it's true that we didn't know about Xinia. I found out only later that the boy's aunt had survived."

I didn't say anything for a moment. Santos was watching me. "Where was she?" I asked. "Where were all the people who are here now?"

"Hiding, the ones that could."

"But if you didn't know about her, how did you come to Río Roto to find her?"

"I didn't come to find her. I only thought of talking to Xinia after you told me about her."

"But what did I say? I didn't know about Hilario."

"Nítido," Santos said. He looked at me for a moment without saying anything. Then he spoke quietly. "You've told me a great deal about Xinia. Perhaps without realizing it."

"Have I?" My voice sounded hollow.

He nodded. "I didn't see why. But things got a little clearer when she came to talk to me. In the way she mentioned you. Things got a little clearer."

I looked away from him. I felt suddenly constricted in the cramped room, the unbearably tiny house. Santos watched me and I sat silently, not asking anything.

"It worries me," Santos said, shaking his head. "It will be difficult for her alone."

"She won't go with you?"

He smiled, not looking at me, as if embarrassed. "Of course. But an injured old man can only do so much."

For several minutes we were both silent. I drew and redrew a tiny circle with my finger on the blanket. Almost all of what Santos had told me was still incomprehensible to me. I could not even begin to make sense of it. Only his last point, the image of Xinia going to Naranjo, alone among strangers there, seemed clear. When I looked up at Santos he seemed lost in thought. "When were you thinking of leaving for Naranjo?" I asked him.

"In another week—at most."

"You won't be well enough in a week."

"I will." He hesitated, and when he spoke again his tone had changed. "Just stay another week."

"Let me think about it," I said.

"Think about it. Think about it for a week. That will give you time."

THAT NIGHT I took the pillows and blankets I'd used in the front room of the sacristy and took them to the vestry. I put the cushions from the changing-room sofa end to end on the floor and covered them with a sheet. There were handbells in the closet next to the electric keyboard and I took one back to the house.

Santos was falling asleep. I put the bell on the table by his bed. Only the top of his head still required bandages. The stitches on his face held the skin of his cheeks, nose, and forehead in place. One of his eyes had begun to heal and turn green. His good eye flickered as I stood by the bed. I leaned in, waiting to see if he was awake.

He nodded softly.

"Just one more thing," I said.

"Hm," he said, without opening his eyes.

"If you didn't come for Xinia, why did you come to Río Roto?"

He was silent, and I thought for a moment that he'd fallen asleep. I heard a soft brushing of wings at the window. The insects were already drawing toward the light. I turned to go and I was at the door when Santos said, "To see you."

SATURDAY PASSED SLOWLY. At ten I heard the doctor come and go from Santos's room. I spent the morning going through the ledger of names and staring at the patch of grass outside the window. At noon I forced myself to go to Cruz's house but no one came to the door. I walked with my head down to the other end of town and found no one at Aurelio's house either. The town seemed deserted, and I had the feeling, as I saw one closed door after another, that everyone stayed indoors as I walked by. A boy who watched me pass from his front window shot stones into the street with a slingshot and the stones fell three feet, then two feet, and then one foot ahead of me. When I stopped to look back at him he had disappeared.

I realized, when I saw an empty crate that had fallen in the road, that most people had left town to go to the market. The explanation was that simple. I lifted the crate and stared at its stained interior and put it by the side of the road. At the cemetery the fountain had drawn the birds. The crows pushed aside the smaller birds, toppling against one another midair. Aurelio had scattered seed in the basin at the top of the fountain.

Starting with the northeast quadrant of the cemetery, I walked row by row, recording the names and dates. Some of the stones bore names identical to those that I'd copied from the ledger, but it seemed to me that they didn't belong to the same people. Those in the cemetery had died decades ago, or in the last three years. There was a gap—not immediately apparent, but discernible nonetheless—an absence of burials roughly ten years earlier. Many of the older and very recent stones were marked with surnames I was familiar with from visits to Los Cielos and Murcia. I found Baer's palatial mausoleum in the northwest corner, the closest corner, I noticed, to his land. An angel perched uncertainly on the roof. The glass of the mausoleum door was cracked and inside a dusty vase lay on the floor. A velvet curtain that hung on the left-hand side had been shredded at the bottom.

The walkways were much cleaner than they'd been when I'd first seen them. Bougainvillea and jasmine, their dense surfaces cleared of weeds, covered the perimeter walls. The bushes that lined the main avenues, which rolled out away from the fountain in a cross, had been trimmed so that they formed curved walls on either side. The earliest legible stone belonged to Adelfo Barrios, who had died in 1912 at the age of fifty-seven. The stone leaned facedown toward the ground, as if trying to peer into the earth. After his name there was a little mark that looked like a comma.

It took me several hours to record all the names, but when I returned to the vestry the sun was still high. I realized when I reached the study that I hadn't translated another sermon. Part of me probably assumed I wouldn't give another sermon. Nevertheless I would have to give at least one more. I imagined myself opening the door behind the altar the next morning and finding the pews empty. A few weeks earlier the sight would have relieved me. I can't explain to you exactly why, but after the wedding in Murcia I only wanted to do it well, without mistakes. I'd made other mistakes, I thought; many others. I sat down and spent the afternoon comparing the names I'd recorded with those in the ledger, but I was easily distracted and found myself repeatedly at the window, staring at the unmarked patch of grass.

DURING THE SERVICE it seemed as though the room had been emptied and filled with people from another town, but it was only because the people I wanted to see weren't there. I experienced something similar to what I felt reading the names: a spark of recognition, and then a feeling of disorientation when I realized I was wrong. I confused the people I'd seen in confession with the people who'd given me names on Monday, and I even momentarily mistook people in the pews for people I knew from other places and times. I always became used to a place in the same way; in Río Roto, as in the past, what had struck me from the beginning was not so much its newness, but its extreme similarity, through analogy, to places I'd been before. Perhaps the sense of familiarity resulted from my tendency to navigate an unknown place by assigning an antecedent to everyone and everything in it. I'd seen that shake of the head, that way of turning away, that manner of slow step, before; in according each its place I couldn't help think- ing of the person it had first belonged to. I often thought I'd seen someone familiar on the street or in the congregation, only to realize a moment later that the person I was thinking of was thousands of miles away.

I'd hoped at first that glimpsing you and Mamá in the congre- gation pointed to a genuine similarity—a family resemblance. Then I realized that I only seemed to see you everywhere because you were both so often on my mind. On that Sunday afternoon, it was Xinia whom I thought I saw several times during the sermon even though she wasn't present. I was convinced, when I looked up in the middle of the first section, that she'd walked in quietly and taken a seat in the last pew. She was wearing a blue dress and lipstick, which surprised me. I looked at her for a moment, paus- ing, and the church was silent. Then I realized that it wasn't her. I turned back to the sermon and found my place. Only a few min- utes later I noticed a woman who hadn't been there earlier sitting by the windows. I forced myself to go on reading, and when I reached the end of the paragraph I paused, looked up, and turned to her side of the room. She looked nothing like Xinia; only her way of standing—her arms crossed, her head bent somewhat downward—had made me mistake who she was. But Xinia was nowhere in the church, and neither were Luz, nor Aurelio, nor his family. I read on, rushing somewhat, feeling a sudden anxiety to be done with the sermon.

When I returned to the house, Santos sat on the edge of his bed. He still wore thin bandages, but his face was clear and his injured eye could open partway. "Take me for a walk?" he said. I put his shoes on and covered him with a blanket. We walked out the side door and into the passageway between the house and the vestry. He held on to my shoulder. His breathing came in short, shallow gasps. "I'll get my strength back," he said. We walked out to the road and stood there for some time, Santos closing his eyes against the sun. "I'm much better," he murmured, holding his face up.

"Let me get some chairs," I said. I walked him back to the house and left him resting against the wall. I brought the chair from the bedroom and a stool and set them on the walkway. We sat down and Santos sat with his eyes closed and his hands on his knees.

Inexplicably restless, I looked up and down the road, watching the boys on their bicycles circling the plaza. We'd been sitting in the walkway for several minutes when I heard Luz's door open. Luz came out of her house and sat on the doorstep. I waved to her and she waved back with two fingers without lifting her arm. I don't know why it surprised me so much to see Xinia coming out of Luz's door afterward. She stepped around Luz and walked toward us.

I stood up as she approached us. Santos stayed in his chair. "Good afternoon," Santos and I said.

"Good afternoon." Xinia pressed her heel into the dirt of the road, looked down, and looked up again. "You look well," she said to Santos.

"I'm much better," he said.

She nodded. "Will you be able to make the trip back soon?"

"Next week," Santos said, "I think."

"Let me know when you're planning to go. I'll be going with you."

Santos stood up. "Well, watch me. You'll see for yourself." He put his hand on my shoulder. "I'm going to try walking around on my own."

"I don't think—"

He interrupted me. "I'm only going to walk around the house, behind the church."

I nodded. "All right."

Xinia and I watched him walk down the walkway and then onto the grass, around the corner of the house. We stared at the house for a moment longer after he'd disappeared.

"He does seem much better," I said. I turned back to Xinia.

She nodded. "Yes."

"Definitely better."

"He's much older than he looks, though."

"Is he?" I crossed my arms.

"I'm worried that something will happen on the way. I won't be able to help him."

"It's a two-day walk?"

"Yes—at a normal pace. It will probably take him longer."

"Well, better to take it slow. He never complains, so you can't tell how he's doing."

"But you can tell? After being with him all this time?"

I'd only heard her speak in the same way once before, when she'd attempted to thank me for the meeting with Santos. Her voice seemed lighter, softer, but her expression remained the same. "Not really," I said. "I just know he often says he's fine when he isn't."

She looked me in the eye. "It's too bad you can't come with us."

I was silent for a moment. She blinked once, slowly. "I was considering it," I said.

"He's used to you. It would be such a help." She looked down again.

"I was considering it," I said again, lamely.

"I would certainly— It would make the trip a lot easier."

I waited, but she wouldn't look up at me. "I don't know what good I'd be, but if it makes you feel better I'll go."

Xinia turned her head quickly and I looked in the same direction. Santos had appeared on the other side of the house. He smiled at us. When he walked up to us Xinia gave him a rare smile. "Father Amán is coming with us to Naranjo," she said.

ON MONDAY MORNING I went to Xinia's house early, at eight. I didn't hear anything from outside, though I stood by the window of the front room listening for a few minutes. I ducked under a laundry line and looked into the kitchen through the open door. No one was there, but through it I could see into the living room. Eliseo sat with his back to me on a low stool, and I felt a flash of envy. But then I noticed the children sitting on the floor in front of him. There were ten or twelve of them, and Eliseo was reading to them aloud. I stood outside, watching their intent faces. He was really reading to them. It took me some time to believe it. Was it possible, I asked myself, that *this* was what occurred behind the red curtains?

Eliseo, with his back to me and his mind on the reading, didn't hear me walk into the kitchen. I stood in the doorway of the living room, looking over his shoulder.

"'Very well, my grandsons,' the old woman replied. Soon they came to the field. And as they plunged the pick into the earth, it worked the earth; it did the work alone. In the same way they put the ax in the trunks of the trees and in the branches, and instantly they fell and all the trees and vines were lying on the ground. The trees fell quickly, with only one stroke of the ax. The pick also dug a great deal. One could not count the thistles and brambles which had been felled with one blow of the pick. Neither was it possible to tell what it had dug and broken up, in all the large and small woods."

You will doubtlessly recognize it. It took me only a moment; as I heard the passage of the Popol Vuh, familiar to me from your reading of it and so many of my own, and felt a surge of laughter rising in my stomach. The children turned to stare at me as they'd been staring at Eliseo. One of them smiled and another put his finger to his lips. At that Eliseo stopped and looked over his shoulder. He stared at me for a moment. "Father Amán," he said. "I didn't hear you come in." I hadn't noticed when I'd first met him how thin he was, or how his feet pointed out like a clown's.

"Eliseo," I said.

"Xinia," he called. "Father Amán is here." He half-smiled at me and held the book up. "Do you want to take over for a while?"

"Ah." I laughed. It struck me as very funny. I laughed again, more loudly, and then cleared my throat. "I'd like that. But no, thank you."

He smiled vaguely and turned back to the book, picking up where he'd left off.

Even if I'd seen it empty, I would have thought Xinia's house resembled a schoolroom. Unlike most of the houses in Río Roto, it had walls and floors of wood—cedar, it appeared, and cypress. The floorboards had bent and bowed in places, showing the ground a yard below. Needles of light hung in the cracks where the planks had shrunk in the walls. There was no sofa, but an odd assortment of wooden chairs. The rocking chairs had cushions on them and larger cushions had been left on the floor for the children. The shelves on the walls were lined with wooden masks: a hook-nosed clown with horns, a rabbit with buck teeth, a monkey with his eyes closed.

And yet in other ways the room seemed totally unlike a classroom. The children on their cushions sat under improvised tables that fit like trays over their extended legs. The older ones had squares of paper and pencils before them. The red curtains I'd seen so often from the outside gave the room a peculiar color. The absence of proper desks, the crimson darkness, the children reclining on their pillows, and Eliseo hunching over his book all served to give the impression that the class had been assembled in the middle of the night for some unexpected lesson.

I watched and waited for Xinia in the kitchen. The children in her room were older; I listened to their slow, hesitant monotones as they took turns reading aloud. She'd raised a finger, asking me to wait when Eliseo called her, and I watched her with the book in her hands, reading silently to herself as her student finished the sentence.

"Keep reading," she said. She closed the door to the back bedroom and walked out toward me.

She passed me without looking up and went through the kitchen and out onto the grass. I followed her. "You shouldn't be here," she said.

I looked at her as if seeing her for the first time. Her mouth was set in a hard line, and her eyes seemed worried as they moved over my shoulders, avoiding my face. I hadn't noticed before that the middle finger of her right hand was callused from writing.

She clasped her hands over her stomach and stood with her feet squared defensively. I felt the urge to laugh again. "You're a teacher," I said.

She glanced at me and then looked away. "Yes, Father Amán."

"I didn't know."

She was silent for a moment, looking at the ground. "We don't like to draw attention," she said. "Teaching is," she glanced at me again, "not as harmless as it is in other parts of the world."

I smiled. "Excuse me," I said.

"I hope you see that."

"Eliseo's a teacher too," I said.

"Yes."

I smiled, but the feeling of hilarity was dying away, leaving me thoughtful, and I looked in through the doorway at the raised faces of the children. One of them was falling asleep with his elbows on the little bench over his legs. "Do you know," I said, turning to her, "I was led to believe this whole time that there wasn't a school in Río Roto."

She crossed her arms. "Yes, I know." She looked at me. I didn't say anything and she looked away. "I should get back," she said. "Is there something you wanted?"

"No, it—" I paused, watching her eyelashes flicker. "It doesn't matter. I'll see you in the afternoon."

"This afternoon?" Her face was blank.

"If you like, stay here. I'll take the names for Sunday."

"Oh," she said. "No, I'll be there."

"Well, I was going to ask you— I'm not sure if many people will come."

She didn't look at me. "I'll be there."

"All right." I paused. "Thanks." Xinia stepped into the kitchen and Eliseo turned as he heard her and waved goodbye to me. I lingered a moment longer in the doorway. Eliseo reached out to wake the boy who'd been sleeping, and the boy sat up straight and rubbed his eyes. The murmurs of reading from the other room paused for just a moment as Xinia reentered it. I stood with my back against the wall of the house for some time, listening to the uncertain voices moving slowly over the new words.

PART III

Fourteen

A WEEK LATER we left Río Roto for Naranjo. We walked south and crossed the river at the bridge for Murcia. After side-stepping Murcia we headed east. Xinia thought that with Santos walking slowly it would probably take three days to reach our destination. The return would then take two and we would be back before the following Sunday. I carried the supplies Estrada had given me for Santos, along with a bag filled with food and a couple changes of clothes. Xinia carried another bag, a sheet wrapped up like a cocoon and tied across her chest.

We started out before dawn, taking the path to Murcia while the black sky leaned over us heavily. Santos drank water every few minutes from a bottle strung around his waist. As we passed the ascent to Murcia, the sun began to rise, making gray blades of the sugarcane. The sky ahead of us hardened into a pale barrier behind the hills. Naranjo could only be reached from the west by a series of small connecting paths; the town's main link to the rest of the world ran east, in the opposite direction, as if it had turned its back on everything that lay behind it.

At ten in the morning we stopped for lunch by the side of a stream that led to the river. Santos was quiet, sitting off by himself, chewing cold tortilla. Xinia and I sat on the rocks. She opened a cloth napkin on her knees and wrapped tortilla around pieces of cheese and ate in small, inaudible bites. Then she prodded a clod of cold rice apart and ate it with her fingers. I ate quickly and washed my hands in the stream. I drank from the thermos and refilled it with the water that ran over the rocks. Santos stood in the path, waiting for us, his hands on his hips.

Parts of the path had been neglected for years. Mud slides had buried long stretches that were then tamped down again by the feet of the few people who'd passed by. At noon we reached a tunnel cut out of the bramble that had only survived because the bramble had long been dead. The trees around it grew densely, their branches trailing luminous lengths of old-man's-beard. Only weak light came through the trees, but the area above the bramble was clear of branches so that the floor of the tunnel was flecked with brilliant and irregular dabs of sunlight. Near the far end of it, an opening like a manhole had been made in the ceiling by some animal or fallen branch. The sun came through the gap unhindered, and though from a distance it seemed to promise some rare vision, when I looked up through it there was nothing to see but a ragged scrap of sky.

We continued to climb and the air grew colder. The lemon and orange trees dwindled. At a turn in the path where water burst out from under a boulder a cluster of pines grew in the rocky soil. I drank from the boulder and refilled my thermos. Just above, near a bald spot on the hill where the trees could not grow among the rocks, a group of crows worried the base of a spindly thorn bush.

As we approached, the crows' cries became violent. They drew back, hesitated, clambered down again, then flew over us and away. There was nothing by the bush but a hole the width of my fist, and the dry dirt around it had been clawed open.

In the afternoon Santos was forced to stop. We'd reached a flat expanse that had once served as pasture. I wondered who could have lived in such a place but didn't ask. The air was humid, the rocks green with moss. At either extreme of the open field the fences lay broken, covered with pale green fungus. The sun directly overhead reached us weakly, filtered through layer upon layer of the clouds' sodden gauze. The gray sky, the pine trees, the damp cold all reminded me uncannily of Oregon. I had the sense that we had stepped into another time, and that at any moment we would come across the wood-shingled houses and the smooth paved streets where you and Mamá walked silently with your umbrellas.

Santos sat on a rock and rested his head in his hands. Then he turned around and quietly vomited on the soft grass. Xinia crossed her arms and looked east, where the field dissolved into forested hills. I poured water from the thermos into the plastic cup and took it to Santos. He poured it over his face and gave me the cup back and then filled his mouth with water from his own water bottle, spat it out, and drank.

"We should go back," I said. Santos panted into the narrow space between his knees, his hands at his sides. "There's no rush. We can go back and if you feel better we can go next week."

Neither of them said anything. I sat down a few feet from Santos and tried to shake off the humid chill. The air smelled like dirt drenched with rain, but the grass felt dry. "I'll just rest for a while," Santos said, his voice a little hoarse.

"I think we should go back. By the time we get there you'll be as bad as you were two weeks ago."

Xinia spoke without turning to us. "We'll go slowly."

I looked at her back and then at Santos. "What do you think?" I asked him. "You shouldn't push yourself—it's not worth it. And don't rush because of me. If it takes another month, fine."

Santos chuckled softly, then coughed. He heaved again but controlled himself. His eyes were watering and he smiled at me. "This one wants to keep going," he said.

She turned quickly. "We've gone a quarter of the way."

"Then we're still closer to home," I said.

"We wouldn't get back now by nightfall."

Santos stood up weakly, tottered. I stood up and took his arm. He walked to a spot with more grass than rocks and sat down, and then he let his head drop onto the ground and sighed. I stood over him, looking down at his thin limbs spread out over the grass. His arms and legs were dark at the joints, as if the skin concealed hard, troubled knots at his knees and elbows. "Look at him," I said.

I walked over to Xinia and spoke to her quietly. "I thought you wanted my help."

She didn't say anything and went on looking east, her arms crossed.

"You should go ahead of us," Santos said, from under his elbow.

"No one knows me," Xinia said.

Santos lifted his head suddenly and regarded her seriously. "I can't make any promises," he said. He put his hand to his forehead. "I'm worn-out." He dropped back down and closed his eyes.

I stood over him anxiously, watching Xinia out of the corner of my eye. She remained standing for nearly fifteen minutes. Then she turned around and took off her bundle and began unpacking. "All right," she said. "Let's sleep here tonight. We'll sleep early and get up early and we'll be halfway there tomorrow."

I looked to Santos, but he was either sleeping or pretending to be. "Xinia," I said. "It will take us four days to get there." She shrugged. "If one day wiped him out like this, think what he'll be like after four."

"We can carry him."

I stared at her.

"I have a sheet. It won't be hard. He hardly weighs anything."

"I think we should go back and try this again in a few weeks. He just never complains—I had no idea how hard he was pushing himself."

Xinia sat down suddenly on the wool blanket she'd spread over the grass. Next to her was a machete in a leather sheath that I hadn't noticed before. Her thermos, her bundle of clothes, her packs of food were piled up in front of her. She looked at me for a minute. Then she said, "Either way we have to sleep. If he's worse tomorrow, we'll go back. If he's okay, we'll go on."

"He's going to say he's okay."

"Then you can decide." She made a little motion with her hands as if she were shaking water from them. "You can decide tomorrow if you think he's better or worse. But either way we have to sleep."

"All right. All right, that's true." I took my blankets out slowly and laid them over the grass. I took one to Santos and spread it out next to him and lifted him onto it. I put a roll of clothes under his head and covered him with a second blanket. While he lay on his back I changed the bandage on his head and threw away the

old one in a plastic bag. Then I washed my hands with water from
the thermos and took out the cans of soup and the bread. Xinia
made a fire with the driest kindling she could find and we warmed
the cans by setting them in the feeble fire and then ate out of the
cans with spoons. I ate the bread and the last of the cheese. When
Santos woke up I gave him a can of soup wrapped in a rag. He ate
slowly and fell asleep again without finishing. We left the fire
burning weakly; it popped and sizzled as it consumed the damp
wood and I fell asleep watching it shrink in the moist air.

I CONFUSED YOU with Santos in my dreams, and I labored half
the night under the imagined weight of you, wrapped in a sheet,
strung over my shoulder. I carried you the way I'd seen women in
Río Roto carrying their children: the cloth tied diagonally across
the back, the weight of the child falling naturally across the chest.
The wounds and clothing were Santos's, but the voiceless, meaning expression of the face was yours. I walked along stony paths,
upward and upward, your bulk blocking the path from sight and
making me stumble. The route went on and on, monotonously,
and then I noticed that you'd begun to grow smaller. Your weight
hadn't changed, but you were receding within the sheet. I walked
on, faster, as if doing so would prevent you from diminishing. It
was no use. You grew smaller and smaller until you nearly fit in
my palm. But the weight, if anything, seemed to increase. I finally
set you down, exhausted, to catch my breath. You lay on the
sheet, so diminutive that you seemed to be miles away. I turned
my head for only an instant, but when I looked back you'd disappeared altogether, and a black crow had alighted in your place. It
examined me, its head cocked, its eye wide. I shouted for you, a

terrible anxiety bursting out in my voice, but there was no trace of you, and the crow took off, frightened by my cries.

I awoke after dawn, and when I opened my eyes it took some time to extract the pieces of waking life from the dream. I'd slept for nearly twelve hours. I remembered that Xinia had said we would start early, and I started up, panicked. Santos's blanket was empty. The other blanket that had covered him lay a few yards away, crumpled on the ground. Xinia's spot was empty as well, but her blanket had been folded and her things, other than her machete, were stacked around it. I put on my sweater; the damp air had left me chilled. I tied my boots and folded my blanket and put it in my pack along with the bag of trash and the leftover food. Then I stood in the pasture waiting for the dim sunlight to warm me.

After twenty minutes I began to feel restless. I looked into the trees at the edges of the pasture and saw no sign of either of them. When ten minutes more had passed I tied my pack on and walked to the edge of the trees to the north, walking along the fallen fence, trying to catch a glimpse of one of them through the trunks. I'd reached the eastern edge of the enclosure when I heard a call from the other corner. From a distance I could see Xinia walking across the field toward me. I turned back and we met by the remains of the dead fire. "I thought he'd gone into the woods to be sick," she said. Her breathing came in gasps; her cheeks were pink with cold and exertion. Around the handle of the machete her fingers were tinged with blue. I looked at the blade and saw bits of wet grass, leaves, plastered on its edge.

"You can't find him?"

"I've been looking for two hours."

"Two hours. Xinia."

"I don't know where he could be."

"You should have woken me."

"I didn't think it would take so long." Xinia moved over to her blanket and began to pack her things quickly, deliberately. "Pack his blankets. We'll have to keep looking. He might have a fever."

I watched her. "He might be lost."

"Yes." She rolled her things up and tied the cloth over her chest. She sheathed the machete and strung it around her waist and then took it out as we approached the line of trees to the north. She stooped down, touched the grass, pushed past a low branch. "He came this way," she said. "But then a few yards in I can't tell." We walked on through the trees, Xinia cutting the thin branches aside occasionally with quick swipes. I followed her at some distance, trying to keep my bearings.

We'd been moving north slowly for about half an hour when she stopped. "Can you smell that?"

"No. What?"

"Smell." Xinia pushed through the leaves tentatively in two or three directions, then moved to the right. "Here," she said. I looked past her at the trunk of a tree that held a little pool of vomit in its roots.

"Did you see this before?"

"No, I didn't get this far."

"But he's not here."

"No. He may not be nearby at all. This has been here for hours. He must have gotten up earlier than I thought."

She turned and headed east. I followed her in a straight line for half an hour. We made little progress; Xinia stopped every other step to cut at the branches and then we began alternating, and whenever I had the machete it took longer. At mid-morning she stopped and without turning around said, "I'm not sure he went this way."

"How could he?"

"He couldn't have gone any other way."

"What if he went back to the middle and then off in a different direction?"

"I checked."

I looked ahead of us. The vines grew as much from above as they did from below, so that we seemed to be not so much among many plants as inside one colossal plant, traveling farther and farther into it. "Then we have to go this way."

She nodded absently and walked on. The trees grew thicker as we progressed, and she used the machete at every step so that the thwacking sound cut a rhythm in the air that echoed among the trees. Behind us the branches collapsed toward each other again, as if no one had passed there. At about noon we neared the edge of the trees and stepped out onto a narrow path that came from behind us toward the northeast. It led away from the trees through a small clearing and then into a ravine.

"This is the path to Naranjo," she said.

"The same one we were on?"

"Yes."

We sat in the clearing to eat. Xinia was silent. When we were through we packed our things and remained sitting on the rocks, as if waiting for something more to happen. "He left us," Xinia said.

"He didn't know what he was doing. He probably had a fever, got up, wandered off without knowing it."

"Then he would have turned around to wait when he realized."

"Maybe he did and we were gone."

She squinted up at the sky. There was no sound in the air. The

rock underneath me was warm from the sun. I resisted the
impulse to lie down on it. Xinia had taken off her rubber boots.
Her knees were lined with long scratches. One of them had bled
and the cut was encrusted with dirt. I opened the bag Estrada had
given me and wet a piece of cotton with antiseptic and reached
over. She flinched. "I'll do that," she said. I wiped the dirt away
anyway and threw away the cotton in the plastic bag full of trash
and then taped a narrow strip of gauze over the cut. She pulled
her legs away and stepped into her boots.

"Let's go," she said.

I nodded.

The path had ceased to climb. After passing through the
ravine, it leveled out into a sparse forest. We walked through it
for hours, coming across no other trace of Santos. When the light
faded we stopped where we were, in a tiny clearing with barely
enough room for our blankets, and lit a fire. We shared a can of
soup and ate hard bread. "We'll reach Naranjo tomorrow," Xinia
said. She held her feet up to the fire.

I fell asleep as soon as I lay down. When I woke up in the
middle of the night the fire was still high and Xinia was still sitting by it, her legs pulled up under her, her chin resting on her
knees.

"Xinia," I said.

"Yes."

I looked at her legs, her tapered fingers, which in the light
of the fire seemed made of amber. There was no sound beyond the fire, and it seemed to me momentarily that we sat not
on the mountain but in it, at its volcanic core, surrounded by its
dark walls, beside its dying fire. "What about the men from the
mountain?"

She didn't speak for a minute. Then she said, "There aren't any."

"I mean before."

She lifted her chin and put it down again on her knees. "I don't know."

I turned over on my back and watched the light from the fire on the branches overhead. "Santos told me about them."

She stretched one of her legs out so that her foot was by the fire. Her head lay sideways in her palm against her raised knee. "What does Santos know? He wasn't there."

I thought about that. I tried to remember the things Santos had told me, but I kept thinking of Baer and his mute bodyguards. Santos hadn't been there for that either. "It sounded like he was," I said.

"Yes," she said.

I turned on my side, facing the fire. Then I reached out and put my hand around her ankle. It was small; my thumb and forefinger touched. For a moment I felt the warm skin in my grasp.

Then Xinia dropped her hand from her knee and plucked my fingers away. She took my thumb and held on to it and our hands lay together on the dirt.

"Tell me about it," I said.

"I don't like making things up."

I was silent.

"I'd have to, to tell you about it."

I didn't say anything.

"People think they know what they've only heard about. Things they haven't seen with their own eyes."

"Like Santos."

"But it's impossible."

"I know," I said, after a pause.

She was silent for a while. "Strange for a priest to say," she finally said. I shifted, and she let my thumb pull away only to catch my hand again and lace her fingers through mine. "Be still," she said quietly.

The sky above the trees seemed very close. It reminded me of how, in the desert, we sometimes slept outside during the summer. You and Mamá would spread out the sleeping bags, and we would lie with our heads together in the center, like spokes of a wheel. When the lights were out and our voices had drifted away on the constant wind, we rolled up the bags and reclined against them. Even when the sky had blackened entirely the air would still be warm and the wind that rattled the loose rain pipe would not cool us. I would hear dogs barking and then, sometimes, a coyote sounding not so far away. Long after both of you had fallen asleep I would still be awake, my senses stirred by being out in the open. You and Mamá seemed very small, and I would sometimes sit up to watch you; the strangeness of how I could be suddenly alone while you both slept gave me a thrill. In the middle of the night I would wake up to see Mamá pulling up her bag and walking into the house. You stayed where you were, snoring, and I finally felt cold enough to roll into the sleeping bag. In the morning, the light would interrupt my dreams long before I woke up. Then when I opened my eyes I would have the feeling that I'd been awake for hours.

Xinia pressed her thumb into my palm, as if feeling for the bones in it. "It all happened in little over a year." She looked at her fingers. "Vicente got married in nineteen-eighty, when I was seventeen. Then the next year Hilario was born. Since it was only me and Vicente I lived with them."

"Vicente and Constancia," I said.

"Yes," she said. "Hilario was still a baby." Her fingers went limp, and it took some time for her to clasp them around my hand again. "We were close. It was almost like he had two mothers. I took care of him at the beginning because Constancia was sick, and even when she got better she was never jealous—we both looked after him. When Hilario cried for me she would just hand him over, and then she would watch us and smile. As if it made her happy. She was a little older than me but sometimes she seemed much younger."

I sat up, still holding her hand, but she turned away as though wanting to hide her face. When I moved to sit behind her she relaxed and leaned back against me, so that I rested my chin on her head, and as she spoke I felt the sound against my chest.

"She had a funny way about her," she said. "Sweet but strange. She would hide things in my books—little notes, pressed flowers, sticks of gum. Then she would pretend she hadn't put them there. As if it were mischief. Once she put bows around the necks of all the cows. Which was funny until the cows ate them and got sick. At night she and Vicente would sit in the living room, talking a little stiffly, like they had only just met; they were always shy together. And I would play with Hilario. When it was time to sleep she would put him in his bed—for a while it was in my room—and then go to bed herself and call out in the dark. Across the hallway. 'Rooou, roou,' like a pigeon.

"Hilario had a swing Vicente had made. It was on the door frame between the kitchen and the living room. There were four cords on a ring connected to a kind of cloth saddle—like a bucket with holes for his legs. Hilario's feet would just touch the ground and he could paddle in the air. There was nothing for the two of us to do other than take care of him, but we could have left him in the saddle all day and he would have been happy.

"It was always the first thing I saw when I walked into the kitchen—his swing in the doorway. It made me smile; I thought it was another one of Constancia's pranks when I saw a pile of orchids sitting in the saddle. They filled the seat, their roots on top of one another. The flowers leaned out like they wanted to jump. Vicente and Constancia sat in the living room, with Hilario on my brother's lap. They were talking to a woman who was wearing pants. It was the first thing I noticed about Ana— her pants, and her boots. They were even stranger. Black and up to her knees. Her hair was pulled back in a braid. Her fingernails looked like they hadn't been washed in years. She smiled at me. Then my brother and Constancia smiled at me in the same way. Politely. It made me nervous.

"That was in October. The year after Hilario was born. Ana didn't come without being invited. Vicente had met her with his teacher, the one we called the dreamer, and he told her to come. I don't remember what she said that first day; I only remember that she brought the orchids and put them in Hilario's swing. Later on Constancia let her and others sleep on the floor in the living room. But the first day we didn't know how far she'd come from, and Ana left when it was almost dark. When she put her hat and coat on and walked away in her heavy boots, she looked like a man to anyone who saw her from behind.

"Another time we talked alone, and I remember what we talked about because she never mentioned it again. We were sitting on the porch at the back of the house. Vicente was working and Constancia had fallen asleep with Hilario. It was so hot I'd just put my head under the faucet to cool off. I didn't know her well, so we just sat there, not talking. I got sleepy. The heat went to my head, and I said what I was thinking before I realized I'd said it. I said, 'Are you the only woman?' Ana didn't seem surprised. She said no, there were several, but she was the only one nearby and she'd come with her husband. I asked her, 'What were you before?' 'I'm a music teacher,' she said. It made my eyes tear up, maybe because I'd asked about the past and she'd answered in the present. She said her husband taught languages. French and Latin. It made me think of a little man with glasses, reading in the middle of the jungle with a flashlight. She said she'd been in a chorus. She'd wanted to start a singing group with some other women but it hadn't worked out. 'Now I'm doing something better.' She smiled when she said it. But then she sang for me. Her voice was low and she sang quietly, looking at me all the while, as if it was just another way of talking. I didn't understand the words. She said it was Latin.

"Only a few of them ever stayed at a time, and I never met Zúñiga. After the first few visits they asked if we'd sell them food—they always paid for everything—and my brother said he would, so he began getting things together for them in the pantry, and then when they came through he would sell them beans, maize, ground coffee, rice, tinned meat, sugar, and flour. Sometimes they met at the sacristy—Father Neto knew Zúñiga from when they were at the university—but more often Father Neto came to the house when they were there. They would all stay up together with Vicente, talking."

Xinia got up and walked a few feet away. She returned with fallen branches that she'd cut with the machete and she put them on the fire and after a few moments the flames climbed up through them, setting the dry leaves that clung to the branches trembling. She sat next to me on the wool blanket and leaned forward over her bent knees, so that her hands fell over her ankles. She watched the fire and I watched the light change the expression on her motionless face.

"Have you talked about it before?"

The corner of her mouth tightened and she glanced at me, but in the dark I couldn't see her eyes. "I've been thinking of how to explain it to you."

I smiled. "Practicing."

She frowned. "I didn't say that."

"What happened to Vicente?" I asked.

"I don't know," she said.

"Xinia," I said.

"I wasn't there. I saw him afterward."

"So you don't know who it was?"

She frowned, and her eyes sockets fell into shadow. She rested her head on her knees again, so that her face, in darkness, was turned toward me. "He was the first one. We didn't know what it meant."

"Someone knew about the supplies."

"I think most people knew. They'd been staying with us—two or three times a month—for so long. Almost half a year. Ana first came in October and Vicente was killed in April." She paused. She said it under her breath, as if saying it louder was too difficult, and she looked at me briefly. "We never imagined—we were blind. It just seemed as though everyone saw it the same way. Other people were helping them too, and it just seemed—I thought—the way people talked it seemed like it was all of us." I watched her face. Her eyes were closed. Then she opened them and said, "It wasn't Aurelio."

"It wasn't?"

"I'm sure it wasn't. Father Neto didn't believe it, and he knew Aurelio better than anyone. He won't talk about it. I don't see why he has to."

"So you don't believe what they say?"

"I think—I don't know, but it's what I think—that Felix or Bartolomé found a way to spare him, and Aurelio has never forgiven himself. For letting them; for surviving." She pressed her closed eyes with her fingers and let out a breath. "None of us has."

I lay down flat on my back and Xinia lay next to me with her head a little above mine on the blanket, so that when she spoke she sounded like a voice coming out of the top of my head. Every once in a while she would lift her hand over her head and gesture, and the sudden, inarticulate movements would remind me of the effort she was making.

There was later, she told me, little doubt about who had killed Vicente and disappeared the men at the sugar mill. "I didn't see Ana for a long time," she said, "we heard rumors that something had happened to them. They came a few times after Vicente was killed, but they didn't stay with us, and there were fewer of them. Ana only said they were close by. 'Have they found you?' I asked. She made a face like she didn't know what that meant. But in any case we didn't see them after what happened at the sugar mill. Then the next time I saw her she was like another person. She had almost passed—part of her—partly passed away. For the third day in a row it was raining hard. The rainy season had begun early in August. The water crashed on the roof and everything was slow. And everything but the rain was silent. Hilario was crying but I just watched his mouth open, his face red, with no sound. I went to stand in the doorway and I watched the water fall in a sheet from the roof. On the other side of it everything was blurry. The world dissolving. The ground had all turned to mud. Constancia never left the house after they found Vicente. She stayed inside and sat in the living room, watching Hilario in the saddle. I felt the same way, unfastened. I'd look up and be somewhere and I'd been there for hours. Not doing anything. Nothing changed on the other side of the sheet of water. And then suddenly I saw something—a shape moving up the road past the house. It was a strange size—too large to be a person, too small to be anything else—and the way it moved. I still couldn't see it from the walkway. I walked closer. Then I was just a couple feet away from it.

"I don't know what I thought I was going to see. I thought at first they were carrying something and that's why they walked so close together. They seemed hunched over like a procession. If I expected anything I expected the long robes and the platform on their shoulders. I even had time to wonder why they were having a procession in the rain. They were lurching this way and that way. I was in the road, right next to them, when I realized why. It was the wire on their necks and wrists that made them stumble. Ana walked in front; her hair was matted down. Her face torn. She had no shirt—only pants and boots. The men behind her were the same. As I watched them, the one in the middle tripped. He tripped forward and choked on the wire and the others all jerked toward him. They swayed, about to collapse. Then he pulled himself up and they all leaned away and got their balance. They ignored me. I went up to Ana and lifted her hair out of her face and she started walking again. She said something I couldn't hear. I shouted at her, 'What, Ana, what?' 'Get away,' she said.

"Just then I heard the jeeps. The soldiers who came on foot cleared the hill. Still about a hundred meters away. They moved slowly, or seemed to. I stood back toward the walkway, watching Ana walk on. The soldiers passed by and didn't even glance in my direction. They marched behind Ana, toward the center of town. Then the jeeps came by, three of them, one after another, throwing up mud.

"Constancia was screaming my name from the doorway of the house but I ignored her. I followed the others who'd come out to the road. We stayed at a distance, not talking. The rain kept us apart. The soldiers moved off and we followed them, not too closely. I couldn't turn back. I wanted to but couldn't. The water pulled at my heels and dragged me on. I lost one shoe and then the other, and I felt the ground giving way beneath my feet. The dirt fell apart and drifted down through the streets, down, down all the way to the river.

"There was already a crowd by the side of the church when I reached it. The rain was lighter for a moment. I could see four others, kneeling in the grass next to Ana and the five men. I couldn't tell who they were. I didn't mean to but I looked around to see who was missing. The officer had started speaking, shouting over the rain. I didn't understand what he was saying. He kept shouting for things—a rope, buckets. He pointed to Tulio, who was standing in front, and Tulio went off. There was no talking. For several minutes the only sound was the rain. We all stood there waiting. Then Tulio came back with an armload of metal. He handed it over and the officer gave a command. The soldiers used their machetes, not guns. I could hear the sound over the rain. Everyone began moving toward the sacristy. The knot of people broke up, and I could suddenly see where they'd been a moment earlier. I caught a glimpse of one of them being dragged, still trying to walk, over the mud.

"I turned my back to it. I faced the plaza. The flooded plaza. The rain splashed on it like the surface of a lake. I hadn't noticed until then the soldiers who were around us, closing in. The water came up to my ankles. My thought was to walk away, past the soldiers and back to Constancia. Then I looked to the side and I saw Luz vomiting into the water. It poured out of her and floated. Spreading out until it reached my ankles. I felt dizzy, and then I retched over and over until I was only spilling my own spit. My head throbbed. The vomit made the water cloudy and I couldn't see my feet.

"When I straightened up the soldiers turned and started filing off. Everyone else was walking away, away from the sacristy. They were slowed by the rain, but within minutes they'd disappeared, and I turned back to the church, to where the jeeps were rolling off and the soldiers had started marching south. They disappeared into the rain. Only a few of us were left standing in the road. When the sound of the jeeps died away I followed the others to where the scraps of wire were left in the stained mud.

"I stood in the road in front of the sacristy, watching the doorway. The men guarding the door weren't in uniform; I didn't recognize them. It was the first time I'd seen the patrol from Naranjo. The door to the sacristy stood open, and we couldn't see anything but we could see the color of the house draining away over the doorway. It looked as if the red walls were dissolving in the rain. The whole thing was coming apart in pieces—plaster, paint—that spread out into the flooded street. Over the boots of the men and over the grass and toward us standing in the road. But the house wasn't really coming apart, because when I knelt in the rain, there was nothing in the red water."

She stopped speaking and was silent for a minute, and I asked her if she'd seen them. She shook her head. "Only later. When we were allowed to take them down." She was quiet and I turned my head toward her. She looked up at the sky, her expression blank.

"What about the priest?"

"Yes. Father Neto and three teachers. They were on the butcher hooks Tulio had brought. Like meat."

She turned her face toward the trees again. "I tried to find a way for us to leave. From the middle of August until November I went to the city almost every day. Most of the people who could leave, did. The town emptied out overnight, and no one talked to anyone else in the street. I rode the bus in the morning, before it was light out, and got back at four. In the city no one wanted to hire me, though I was willing to work for cheap. I had short jobs but nothing permanent. Nothing for more than a week or two at a time. I tried at a bottling company and an underwear factory. There were days when at four, despite Hilario and Constancia, and despite the fact that I hated the city already, I had to talk myself into getting on the bus. By that time every tree was covered with dust; the air smelled like gasoline; the bus motors sounded like dying things. The filth of the place disgusted me. The ditches were filled with things I couldn't name. By the side of the street like trenches. The trash floated on the wind and stuck to the sides of the buildings and glued itself down on the streets and sidewalks when it rained.

"In November I met with a woman whose husband was in a wheelchair. She had a grave face and fierce little eyes. Both of them very white and smelling of talcum. The man in the wheelchair smiled at me and held his clean hands on his knees. Every corner of their house was filled with tiny, breakable things—vases and paintings and porcelain teacups and dolls from Japan and paper flowers. Everything orderly; everything in its place.

The woman explained how, to save water, she filled a bucket in the sink, soaped all the dishes, then rinsed them off in the bucket. They'd eat breakfast at eight, lunch at one, coffee at four, and supper at seven every day. The plants, she told me, had to be wiped down with a sponge because the dust from the road managed to get in.

"She showed me a little pitcher in the shape of a cat. 'Look,' she said, 'it's already covered with dust,' and it was true that the cat's tongue—the pitcher's spout—was yellow, as if the cat had gotten sick. 'I don't expect you to be a nurse,' the woman said to me. 'We have someone who comes twice a week and helps him do his exercises. But if you see that he needs something, hand it to him, won't you?' She smiled at me, and though I'd been worried about her hard eyes from the start, I realized then it might not be a bad place to work. It was unlike any house I'd ever seen. But it felt safe, totally removed from the city, and on that day it was harder than ever to go home. 'Come back in a couple days,' the woman said to me as I left, 'and I'll tell you if I can hire you.'

"I walked from their house to the bus station, and a few blocks from their house I went through a park lined by palm trees. I was crossing it when a crowd of pigeons sprang up and clattered into the air. Up, in a long, vanishing spiral. When they were gone the park was quiet. I stopped for a moment and sat on a bench under the palms. I tried to remind myself that the silence there, too, wasn't permanent.

"The bus I took from the city didn't go all the way to town, and I walked the last two miles. So it was about four-thirty when I reached the top of the hill from the direction of Los Cielos and saw the column of smoke coming from the school building that reminded me immediately of the pigeons, scattering in every direction as they neared the clouds. I started to run. I was only half a mile from the house. As soon as I reached it I heard Hilario's screams. I could see him from the doorway of the kitchen—he was in his saddle, facing the wrong way, facing me. His fists were balled up, his face red and stiff.

"Behind him, in the living room, a man in uniform crouched on the floor, tearing up the wooden floorboards with a crowbar. Next to him was a pile of floorboards. I picked up the closest thing, a pan from the stove, and I stepped past Hilario and walked up behind the man and dropped the pan on his head. He stopped for a moment, as if he'd just remembered something. Then he pushed himself up and before I could step away he lifted the table that stood just in front of him and got up, throwing the table away from him and into my stomach. I fell against the wall, with the table pinning me to the floor, and the man picked up the crowbar and hit the side of my head.

"When I opened my eyes again there were two other men in the room. They weren't soldiers; the soldiers were gone. I didn't recognize them. One of them was setting fire to the curtains. The other one was taking Hilario out of his saddle. From where I was I could see into the bedroom on the other side of the house. Constancia's legs were on the floor; the rest of her lay behind the door. I coughed, and the men stopped and turned to look at me. 'Don't,' I said. I tried to push the table off but I could barely move it.

"For a second they both stared at me. Then one man turned to the other and said, 'Leave well enough alone,' and the other man looked at me and nodded and they stepped out of the room. They left by the kitchen door. I could hear where they were by the sound of Hilario's screams, which grew fainter and fainter until they died away.

"I managed to tilt the table to one side, and then I pushed up as hard as I could and the table dropped again on my hips. The fire had spread to the window frame and almost reached the ceiling. I lifted again and got one of my legs free by pulling it up against me. Then I rolled onto my side and dragged myself over the floor, out from under the table, so that the side of it finally crashed off my hip onto the floor, pinning my skirt. I ripped it free. I limped to the kitchen and took the pot from the stove and carried water from the faucet into the living room, tossing it up over the window and all over the wall until the fire was contained and the smoke filled the eaves.

"Only then could I go see Constancia, who'd long since left me behind. The skin around her eyes was blue. Her right hand was closed tight, and I had to pull to get her fingers open. The nails had dug into her skin so hard that there were little crescents of blood across the wrinkles of her palm. There was nothing in her hand. But later, when I washed her and changed her clothes, I turned her over and heard something fall on the bed. I looked and saw her wedding band, and for a while I couldn't figure out where it had been, until I realized from the imprint on her tongue that she'd been holding it in her mouth."

Fifteen

IT'S THE SENSE of the words, not the words themselves, that one remembers. And it's doubtlessly easier to remember what one believes. Whatever seems improbable or false is gradually forgotten, but ideas that ring true tend to resound again and again in one's thoughts. I would never say that I remember Xinia's exact words. But she must have said some of the things I recall, because they found their way into my thoughts. Likewise the ideas I encountered in MacLeod, Tedlock, and Thompson inevitably surface here and there in my own thinking and writing. They can't be neatly contained; they are all intermingled. I can't distinguish now, for instance, between certain ideas of Tedlock's and ideas of mine, even though I remember when her ideas seemed new to me. It's because she altered my thinking that I can't see where her ideas end and mine begin. I don't know how it's possible to distinguish one from the other. I don't know what purpose it would even serve, when so many of the things we think about came from somewhere else. From this perspective, it's impossible to avoid being a compilation of stolen words and ideas.

In recalling what Xinia told me, I realize that her thoughts have surfaced repeatedly as I write; perhaps I've passed them off as mine. The very notion that things can't be invented, I recognize now, came up for the first time that night—and it came from her. But I can't say whether it was simply her way of talking, or everything that happened to me in Río Roto, or both taken together that made me believe the idea myself. When I consider this, that ideas can be borrowed as much from people as from pages, I find it difficult to understand where to draw the line. It might be that nothing I've written is really mine, and the only novelty is one of combination. If this is true, it's not possible to steal ideas; it's only possible to plagiarize patterns of accumulation, arrangements and rearrangements of words and thoughts blackened from use.

No doubt by the time they reached me, both Santos's and Xinia's words were worn from repeated consideration and adjustment. It would have fallen to me, then, to create something unique by combining them, but I wasn't able to. At first I spent countless hours considering one alongside the other, attempting to reconcile them. I would sometimes discard one or the other entirely, and I would sometimes decide on an unlikely amalgamation. But with time I found myself increasingly unwilling to do this violence to either. There was no doubt that neither was entirely true or entirely untrue; in all their reasons for being so, there were causes far beyond my judgment.

I can only tell you that while what Santos told me was almost certainly a concealment of the truth assembled out of true and untrue pieces, he lied with my interest at heart. What Xinia told me was probably more true, but she told me the truth for her own sake—not for mine.

◆ ◆ ◆

I awoke before Xinia and watched her sleep. The blanket was wrapped tightly around her and she lay very still. With her eyes closed she seemed like another version of herself. Her breathing was light. The sun came into the clearing slowly and when it touched her face her eyelids trembled. I traced the knuckles of her right hand, which lay on the outside of the blanket. Her fingers were very small. I pressed the callus on the first knuckle of her middle finger softly, like a button, and she woke up all at once.

We packed without speaking and covered the fire with dirt and started out of the clearing and toward Naranjo. The first sign we had of the town was a black dog who ran out of the woods to our left and pawed at us without barking. Its mouth and coat were dirty. An old cut ran halfway through its left ear, making the end of it flutter like a dead leaf. We expected the people with him to be nearby, and so for some minutes we stood waiting. The dog waited too and finally dropped to the ground and rested with its head over its paws. Xinia stared intently into the trees. The muscles around her mouth tightened and I began to feel nervous, standing in the quiet, watching her. "Let's keep going," I said.

Xinia glanced at me, nodded, and turned away. The dog got up and followed her, hanging its head and panting. I walked behind it and watched its tail wag spasmodically. We'd gone only a few paces when she stopped and turned to face me. "It won't be like arriving with Santos," she said.

I looked at her. "Yes, I know. What do you want to say?"

"You shouldn't say anything. As little as possible."

I hadn't heard her. I was watching the dog, who stared with interest into the trees. "Xinia."

"What?"

"Maybe we shouldn't say we're from Río Roto."

"Yes, I know." She waited.

"Would you recognize them?"

As of the previous night she no longer avoided my eyes. Nevertheless I could see no more in those flat surfaces than I had before in her withdrawn nods. She blinked slowly, as if waiting for me to say something more. "I'm not sure," she said.

The dog pawed her foot and then walked around her. "Maybe Santos is there ahead of us," I said.

She shook her head, but I couldn't tell whether she meant that he wasn't or that she didn't know. Then she turned and walked after the dog, who was waiting for us at the turn.

We reached Naranjo in the afternoon. I want you to see it exactly as I did, because I can see how, if I'd come at another time, as someone else, even from another direction, it could have appeared very different. I know that for some people, as Santos related, Naranjo once felt like a refuge. If you imagine yourself arriving as I did, you may be able to understand why it could never have been that for me. We could see nothing of the town until we reached the crest of the hill, and then the cluster of houses appeared below us, on the decline, scattered among a few trees that seemed to lean out away from them. There was no order to them and no connecting path. More or less in the center, a flattened pile of dried cornstalks carpeted a wide, level space. Two children sat in the doorway of the house closest to us holding their knees. They watched us silently as we walked past them. Downhill from us a woman came out of her house carrying an armful of clothes and when she saw us she stopped and turned around and walked back into her house. A moment later she walked out of the back door and walked away hurriedly. "Xinia," I said.

She silenced me. We stood on the cornstalks and looked at the two dozen encircling houses. There were more in the trees behind them. From farther downhill I heard the squeals of a pig. A moment later a man walked out from behind one of the houses and walked straight toward us. He wore his straw hat angled down and his arms hung at his sides as if sore from work. The front of his shirt was stained with sweat. When he reached us, he lifted his head and tucked his thumbs into his belt loops. "Afternoon," he said.

"Good afternoon," Xinia replied.

"Where you from?" he asked. His face was calm. The woman who'd abandoned her laundry stood in her doorway and watched.

"We came to see Santos," Xinia said.

He blinked. "Where from?"

"We're from Rabinal."

The man nodded and looked down at his boots. "Santos has never been to Rabinal."

"We met him in Río Roto. When he left he said to find him here."

He shifted his weight, crossed his arms. "When was that?"

Xinia looked at me, squinting, as if trying to remember. I squinted back and she turned to him again. "Four days ago?" she said.

"You left with him?"

She shook her head. "Two days later."

The man nodded without looking at us. "You can wait at his house." He walked away and we followed him downhill on a narrow path that curved south. Without glancing back he pointed at a one-room house that stood back from the path. "Over there," he said over his shoulder. We stopped by the open doorway.

It was hard to tell what had happened inside. The mess covered the floor and spilled out onto the walkway. A dented coffeepot held the door open. I glanced into the room and then took a step back. Xinia looked away and put her bag down.

The man who'd spoken to us had already disappeared. I put my bag next to Xinia's and stood with my arms crossed. The roofs of the houses around us glared in the sun. I stepped into the shadows of the trees behind me, but the air was damp and smelled of rot. From the house next door I heard the sound of wet clothes being pounded clean. Minutes later, five men came out from around the corner of one of the houses near the center of the village. They didn't talk to one another. The one in front walked lazily with his arms swinging and the others hung back. He wore a bandana tied loosely around his neck and as he came toward us he lifted it to wipe the sweat from his chin.

When they reached us, the man with the bandana took off his hat and wiped his forehead with his hand and squinted at us. "Afternoon. Where are you from?" he asked.

"From Rabinal," Xinia said. "We're here to see Santos."

The man waved at the air with his hat and then held it against his stomach. "He's not here."

"Do you know when he'll be back?"

"He's been gone for weeks."

"We saw him in Río Roto a few days ago. He said he was coming here."

"We haven't seen him."

Xinia shifted her weight and glanced at me. I looked back at her blankly. "Maybe someone should go look for him," she said. "He should have been here by now."

"Maybe," the man said. He didn't move.

A few houses away a dog began to whine. The man with the bandana was staring at Xinia. He turned around and looked at one of the men behind him. "Leave well enough alone?" he asked quietly and with mild surprise, as if the phrase were a name he was trying to place. The man gave a small nod in response. Then the man with the bandana turned back to Xinia. He looked back and forth from me to her and then smiled. "You must be tired," he said to Xinia.

"A little," she said.

"Well," he said, "you're welcome to stay here until we find Santos or he comes back."

"Thank you."

He turned and looked downhill. "We don't have much, but you're welcome to what we have. The main road's off that way. My house is at the top of the hill. You can stay with me and my wife," he said to Xinia, "and you can stay with my brother," he said to me.

"Thank you," Xinia said. "We'll be fine here."

"As you like," he said. "Santos won't mind. Leave your things and we'll go have lunch."

We followed him up the hill and the other men walked behind us. When we reached his house, the man told the others to go eat, and after a pause they each drifted away in different directions at the top of the hill. The inside of the house was dark. The woman at the fire turned abruptly when we walked in and held the wet tortilla in her hand as she stared at us. Her husband threw his hat on a chair and sat in another one and waved to two others that stood by the table. He rested his elbows on the table and sighed.

"Noé?" the woman said quietly.

He glanced at her. "They're looking for Santos. Going to wait for him until he comes back."

"I'm Xinia. This is Father Amán," Xinia said, still standing.

The woman looked us over and then half her mouth smiled. "Please sit down," she said, gesturing with the wet tortilla.

We sat by the table and listened in silence as she slapped the wet dough and laid it on the *comal.* A minute later she brought a bowl of broth and set it in front of Noé and then she brought two others. We thanked her and she nodded, looking at us sideways as she left the table. She brought her bowl and then a stack of tortillas folded in a cloth. Noé opened the bundle and took one and folded it and jabbed at the soup. The woman chewed without taking her eyes off us, and I watched Noé as he spoke to Xinia. I would later learn that he was much younger, but he appeared to be an old man. Not knowing him, you would have guessed he was past seventy when in fact he hadn't even reached sixty. His gestures were slow and deliberate but not hampered; it seemed rather as though decades of practice had pared his activities down to a handful of simple movements.

"I've been to Río Roto," Noé said, without looking up.

Xinia and I didn't say anything. Noé's wife stared at him.

"The houses there are bigger," he said.

Xinia cleared her throat. "Some of them are. This is delicious," she said, turning to the woman. The woman nodded hesitantly.

"What about by the river?" Noé asked.

Xinia looked at him. "In Río Roto?"

He nodded.

"I think they're more like here."

"Dirt floor?"

"Dirt floor and made of wood. In town they're cement."

"They have the *milpa* nearby?"

"Most people work farther out of town. There's nothing but cacao by the river."

"Not a good place to live there." He spoke with his mouth full of tortilla. His wife sipped the broth from the side of the bowl, looking out at us over the rim.

"It's very damp," Xinia said.

"And then the river floods," he said.

Xinia stirred her soup. She hadn't eaten more than a spoonful and she sat tensely, watching Noé eat and waiting each time for him to speak again. "Sometimes. The whole town gets a lot of water. The clouds get trapped."

Noé shook his head, swallowed. "I don't envy you in the winter, that's for sure."

"Well," Xinia said, "I live in Rabinal."

"That's right," Noé said. He smiled and took another tortilla. "I like the old wooden houses, even if they do get moldy. I'd build on the northeast corner by the road to Los Cielos, and I'd build all out of wood. Mahogany and cedar. Wouldn't you like that, Ester?" His wife stared at him. Xinia stopped stirring and looked down into her bowl. "Of course the problem with a wooden house is that it catches fire so easily."

Xinia dropped her spoon into the bowl. I took another tortilla and folded it and refolded it until it broke into twelve pieces. I glanced at Xinia, who hadn't moved. Noé and his wife were watching her. "Did you build this house?" I asked.

Noé glanced at me briefly, as if seeing for the first time that I was there. "With some help," he said. We continued eating in silence. The spoons clattered against the bowls and Noé sipped noisily. His wife hadn't eaten half her food but she began picking up the dishes and stacking them in a bucket. "Ester?" Noé said.

She turned quickly and looked at him. "Yes?" she said.

"Where's Roy?"

"I don't know. He's out working." She hesitated. "Isn't he?"

"I don't know, that's why I'm asking you."

"But he went with you this morning."

"Well, he isn't with me now."

She swallowed. "Then he's out working, Noé."

"That boy." He smiled at us. "My son never works." Xinia was staring at Ester or at the wall behind her.

"How old is Roy?" I asked.

"Twelve."

"Young to be working."

"Not really." He stood up. "I'll be getting back."

I stood up as well. "Thank you for lunch." I turned to Ester. "It's very kind of you to feed us on such short notice."

"You can eat with us as long as you're here," Noé said.

"That's very generous," I said. "Thank you." Xinia was still sitting at the table. I put my hand on her shoulder. "Xinia," I said. "Let's go see Santos's place."

She pushed herself up and nodded. "Thank you," she murmured. We walked out of the house and down the hill to Santos's house. I watched the door of Noé's house from the window and fifteen minutes later he left, wearing his hat and his bandana.

AFTER WE cleaned Santos's house, Xinia laid a wool blanket over the mattress and sat on it with her back against the wall. I asked her what she wanted to do and she said rest, so I walked out of the house and downhill to what Noé had called the main road, a strip of dirt that began in a patch of half-dead grass and disappeared to the east among the trees. A quarter of a mile along, a broken wall stood engulfed by a jasmine plant. A pair of hummingbirds darted in and out of it. I sat in the road to breathe in the scent and watch the birds and try to recall what you'd written that reminded me of the broken wall.

It was a passage in one of your notebooks that you repeated more than half a dozen times in various ways. You described a house with an outer wall covered with jasmine—so covered that the shutters on the inside opened out onto a mass of vines. The house belonged to a woman named Hortensia. The base of the plant was a skeletal clutter, but the leaves farther up were dark and waxy; the flowers spread like white confetti on the crowded vines when they blossomed. At first the buds appeared only as tiny spears—little rolls of white paper. Then they opened overnight, and by the next day the edges of the trumpet-shaped flowers turned brown, as if the paper had been too close to a fire, and the following day they fell to the ground. But they didn't all bloom at once, and so for weeks the air smelled of jasmine oil, and at night the scent drifted in and out of the rooms, giving the impression that an unseen woman was moving silently through Hortensia's house. When I'd first read the passage, I hadn't given much thought to who Hortensia was or why you recalled the scent of her rooms at night.

I didn't hear her step and didn't see her until the flight of the hummingbirds drew my eyes to the left. The old woman had come up the main road from the east. She stood still, holding her heavy bag and watching me. For some moments we stared at each other.

My mind was still on the passage in your notebook. While reading the notebooks in Oregon I'd looked up once to see Mamá standing in the doorway. On that occasion she either didn't realize what I was reading or decided to overlook it. After a pause she said, "You're always reading," and then she smiled and left the room. The woman standing in the road was thinner and more worn, but her face was the same. It might have been Mamá stand-ing in front of me. For a moment I thought she would smile and say, "You're always reading." I stood up and the woman smiled at me and a heavy pain passed over my chest, as if my ribs were pressing inward. I waited to hear what she would say.

"Do you remember?" she asked.

"What?" I said.

Her smile faded. "Who are you?" she asked quietly.

I hesitated. "Father Amán," I said, "from Rabinal."

"Oh," she said. "A pleasure, Father Amán. I'm Tencha." She shook her head and smiled. "I get confused these days."

I swallowed hard over a knot in my throat and the pain brought tears to my eyes. I smiled back at her. "I do, too," I said.

She laughed and picked her bag up and with the brown wrin-kles around her eyes she no longer looked so much like Mamá. "That used to be my house," she said, pointing with her other hand.

"Let me take that," I said. She patted my arm as I took the bag. "What happened to it?"

We walked past the broken wall and toward Naranjo. She looked back at it once, as if to remind herself of what had occurred. "It just fell over. The whole front wall used to be covered with jasmine. When I opened the shutters on the inside all you could see was the mess of green vines."

"Yes," I said. "Not much light. It probably smelled good."

She sighed. "The smell was so sweet it kept me awake at night."

XINIA WAS SITTING on the bed where I'd left her when I returned. She seemed not to see me walk in and pull a chair up to the bed. I watched her for a moment before speaking. "Xinia," I said. "Someone asked us to lunch." She stared at her knees without speaking. "She especially wants to meet you."

At that Xinia's eyes flickered and without moving her head she looked at me.

"Santos told her about you."

She blinked. "What's her name?"

"Tencha."

Xinia looked at me in silence for a moment. "What else did she say?"

"Nothing." Her eyes stayed on my face, watching me warily. "Are you okay?" I moved onto the bed next to her.

She sat stiffly, pulling away a little, and turned to look out through the small window. Her jaw was clenched and she took quick, tense breaths. "I don't like being alone here," she said.

I looked at her closely but she wouldn't turn her face. "I'm sorry." I took her limp hand and held it. She stared expressionlessly at the window. After a time her breathing slowed and she leaned her head back against the wall, staring out at the room with glazed eyes.

Noé came by in the late morning and told us that his brothers would leave to look for Santos after lunch. He smiled. "I'm sorry you won't have a chance to meet my son, Roy," he said. "He's going with them."

Xinia didn't say anything. "Yes," I said. "We would've liked that."

"I'll come around later to see if you need anything."

"Thank you."

When he was gone we left for Tencha's. Her two-room house was painted turquoise and sat close to the main road. She cooked on a wood-burning stove that stood behind the house under a sheet of zinc. Four plastic tarps the color of pool water were rolled up by the edge to be unfurled and secured to the ground when it rained. Tencha wore an apron with a deep pocket from which she drew a spoon, a chunk of lard wrapped in waxed paper, a potato, and a blunt knife. Xinia sat on a stool staring out onto the road and I peeled the potato with the knife by chipping away dime-sized pieces of peel. Tencha smiled as she watched me and pounded at the meat on the cutting board. She seemed to like watching my clumsy efforts.

While we were eating she appeared to be lost in thought. At one point she looked up suddenly. "I'm so glad you came," she said. She turned to Xinia. "We never see people from other parts." She smiled and spooned the rice and beans into her mouth mechanically.

I nodded and smiled back. We went on eating in silence. A moment later she put down her spoon and looked up again. She leaned forward, speaking under her breath. "Did Santos stay in Río Roto?"

Xinia and I looked at each other. "No," I said. "We don't know where he is."

"You don't have to tell me what you told Noé." Her brow furrowed. "I just want to know if he's all right."

Xinia put her spoon down. "We really don't know. He came with us partway, but yesterday we lost him."

Tencha's face fell. She seemed suddenly, deeply grieved. "You lost him," she echoed.

"We still hope they'll find him," I said.

Tencha shook her head. She spoke softly, as if to herself. "It's just a gesture." She smiled sadly. "I'm sure Noé knows exactly where he is."

I looked at Xinia in silence for a moment. "Noé wasn't with us," I said. "He would have no way to know."

Tencha pushed her unfinished beans away. "But he knows, nonetheless."

Xinia opened her mouth to say something, but Tencha cut her off. "Believe me." Xinia stared at the table. "Finish your food," Tencha said quietly. "I want to show you the greenhouse my son made."

Tencha's gray hair was gathered at the base of her neck and separated into two braids that coiled over the crest of her head. She used the braids like the apron pocket, to collect things she wanted to hang on to. When we stepped into the greenhouse she picked up an orchid from the dirt floor and tucked it into the braid over her left ear. The orchids hung on the left wall, their roots bundled together. On the other side ferns grew thickly in the humid air and pressed against the walls of the greenhouse. It was past noon, but the sun shone strongly through the green plastic and the air in the greenhouse felt overripe, as if about to burst. Tencha opened a window in the roof with the handle of a broom and showed us a purple orchid in the corner entwined with a fern. The back wall lay in shadow from a plant that grew against it, and she took us around to the outside to see the jasmine that sprawled over it and onto the roof. "I have to get up there and prune it," she said, "so it doesn't block the light."

She looked around as if trying to remember where she'd left something. "If you'd help me with this," she said to me. I followed her to the side of the greenhouse and she pointed to a wooden ladder. I lifted it and rested it against the wall covered with jasmine. Tencha grunted as she stooped to unlock a wooden tool chest and pulled out a pair of shears. I took them and put my foot on the ladder but she stopped me. "You'd break every rung and then your neck. Just one more thing." Xinia stood a few feet away with her arms crossed, looking out toward the road. Tencha patted her arm as she walked past her and into the house, coming back a moment later.

A skinny boy with wide eyes and a shock of black hair followed her closely, peering out from behind her. Xinia made a little sound. "Now, Roy," Tencha said, "take these shears and trim the top. I know you're leaving so make it quick. Xinia and Father Amán will tell you where to cut." The boy took the shears and his face tried a smile that ended in a grimace as he looked at us. I held the ladder for him to climb up and Tencha turned away, taking the orchid out from behind her ear as she walked into the house.

ONLY ONE passage in your journals refers to something that I remember. I'd assumed the entries described things you experienced alone, because they sounded as though they'd been written in the moment and I'd never seen you writing. They seemed, as the description of the train trip through Martinez did, attempts to record, not invent. I came to believe that the repetitions were revisions you made later as efforts of recollection. But the entry that seems familiar, if it pertains to the place I remember, would describe something you saw more than ten years before writing of it. You drafted it several times, as though trying to remember how it happened or proposing to yourself different alternatives of what might have happened differently.

You described a place close to the water, where the grass grew in sandy soil, bent seaward by the wind. The trees were pale and dusty. Immense bay trees and eucalyptus filled the air with their scents and opened into sandy clearings. The path had eroded in places. Halfway down it a bench made from half a redwood trunk lay by the side, as if by accident. The sand beneath the bench had given way, so that it rocked gently if more than one person sat on it. Then, a quarter of a mile along, the woods ended in a dry field high above the water. As we came out from among the eucalyptus trees, the most unlikely thing occurred: a hot-air balloon lifted over the field and toward the water, trailing four ropes. A cluster of men ran after it and then stopped, watching it rise and drift. What had seemed like a sudden movement became slow, and the balloon eased lazily over the water and along the coast, until it was impossible to see whether it moved at all. The men on the ground watched it, and we walked along the edge of the trees until we came to the wooden walkway that led down to the sea.

In the version that follows, there is no sea. And in the third version, there is no balloon. In the fourth version, the bench has vanished. And in the last version, the longest, there are only bay trees and eucalyptus, crows that peck at the sandy ground, and the still air smelling of sap and earth. It was the last version that I immediately found familiar when I first read the entry. I remembered too the gate at the entrance and the house converted into a museum and the pine benches near the parking lot—none of which you mentioned. We visited the park when I was about ten. Mamá had decided not to go with us that day. We ate sandwiches wrapped in waxed paper and you tossed your crumbs to the blue jays that crowded the wooden table. As soon as I recalled that day—the overcast sky and the sharp smell of the trees—I remembered, too, the pieces from the other versions and realized why I hadn't recognized them.

The trip to the seaside took place on a different day. There, too, eucalyptus trees grew in the sandy soil, but they ended abruptly at the edge of a circular lawn with a stone border that overlooked the sea. Facing the lawn, a Gilded Age mansion sat decaying imperceptibly, and from its upper windows we saw the ships that glided over the slice of ocean visible in the gap between the trees. On that day, too, the sky was overcast, and the gulls dipped toward us as we walked to the edge of the lawn and stared down at the narrow stairs stapled onto the cliff side and leading down to the water.

The balloon we saw at the seminary, on a hot day in July one week before the annual competition. The green hills of the seminary opened out onto a flat expanse where all the balloons waited to take flight. I hadn't recognized your description because on the occasion of the trial run, as I recalled, the white balloon lifted into the air carrying one of the men with it. He clung to the trailing rope as the men on the ground ran after him, shouting. Some told him to drop and others told him to climb up in the moments after the balloon lifted. Within seconds he was high above the ground. The men went on shouting and all at once he let go. The balloon shuddered slightly and the white figure fell to the ground. They ran over to where he'd fallen and crowded around him, and then one of them ran away from the others, downhill. We walked toward them slowly and waited at a distance. I turned to look at the balloon, which already floated high above the trees of the seminary. One of the men in white stood back from the group and looked downhill. He saw us, waved, and shouted, "Okay." We waved back, being too far away to say anything, and then we turned around and walked back into the trees. You didn't speak as we walked along one of the paths to the entrance of the seminary. Finally I asked you, "Have you ever been in a balloon?" You shook your head. You said, "I've only seen someone fall like that once. From a helicopter." And I said, "So you've never been in a balloon." You looked at me and after a moment you said, "No, I haven't."

Perhaps you'd forgotten the man who fell from the balloon. For my part, it seemed I'd forgotten the bench made of redwood. I remembered nothing like it at the seminary or the eucalyptus park or the mansion by the sea. Nevertheless it seemed familiar, and for some time I tried to remember where I'd seen it, thinking that if I could pinpoint the origin of that final detail I would be able to make sense of why you'd written of the four places together. At times, when I thought about the three days as I remembered them, it seemed to me that you'd grouped them intentionally, and that if I could remember them exactly as they'd occurred, their combined meaning would become clear.

But I felt unable to put the pieces together until, in Naranjo, I found the split trunk near the road that led east, away from the village. It was exactly like the one you described—only it was mahogany rather than redwood. But it, too, had been split in half, and it sat wedged into the weeds: a half-cylinder blackened with age and moss that rocked slightly when I sat on it. As soon as I saw it I thought of the journal entry. It seemed suddenly clear to me that you were grouping, fictionally, different places and times. You were writing your history in the same way I had: by letting images and impressions overlap freely to invent a single past. On the day that I found the bench and for many months afterward, I struggled to decipher what the grouping of events into a single passage could mean. The park, the seaside, the seminary, and the log leading out of Naranjo: they seemed to contain infinite possibilities. Perhaps you remembered what I'd asked you about falling from the balloon as well. Perhaps you wanted to both preserve and rewrite that moment, memorializing it in a way that softened its mistakes.

But as the months passed, and I thought about them more, the pieces you wrote have grown less rather than more distinct, and it began to seem likely that you simply collected the four days in one out of confusion. The log in Naranjo strikes me now as nothing more than a coincidence. There must be one like it in California that you sat on briefly or saw from a passing train. Then when you attempted to recall a day you and I spent together, you inadvertently combined one occasion with another. You were only recording the deterioration of your memory.

Sixteen

I'd hoped to talk to Tencha alone, but I couldn't leave Xinia by herself. Since we'd arrived in Naranjo she'd spoken less and less, even while we were alone. She sat on the bed, her knees curled up to her chest, and whenever we left the house she followed me sullenly, as if obliged to. So I had to speak to Tencha in front of Xinia, and we both spoke carefully, unsure of how much Xinia heard when she sat staring blankly ahead of her. Tencha asked us how long we were staying and I looked at Xinia. She shrugged and gazed into her lap. "We haven't decided," I said.

"I wish you could stay," Tencha said, "but if you have to go, no one needs to know about it."

You'll find it hard to believe, but I only mean to describe to you what it was like: everyone in Naranjo had assumed Santos wouldn't return because of Noé. The idea seemed plausible to me, too. Nevertheless, I couldn't see how Noé would have had the time. The distances were still unfamiliar to me, but watching Xinia had given me some sense of how quickly people who knew the mountains could travel. When I told Tencha that Santos had been hurt just outside of Río Roto and had spent a month with me, she didn't immediately understand. I explained to her that if he'd followed Santos to Río Roto, Noé would have been gone for days; his absence would have been noticed. Tencha appeared not to hear me. "Santos told me he might not come back."

"Why did he say that?"

"*La oreja,*" she said in a low voice. "Those were his words. And he could see that kind of thing, things that hadn't happened yet."

"The ear?" I asked, not understanding.

"That's what he said."

"Why do you call Noé *la oreja?*"

Xinia looked up sharply and Tencha put her hand up to quiet me. "Quietly."

"I'm sorry. What?"

Tencha shook her head and turned away. My words seemed to plunge her into thought. The clothes she was washing lay piled in a plastic bucket. She took a shirt out of the bucket and wrung it slowly, letting the water fall onto the grass. Then she shook it out and clipped it to the laundry line with plastic clothespins. I watched her move slowly through the pile, until all the clothes hung stiffly from the line. The smell of wood smoke from the stove mixed with the sharp smell of soap. She sat back on a stool, absentmindedly clipping and unclipping the plastic clothespins to the edge of her apron. She grimaced and passed a hand over her hair. "Can you believe there was a time, ages ago, when Noé wanted to marry me?"

Xinia didn't stir. She was looking out toward the road again, her hands limp in her lap. "Really?" I said.

"Yes. My sister married his brother Diego when they were very young." She smiled at me.

I looked at her and suddenly felt the rush of blood in my ears, blocking out every sound. I hadn't thought of Noé as connected to anything. You'll wonder how it didn't occur to me sooner, and I don't know. Noé was simply the one who'd gone to Río Roto, the one who'd taken Hilario, and my mind hadn't allowed for him to be anything else. I had no reason to think of him any other way. All I knew of him came from Santos and Xinia. For a moment I only watched Tencha's smile fall at the corners. I leaned back against the wall of the house. "I didn't know," I said.

She raised her eyebrows and looked at me with concern. "I thought you did," she murmured.

"No," I said faintly.

Tencha waited a moment, watching me. "Yes, that's how it happened. Noé thought it would help things along. That they were married. But they couldn't have been more different. Believe me. Diego was totally unlike the other three. I'd like to think I'm more like Iris than Noé is like his brother." She looked at Xinia, who was still staring at the road, and then looked at me questioningly.

I shook my head. "What is your sister like and what was Diego like?"

She tilted her head and smiled at me sadly. For a moment she didn't say anything. "Is and was." She sighed. "Quiet and stubborn, the one. Quiet and complicated, the other. Both in a good way."

I nodded. Xinia glanced up at us then, and when I looked her in the eye she turned away.

We sat silently, watching the trees, and tiny flecks of rain like fine hair began to fall. The smoke from the stove piled up and then dislimned against the clouds. Tencha unfurled the tarp to protect the clothes she'd just hung to dry. She took a handful of peanuts out of her pocket and began cracking the shells and eating the nuts. The shells fell about her bare feet. "When Santos was younger," she said, "he was good friends with Noé and Diego. With Diego especially. Santos was even more sure of himself then. In the last few years he's been full of doubts, but then, he was sure. He knew things. He talked about Río Roto in the past, however many centuries ago, and he said it would all happen again, but in reverse." Tencha smiled. "None of us understood what he meant. He talked about Spanish invaders, conquerors. Soldiers with guns. Betrayals, massacres, illnesses—death everywhere. 'Yes,' we said to him. 'But that was all in the past. Ages ago.' 'It will happen again,' he said. 'And everything will be overturned. Everything will be put right.'" She looked at me. "Did he tell you about what he saw would happen?"

"No, he didn't."

She winced. She shook out her apron and a flurry of shells pattered onto the floor. "It's because he realized he was wrong. Not wrong. Everything happened as he said it would. But we—" She paused. "We were not who he thought we were." She looked down at the shells around her feet and smiled sadly. "We were the soldiers. Conquerors.

"There'd always been boys leaving. The army took them when they were fifteen or sixteen. We thought it was the same thing when the colonel came. But it was different." She spoke quietly. "*La oreja* made it different." For a moment she was silent, and she shook her head. "It's not a good expression. Because we all hear things. We all listen, even when we don't want to. But," she said, tilting her head, "we don't all repeat what we hear."

I stared at her intently, trying to follow.

"*La oreja* heard everything," she said. "He heard when you

didn't go to work one day, and he heard when you spent the night somewhere, and he heard if you fought with your husband or dropped a pot in your kitchen. He heard the guerrilla in Río Roto, and he heard what they said to one another when they were there. And every word *la oreja* heard made it back to the colonel."

Tencha paused and sat without speaking.

"Who was it?" I asked.

She shrugged. "Some people still say Santos is the only one who really knows. Maybe they are right; Santos never told me himself. He did tell me much later that he and *la oreja* had come to terms. I suppose *la oreja* promised to stop up his ears, and Santos promised never to say his name. It didn't matter. Most of us knew who it was.

"All the words *la oreja* repeated to the colonel worried him. You could see it in his face—frowning. But the colonel had a solution: soldiers, who weren't really soldiers; guards, who weren't really guards; men from Naranjo, who, after a time, were not really men from Naranjo. The colonel told us towns everywhere were doing it—starting their patrols. For protection. It was the colonel who suggested it, and it was Noé who took charge of it, but it was everyone in Naranjo who wanted it." She shook her head. "Almost everyone. I did." Then she looked down into her lap. "My husband Josef didn't. I never contradicted him out loud. But he didn't like it. Josef said Noé was just letting the colonel scare him. That made Noé really angry. They stopped speaking about it, stopped speaking altogether.

"The patrol had no uniforms; Noé made them wear bandanas. They stood on the main road, holding their old rifles, waiting for something. The next time the colonel came through Noé said there'd been no sign of the guerrilla. They stood there with their bandanas, eyeing the soldiers' uniforms. Standing as straight as they could, envious. Envious of what? Take the uniforms off and they were just the same men, scratching their lives out of the ground with a hoe.

"The colonel—with his big belly and boots laced up to his knees—pulled a fishhook out of his pocket and started cleaning his nails with it. We all stood there, watching, wondering what more there was to say. When the colonel was done cleaning his nails he sighed and looked around and said to Noé he was worried the patrol wasn't doing its job. Noé said, 'Colonel, we are.' The colonel shook his head and kicked at the dirt and said it was no good trying to hide it when people in Naranjo were 'assisting the enemy.' Noé said he hadn't seen anyone assisting the enemy. The colonel pointed the fishhook at Noé and said, 'You may not have. But your brother has.' And he looked at Noé's brother, Otilio, standing next to him. Otilio shook his head, and just as he was shaking it the colonel reached up and pushed the fishhook through his nose. Noé stepped forward toward them, and the colonel took the knife out of his belt without even looking and pushed the knife through Noé's shoe, into the ground. Noé fell over his foot, trying to pull the knife out. Otilio jerked one way and then the other and the colonel held the fishing line and pulled down slowly, so Otilio had to lower and lower his head until he was kneeling. And then the colonel asked Otilio who he'd seen taking food to the guerrilla and Otilio didn't say anything. The colonel pulled on the fishing line and Otilio made a noise. 'What?' the colonel asked and pulled again. Otilio finally shot his hand out. 'Who?' the colonel acted surprised. Otilio pointed blindly— we were all standing there watching, where else would we be—

saying, 'Him, him.' The colonel dropped the fishing line and walked toward us and took an old man by the shoulder. Hernán looked at him with a serious expression and said, 'I don't know any guerrilla, Colonel. But I hear they can change shape like the *brujos*. I might have come across one without knowing it,' and the colonel smiled and said, 'I'm sure you have.'

"The colonel left with Hernán, who never came back. The patrollers understood better then what they were supposed to do. Hernán's wife told them once on her way to the city that they were too lazy to work like everyone else. They didn't say anything. But when she got home her chicken coop had burned to the ground and her pig lay dead on her doorstep. Then the man who helped her rebuild the chicken coop had his *milpa* burned the following week. On and on that way until Josef talked to Noé. I never knew what they said to each other, because Josef came home and wouldn't talk; he just sat at the table staring at his hands. He went to bed while it was still light out and all night I heard him sighing. The next morning, Tulio came from Río Roto, and only a few hours later the colonel came again. This time and every time the colonel returned Noé knew better than to hesitate. Sometimes it would be something small—hardly a reason at all—but there would always be someone to single out. Noé didn't have to think a second before pointing to Josef and Tulio. When the colonel asked him why he hadn't done anything about it, Noé said he'd only just found out. You see, there didn't seem to be any doubt, then, who *la oreja* was.

"They tied their hands and Tulio didn't say anything. Josef was still calm. He said to the colonel that he hadn't done anything wrong and the colonel came right up to him and stood there in his face, staring at him. Josef didn't look away. Then who was feeding the guerrilla?' the colonel asked. And Josef said the truth—no one. He said no one had even seen the guerrilla. The colonel spat on the ground and looked around disgusted. Then he said, 'One of the guerrilla told me himself he'd gotten food here and it wasn't my fault he died before saying who. So if it wasn't you,' the colonel said, 'who was it?' 'No one,' Josef said. 'It was someone,' the colonel said, smiling. 'Guerrilla don't live off air. If I don't take you, who else am I going to take?' Josef looked him in the eye, and then he looked at Noé, and then he looked at the ground. He was quiet for a while. The colonel liked it, watching Josef. He had all the time in the world. And then without looking up Josef shook his head. The colonel grinned and waved his hand, and they started off out of town.

"I followed about a quarter-mile back, stopping to slow myself down because I kept catching sight of them. Then when we'd gone about four miles I saw someone coming back along the road. Just an outline—the shape of a man, coming up the road toward me. My heart jumped—I thought, It's all right, they've let him go. I ran so that I couldn't feel anything but my blood pounding. When he was close enough to see I felt the ground drop out under me. Tulio walked with his arms at his sides. Not even bound.

"He said they'd let him go, he didn't know why. I didn't say a word; I made to walk on and he said, 'Where are you going?' I said I was going after my husband. And he said, 'You don't want to do that.' I looked at him and said I did. He took my arm to draw me back and I pulled my arm away and he took hold of it again and held on tighter. We fell in the dirt, fighting, me punching out every way I could and biting when I had the chance and him trying to hold me still. When he pinned me facedown on the road I couldn't see from the dust. He said, still keeping me pinned with his knee in my back, that Josef was already dead, he'd seen it. And I screamed that I wanted to go. He waited, just keeping me flat on the ground, until I was tired. He picked me up and said, 'We're going back to Naranjo now.' I wouldn't move my feet—I wouldn't stand, even. He had to drag me, pulling me by the armpits. My feet scraped over the dirt, moving backward."

THE WOMEN in Naranjo burned trash by piling it onto the mat of dry cornstalks and raking the garbage from the outside in. The bitter smoke crowded the air over the houses and headed east and dissipated over the main road. I awoke to the sound of a hoe scratching at the clumps of trash. A woman stood with her back to me and moved her large shoulders only slightly, so that the hoe nudged the garbage inch by inch. At the center of the mound, the charred remains of bones and vegetable stalks, peelings and coffee grounds were gradually buried. As the woman picked at the earth, immovable, a child wearing a long shirt darted behind her and tumbled onto the dirt a few steps away. She took her hoe in her hand and lifted the child by the back of his shirt and propped him up, unhurriedly, like an overturned stool. He ran ahead without turning back or making a sound and she watched him go, holding the hoe on her shoulder. Bit by bit the garbage disappeared, until all that was left in the center of the burnt ground was a tiny pile of plantain peels that shriveled and browned in the embers. The woman tossed dirt on them and patted the dirt down with the hoe, watching the smoke extinguish itself. Then she tipped a bucket of water over the black mound. She stooped carefully, propping herself on her knee, to pick up the rocks that lay next to the bucket one by one. These she placed around the wet ashes, so that when she left they resembled more pieces of something unearthed by the scouring fire than markers placed over it.

AT SEVEN in the evening Noé stood in the doorway of Santos's house with his hands on either side of the door frame. The drizzle had only just stopped and the clouds wouldn't clear before sunset. I'd been watching the trees darken while sitting on a chair by the window. Xinia sat on the bed with her feet on the floor and her hands on her knees. She sat so hunched that her elbows rested on her thighs. When Noé rapped on the door frame she turned her head slowly and stared at him. I stood up and crossed my arms and took a few steps toward the door.

"Well, they've come back." Noé pulled his face down, looking serious or like he'd swallowed wrong. "We're not going to see Santos again," he said. "I'm guessing he went back to Río Roto." Perhaps to you his expression would have seemed sincere. I couldn't see it.

"Yes," I said. "It'll take us a day or so to get our things together."

Noé nodded. "We'll send someone back halfway with you."

"I don't think we'll need it. But thanks."

He crossed his arms and leaned against the door frame. "You'll want to say your goodbyes. Tencha will be sad to see you go," he said.

"We'll come by to see you before leaving," I said.

He smiled, uncrossed his arms, and half-turned in the doorway. "Well," he said. He nodded at us and in passing looked down at the floor in front of him. His smile faded. He shifted his jaw and frowned. I looked at the dirt floor and saw what he saw: the dusty print of a small, bare foot.

I'd gotten used to watching his slow, deliberate steps. His belly weighed him down. I'd underestimated how quickly he could move, how deftly his thick arms could wind and unwind. Before I took a single step he'd crossed the room and pushed Xinia aside. She fell sideways onto the bed and at once pushed herself up again but not before he'd reached under the bed and pulled Hilario out by the leg. Hilario wriggled and then let himself go limp. Xinia stood up and tried to grab Noé's shoulders. "Let him go," she said. He pushed her roughly, so that she fell back on the bed and knocked her head on the wall. He dragged Hilario by the ankle to the middle of the room. I was just at his back and I wrapped my arms around him from behind, pinning his elbows. He lifted his leg and kicked me swiftly and with the next motion struck Hilario in the side. Hilario grunted. I didn't let go. Noé threw his head back, trying to hit mine, and I moved aside. He released Hilario's ankle, and Xinia reached out and pulled him up off the floor. Noé jerked his head back again and hit my nose and I let go. He spun around and pushed me up against the wall. My head snapped back against it. I kneed him in the stomach and he grunted but kept pressing his fingers into my throat. I tried to get air, tried to knee him again, but he barely grimaced and I couldn't feel my leg lifting. The room blackened from the outside in.

Xinia had already packed her things in her sheet when I woke up, and the room was dark. I sat on the edge of the bed and held my forehead. Xinia brought me a wet cloth and then crouched by her bundle, tying and retying it impatiently. I wasn't thinking clearly, but she'd already thought it all through. You may think that I should have stopped her, or that I should have waited to consider. But I couldn't be certain what to expect, and Xinia seemed to know what would happen down to the last detail. Noé had said to her only that we had to leave by nightfall, and I half-believed he just wanted us gone. But Xinia said the whole point was to follow and find us alone. I packed my bag while she knelt next to me, whispering, her hands trembling a little as they clenched her knees. We hadn't seen Tencha again, and no one had come near the house since Noé had left us. I'd missed the sunset, and it gave me the feeling that I'd missed a whole day. The town seemed quieter than usual.

Two hours later we left through the back door and walked quietly uphill to the path that led back to Río Roto. In the darkness the path was hard to see, and I had to follow the white band of Xinia's sheet to keep on course. After several minutes my eyes adjusted, and I turned to glance back behind us.

"I can't see or hear anything," I whispered to her.

"They're there," she said.

"They may not have heard us leaving."

She stopped. "Listen, then. We would stop to listen anyway."

We stood still and I could hear nothing but the trees above us and our breathing. "I don't know," I said.

She shook her head. "I'm sure. Now we think we're alone and keep going."

She turned around and walked on and I followed her, stepping less carefully, brushing up against the branches on either side of the path. We made slow progress. After nearly an hour the trees began to thin as we approached the edge of the ravine. Xinia spoke quietly. "Here is where they'll think we got lost. Don't stop or they'll spend more time looking around this spot. And talk to me once in a while."

"All right," I said. "Be careful."

"I know."

I reached out and clasped her shoulder. "Don't wait too long tomorrow."

She didn't say anything.

"I said don't wait too long. Take the bus if I'm not there."

"We will," she said. "I'm stopping here."

She stepped to the right, off the path, and vanished. I kept walking. "We have to hurry," I whispered aloud. The trees cleared at the edge of the ravine and the moonlight illuminated the route heading downhill. "This is it," I said. I plunged downward, slipping on the loose rocks, making even more noise than I intended to. The path plunged more than a hundred meters. At the bottom I paused. I could hear nothing behind me, but I went on, hoping that it was only because they knew the path and could negotiate it silently. I climbed up the other side of the ravine, scrambling over the torn vines, and when I reached the other side I checked my watch in the moonlight. I still had to give Xinia another hour. The path led me into the trees and I walked almost blindly, the moonlight that had guided me in the ravine disappearing behind the thick canopy. "Several hours left before dawn," I whispered. "Several hours to walk in."

Xinia had estimated that it would take her almost two hours, in the darkness, to return to Naranjo and then reach a safe distance along the path running east out of Naranjo. I had to walk slowly to give her enough time, but I had to stay far enough ahead to keep them from noticing that I was alone. The path seemed utterly unlike the one we'd taken into Naranjo, but I knew it was only the darkness that distorted it beyond recognition. I had difficulty seeing the narrow dirt groove at my feet and I walked slowly, stopping every so often to check the time.

When more than two hours had passed I stopped. I had almost missed the path, where it dove off downhill between two slender trees, and it seemed a likely place in which to get lost. For several minutes I rustled the branches, wondering aloud where the path continued. Then I turned around and headed back the way I'd come. I stepped loudly, worrying that they hadn't heard me turn and that I would stumble upon them. But either they kept a good distance or they were never there to begin with, because I saw and heard no one. Only once or twice did I hear anything from among the trees, sounds so indistinct that they could easily have been caused by the wind.

I returned to Naranjo with still a few hours left before dawn. I sat against the front wall of Santos's house, where I could see Noé's house clearly. The night was cloudy and still. I'd been wide awake while walking through the woods, but as I sat against the house I began to feel exhausted. My neck ached from where Noé had pressed it, and the pain was spreading to the back of my head. I watched the purpled sky and thought I saw birds overhead. Their wings rustled as they dipped down to the rooftops. But they were bats, and as one skimmed over my head I heard the air thud slowly under the wings of an owl. A moment later its cry sounded from everywhere at once.

The clouds broke up and a pale, gigantic moon clung to the edge of the trees. Noé's house was quiet. I stood up and took my blanket out of my bag and wrapped it over my knees. An hour and then a half hour passed and I figured that Xinia would be well on her way. Either that, or they'd found her. I didn't sleep, but I rested my head against the wall for a moment, and when I opened my eyes again I saw a shadow moving downhill from the direction of Noé's house. The figure stopped by the remains of the burnt garbage and as it stopped another shadow to my left moved into the moonlight. They stepped softly toward each other. I held my breath. When they reached each other they paused. I tensed my legs, ready to spring up. A moment later they were embracing, clinging so fiercely that they fell to the ground. They rolled over the new mat of cornstalks, their breathing sharp and fierce, their kisses vicious. After a moment they picked themselves up and fled hand in hand away from the open space and downhill, and as they disappeared into the shadows I heard their urgent whispers, hurried but vague, like the rustling of paper.

When another hour had passed I stood up and wrapped the blanket over my shoulders, picked up my bag, and walked back into Santos's house. I let myself in through the back and unpacked my things in the dark. Then I got into bed and curled up against the wall where Xinia had the night before. It seemed that I could still smell her on the mattress, but it might have only been the jasmine, whose perfume leaked into the night air, stealing through the open windows of Naranjo and unsettling everyone's dreams.

I AWOKE ONCE, when we lived in the desert, without knowing why. I had the sense that it was still the middle of the night. Instead of falling back asleep I sat up and looked out into the room. The book you'd been reading to me sat on the bedside table, illuminated by the light that came in from the partly opened door. I walked out into the hallway and saw that the light came from your bedroom. In that half-sleeping state, I walked to your bedroom and looked in through the open door.

Everyone has experienced how day and night seem to inhabit different spheres. Sensations and thoughts that take firm hold in the middle of the night seem, by day, unimaginable, and likewise awaking in the dark, as I did, can sometimes temporarily erase the ordinariness of daylight. The experience is so universal that we can speak of it without explaining. As a matter of course, we describe fears that spring up only at night and decisions that can be taken only with the light of morning. The evening I looked into your bedroom—I must have been seven or eight—was the first time I became aware of how day and night can seem like separate worlds. I'd never heard it or read it elsewhere. Perhaps some of the ideas and sensations that we seem to copy from others are, in reality, experienced the same way by people in general. Though over the years the idea has matured in my mind, the notion of day and night as bounded did occur to me on my own. It may be that in echoing others we aren't copying or reusing the same ideas so much as reinventing them: for each person a new idea exists—once again—for the first time.

I stood in the doorway of your bedroom and saw you and Mamá fully dressed, sitting on the bed, speaking quietly to each other. You held a small box in your right hand and Mamá's chin with your left. I couldn't hear what you were saying because you spoke quietly, murmuring. Then you gave Mamá the box and she opened it slowly, pulling on a blue ribbon that held it together. She opened it, took something out, and stared at it for a moment.

"Open it," you said.

Her right hand fumbled with it and stopped, suddenly. Then she bent over it and fell toward you, weeping. You laughed lightly. "Don't cry," you exclaimed. Mamá shook her head. "Don't cry," you said again. "Listen," you said. "I've been meaning to give them to you for a long time."

Mamá sat up and wiped her eyes and kissed you on the cheek. Then you opened her clenched fingers and took from her trembling hands a thin silver chain with a locket. Mamá bent forward and you closed the clasp. She sat back and looked at the locket and turned to you suddenly. "It's superstitious."

"Don't be silly."

"You're sure?"

"Of course. It's just to remember her by."

Mamá nodded and looked down at the locket again. She opened it and carefully took out a speck of gold that tinkled softly when she placed it back inside the locket. "I'll be afraid to wear it in case they fall out," she said.

"Go look at yourself in the mirror," you said.

Mamá stood up and walked toward the mirror and that's when both of you saw me in the doorway.

"Nítido," you said, standing up. "What's the matter? Can't you sleep?"

I shook my head. "The light was on."

You laughed. "All right, then. But you don't like your door closed. We'll turn out the light in a minute. Go back to bed and I'll be right there."

I went back to my room with the feeling that I'd stumbled into another world. It was as though you and Mamá became different people during the night, and I'd accidentally seen you, transformed, into your other selves. By the time you came in to see that I was in bed, the sight of you and Mamá sitting on the bed was growing confused with other thoughts, and I hardly heard you when you whispered, kissing me on the forehead, "You're much happier not knowing."

I WOKE UP with Noé's knee in my stomach. He had his hands wrapped around my throat and his back to his brothers, who hovered behind him. Only because their shadows crowded the windows could I tell that people had already gathered around the house. I wondered whether the figures I'd seen during the night in the moonlight were among them. The thought made me smile. Noé pushed my head back so that my eyes faced the wall. "Where is he?" he asked. His spit hit my cheek and I grimaced. One of his brothers said, "Noé," and stepped forward. Noé ignored him. He pulled my hair back with one hand and with the other hit my jaw, not too hard. I felt my teeth ring.

I heard the commotion outside and saw, out of the corner of my eye, the patterns of the moving shadows. Noé seemed not to notice. His brothers had walked to the door; they were trying to keep someone out. "Nítido," she shouted. My pulse seemed to pause. I thought for a moment that it was Xinia. I felt afraid suddenly. My stomach dropped. "Nítido," she screamed again. But it wasn't Xinia; it was Tencha. Noé's face crumpled in on itself and he let go of my hair. He still held my shirtfront with his other hand and he looked at me with horror, as if he recognized in me the contagion that announced his own death. "What," he said.

I pushed his hands off of my shirt and they fell away without resisting. "I—" I said. I choked and put my hands to my neck and coughed. My breath moved through something like a broken sieve in my throat. "Nítido. Diego's son." I choked on my breath. "Your brother's son."

I DO HAVE one memory of Guatemala from when I was younger, but I'm never certain whether it's a memory or a dream that I confused with a memory or a recollection of some other time and place that I wrongly slipped into the first three years of my life. The more I think of it, the more tenuous it becomes.

I am sitting in the dirt. Hot air undulates over the road ahead of me and through it, in the distance, a pale figure moves toward me. Walking brings me no closer to it, and I sit down again in the dirt road, the dahlias and zinnias hanging over the low wooden fence to my right. As I watch, the luminous shape grows larger until it splits in two: a man and a woman, walking toward me, their heads together, their faces a blur, their bodies rippling uncertainly in the heat so that they seem on the verge of coming apart and vanishing. The blue sky presses down on them and the road trembles and unravels briefly and redraws itself. The only sound, a constant buzzing that rises and falls as if riding the heat waves, comes from the heavy flowers that lie just out of reach. Before the figures can reach me, a door slams, and a moment later a woman says my name. Her voice brings me to myself and I look down, only to find my arms and legs disappearing in the heat, splintering into a hundred pieces of blackness. The woman pulls me up and roughly brushes my arms and legs with her hands. The ants began to fall away, clinging to her fingers and then tumbling to the ground so that they form a quivering carpet. I stand mesmerized, immobile, watching the ants that still crawl furiously over my skin.

I have no recollection of the moment when you and Mamá finally reached us, or of what Hortensia said to you. And for many years I hadn't known who the woman was or why she was there. As with so many other less certain things—not images but indistinct echoes that unexpectedly expand around a thought or a sensation, filling the space around it with vague suggestions—I only know that it doesn't belong to my later life because of its discordance. Without knowing precisely why, I know the dahlias, the buzzing, the heavy sky all belong elsewhere. Had I not known that I'd spent my first three years in another country, I might have concluded that they were left over from another life.

In some sense I envy you and Mamá, because you became adults in the other life and could remember clearly what did or didn't belong in it. I thought there were no photographs, letters, or physical mementos of that other time, but I see now that, like the locket, they may have been all around me, unintelligible to me but weighted with meaning to you. Only rarely did I recognize references to the past. There were moments when you looked over at Mamá and said, "Iris," and she would look up, and I knew that you'd dropped away, as if through a slit in the net that held you in place, and that your way of saying her name and her answering look belonged to that prior life. When something similar occurred to either of you alone, you seemed liminal and undefined, as though I'd caught sight of you through a revolving door. Over time it happened less often, so that during the last year in Oregon, while you drifted off by yourself to somewhere new, Mamá, perhaps in her bewildered attempt to stay with you, gradually closed off everything but the present. Only on her birthday, when I bought her a gardenia and set it on her chair in the morning, did she seem to slip away as I'd seen her do in the past. She leaned into the plant, even though the flowers were still only tight buds, and inhaled deeply, and when she stood up again her blithe smile was like a child's, so that I almost wished she could remain in the remote place the gardenia had taken her to, however distant it might be.

Seventeen

TENCHA'S SON led the way through the trees along a path that ran south. I wondered who had last passed that way and when; Helbert had to carve a route with his machete. The place was less than a quarter of a mile from Naranjo, but the stillness made it seem farther. The clearing was nothing but a patch of uneven ground. Pale, wilted grass grew sparsely to the edges. The few saplings that dotted the grass appeared scorched by the sun, and the trees at the edges leaned away as if trying to flee, straining against their manacled roots. No mound or sign marked the place. Helbert crouched by one of the saplings and tore it up carefully with both hands. "No one comes here," he said.

I crouched next to him, gazing over the tangled plants, their dusty leaves. "How many are here?" I asked.

"We don't know."

"Anyone for sure?"

He wiped the dirt on his palms. "Like my father?"

"Like him."

"Don't know." He smiled at me briefly and reached for another sapling. "We didn't find it for a while."

"He could be here," I said.

"Maybe. He could be anywhere." He took the pieces of the sapling and bundled them together and threw them behind him into the trees. "I've heard there's people who excavate. They can tell from the bones who they were. What happened to them."

"They might come this way."

"Up here? They wouldn't even know to come. No one knows."

I walked carefully around the clearing, staying close to the trees, until I was on the other side, across from Helbert. I crouched down, facing him over the sparse grass. The ground beneath my hand was cold. "Jasmine?" I asked. It grew in the center, leaning weakly, tossing only a few white blossoms into the air.

Helbert nodded. "It needs more shade."

I stood up. A breeze came through the trees and tugged at the thin grass. It nodded and swayed and a moment later drooped again. I smiled. "I would have left without knowing."

He smiled back. "Let's go," he said.

Hortensia was waiting for us to eat. "Tencha," I said, when I saw what she was doing, "Noé doesn't like me to eat here so often."

She brushed the air with her hand. "You'll be hungry again in an hour," she said. She opened the tamales and put them on plates and carried them to the table. Helbert stood outside washing his hands with a bar of soap and water from the spigot.

"All right," I said.

We sat down to eat and Helbert chewed silently, cutting the tamale into eight pieces with his fork and spearing the pieces one by one. Tencha ate slowly, watching me the whole time. "Do you know where your name comes from?" she asked.

Helbert swallowed. "I know."

"I asked Nítido," she said.

"No," I said. "It's been a problem."

"What is it in English?"

"Nothing. Everyone called me 'Ditto.'"

"What's that?"

"It means the same thing."

"The same as Nítido?"

"No, it means the same thing over again."

"That has nothing to do with Nítido."

"I know. It's just the sound."

Tencha frowned and took a few bites of tamale. "Well, I can tell you."

I nodded, swallowing.

"When you were born there wasn't a spot on you."

"Of what?"

"No blood. We pulled you out. My sister was a mess but you looked washed. Not a drop. Not even on the cord."

"That's impossible," I said.

She shrugged. "Don't believe me."

Helbert finished his tamale and began peeling the plantain leaf into narrow strips. Tencha and I ate in silence. When we were finished I reached for my wallet and looked through it until I found the photograph. I propped it up on the table in front of Tencha.

"That's before he got sick," I said.

Tencha's chin trembled and she tried to smile. She put the photograph down and pressed her eyelids with her fingertips. "They're so old. And look so young. Younger than me."

I laughed and leaned over and kissed her on the cheek. "Well, it was several years ago." I think I took the photograph the first year you moved to Oregon. In it, you and Mamá stand by the door of the new house. Mamá looks serious, a little annoyed; she was in the middle of cooking when I pulled her out for the photo. You are smiling slightly, seeming at ease. Even to my eyes, in Naranjo, your corduroys, flannel shirt, and leather shoes have an air of comfort and wealth about them. Above you both a block of sunlight falls on the wood shingle of the house, but neither of you seems to notice.

Tencha looked at the photograph again. "I guess life is easier there."

I didn't say anything.

"Let me see," Helbert said. He studied the picture, frowning, and when he finally handed it back he looked at me closely. "How long are you going back to Río Roto for?" he asked.

"I promised I wouldn't stay long," I said. "Just do a few things."

Tencha chewed quietly, watching us. "No one there knows?" Helbert asked.

"No one."

"Not even Xinia?"

I shook my head. "I'll tell her. When I go back."

We sat quietly for a while, listening to the fire in the stove and the zinc overhead tinkling under the drizzle that had started. Tencha began picking things up. I left them sitting by the stove behind the house, waiting for the darkness.

I SPENT most of the time at Noé's house with Ester, whom I'd discovered the first morning in the back room, crying over the narrow stuffed mattress where Hilario's few belongings remained. She'd refused to speak of what had happened, her agonized face expressing a generalized shame in everything pertaining to him, as if she were torn between the remorse caused by keeping him so long and the guilty wish that he'd never escaped. Knowing well she'd probably been Hilario's only comfort in the house, I tried to set her at ease, but she seemed to feel that however much his presence had justified her affections, his absence rendered them invalid, and when I finally coaxed her to speak about him she apologized brokenheartedly at every turn for missing him when she had no right to. I don't know what mistaken association made me think that describing myself at Hilario's age would lighten her thoughts, but what I told her caught her interest, and she surprised me by asking the questions no one else had. I told her about our time in Los Angeles and Pear Blossom, Santa Cruz, Palo Alto, and Oregon, and then about Mamá living in Washington state, which she listened to with a kind of fervor that made me exaggerate the dampness and the loneliness and the inconveniences of the winters. We were alone much of the time, as Noé stayed out, content to have everyone see that I was staying in his house. Nevertheless when he returned in the evenings to find me deep in conversation with Ester, he couldn't help listening, and after eating he sat in a chair against the wall, smoking and watching us talk.

I don't mean to dwell on the things Noé said about you, but perhaps, by mentioning them, I can give you some idea of the person he'd become. I have no idea if he spoke to you then as critically as he spoke of you to me—perhaps it was only envy that made him so disparaging. Or perhaps everything that happened while you were away left him so altered that even his recollection of you was marred. It's difficult to say, because his disdain—not just for you, but for everyone—is at once so widespread and so unpredictably interrupted by affection and sincerity.

"Papá would have liked Bainbridge," I said to Ester, "because as he got older he started fishing. He spent hours outside, sitting alone on the bank with a line in the water. He never had time when he worked. Then once he retired only a couple years passed before he was too sick to fish by himself."

Noé shuffled in his chair. "He was sick then?" he asked.

Ester looked at him and allowed a look of the slightest reproach to pass over her face.

"Yes," I said.

"Bedridden?" he asked.

"Not at first. At first you couldn't tell, to look at him. It just made him forget things. And later on, then you could tell. We got him a wheelchair."

"Everyone gets old," he said easily. "Some before others."

"It wasn't like that," I said. "He wasn't senile. He was a different person."

Noé nodded. "You mean his character. I've heard people get soft in the States. But you know—he wasn't tough to begin with."

I watched the smoke rising up around his mouth and over his head. Ester stared down at her lap. "Probably." I looked at my hands on the table, my fingers smooth and soft next to Ester's. "Maybe he didn't change." I smiled.

Noé nodded, as though he knew what I meant. "But he understood what you were saying," he said.

"I don't know." I hesitated. "I hope he didn't."

"You haven't said," Ester said to me, "whether he knew, at least."

"That he was sick?"

She nodded.

I pulled my hands away from the tabletop and Ester watched me. The smoke hid Noé's face. I still think that it was better for you to not know—not understand the illness for what it was. But you never told me how you felt about it. Perhaps you told Mamá, at some point, how much you wanted to know. But I never heard it from you—or from her. And I wonder whether you would have known what you were asking. Even when you spoke to me on the phone and described your changing symptoms, you didn't anticipate what was to come. When you apologized to Mamá by describing to me the sudden lapses, the uncontrollable outbursts, you weren't sure what you were apologizing for. It wasn't until I spoke with Ester that I began to understand the nature of those conversations—those confessions.

"It's hard to say," I said. "We couldn't tell. What he knew and didn't. What he thought."

She tilted her head to the side and looked at me closely. "You think he minded?"

"Don't be stupid," Noé said.

I ignored him. "What do you mean?" I asked Ester.

"If he accepted it."

I didn't understand her. She held one hand on the tabletop, palm-up, as if waiting for something to fall there. Her hand was callused, her fingers bent. "You mean that he gave up?" I asked her.

"No," she said, uncertainly. "I just mean he may have expected it. From that feeling of having been passed over." She clenched her open hand and then slowly opened it again. "You feel there's been some mistake."

I watched Ester, whose lined face was so calm. Her eyes were bright and she spoke with unusual certainty. "He may have felt that way," I said. "I don't know."

Noé stood up and made a good deal of noise stamping out the cigarette. "I'm going to bed," he said. "Ester."

She looked at him briefly. "Yes, all right. I still have to clean up."

Noé left the room and Ester began picking up the plates. I helped her carry them to the bucket of water. "You don't have to do that," she said, but she didn't object when I picked up a towel. Her face was difficult to see in the dim light as she washed the plates, scrubbing them in one bucket and rinsing them in another and then passing them to me. "That's how it is for me," she suddenly said.

I took the plate she handed me and dried it slowly. "How?"

"I always have pain here." She made a quick, embarrassed gesture toward her apron. The remorse in her voice as she confessed it echoed that of all the confessions I'd heard in Río Roto. I watched her in silence and she went on scrubbing, rinsing. "I could never have children." She handed me a plate. "It's only fair. Other people have them and lose them."

AFTER THE FIRST WEEK I went with Noé in the mornings to his *milpa* and helped clear the ground with a hoe. At the beginning he watched me to make sure I worked right, stopping me every other minute to show me again how to make the quick motions with the blade into the ground, the weeds. I took my shirt off and wrapped it around my waist to catch the sweat. My fingers burned and blistered from the rough handle of the hoe, and on the next day I wore scraps of cloth around my palms. The other men all found their way there at one point or another because they happened to be nearby or had to walk past to get to where they were going. They stopped by the edge of the *milpa* and Noé went to talk to them, resting his wrists on the handle of his hoe, laughing as he pointed up at me. They all listened, watched me working clumsily, and went on their way.

At the end of the week my back was past burnt, my skin falling off in ragged white sheets. Noé worked alongside me then as my efforts improved, scarcely moving the hoe but turning the soil more than I could by heaving with my whole shoulder. The sweat ran over my brow and into my eyes. Noé reached into his pocket and pulled out a bandana and held it out to me. I shook my head. He shrugged and stood back to watch as I finished the row. "You're more like me than him," he said.

I grunted and leaned to pick up a rock and toss it out of the field.

"Aren't you taller?" he pressed.

I stopped and leaned on the hoe and wiped my forehead with the rag around my palm. Noé stood in front of me, his white shirt worn thin over his belly, his smiling face smeared with dirt. "I was taller than him," I said. "By a few inches."

"Even how he walked. Looked like such an *indio*."

I tossed the hoe down lightly and looked at it, the cracked brown handle on brown dirt. "Really," I said. "So do I."

"What?"

"Look like such an *indio*. Am such an *indio*." I laughed dryly, not looking at him.

He frowned. "If he said that he told you wrong."

I picked up the hoe again and held it loosely in my palms. "Forget it. I meant it differently."

He squinted at me. "You wouldn't have come out bad if you'd stayed here."

I looked over his head at the crows that fought among the corn-stalks. They jabbed noiselessly, their wings scattering into the air as if the birds were coming apart. "I don't know," I said. "Maybe."

Noé frowned. "You get soft in the city. He did."

I shrugged. I wiped my brow again and looked up as a cloud passed over us.

Noé reached out without moving his feet so that he almost tipped over and he patted my arm. "You're getting better at it."

I stood still as long as I could and then pulled away and started working again. The cloud passed and the sun hit me and I worked for some minutes until I'd reached a distance. I looked out of the corner of my eye to where Noé was still standing, watching.

He unnerved me most when he reminded me of you, rare as that was. At times he seemed to have a similar way of holding himself back. But his preoccupations were completely different. More than once he said, after a long silence, "Tencha must have told you a lot about me."

"Not much," I would say, but he would remain thoughtful.

"People here talk a lot," he would say lightly. It was one of his refrains. "And when there's nothing to talk about they make things up."

I nodded, agreeing.

On other days I tried to get away during the lunch hour, after we'd been home to eat with Ester and before returning to work. He followed me closely and I rarely got out of his sight. One afternoon he stopped me in the middle of a row and held out a thermos of water. "Take a break," he said. He walked away hold-ing the thermos aloft, as if luring me out. We sat on the stones in the shade and drank water and he wiped his neck and chin elaborately with his bandana. "It's coming along well," he said.

I nodded. We'd cleared the field of cornstalks, and their hard stubble covered the hillside.

"I guess Diego didn't keep *milpa*," he said.

"He grew tomatoes a few times."

I took another drink of water and handed it back to him.

He sighed. "I couldn't abandon a thing like that."

I blinked the sweat away, watching a clot of tiny birds peck at the *milpa* downhill. "Land is too expensive."

"What did he do then?"

"He drove a truck."

"For money?"

"Yes. A transport truck."

"Was he any good at it?"

"He was."

He shook his head. "It's not right. He didn't belong in a truck."

I stood up. "I'm going to piss." He nodded and I walked into the woods, away from him, away from the hot sun. I walked quickly, breathing heavily, letting my feet follow their own course. A few minutes later I stopped and looked up at the canopy and focused on the lapses of sunlight between the trees. I let myself get dizzy. The trunks swayed. I sat down on the ground and watched the wind move occasionally overhead through the branches. I hadn't been away ten minutes when he began calling me. "Nítido," he shouted, absently at first. "Where are you?"

I stood up and listened to him. I would have turned back in a moment; I'd only wanted a brief respite. But the sound of his voice seemed to push me away. I took a few steps in the other direction. "Nítido." His tone grew more urgent. It was all I could do, while struggling with the irritation, to keep from bolting. I stood still, waiting, ashamed and repulsed at the same time.

"Nítido. *Nítido.*" He hadn't seen me yet. He'd begun calling my name wildly, and I could hear him crashing through the trees, heading roughly in my direction. Still I stood impassively, the sound of his voice filling me with disgust. "Nítido!" He saw me. His feet pounded over the short distance between us. He rushed up to me from the side, threw his arm around me, and pulled me back so roughly that we fell to the ground.

"What, what!" I flung him off.

We lay on the ground, our legs entangled. He clung to my arm, breathing raggedly. "Don't," he gasped. "Don't get up yet."

I carefully pulled my legs free and when he assured himself that I wasn't going to stand up he leaned over his knees and took great gulps of air. His heavy stomach shuddered. "Nítido," he said again, as if to himself.

"What is it?"

He stood up slowly, holding my arm, when his breathing had returned to normal. Without letting go of me he reached for a broken log and grunted as he rolled it over the ground toward the spot where I'd stood minutes earlier. The log wobbled, paused, wobbled again, and suddenly it was gone. It sounded moments later with a crash, having vanished through the leaves. "Don't go near it," he said, clinging to my arm.

I hadn't yet understood.

"We built it. I built it. My brothers and I. A long time ago."

"A hole," I said, blankly.

He took a deep breath and shook his head. "Nítido, Nítido."

"Like the boy and the ants."

"What?

"Nothing." I turned to look at him. His mustache gleamed with perspiration. The scar above his right brow was white against his reddened face. I avoided his gaze so frequently that I hadn't noticed how his eyes were milky.

He sensed my scrutiny and looked away, embarrassed. "Have to look out for you," he said. "It's not like you can be here a day and know the place."

At MIDNIGHT on the last night of my stay in Naranjo, the deafening rain coursed around the houses as if over pebbles midstream. I imagined them all swept downhill, pressed against the trees by the flood of water that invaded the main road on its way to conquering the east. I got out of bed and put on a pair of rubber boots. When I first stepped out into the mud the heaviness and coldness of the rain shocked me, and I struggled to overcome the illusion that I was walking underwater. Within seconds the rain had filled my boots, and I took them off and left them at the edge of the trees. I followed the path Helbert had cut a few days earlier, walking at first carefully and then without restraint as I felt nothing underfoot but mud and flattened leaves. It took me almost half an hour to reach the clearing. I took off my shirt and draped it over my neck and sat in the mud. Streaks of dirt coated my legs and feet. Within seconds they were clean. My head and back began to tingle from the pressure of the water. The grass clung to the ground like thinning hair pasted onto a skull. I hadn't noticed on the last visit that the ground tilted west, away from me. I watched the water dissolving the earth around the roots of the plants and carrying them away, haltingly when branches choked its flow and then sweepingly as the tangled boughs lost their hold and gave way. The ground seemed to disintegrate beneath me inch by inch, and I imagined that it wouldn't be long before the bones would begin to show, gleaming white as the rain washed them clean.

I'd anticipated almost none of what Tencha told me during our conversations. The past I'd invented for you and Mamá had already begun to grow indistinct. I saw the images and explanations I'd carefully composed during the last years blurring before me, like so much ink running on the page. What Tencha told me seemed not so much beyond imagining as beneath it. I might have divined the tedious details of your early history had I thought less, imagined less, believed less. Nothing that had happened seemed exceptional and yet your lives, in their ordinary specificity, had eluded me.

It had never occurred to me that you'd changed your name, but I could see why you dropped "Rodríguez" for the more unusual "Amán." Tencha told me that your father, Noé Rodríguez, had died young. Noé was already fifteen when he died and you were thirteen. The other two, the twins, were ten. The year after his death, the land the family had been granted was reappropriated. You'd survived, Tencha said, only because your mother Vira had gone to the city to work as a maid, leaving the four of you to work the tiny *milpa* that remained.

She saw you once a month by saving her Sunday afternoons, which the woman in the capital allowed her to accumulate, so that by the end of the month she had two full days to herself. She left the woman's house early on the last Saturday of every month, took the bus for three hours, walked another six hours to Naranjo, and spent the afternoon and evening with you, Noé, and the twins, who with each month seemed less and less familiar. On Sunday morning she slept in until eight, then walked back the six hours and took the bus to the city.

During those first few years, while Vira worked in the city, Noé taught you and the twins to work with him. The first summer the corn spoiled and you lived off beans and anything the others in Naranjo could spare. You suggested more than once, Tencha said, that working for other men in Naranjo would let you share in their yield, but Noé didn't like to see the *milpa* abandoned, and he knew there wouldn't be time to do both. The twins did what Noé asked them to. You worked along with them and in the evening you worked for another family—for Iris and Hortensia and their father—though it meant that you worked a longer day.

Vira's situation was considered temporary, but after six years of working in the city her wages could still not be dispensed with and the yield from the *milpa* never allowed for savings. You were nineteen that year and Mamá was a year younger. When Vira arrived at the end of June you told her you'd be married on her next visit. Vira was only forty-three, but her ankles had swelled so that she couldn't wear anything but sandals. The veins marbled her legs, fighting to reach the surface. The six-hour walk took her much longer, but the narrow road could only be covered on foot and no one could do anything to make it shorter for her. She promised to ask for an extra day the following month, though she couldn't guarantee that she'd get it. At the end of July, the weekend for her visit arrived but Vira did not. The ceremony was put off—you couldn't think of being married without her—and on the Monday following you took the long walk to the bus stop and rode the bus to the city and found your way, after making several wrong turns, to the house where your mother had lived for the past six years.

The house, as you told Tencha later, had an inner courtyard choked with bougainvillea. The cold, dark rooms around the patio smelled of old wool and damp plaster. You waited in the anteroom, where the partly closed shutters dropped pieces of light on the carpets. You waited half an hour before a tiny woman with white hair tinted a purplish black came to see you. She offered you a seat and sat some distance away from you on the edge of her chair. Her legs barely reached the floor. She played absently with her rings as she spoke. You told her why you were there, and the woman said that she was very sorry, but that your mother had suffered a heart attack weeks earlier. She'd wanted to contact the family, she said, but Vira had never told her where she lived, and she'd been forced to bury her in the city cemetery at her own expense. If you knew anyone from your town who might take up her position, she said, she would consider them. You visited the cemetery that afternoon and found your mother in a small niche that read only "Vira" and the year.

I LOST TRACK of time sitting in the clearing, but when the rain stopped the sky held close its heavy darkness. Within minutes the clouds rolled to the east and moonlight flooded the clearing. I began to tremble from the cold. For many years I'd felt the terrible remoteness that came from knowing too little. Having corrected it, I found the distance that once stretched out before me, an expanse of blankness, replaced by another. I'd often imagined Naranjo, and only knowing it revealed how completely I'd failed to approach it. There, in the place I came from, I felt as far as possible from all I knew. Farther uphill slept houses full of strangers. They were unknown to me, and they would remain that way, and I was lost in a place where all the things I'd ever seen, thought, and imagined were lost with me.

Eighteen

THE FOLLOWING DAY Helbert walked halfway back to Río
Roto with me by a different route. He didn't speak much on the
way, and when we stopped to eat at the end of the day, he spent
most of the evening staring into the fire. In the morning he gave
me the food that he'd brought with him and prepared to return
to Naranjo.

"You can't get lost. It's a straight path from here."

"Thank you," I said.

He embraced me briefly and took several steps back. "See you
soon." I didn't say anything. "She'll miss you. But take as long as
you need."

I nodded and moved to embrace him again, and he held on to
me for a moment longer and then turned away abruptly. You
would have been struck by how much he resembled me: his
shoulders a little hunched as he walked away through the tall
grass. He raised his hand when he reached the edge of the clearing. For some minutes I listened to the sound he made pushing

through the trees, and then the sound was gone. I turned the other way and began the walk to Río Roto.

Though I hadn't planned to, I stopped to rest mid-morning in a flat, rocky clearing where the sun shone. I felt cold, and I sat on a stone to let the heat dry my sweat as I listened to the screams of birds in the trees up ahead. For a few minutes I fell asleep. When I awoke the sun struck down from directly above. My shirt was heavy with perspiration. I drank water from the thermos and stood up, shivering. I walked slowly across the patchy grass to the trees, where I expected the path to resume. There was no opening. I walked along the edge of the trees searching for the continuation of the trail and couldn't find it. The way back to Naranjo on the other side was clearly visible, a dusty groove among the rocks. There seemed to be no other traveled route out of the clearing. One or two spots among the trees seemed less impenetrable, but it was clear that no one had passed there recently. Then through a cluster of narrow trees growing not far from where I'd slept, I glimpsed what seemed like another clearing in the distance. I pushed through the branches, searching for solid ground and finding mostly roots.

I made slow progress and was soon shivering again from the cold of the shade and sweating from the effort of pushing through the trees. On either side of me, darkness and dense forest stretched out limitlessly. The birds I'd heard earlier became visible at moments as they dipped above the trees overhead and toward the clearing. Their cries were hoarse; at times they seemed to buzz like heavy insects. After more than an hour I looked back at the way I'd come and it seemed that I'd reached the halfway point. I rested standing up, letting the branches hold me motionless for some minutes. My chin sagged, and I woke up when my bag dropped from my shoulder. As I looked ahead at the slivers of light from the setting sun, I struggled with a sense of panic. I moved on, holding the bag over my head so that I could move more quickly through the clinging branches. My arms grew weary so I held it in front of me like a shield and plunged through the leaves, letting the hard thorns rip at my arms.

When I reached the clearing I found that it was nothing like the rocky expanse I'd left behind. The tall grass grew inward toward a crease in the center, as if the earth had been folded in half there and reopened like a book. I stumbled through the grass and tripped almost at once as my feet tangled in the long blades. The buzzards I'd seen rested on the branches of the trees and stood in the grass, and when I fell I imagined at first that it was one of these I'd collided with. I could tell only that what I'd fallen against was dark and soft and not like grass, and I expected the feathers to fly up into my face and the claws to scratch free at any moment. I put my arm over my face and closed my eyes and waited, and when a moment later the birds had flown off not from under me, as I expected, but from a few feet ahead of me, I opened my eyes and realized I was looking at a boot.

Most of the clothes were shredded and more than half of his flesh was gone. The bones only came through in places, though the birds had cleaned his face off long before; the rain and sun had already polished and blanched his skull. I tried to rise and couldn't. I crawled through the grass as quickly as I could and I didn't get far before I reached the other one, who lay facedown. This time I made every effort to stand, and by dropping my bag I was able to take a few steps before I fell again and vomited into the grass. It took everything out of me, and I rolled over next to where I'd retched, unconscious of the corpses' stench and my own. I took deep breaths and stared at the sun overhead that the passing bodies of the buzzards blackened in fragments.

I don't know whether I slept or simply failed to keep track of time, but when I looked at the sky again the sun crouched just above the trees. A buzzard stood by my foot, tapping at my boot. I kicked feebly and the animal backed off, flapping indifferently. Before sitting up I rolled over and pulled a blanket out of the bag and wrapped it around my shoulders. Several minutes passed and I felt well enough to try standing. I staggered to my feet, putting my hand out before me to keep my balance. *La oreja* and Santos had finally collapsed under the burden of their mutual promises. Neither of them had enough flesh remaining to give me any idea of how they'd died, and the machete that lay on the ground next to Tulio might as well have been to cut through the grass as for anything else. Santos's left arm lay some distance away; it seemed possible that the buzzards had dragged it from him.

I pulled my bag behind me through the grass and looked for a way out of the clearing, but I couldn't find one. By the time I'd walked the perimeter of the clearing, I felt I couldn't go another step. The sun had dropped below the trees. Its orange light filtered onto the high grass like liquid rust. From where I'd fallen I couldn't see Tulio and Santos. The buzzards' dim shadows moved from the trees to the grass and back again. Their wings were slow, their eyes blind. The sun would set on them and I would wake up to find them gone. I pulled the blanket over my head and fell halfway into sleep.

IN THE MORNING my fever continued. All that day I walked through the trees around the clearing, thinking that if I walked in a circle I would come across the path leading from it. There was no such path, or perhaps the only path was the circular path winding around the clearing that I was walking on. By moving in ever-widening arcs I found myself near nightfall in the clearing I'd left the day before. I slept between two rocks, troubled by thoughts of the buzzards. I found that despite the fever I couldn't sleep through the night, as cries that I heard or imagined drifted in on the wind and seemed to take the shape of rocks that moved toward me when I didn't watch them. In the middle of the night I wrapped myself in the blankets and took up the bag and began walking back along the path that had first led me to the clearing, thinking that if I could do nothing else I would return to Naranjo.

And yet I must have taken a different path, or else I took the path to Naranjo and then wandered off on an adjoining trail, because when the sun rose I found myself lying facedown, the bag still attached to my shoulders, in the damp meadow that I'd slept in with Xinia and Santos weeks earlier. I still had a fever, and the hunger began to make my legs tremble. I found the path we'd taken from Río Roto and set off down it, dizzy with the effort of trying to remember how many hours we'd taken to reach the spot on the first day. When I stopped to drink I found the thermos empty. I walked on, trying not to rest so that I wouldn't fall asleep on my feet.

I reached Río Roto as the sun was setting. From the decline that followed the bridge to Murcia I saw a thing that made me stop in the road. I thought for a confused moment that the town was a lake whose mirroring surface reflected the constellations. The small lights wavered and disappeared and returned as if touched by ripples of water. But they could not be stars, because they moved—slowly, almost imperceptibly—toward the southwest corner of town, where they already formed a flickering, roving cluster. I walked on, perplexed, and only when I reached the entrance to the cemetery and saw the people filing in, holding their candles aloft, did I remember that it was the first of November, the day of the dead. For some minutes I stood beyond the reach of the candlelight, watching the slow procession and the lights gathering and vanishing among the tombs. Then I turned east to avoid them.

The air smelled of wood smoke and rain. I took the main road to Xinia's house, and when I saw the front door closed, the thought of opening it seemed too great an effort. The door at the side of the house stood open, and I walked in through the kitchen and then into the living room, where pale lights on the end tables made the wooden chairs, the floorboards, and the rafters all yellow. She must not have recognized me, because she stood in the door of her room staring out at me with a frozen look. I was still wrapped in the blankets and I'd emptied the bag the night before to warm my head with it. When I turned to look at her she made a choking noise and took a step forward. "Hilario," she said, and the boy came to the doorway and she said something to him and after glancing at me he ran out of the house through the side door. I let my knees sag and sighed and felt the floor underneath me.

THE CHURCH we went to in Palo Alto was in the hills, which during the summer droughts broke out, every few years, in widespread fires. Even during the months of rain, the world outside seemed suffused with a pale sunlight that the brass-fitted door, swinging on its soundless hinges, extinguished in a brief sweep.

The chapel smelled of floor cleaner and dust. A triangle of glass in the wooden dome of the ceiling dropped a shaft of light on the altar. The pews were blackened with use, and when we sat in the back I slid on their polished surface, resting my head on Mamá's lap and listening to the voices echo off the walls. You sat solemnly next to her, listening to the sermon. I flipped through the hymnal, hearing the lyrics in my mind to a single melody of slow, dirge-like chanting.

In the confessional Father Joe's face was gray and impassive. "Forgive me, Father, for I have sinned," I said.

He leaned in close to me and put his hand on my forehead. "Don't think about it now," he said lightly.

I shook my head and pushed his hand away. "You must hear my confession," I said. I felt as though I wanted to weep but my throat and eyes were dry. "I'm sick, Father."

I thought I heard him laugh. "Yes, you are."

"I made mistakes. I wanted it to be different—" He reached for my forehead again and put his hand against it. His palm was cool and damp. I took a deep breath. "And I'm still here. I'm still here." The thought made my heart break. I felt a pain so sharp that my chest seemed to split open. "Forgive me, Father."

Father Joe shook his head. "You have to drink this water," he said. "And then you're having some soup." He turned to look over his shoulder, his hand still pressed to my head. "Luz," he called.

I tried to push him away. "Father, I've lied. About everything."

"Drink, Amán." I had no energy to resist him. I drank the water he held up to me and then closed my mouth around the spoon. The clear broth tasted of cilantro. He brought the spoon to my mouth again and again, and I fell asleep with the feeling of the spoon hitting my teeth.

When I awoke I was lying on the altar. The sun came through the skylight and made a triangle of light on my stomach. Two boys rested their chins on the edge by my feet. I didn't recognize them. I thought one of them might be me, but I wasn't sure. I stared at them and they stared back. There were no boys, I realized, but only a mirror: a split mirror, one side reflecting the other, both sides reflecting me. I moved my head experimentally. The two sides of the mirror conferred with each other in whispers. I waited for them to decide. They could do as I did or not; I didn't care. If they didn't, all the better. I could get up and leave the altar and leave them there, their flat faces trained on the cut-out sun. The boys blinked and looked at me and one of them tried to smile. "Are you better?" he whispered.

A step sounded behind them in the darkness. They started. I felt a spasm of anxiety and tried to lift my head, to look into the darkness behind them, but I could see nothing.

"Quick, hide," one said to the other. They ducked their heads and vanished.

WHEN I AWOKE again only one of them was there. He sat in a chair by the side of the bed. He smiled, seeing my eyes open, and leaned forward. This time there was no mistaking him: my son, Nítido. I hadn't recognized him because my memory was slipping. Just a moment earlier I'd thought he was someone else. It wouldn't be long before I opened my eyes to find a nameless boy whose face meant nothing. In time, he would speak to me and see in my face that I thought him a stranger. There would be a loss, and it wouldn't be mine. I wouldn't miss all the things I was forgetting, but he would, and remembering them himself would not restore them. Only he would have them, and then they would be as if they'd never been. They would be, in truth, his inventions. He would be left alone in every moment but the present.

"Don't cry, don't cry," he whispered. "You'll be better soon."

"I won't," I said. "I've already forgotten almost everything."

His face was troubled. "You'll be fine."

"When I've forgotten everything," I said, "you'll still remember. It won't be the same, but it'll be something." He sat back, his expression uncertain. "Just pretend I remember it."

He shook his head. "You should rest," he said.

"I don't want to fall asleep. I forget something each time I fall asleep."

He touched my forehead and got up and walked toward the door.

"Nítido," I said.

He stared at me from the doorway. "I'll be right back," he whispered.

I listened to the rain beating against the window and I knew that the lawn would be under an inch of water and the bird feeder would be clogged with wet seeds. I would be awake only at moments, and I might not remember the waking moments. There was no way to be sure, I realized, struggling with my heavy eyes, that this wouldn't be the last thing I would remember—or that I would be awake for. I couldn't say, then, whether they were the same thing. I might be awake but not remember, and I might remember but not be awake; the possibilities confused me. But I could still hear the rain, so I hadn't fallen asleep. Or perhaps I had fallen asleep and was only remembering the rain. There was no way to be certain, but I knew what would happen. When the rain stopped, the mist would hang over the trees for days and then the sun would break through weakly, as if reaching for us at the bottom of the ocean.

DR. ESTRADA had left aspirin by the side of the table. I was in the back room of Xinia's house. Claudio and Hilario sat on the floor at the foot of the bed with their backs to me. I could hear them talking in whispers. The red curtains were closed, bleeding a pink sunlight into the room. I lifted my hand and looked at it. My fingers were thin and strangely pinched. I tried to sit up and as I did the two boys turned around to stare at me.

"Hi," I said.

"Hi," Claudio said. Hilario nodded. They moved cautiously, each taking a corner on the far end of the bed, watching me.

"I guess I'm better," I said.

"Estrada said you had amoebas," Claudio said. "He says it's something Americans get. I didn't know you were American."

Hilario looked at him. "Only his neck up. Xinia said."

"You think the amoebas were in his head?"

Hilario shrugged. "Maybe."

"I think they got to all of me," I said.

Claudio smiled. "You have no more muscles."

"Father Amán." They looked up quickly. Luz stood in the doorway. "How are you?"

"All right."

"Help me bring the lunch in." She left the room and the two of them left after her, both talking at once.

I'd been sick for nine days. They'd kept me at Xinia's to be near Estrada. When he came in that evening he said the only consequence was the lost weight. "Are you sure it was amoebas?" I asked him.

"Why?"

"I thought it might be vertigo. I've had it before. I get dehydrated."

"Might be. But I think amoebas."

I'd planned on spending only a few days in Río Roto, and I'd already lost ten days, but Estrada told me I would need at least another week or two to recuperate. I had to follow his recommendation, regardless of how much it delayed me, because the sickness had left me debilitated. On the second day of my recovery I was able to get out of bed with Xinia's help and for a while we sat on wooden chairs on the back porch, looking out over the flat expanse of grass between her house and the doctor's. I'd thought she wouldn't know what to do with Hilario, but I was wrong. She watched him appear and disappear throughout the day without concern, and when she held on to him too long, her arms folded over his slim back, Hilario stood with his head resting on her shoulder, waiting patiently. In no small part she owed it to Santos, who according to Hilario had been telling him for years who he was, promising him that someone would come. We didn't talk about Naranjo until the third day I was well. It was me who brought it up.

"I'm sorry I didn't meet you on the way back," I said.

She shrugged. We were sitting behind the house again and she looked out over the grass without changing her expression. "I figured you'd want to stay for a while," she said.

I faltered. "Did you?"

She glanced at me. "I didn't think they would recognize you, but I knew." I was silent as she continued to look away. "From Santos."

I was still not entirely well. At times I would feel waves of dizziness, as I did at that moment. You will say that I shouldn't have been surprised, but I hadn't yet had time to think through everything that Santos could have said. "I have a confession to make," I said.

She exhaled quietly and gave me a long look. "Don't. I know."

I felt the blood rush to my face. "What do you know?"

"Who you are."

I looked up at the grass where a cow made her way purposefully toward the doctor's house. The sky over the river was marked by a single cloud that seemed to remain stationary. "You don't think— It wasn't wrong, then, you think?"

She didn't answer for a moment. "That's not the word," she finally said.

The cow reached Estrada's house and stretched its head in through one of the windows. After a moment there was a distant shout and the cow kicked away and trotted off from the window. "I'd like to explain it to you," I said.

"Another time," she said quietly.

I hesitated. "But I'm feeling much better."

"If you're better we should try walking."

I didn't say anything. She was looking away from me, her expression calm or uninterested, I wasn't sure. "Why not," I said.

She went into the house and came back with a walking stick, which she handed me. I pushed myself out of the chair and leaned on the walking stick as the blood rushed to my head. Xinia held my arm until the dizziness passed. Then we made our way down the steps and across the field. The cows, clotted with flies, ignored us as we walked by.

✦ ✦ ✦

FOR THE NEXT FEW DAYS I rested in the mornings while Xinia and Eliseo taught. When I felt up to it I sat in the doorway of my room, listening to them as they read—now in Spanish, now in K'iche'—until the slow, soporific repetition of words made me nod off. But most of the time I went to Xinia's bedroom, which was quieter than mine, and slept. When I couldn't sleep I lay in bed, watching the red curtains move softly against the window frame. The day after we spoke on her porch, it only occurred to me to open the wardrobe in the bedroom because she'd left it partway open. I'd assumed when I first saw it that it served as a dresser. I was surprised to see books through the narrow crack, and I reached in to open the wardrobe without thinking. Some of the books she evidently required for teaching, and the textbooks I recognized as the kind that would have been assigned during her year at the university. But on the top shelf sat a number of books that I hadn't expected to see: several English grammar guides, a Spanish-English dictionary, and a small collection of classic works in English. She had *Ethan Frome* and *Lord of the Flies* and *1984*, among others. For several minutes I simply stood, staring at them, my head spinning. I thought back to the first time I'd seen Xinia, crouching behind the sacristy to examine my books in their broken boxes. She had tried again when the books were on my desk. There was no excuse I could think of for my blindness. I reached out numbly for *1984*, opened it, and glanced at the cramped annotations in the margins. She'd read it carefully. I put it back on the shelf and mechanically opened the composition notebook that sat next to it. Her brief essays in English were graded by an instructor with check marks and plus signs. The marks improved farther into the notebook. Xinia's phrasing was awkward and unsophisticated, but her English was doubtlessly solid and almost always correct. She wrote well enough to compose a memo or a letter; certainly she knew enough English to read one.

It took a great effort to reach up and replace the notebook on the upper shelf. I closed the wardrobe carefully and moved toward the bed. My feet dragged; I felt incredibly heavy, as if all my blood had suddenly turned to sand. I had a similar feeling in my eyes—they felt choked and salty, as if I'd fallen headlong into a powerful wave.

ON MY FOURTEENTH BIRTHDAY I was expecting a bicycle and couldn't hide my disappointment when you stacked three rectangular boxes of diminishing size on the breakfast table. The bottom box, the largest, was full of paperbacks that you'd picked out from the used bookstore. The middle box contained an enormous, somewhat worn dictionary that I used all throughout high school and then took with me to college. The last—and I'm sorry to say, the most infuriating—had two small, clothbound books that each came with a lock and key. I don't know what I was expecting: something else. In any case I didn't appreciate your proposal that we write in the books on alternate weeks, so that when they were full, the books would represent two long, different, but continuous conversations. I'm aware that I agreed to it with little grace, and it's difficult to say who was more aggravated—myself for not getting a bicycle or you for having given me a present at all.

You tried to begin the writing with me again a few months later after giving me a bicycle for Christmas, and feeling conciliatory I tried it, writing a page in my uneven hand about what I'd done that day. You elatedly traded books with me at the end of the week and said nothing about my insignificant efforts, and I attempted to read your five pages of tiny script about the color of the desert at night and the sounds made by the quail and the beauty of tumbleweeds. I think—I'm sure, because I read it again later and hardly recognized any of it—that I didn't read past the second page. Nor did I know what to write in response to your meditations, so when you handed me back the other book and I told you I hadn't done it yet, you smiled woodenly with such unconvincing indifference that I had to look away and put it out of my mind at once.

I found both of them alongside your other journals when I returned to Oregon, and for a moment, as I struggled to open them with the rusty keys, I hoped that you might have written more in them despite my lack of motivation. But either because the failure of the project depressed you or because you felt there was no need to lock up your solitary thoughts, you never wrote beyond the first exchange. I'd always assumed that the silence you and Mamá maintained about your past was of mutual consent, and it never occurred to me until I saw the locked journals again that you might have wanted to speak to me, and that you kept quiet simply out of respect for her wishes.

Perhaps if I'd read past the second page in the notebook when I was fourteen I would have responded. But I doubt that even then I would have felt any stirrings of the curiosity that seized me so entirely years later. By then, the expression of it was incomprehensible to you, like everything else. I did try a few times to ask you questions, and you stared at me blankly, sweetly, even, as if touched that I'd come around and content to reply in silence. The opportunity to write back to you was long lost.

After the second page the description of the desert trailed off into something different.

The dry air makes my throat itch. The earth seems dead, stretching out in every direction like a dusty slab. When the sun sets the world goes blind. On the mountain, in places like Naranjo, it's completely different. The ground turns in its sleep, stretches, and comes awake after dark. It sits back and watches. I can hardly remember anymore what it's like to walk through the trees and feel the wet leaves on me. To put one's hand down on the grass and feel it yield, as warm as flesh from the sun. At night the warmth seeps away, drained into the ground, and the cold wet air breaks against one's face. I would walk out then, while you slept, walking and walking. There would be no moon. I would walk blindly, my feet seeing for me. On the road I walked on and on. When the clouds broke and the stars came into view I sat down—they seemed to press so heavily. Then I felt tired enough to sleep. I turned back and watched the trees turn gray.

DURING THE FIRST WEEK of my recovery Aurelio often sat with me in the evenings, looking out over the trampled pasture behind Xinia's house. Cruz and Sabina had moved to Murcia. They lived under a tarp that tented the foundation while Cruz and Aurelio finished putting the house together. After we'd been sitting in silence for half an hour on the first night, he pulled a toothbrush from the pocket of his pants and spent some minutes passing it from hand to hand, as if getting a feel for its dimensions. I asked him if the cows all slept in the barn by the doctor's house and he laughed and said, "Yes, Estrada's clinic."

"Is that what it is?"

He nodded. "Years ago. He gave it to Xinia for the cows when she started the school. He gave her more than one cow, too."

A white light came from the front room of the doctor's house. Estrada had told me that at night he read aloud to himself; perhaps after playing the guitar for an hour he found the silence too weighty.

I heard a soft brushing sound and glanced around quickly, thinking of moths. But it was only Aurelio, scrubbing his fingers gently with the brush. He pretended not to see me staring, and I caught myself and looked away. He brushed for hours, first spitting on the brush or holding it out in the rain when the night was wet and then working away at the black lines that laced his nails and filled every deep wrinkle. He liked to tell me about what he'd done in the cemetery, which part he'd cleared, which stones he'd unearthed under the moss. And on the days he spent with Cruz he told me how the house was coming along, the cement they poured, the bars for the windows, the floor tiles he'd bought himself in Rabinal. They'd left their house of a few hours in Río Roto intact, though they might have pillaged it for supplies, because none of them could bring themselves to tear out a single tile. Aurelio told me on the first night that he'd collected the furniture, and that the rest of the house would remain untouched.

"She won't go back there," Aurelio said.

"Sabina? I don't blame her."

He shook his head, smiling. "You don't know her yet. Sabina went with me to pick the things up. She doesn't think like that. I mean Sonia."

"Well, she has good reason, too."

He ran the toothbrush over his knuckle, still smiling. "She's all worries. Can't believe how on the outside they look the same. Just like Sonia looked twenty years ago."

For a moment he didn't speak. On the other side of the field the doctor turned out his light, and the sound of the churning river struck me, though it had been there all along. A fringe of blue sky gleamed dully between the black of the hills and the black of the sky overhead, as bleak and uncertain as a light underwater. "But she's like me," Aurelio said then. "Doesn't talk about it." He put the toothbrush away and settled his hands on his lap. "Harder to do anything for her that way."

That night, after Aurelio left, I lay in bed listening to the cries of the insects that moved past the window. A cockroach in the wardrobe scrabbled along the wooden door. I got up and walked barefoot to the front of the house. Xinia always left her door open so she could see into Hilario's room across the hall. I stood in the doorway, trying to make out her shape in the folds of the bedclothes. She slept facing the wall, as she had in Naranjo. I could hear her easy breathing when I reached the edge of the bed. Her hair fanned out over the blankets, the only dark spot on the white bed, in the white room. Kneeling by the bed I leaned forward until my cheek was against her hair. I wasn't looking for anything but the familiarity of it, the smell of smoke, the elusive warmth. Then I stood up suddenly, reminded of how I'd sometimes seen Mamá, during the last year, sitting watchfully by your bed. But Xinia hadn't forgotten me yet, I said to myself, as I stopped to look at her once more from the doorway.

Nineteen

Since i'd left her on Bainbridge Island, Mamá had sent eight letters, and they'd all reached Río Roto while I was away. Tomás Morelio said they'd arrived out of order and he couldn't promise me there hadn't been others. She sent the first letter in August and the last one was dated September 27, the day I left for Naranjo. She had been careful not to ask me anything about exactly where I was or what I was doing. The closest she came was to say, "I hope you found a nice school and that it hasn't been too hard in Spanish." She told me of the people she'd met on the island, of the landlord who'd given her a cocker spaniel for her birthday, of how she was getting around on a bicycle that she'd bought from a fireman, of how her hip had begun hurting too much to use the bicycle, of how she'd read that keeping her mind active would prevent memory loss. She acknowledged the letters I'd sent by saying, "Thank you for writing and I'm glad to hear you're well."

The last and shortest letter said of herself only that she'd taken to walking the dog by the water in the mornings and that the weather had grown colder. The remainder of the letter, however much it preserved her usual tone, took me by surprise by touching on the one subject she always avoided. "I never thought it was a good idea for you to go, and I still wish you hadn't. Knowing you are there has made me think about things I haven't thought of for years. I think if you hadn't gone they wouldn't even have come to mind. Now I have to think about them whether I want to or not. And with Diego gone, who am I going to talk to? Not people here. When your father was alive it never bothered me, knowing people knew nothing about me. It's strange how it happens. I don't mean that I am lonely, I don't want you to think that. But when you come in December you will tell me all about your trip, and we will talk about how things have changed since the last time I was there."

Had there been a telephone in Río Roto I would have called her, whatever the expense. After reading the letters I sat at the table in Xinia's kitchen and wrote her a short reply. I didn't want to tell her that I'd been sick, and I couldn't make up my mind to say anything about Naranjo, so I wrote only that I had many things to tell her and that I would see her in December.

Tencha told me that you'd slept in the park across from the woman's house, and the following morning you stopped by to see the niche marked "Vira" once more before going back to Naranjo. The following weekend you and Iris were married and the week after that you went against your will to the house in the city and proposed, as Iris had urged you to, that she take your mother's place. The woman even agreed to take you on as a gardener on the condition that you and Mamá share the salary.

As she pointed out, she would have the additional cost of having to provide more meals, and she couldn't be expected to give away something for nothing.

Every three months you and Mamá returned to Naranjo. You learned to drive and drove Julieta's car when she had to leave the city. The two of you shared the housework and Mamá worked in the kitchen. Julieta provided uniforms, so you only had to buy shoes, socks, and underclothes. It seemed likely that Julieta had gotten along with your mother because she too was a widow, since it was the only similarity between them that you could perceive. The old woman wore tiny high heels that clattered on the tiles of the corridor. In the afternoons she sat in the dark anteroom and drank a glass of whiskey with ice. Occasionally she asked you and Mamá to eat with her, though when she did, she ate in silence and only looked up at the end to excuse herself. Lying with Mamá in your narrow room's single bed, you could hear Julieta's radio playing on the other side of the house until midnight. She listened to classical music and call-in talk shows that gave advice to the lovelorn.

Julieta's only son lived in Texas and called her twice a month. During these conversations she said very little; she held the phone to her ear with both hands and made exclamations of appreciation and surprise. She asked questions about whether it was cold and what he was eating. This stranger's books, which Julieta seemed to regard as family heirlooms, came into your hands by chance. Julieta admitted that they were rotting, and by agreeing to let them be sunned and aired she unwittingly allowed them to circulate from her son's old bedroom, to the patio tiles, to the narrow back room, and back to her son's shelf. The books in themselves were valueless: cheap textbooks, grammar guides, primers, and outdated reference books. You and Mamá worked your way through them and spent some of your salary on pencils and lined paper and note-books for practicing cursive. By the third year you'd finished the books in the bedroom and begun using the library.

Julieta, who had seemed so accommodating in comparison with what you'd heard of other domestic employers, lost her patience when Mamá told her that she had become pregnant. She didn't run a charity, she argued, and when the baby was born she would be feeding three people and paying as much for less work. For weeks she maintained that she would dismiss you both at the sixth month, and she interviewed women from the city who stood in the dark anteroom, watching Mamá cautiously as she moved through the corridors. Perhaps the anxiety of losing her job was too great a strain, or perhaps, as you noted to Ten-cha, Mamá didn't eat enough during those months. For whatever reason, Mamá miscarried in the third month.

Julieta at first appeared willing to dismiss you both regardless, because Mamá remained bedridden for more than a week. Tencha told me how you made up for it by doing all the work yourself and how, if you showed any signs of being dejected, Julieta would become offended and point out how fortunate you were to have an employer who let her servants work from bed. After some time, Mamá recuperated her physical health but seemed, in other ways, altered for the worse. Perhaps she'd begun planning for the baby too soon. From the very first she started knitting clothes and blankets; and convinced that it would be a girl, she'd saved money for a pair of earrings—tiny gold studs that fit on a fingertip. You often found her in the back room, contemplating the unfinished pieces of knitting like treasures. On the first trip back to Naranjo, you took all of it back with you and left it with Tencha for safekeeping.

It seemed too good to be true when, the following year, Mamá realized she was once again pregnant. Tencha surmised from the thinness of your face alone how you ensured that Mamá maintained enough weight. You did admit to her, at least, that you'd managed to reorganize the work so that Mamá did less without Julieta knowing. This time when she found out, Julieta didn't threaten dismissal, but she did argue that she would have to lower your wages. Since you were still in debt to Julieta for Mamá's hospital bills, lower wages meant that the debt would not be paid off, and there would be nothing to rely on for future expenses. For some months, you told Tencha, it almost seemed as though returning to Naranjo would be the better alternative. You'd wanted to return at the beginning of the pregnancy but Mamá, inexplicably, said she couldn't go back to living in Naranjo. From the way you described it, Tencha felt that Mamá had picked up a dislike for the way people there walked barefoot and smelled of smoke and slept with only straw mats between themselves and the dirt floor.

Toward the end of Mamá's pregnancy, you persuaded Julieta to keep her on with the same wages. By letting you go elsewhere to live with the child, Julieta would economize on your meals, and when she needed you for extra work she would pay you by the hour. As was to be expected, the place you found cost as much as Mamá's entire salary, and whatever money you had for meals came from the extra money you could earn from week to week. At the end of the second month you had to acknowledge that the baby wasn't gaining enough weight. In a sense you were lucky, because Hortensia was still breast-feeding Helbert. You returned to Naranjo, and Tencha took care of both children. For a time, Tencha and Josef, and Ester and Noé were all like second parents. When I wasn't with you, Noé took me everywhere; he had called me by a nickname, "Todito." You—and I—saw Mamá every four weeks, and just as you had in the past, you waited on the last Saturday of every month by waking up early and standing on the main road, taking a few steps every few minutes until you were halfway to the bus stop and could finally see her coming around the corner.

Tencha noticed when, during the second year, you began mentioning the old woman's son in Texas. Having read his books, you no doubt began to speculate, imagining someone with no more than what you had in your head, making his way in Texas. As soon as she'd gotten hold of the idea, Mamá was even more desperate to leave than you were. Tencha thought you talked about it—as a recurring fantasy—to prolong the Saturday evenings at the end of the month. You had no sense of cost, of distance, of what the places were like. It never occurred to Tencha to take the plan seriously. Even when Mamá said, at the end of August, "I have to tell you something, Tencha," she'd listened to her talk about Los Angeles without the slightest concern. When Tencha asked good-humoredly how you would get there, Mamá shrugged and said you would take the bus. Nevertheless, halfway through September, you stopped by to tell Tencha you were going to the city. You were taking me with you, and you needed the gold studs that Tencha had in safekeeping.

"Don't sell them yet," she'd urged you. "There might be another girl—later on."

She said she felt a little frightened by the way you looked at her then, saying, "I won't sell them, Hortensia. But give them to me anyhow." It was the thing she worried about most when you and I didn't return from the city the next day.

Tencha knew for certain that you'd left the country only

months later, when she found a crumpled ball of paper at the bottom of the sugar sack. When she smoothed it out the magazine photograph showed a silver city chiseled out of a crimson sunset. On the back you'd written "love, Diego, Iris, Nítido." They all took it hard, Noé especially. Hortensia went to see Doña Julieta in the city, who told her that Iris had disappeared without giving notice. She spoke to her on the doorstep, the door open only a few inches. "After everything I did for them," she said bitterly. "I don't want to see anyone from your little shit village ever again."

XINIA HAD ASKED me if I wanted books brought from the vestry, and I'd told her I didn't feel like reading. But I did want to pick up some of your journals, and when I felt well enough to walk I went to the vestry on my own, stopping several times along the way to talk to people I hadn't seen since I'd left. Perhaps they felt sorry, seeing me as wasted as I was, because many who hadn't been speaking to me when I left for Naranjo stopped to ask me how I was and to say how glad they were to see me again. "Amán," the blind grocer said when I stopped to rest in the shade of his awning, "we've missed you Sundays."

"I'm glad only Sundays."

He laughed, his white hair falling over his eyes. He reached out for me with a wrinkled hand and patted my back. "Have a coffee," he said.

"On the way back. If I stop now I won't get there."

"I know how that is. On the way back, then."

While I'd been lying sick at Xinia's house, perhaps still under the influence of the fever, I'd finally concluded that there was only one way to read your journals. The absence of dates, the varying repetitions, the precise but disorganized descriptions all required a particular kind of reading. I couldn't be sure that it was the reading you intended, but it was the only reading I felt was right.

The section I was looking for was at the beginning of one of the newer notebooks:

Little of the ruined convent remains standing. A vaulted chapel, a couple courtyards with crumbling stone fountains. The bougainvillea roams wildly over the broken staircases. The nuns' cells are slim stone niches arranged in a circle, like spokes on a wheel, under what was once a dome. Each has a single tiny window, barely large enough for a hand to slip through. The convent storeroom is by the entrance to the rear garden. A narrow curving set of stone steps, and then the dark storeroom, under-ground. Enormous, almost the size of the chapel. The air is musty and cool. At the center of the circular room, a tall pillar that rises to meet the curved ceiling. The floor is packed dirt. A window in the back, high up, cuts into the wall. The light from it is pale green, filtered by the grass. Standing near the center, by the pillar, there is near silence. No sound from beyond the storeroom reaches me—it is a void. Centuries ago, there would have been the soft rustle of skirts, the nuns moving mutely through the room and up the steps. My steps echo as I walk to the wall. From that white, curved wall, a whisper travels across the room, from one ear to another, invisibly. The sound is incredible, perfectly clear, defying under-standing. There is no explaining the wall's mysterious properties. It is as though the person at such a distance and hidden from sight is right there, whispering into your ear.

You may never have meant for the passage to be read. You may have meant it only for yourself. But it meant something to me nonetheless. I understood the amazement you described—the experience of wonder, the thrill of finding something inexplicable—

as if you had related it to me in person, with your eyes alight and your voice trembling. Something similar had happened to me at the San Francisco Columbarium, which I visited when parts of the building had yet to be renovated. Condensation clouded the glass panes of the niches, and the fabric lining the interiors had shredded and curled. I thought the fantastic growths that trailed over the urns were spiderwebs, and only when I read a pamphlet on the renovation project did I realize that the omnipresent veils of pale green and blue were mold. The older niches, from the late nineteenth century, contained only the stained urns, the rotting fabric, and the occasional etched placard: "In the midst of life we are in death." If their occupants had suffered from an exaggerated austerity, the inhabitants of the more recent niches—most dated from the 1980s—had embraced the opposite extreme: they seemed burdened by a fevered impulse of accumulation, an inability to disconnect from the frivolity of life. Perfume bottles, teddy bears, a tape measure, a whisk, ceramic figurines, costume jewelry, and any number of faded photographs, the people in them frozen in extreme gaiety, filled the recent niches.

I'd found the Columbarium door open and no one inside. I went up from one circular floor to the next, until I reached the top floor, which had no view into the central dome. A woman there kept a journal on a string in which she wrote letters to her father. He sat looking out from the photograph, seated on a motorcycle, grinning and raising his right thumb. She left him unopened bottles of beer that stood, dusty and warm, just out of reach of his niche. Toward the top of the building the heat was oppressive; I worked my way downward again, stopping on each floor. I'd wanted to test the Columbarium's unique acoustics: the circular walls enabled sound to carry from one side of the building to the other. But I'd come by

myself, and there was no one I could send to the other end of the
building. I was leaning in toward one of the glass-paned niches,
examining a collection of seashells, when I suddenly heard a voice
that seemed to come from the niche in front of me. "It isn't here.
It's farther along." I stood back, stunned, and looked around.
There was no one in sight. Leaning back in toward the niche, I
picked up the voice again: "can't put in anything valuable. Only
little things that meant something to them. Look at that." The
voice was so clear, so immediate, that it took me several seconds to
realize what I was experiencing. I spent a quarter of an hour walking around to the other side of the building, to see if I might catch
a glimpse of my invisible interlocutor. But the building seemed as
empty as I'd found it.

Even the passages in your journals that I cannot match exactly
with experiences of my own have a definite significance. Though
in most cases it is hard to place them in context, they are not
lacking in meaning as a consequence. They have the quality of
the voice at the Columbarium: an immediacy and vividness over-
coming all distance. Your passages sound as though you were
really present, reading aloud from over my shoulder.

I HADN'T PLANNED on taking up my responsibilities at the
church again, but when Xinia told me that people had been
waiting at the confessional almost every day since my return, I
reconsidered. "You think I should go?" I asked her.

She looked at me and said without sarcasm, "If you feel up
to it."

I felt well enough on Tuesday and I made my way to the
church after lunch. I left the door open and sat in the cool

wooden box, resting my head against the seatback. I woke up to a chair scraping over the floor and I saw the grocer's wife settling in next to the confessional. She smiled at me and sat down and I opened the oval shutter and looked at her through the broken screen. "Father Amán," she said. "I'm glad you're feeling better."

She put her swollen ankles out next to each other, her feet pointing up, and fanned herself with her handkerchief. I offered her water and we both drank from the thermos cup. She told me that the doctor had advised her to drink ten glasses of water a day in order to lose weight. The sweat clung in beads to her upper lip. I stood up and dragged the fan over to where we were sitting. I angled it toward us and flipped it on.

Dalia told me that she worried about her husband's condition. "Blindness isn't usually contagious, is it, Father?"

"No, it's not."

"I know," she said, as if the fact disappointed her. "Nevertheless, it sometimes is."

"I suppose if it results from a contagious illness, then it could be," I said. "But Arturo has cataracts, doesn't he?"

She shook her head. "I think I caught whatever he has." She patted her forehead with the handkerchief and covered her eyes with it briefly.

I nodded. "Your vision is failing you?"

"Yes, Father. I'm sure I'm going blind. It's hard to describe. All I can say is that it's like a cloud. All around the edges, a cloud."

"Things look different?"

"Not everything. Details. They blur. Sometimes colors are hard. It's not all the time. At night is when it's worst. The other night I looked over at Arturo sitting in his chair, listening to the radio. He looked like he was in a snow cloud—white all over. The skin of his face a little green. I felt too afraid to say anything. He didn't move, he only sat there, listening to the radio, and I thought for a moment: When did he last speak? Is he alive? And I closed my eyes to clear them, and when I opened them again he turned toward me and said, 'Dalia?' with his chin in the air. He looked the same as always. But I knew the cloud was still there. Only on the other side of my eye."

"Is that where it goes?"

"I think so."

"It's a terrible thing to lose one's vision."

"Yes, Father." She looked into her lap.

I had on a few occasions caught Mamá, when she sat next to you with her knitting or stood beside your chair, looking at you with something very close to envy. She could often seem wistful or frustrated, which didn't surprise me, but there were times when it seemed for all the world as though she was begging you to switch places with her. At the time I'd been unable to understand it. "I know," I said to Dalia. "The person who loses his sight loses a whole world, and the people around him lose all that he saw in it."

"Yes, Father." She pressed her eyes with the handkerchief.

"They feel so lucky to see things still. But they feel so put-upon by the very things they have to see. He escapes into darkness. The others go on, feeling guilty every time they look at him, wondering what it would be like to follow him. Into that sightless place."

"Yes, Father," she whispered.

"It's enough to make you want to close your eyes for good."

She bit her lip and nodded. I handed the cup around to her

and she poured some of the water onto her open handkerchief and then pressed it against her face with her fingertips. Under the white cotton her eye sockets made dark shadows. She pulled it away and held it to her neck and as she handed the cup back to me her fingers trembled.

I BROUGHT two history books written in fairly elementary English back from the vestry. When Xinia and I were alone in the house, I brought them out to her and put them between us on the kitchen table. She glanced at them and continued cleaning the pineapple she had half-dismembered on the cutting board.

"I thought you might want some new books in English," I said.

She looked at me quickly and then half-smiled. "You saw them."

"You can't have learned to read Orwell in one year of university."

She shook her head. "I started out studying on my own. Then I took an advanced course."

"Just because?"

She brushed all the pieces of hard husk from the pineapple onto the table and stacked the cleaned slices on a plate. "I had plans to keep studying, but they didn't work out."

"You took up teaching."

"Yes."

I nodded. "The same thing happened to me." She put the knife down, cleaned her hands on a dishcloth, and looked up at me attentively. "I was planning to go on with my studies," I said. "Instead I became a teacher. But it was for the best; in the end I loved teaching."

She nodded. "Me too," she said. "Now I wouldn't think of going back to school. I would miss teaching." She folded her hands and spoke quietly. "You must miss it."

"When I was with my parents, all last year, I didn't miss it so much. But now I do." I didn't tell her that what I missed wasn't so much teaching as the time when I was teaching: you were still well and I had found something to do that did not yet feel meaningless. Xinia didn't say anything. She sat watching me. "So everyone here knows?" I finally asked.

A slow smile crept over her face. "No, you haven't understood at all." She looked at me thoughtfully. "Maybe one or two people guessed. I never mentioned it to anyone."

I shook my head. "You had every reason to."

She looked out through the doorway to the patch of dirt where a group of hens were quietly picking their way through a smattering of corn. When she spoke, her words seemed unrelated to my question, as though she were voicing something that had suddenly occurred to her. "When I was first getting to know you I often thought about something that happened last November. Father Antonio had already been gone about two years. There was a woman named Laura, who lived on the edge of town. When she was younger she lived with her uncle, but then her uncle died and she was left by herself. Sometimes men would go see her; it was an isolated place, off the road that goes down to the river. No one else would have anything to do with her. When she got pregnant I would see her on Fridays walking into town. Everyone in the plaza would sit and watch her. In November she died giving birth. We all knew, but no one went to her. No one laid her out or held a wake. If there'd been a priest at the sacristy—even the most incompetent priest—it would have been unimaginable.

There would have been steps we had to take. Women from the church would have gone to wash her and change her and light candles. Someone would have had the task of carrying her to the cemetery, putting her in the earth. When a person with friends and family dies, these things happen of themselves. But if you are alone," she paused, "they do not. Something else has to make them happen."

"But still," I said. And then I paused, reflecting. "You mean what you did for me, you would have done for anyone?"

She looked at me, turning away from the doorway, and put her hand out across the narrow table. I took her hand in both of mine. "When you told me your father had died," she said, "I knew you would be all right." I didn't say anything. "You must have come for a reason," she went on. I nodded. She held my hand tightly. Without dropping it she stood up and walked around the table and stood behind me. She bent forward and pressed her cheek against mine. I held her hand against my chest. Her hair fell over my face and I lifted my hand to press it against my mouth. As I turned in my chair her hair slid away and I found her eyes only an inch away.

I GAVE my last sermon in Río Roto that week, a short sermon that I wrote myself, based on two lines from 1 Corinthians: "There are, it may be, so many kinds of voices in the world, and none of them is without signification. Therefore if I know not the meaning of the voice, I shall be unto him that speaketh a barbarian, and he that speaketh shall be a barbarian unto me."

With an apology to the congregation, I also read from the diary of Christopher Columbus. From the first I'd been struck by the peculiar wonder mixed with avarice that marked Columbus's entries, the strange sorrow that he felt—"the greatest sorrow in the world"—at realizing that the trees and birds he saw on his first voyage were unfamiliar to him. His descriptions of the people he encountered were even more moving. "Also I do not know the language," he wrote, as he explained why he could not delay over-much in one harbor or another, "and the people of these lands do not understand me nor do I, nor anyone else that I have with me, them. And many times I understand one thing said by these Indians that I bring for another, its contrary; nor do I trust them much, because many times they have tried to flee. But now, pleasing Our Lord, I will see the most that I can and little by little I will progress in understanding and acquaintance."

Who is the barbarian, I asked, when two people do not understand each other? It was no coincidence, I said, that people who spoke different languages often began, in those first moments of attempted communication, by naming themselves. Placing a hand on the heart or chest, we repeat our names, as if providing an anchor for whatever incomprehensible swell of language might afterward wash over us. The other person repeats our name and says his own. And we are suddenly holding two ends of the same line. We can bear to leave many other aspects of our-selves unintelligible, inexpressible, and unknown, but we have difficulty cutting loose from that most basic description of our-selves. And in remembering others, I said, recalling a name can be the means of holding that line to preserve ourselves: a way to stay afloat.

As I read the names aloud after the sermon, the congregation sat attentively just as it had in the weeks before I'd gone to Naranjo. The list of names was almost exactly the same as it had been on those occasions, but to me it appeared very different. I was able in most cases to recollect who had given me the names, and I seemed to see each person in the congregation accompanied by those he or she was remembering. Toward the middle of the hour, when the room had settled into its most profound stillness, I read your name, dwelling on it no more and no less than on the others. I understood, hearing it hang in the air before the lectern, how one might wait an entire week simply to hear a name spoken into such silence.

TOMÁS MORELIO chose to come by on Sunday afternoon, when he knew Xinia would be away. He placed a tin of teabags on the table between us and asked how I was doing. I made the tea he'd brought and gave him coffee from the stove and we sat over the table, myself hunched and Tomás straight with his elbows carefully at his sides. The tea tasted like rock moss. He watched me sip and I told him how good it was. He said it would clean my system out. I nodded. Before taking the envelope out of his shirt pocket he reminded me good-humoredly but firmly that I hadn't yet been to his house for dinner and that he expected me to accept his invitation once I felt well. I agreed and apologized. He waved his hand and repeated that he and his wife looked forward to having me as their guest. Then he took the letter out of his shirt pocket and slid it across the table. His face lit up as though he'd just thought of something.

"I heard you were going to see your mother for Christmas," he said.

I looked at the envelope blankly and then back up at him. "Yes, I promised her I would."

He smiled. "That will leave us in something of a bind for the Christmas celebrations."

I looked down at the table. "I know. I feel bad about it. It's just that I promised her. And the truth is, I haven't announced it yet, but I don't think I'll be able to continue. With the church, I mean." I put my hands in my lap and put them on the table again and took a long gulp of the tea. "I may—I most probably—won't be coming back."

He didn't speak for a moment. He waited for me and when I didn't say anything more he smiled broadly and tapped the envelope. "That's just what I thought," he said.

I looked at the envelope again and stared, not comprehending.

"I don't understand," Tomás said, laughing lightly, "how after years of neglect the bishop can now be so conscientious."

"What?" I asked.

"I wrote to the bishop in May. Just two weeks later I received your letter. I didn't even know and happily never had to worry that the bishop's first appointee had been detained. Here is the letter from Father Quevedo, saying that he couldn't come in August after all, and that he will be here for Christmas. That doesn't surprise me at all. Always late." He laughed again. "But that they should have been so thoughtful as to send you for the interim is beyond me. When we've had no one for so many years."

I swallowed and looked at the neat handwriting of Father Quevedo, who'd filled two pages with his apologies. "I didn't know," I admitted.

He waved the letter with a dismissive gesture. "I have no doubt Father Quevedo has not heard of you either. They work that way. The right hand doesn't know what the left hand is doing. And yet, in this case, they managed to do it correctly." He looked at me and I stared back at him. "Assigning you for a few months, and then Quevedo. It works perfectly, don't you think?"

"I guess so," I said.

"Do you have any more coffee? I will trouble you for some if you do."

I stood up and lifted the pot from the woodstove with a rag and poured the black syrup into his cup. He held the handle with his thumb and forefinger and thanked me. I put the coffeepot back on the stove. In the drawer of the metal cabinet next to the stove I found quesadilla in waxed paper and I cut the cake into four squares and put it on a plate. Tomás ate it with great enjoyment, lifting the crumbs off the plate by pressing them with the tips of his fingers. He shook his head. "Xinia makes excellent quesadilla."

"I guess I should announce that I'm leaving," I said.

Tomás took another piece of cake. "If you like I can give news of the arrival of Father Quevedo."

"I'd appreciate that."

Tomás folded the letter, which I still hadn't read, and he put it in the envelope and then in his shirt pocket. "Well," he said, "I'm glad to see that you're doing so much better. Don't forget about dinner."

"Thank you, I won't."

He stood up. "Perhaps you'd like to come with Xinia and Hilario."

"Thank you," I said again. "If there's time. I'd like that." I stood up and walked with him to the door of the kitchen and he stepped onto the dirt, carefully putting his soles down on the driest spots. "Tomás," I said, "I'd like to apologize."

He put his hand to his shirt pocket and pressed the letter

inside it against his heart, as if to say it meant a great deal to him. "Not at all. There's nothing to forgive." He smiled. Then he turned away and walked on tiptoes through the mud, stepping from one dry patch to another.

THE LETTER I received on Monday had been mailed ten days earlier, and Tomás told me it was the fastest he'd ever known a letter to be delivered. "It had special postage," he said.

I didn't recognize the handwriting, and my name was misspelled, "Nitodo." It took me a moment to realize from the return address that it was from Mamá's landlord. Tomás had brought the letter to me at Xinia's house, and I was alone. When I waited for her I sat on the front step, looking onto the path that led to the road, so that I could see her when she turned the corner.

I'd forgotten the landlord's name—Kathleen. She and her husband Brian had both signed the letter that told me of Mamá's death. The heart attack occurred during the night, and Kathleen hadn't found her until the morning, at which point she called the hospital. Mamá had lived on for some hours but hadn't survived the day. They'd tried to reach me through the embassy, and Kathleen was certain there had to be a telephone number that she couldn't find. In the end they'd decided to write and they were very sorry, extremely sorry, that they'd been forced to undertake the funeral proceedings without me. Mamá hadn't left any instructions, and so they'd chosen the ceremony according to their own tastes. Would I contact her, she asked, at my earliest convenience, as if to say that my convenience had already delayed me enough.

Twenty

I TOOK THE FIRST BUS to Rabinal the following morning, climbing aboard while it was still dark, and I watched the air lighten, as if infused with pale breath, from the open window. At the bus station I stood for some minutes on the curb, letting the gunning motors, the shouts of the drivers, and the squawks of chickens bound in crates atop the buses settle around me so that I could find my way through. I bought a phone card at the bus depot and took it to the splattered pay phone that stood in the park. When the phone began ringing I realized I didn't know what time it was in Seattle.

I could have taken the bus anytime, I was thinking. I might have called her at least once.

The woman who answered sounded half-asleep.

"Yes, hello. This is Nítido. Iris's son."

"Oh, hello. Hi, Nítido. I didn't know if we'd hear from you." She paused. "I'm so very sorry."

"I did get your letter."

"Yes," she hesitated. "I am very sorry we couldn't wait for you."

"I understand. Thank you for all you've done."

"It's no trouble. Your mother"—her voice caught—"was wonderful. We were very fond of her."

"Thank you."

There was a pause. I watched a pack of lean dogs move into the park, hungry and skulking, walking one after another with their heads hanging low. They took no notice of the pigeons. "She said you were going to visit her for Christmas," Kathleen finally said.

"I was going to."

"Well, her place is still here. We have all her things."

"I don't think I'll be able to go."

She paused. "All right."

"I can understand that you want everything cleared out. I'll call someone to have it packed and sent to me."

"To you? There?"

"Don't worry. I'll take care of it."

"Well." She sounded doubtful.

A long tone sounded in my ear and a recording told me that I had half a minute remaining. "My time's up," I said. "Thanks again for all you've done. I'll write so we can arrange about any expenses."

"Nítido," she said.

"Yes."

"I hope we see you again someday."

"That would be nice."

My hand was sweating as I hung up. When I'd finished the errands, I had another hour to wait for the next bus for Río Roto, so I sat in the park and watched the buses pull in and out of the depot, their towering loads pitching as they turned the corner onto the main road. The pigeons picked at the trash: plastic wrappers and paper bags caught in the wickets that bordered the walkways. A woman walked past me with her daughter in hand, their expressions vacant. I watched them cross the park and walk aimlessly back along the perimeter in the opposite direction. At nine-thirty I boarded the bus and within minutes we were on the unpaved road to Río Roto.

On that morning, the view from the window appeared much as I'd expected it to months before. I found myself rewriting it, in the manner of your journal entries. The hills on either side tumbled against one another with a kind of careless grace. There were no clouds in the sky above them. When we reached the river I caught glimpses of it through the trees, its white foam appearing in swift and fluid flight between the trunks, like an enchanted thing too brilliant to be seen. The sound it made was a trembling, febrile pressure against the earth. On the descents the motor quieted and the cries of the birds reached us through the muffling trees. An hour into the drive, the bus slowed at a corner near a cluster of houses, and I watched the driver craning to look in the mirror, anxiously watching the right side of the bus. I leaned my head out through the window, expecting to see the wheels spinning over a chasm of broken road. Instead I saw an old man in a dusty suit and a panama hat holding his left palm against the side of the bus. With an expression of tenderness and great amazement he watched the bus inch away from under his hand, and ten minutes later when the driver finally pulled free, I saw the old man disconnect from the rear of the bus and then gaze at his hand in wonder, as if a sun he'd reached for lay in his palm.

We arrived in Río Roto and I walked up the dusty road to see Xinia, taking an hour to get there as I stopped so many times to lean on the fences, talk through the windows, deliver the fruits of the errands they'd sent me on.

On one of my last days in Río Roto I went with Xinia to Murcia. Hilario walked ahead of us, running and stopping and ducking into the bushes at the side of the road and then reappearing behind us before sprinting ahead again. We walked in silence. Xinia took my hand occasionally and then dropped it when our palms grew damp. Every ten minutes we stopped so I could drink water. The climb up through the cane took almost an hour, and when we reached Murcia, Hilario crouched uncertainly at the edge of the cane, looking out through the stalks at the scattered houses. As we passed him he sprang up to join us. He walked just behind me, peering out to the side every few steps, and then he took my hand and his fingers clenched my palm. I squeezed back and looked at Xinia and she smiled vaguely, turning away.

Cruz and Sabina had built their house at the southern edge of Murcia, behind the church where they'd been married, and before we reached the door we saw Sabina waving from the front window. The two of them came out to stand on the doorstep as we approached. Hilario dragged his feet, pulling me back slightly, and Xinia went on ahead and put her arms around Sabina. Cruz patted me and then Hilario on the shoulder. I gave Sabina the wool coverlet we'd brought and she thanked me and said it would be a relief to them on the nights that it rained. After a moment she left the room with Xinia, and Cruz and Hilario and I sat on the wooden chairs in the front room. Cruz launched into an explanation of how the house had been constructed, beginning with how they'd cleared behind the church to make space for the foundation. After a time Hilario dropped my hand and began kicking his heels against the seat. He'd stopped listening to Cruz; I could see his eyes following the movements of Xinia and Sabina in the kitchen.

"Have you found any other shortcuts through the cane?" I asked.

"What?" Cruz said.

Hilario looked at him.

"We came up through the cane," I said. "I thought there might be other paths through it up here."

"Oh, there's dozens."

Hilario sat up and leaned forward.

"Maybe you could show us," I said. "Hilario and I like those."

Cruz blinked. "Right now?"

"Sure."

"All right." He stood up and Hilario jumped to follow him and I put my head into the kitchen to say where we were going. I followed them at a short distance, watching Hilario trip over Cruz's heels. By the time they'd reached the edge of the cane Hilario was running ahead and he disappeared into the tall stalks as if into a sheet of water. I followed the smoothed dirt path, listening to their steps ahead of me, muffled by the cane. Their voices came to my ears as though delayed.

"Where does this go?"

"To a stream uphill."

"With a pool?"

"Maybe for you it's big enough."

I stopped to rest and I heard their voices and footsteps receding until they seemed only dim echoes confused with the sound the stalks made brushing against one another. I turned around and headed back toward the house, thinking that I would wait for Cruz and Hilario at the start of the path, but when I reached the edge of the cane I heard Xinia calling me, and I walked to the house and stood in the doorway of the kitchen. She smiled. "I thought you might not have gotten far," she said.

"You thought right," I said.

Sabina cleared a chair and put a cup on the counter next to it. "You're too thin, Father Amán. You're going to stay here with us and spend the whole afternoon eating."

"I like it here, Sabina," I said. "Murcia agrees with you."

She smiled. "The women come by all the time—every afternoon."

"I'm glad to hear it. It's hard being the stranger."

"We're not really strangers," she said. She put a plate with a sugared roll next to the coffee and she sat on a stool and Xinia stayed standing with her arms crossed. "Maybe we haven't lived here before but it's not like Murcia and Río Roto are so different. A couple words and you know we're the same. Like you, Father Amán. New but familiar." She smiled and looked at Xinia and Xinia nodded.

I was drinking the hot coffee as she spoke and the burning liquid brought tears to my eyes. I wiped them away with the back of my hand and took a bite of the roll. The women looked away and I swallowed the sugary dough and sipped again at the coffee. "Does Aurelio come often?"

Sabina nodded. "When he comes they're no different. They know him now from the cemetery."

The water on the stove began boiling and Sabina rose to slide the cut vegetables into the pot. I sat in the chair and spoke to them as they moved slowly through the preparations, and an hour later Cruz returned with Hilario. He sat on the floor next to the stove, holding his hands and feet up to warm them; the cold water of the pool had left his skin wrinkled.

THE MORNING after going to Murcia I moved the books that remained in the sacristy. The bedroom seemed empty and foreign without Santos and I'd closed the bedroom door and packed in the hallway. The books took up much more room than they had in Oregon, and it took me some time to realize that the water had so distorted the size and shape of the pages that many of the books were almost twice as thick as they'd been before.

Aurelio found me as I was arranging them on the shelves of the study in the vestry. "I thought I'd help you but you're done."

I looked over my shoulder to where he stood in the doorway. "Will you tell Xinia that these are for her?"

He shifted uncomfortably from one foot to the other. "You haven't told her yet?"

I looked away. "No."

"But you won't leave without talking to her."

"I might forget to mention the books."

"All right." He walked into the room and pointed to a pile on the desk. "You're taking those."

"Yes. Not that many."

He raised his eyebrows. "I don't know how you're going to carry it all."

"I'll manage." The only books that belonged to you, the notebooks and the Perry volumes, I had set aside first. Tedlock,

Thompson, MacLeod, and the Popol Vuh were the obvious other choices. For some time I'd deliberated over other piles, and in particular I thought about bringing at least one book that I hadn't yet read. But in the end I decided it was the ones I knew almost by heart that were most necessary. Though they were old books to me, they were sure soon enough to appear new.

Aurelio watched me in silence as I finished putting the office in order. When I was through I took my things into the changing room and put them near my bag. I closed the door and we walked out of the church and onto the street. I told him there was one more place I had to go that day, and when he heard where it was he paused.

"Well," he said, uncertainly, "it does have the best view to remember us by."

The sugar mill looked as it had on the last occasion, except that Claudio's donkey was standing by the grinder, eating the dry cane that stood in a stack in front of it. Claudio lay on the grassy slope overlooking town. When he saw us he held one hand up in greeting and with the other hand put a finger up to his lips. Next to him a birdcage made of slender bamboo stood with its door open. He'd scattered bits of seed all around the birdcage and on his legs. In the cage a cup of water tilted downhill.

We sat down without speaking. Aurelio lay back on the grass. I sat next to them cross-legged and watched the clouds over the river move south. After some time a pair of gray birds with speckled wings dropped, suddenly, to the ground near me. They made no sound. With rapid movements they stabbed at the seeds and hopped toward each other, then away, then toward the cage, then away from it. One of them stepped quite easily onto my knee. It looked me in the eye, jabbed at my pant leg, and ate the firefly that had crept between the folds of cloth. Then it stepped off my leg and onto the grass. A moment later it was drinking from the cup of water, and Claudio had closed the door of the cage with a sudden click. Its mate rocketed into the air.

The sun had put us all to sleep. We lay very still. Claudio opened a can of soda and passed it around to us. The bird's movements in the cage were frantic. Nevertheless we lay still, with the even stiller machinery of the ruined sugar mill behind us and the unchanging town below. After some time Aurelio began to snore and Claudio snickered, smiled at me. The bird's wings beat noisily against the bamboo bars. I could see, when my eyes were open, the matching flurry of gray feathers that wavered among the trees. Claudio closed his eyes and put his hands over them. The scurrying noise of the bird's claws grew confused in my dreams. I thought the sound came from balls of paper being thrown against my window. I woke up hearing Claudio say, "Shut up, bird." I opened my eyes, looked sideways, saw him opening the door and the bird bursting out in the direction of the trees.

I HAD TO ASK Xinia to go with me to the cemetery once again and this time she walked easily to the rear and sat on the bench across from Vicente and Constancia. She didn't say anything, but rested against me as she sat looking at the stone markers.

"I'm glad Hilario's with you," I said. I put my arm around her waist and felt her head nod against my shoulder.

"Because of you," she said.

I smiled. "You're very cunning," I said.

She turned around to look at me, her face pained. "I knew they wouldn't hurt you. Like carrying a charm. And now you're here and so is Hilario."

I smiled and touched her cheek. "I didn't mean it." She still looked at me, and gradually her face smoothed out. I wanted very much to say nothing else. "Xinia," I said.

Her face tensed and she took my hand. "What."

I was nervous, and my voice broke as I tried to swallow. "My uncle. And Ester. They never had children, and it hasn't been easy. Noé is very determined."

I'd become so accustomed to seeing her unmoved, the moments of chaos going off like remote fires in her eyes, that the panic on her face frightened me. "He's coming back for him. How could you not tell me?"

"Xinia, please, stop. It's not that."

"What is it?"

I looked away from her, turning toward the cemetery. From where I sat the tombs appeared to permit no throughway, intersecting again and again in a labyrinth of stone. Their colors alternated: gray, black, white, black, gray, gray, and gray. I tried to see the farthest one and couldn't make out its color. "Hilario is your son now, and I'd like nothing better than to ask you to accept me, to consider me—not that I could ever take the place of your brother, and I don't mean in the same way—but that I could be Hilario's and yours, as well. But"—I put my hand out to cover hers, though I couldn't draw my eyes away from the maze of stones—"I agreed with Noé. I promised him I'd go back. Just as you've gained a son, he will. It works that way for everyone. I hope"—I paused—"this might let people here, and people there, begin to forget certain things."

Xinia's fingers dug into my palm. I squeezed back as hard as I could.

"I wouldn't ask you to go with me. I'd like to, but I won't." I looked at her then, in the weakness of what I was asking despite myself, and saw her face drained; and for the first time since I'd met her it reflected another blankness, as of a person who wakes up on her feet, sleep having carried her unconscious to a place she never expected.

"Nítido," she said.

I waited, watching her face restore itself, but it was a long time coming. I didn't ask her anything more; I pulled her up and drew her arm through mine. We walked slowly along the rows and I told her all that I'd learned of the people whose graves we passed. Many of the older stones were as new to her as they'd been to me, and only by studying their names and dates in careful synchrony had I been able to resolve the vexed question of who belonged to whom.

ACKNOWLEDGMENTS

It would not have been possible to write this novel without the generosity of people in Guatemala who have spoken to me about their experiences during the armed conflict. I can only thank one, Jesús Tecú Osorio, by name, but I am deeply indebted to all of them.

As always, I am grateful to my family in Guatemala for their continual support. I am particularly obliged to Marina San Román, for the stories, and to Sergio Silva Lorenzana, for opening the trunk. I also wish to thank Evelyn Klüssmann and Edgar Gutiérrez for their advice and insight. Ana Maria and Arnold Erickson have provided more inspiration and support, over the years, than they know. And I am tremendously grateful to friends in Tucurrique, Costa Rica, who made the town a home for me twice. Their kindness is constantly remembered.

I would like to thank the friends in New York, Berkeley, and elsewhere who read earlier drafts and offered their comments and encouragement. Lisa Young's insightful observations on a very early draft are particularly appreciated. Jon Fasman's comments and conversation, over the years, have always been an invaluable source of guidance. Benny Zadik has suffered through more versions of this novel than I ever thought possible, and I am very grateful to him for his humor and his manner of sharing the writing process. I am also indebted to Brianna Leavitt-Alcántara for not only reading, but for her tremendous support as a colleague and friend. It is hard to adequately express my gratitude to William B. Taylor, whose mentorship over the last few years has been so important to me. I am especially grateful to him for such perfectly-timed reading suggestions and unfailingly thoughtful comments on writing.

Of the many books and works of scholarship that informed this project, I am most indebted to those mentioned in the novel: John Perry's *Practical Sermons*; J. Eric Thompson's *The Rise and Fall of Maya Civilization*; Barbara Tedlock's *Time and the Highland Maya*; Murdo MacLeod's *Spanish Central America*; and the translation to English of the Popol Vuh by Delia Goetz and Sylvanus Griswold Morley.

Thanks to Minnie Marie Hayes, my initiation into publishing was a wonderful experience; I am grateful for her advice and for the inspiring energy she brings to every project. I want to thank the people at Riverhead Books, and in particular Sarah Bowlin, for their care in shepherding this novel through to publication. I am extremely grateful to Megan Lynch for her dedication to this work and for bringing the best version of it to fruition. And I am indebted to Dorian Karchmar for her enthusiasm, clear vision, and unshakable confidence; this book has come into being because of what she saw in it.

Lastly, I want to thank my family for their tireless support. I am grateful to Pablo for setting the bar so high. And I am grateful to my brother, Oliver, and my parents, Martha Julia and Stephen, for the unconditional faith that is the foundation of every word, as I hope they know.

Nítido Amán never asked his parents about his Guatemalan birthplace, or why they left. No one spoke of it. But after his father's death, he returns to the tiny town of Río Roto prepared to ask questions. When he's mistaken for the new local priest, Nítido decides to play the part, thinking that the confessional confidences of the townspeople might prove more fruitful in leading him to the answers he seeks. What he finds is a place shrouded in silence and secrets, where every word bears weight. Answering his parishioners' whispered summonses, Nítido catches frightening glimpses of the history he's aching to know. But Nítido must give voice to the unnamed horrors of Río Roto's past, if he's ever to know the truth about his own.

"Meaty and salient...A smart inflection in the searching-for-roots trope."
—*San Francisco Chronicle*

"Some first novels give the feeling of having grown in a chrysalis, only to emerge at the very height of readiness. Sylvia Sellers-García's *When the Ground Turns in Its Sleep* is just that kind of novel." —*BookPage*

"Impressive...Spare...Graceful...Part folktale, part noir mystery, part meditation on the burden of history, this is a remarkable debut."
—*San Francisco* magazine

Courtesy of Pablo Sandoval

Sylvia Sellers-García was born in Boston and grew up in the United States and Central America. A graduate of Brown University and a Marshall Scholar at Oxford, she has interned at *Harper's* and worked at the *New Yorker*. Her fiction has been published in *StoryQuarterly*. She is currently a PhD candidate in Latin American history at the University of California, Berkeley.

ISBN 978-1-59448-336-3
51600
9 781594 483363

FICTION

$16.00 U.S.
$17.50 CAN

www.penguin.com
www.riverheadbooks.com
Cover design: Ben Gibson